The Ti, ...ravellers

Christmas

A Guardian of Scotland Novel

by

Amy Jarecki

Rapture Books

Copyright © 2016, Amy Jarecki

Jarecki, Amy
The Time Traveler's Christmas
Time Traveler's Christmas, The

ISBN: 9781942442233
First Release: October, 2016

Book Cover Design by: Amy Jarecki
Book Cover Photos:
    Djiledesign | Dreamstime.com
    http://www.123rf.com/profile_AnnieAnnie'>AnnieAnni
e / 123RF Stock Photo

Edited by: Scott Moreland

To Bob, who always makes my Christmases interesting and fun.

FOREWORD

In the previous Guardian of Scotland novels, I used the last name "Murray" for William Wallace's comrade in arms Andrew de Moray and his wife, Christina. Through my research, I found texts that used three variations of Andrew's name: Murray, Moray and de Moray. While writing Rise of a Legend, I opted to use Murray. However, in May 2016, Scotland announced the unveiling of the towering steel sculpture, by artist Malcolm Robertson, entitled *Brothers In Arms, the tribute is to William Wallace and Andrew de Moray*. Because of this important sculpture, in *The Time Traveler's Christmas*, I have reverted to using the archaic form of the name, de Moray. The sculpture will be erected on the north bank of the River Forth in Stirling and depicts the two armored heroes, shoulder-to-shoulder, with their arms aloft raising a Scottish flag featuring the Lion Rampant.

CHAPTER ONE

Crouched in a defensive stance, Lachlan Wallace's mind refused to focus. Sweat streamed from his brow, drained into his eyes and blurred his vision. His breathing rushed through his ears like an angry river. Everything around him moved in slow motion. He rubbed his forearm across his face and his white sleeve came back with a swath of blood.

But nothing hurt, except Lachlan's heart.

Shifting his gaze to the time clock—five seconds left—the red numbers frozen in place while the judges consulted with each other to confirm the three points given to the American for his last kick. Maybe that's what caused the bleeding. Lachlan didn't care.

He switched his sights to the scoreboard. Tied, UK nine, US nine. The American contender across the mat stared with the hunger of a rabid dog. Still, Lachlan could take him. He just needed a moment to focus.

Damn. Out of the starting gates, he'd suffered a vicious kick to the gut, but that wasn't the reason for a ton of lead sinking to his toes.

Just hang in there. I have to prove her wrong about something.

The referee sliced his hand downward—the signal to engage. Lachlan's legs moved like four hundred pound weights hung from his thighs. The American approached, growing blurrier by each fraction of a second. Holding his defensive stance, Lachlan shifted for a countermove as his opponent slightly raised his hind foot to his toes.

A kick.

Anticipating the move, years of training took over and Lachlan spun to the right, aiming a left roundhouse kick to the American's head. A millisecond off, the man ducked and rolled away from what could have been the kick to end the fight. Lachlan should have continued with the attack, pinning the man to the mat and issuing a three-point punch to the face, but Angela's voice rang in his head.

"I've filed for divorce. John and I moved your things to Container Village on Falkirk Road. You'll be hearing from my solicitor. You're such a loser. Don't try to call. I've blocked your phone."

The rush of Lachlan's breathing deafened his ears.

Who the fuck is John?

The unanswered question burst into a million stars as the American's heel collided with Lachlan's temple.

***

Back in Scotland with an overstuffed duffle hanging from his shoulder, Lachlan pushed the buzzer to Uncle Walter's Glasgow flat. Walter Tennant wasn't really his uncle, but Lachlan had called the old archaeologist by that moniker ever since he could talk.

"That you, laddie?" the disembodied voice crackled through the ancient speaker.

"Yes, sir," Lachlan said while the buzzer sounded. He pushed through the door and bounded up two flights of stairs. He never used a lift when stairs were available.

Waiting in his doorway, Walter's glasses were thick as Coke-bottle bottoms. The man had to be over eighty. Crusty, he'd lost most of his hair and his back stooped a bit, but other than that, the old archaeologist could pass for sixty-five. Walter's neck craned as Lachlan topped the stairs. "How can you possibly look taller every time I see you?"

˙At thirty, Lachlan had been six-foot-six for a good ten years. "Maybe you're shrinking." He gave the old man a hug. "How's life treating you, Uncle?"

"No complaints. Your mum will be helping with the dig at Avoch Castle in the spring. Do you think you could take a couple weeks to join us?"

Heck, Lachlan could barely think past tomorrow and Walter was asking about a dig that wouldn't start for six months? "I'll have to check my schedule. Avoch? Wasn't it once Ormond Castle, the seat of Andrew de Moray?" Lachlan wasn't a history buff like his mum, but he had a zest for anything about William Wallace and de Moray had been the great legend's comrade in arms.

"You are your mother's son." Walter ushered him inside the flat—threadbare carpet, an old TV, a recliner.

"Hey, did you get a new couch?" Lachlan asked.

"Aye. Figured I needed someplace for the guests to sit."

"You planning on having guests?"

"Nay. Just me and the cat—but it doesn't hurt to be prepared." The cat was the reason for Lachlan's visit. The timing was perfect. After he'd regained consciousness in the Brussels hospital, he'd called his mom who was in London for a series of lectures on Medieval History. By the time he arrived at the Edinburgh airport, he had an offer to cat sit for Uncle Walter for two weeks. Lachlan had changed his flight from Edinburgh to Glasgow, and there he stood with his duffle in tow. All he needed was to do a load or two of washing.

"So where is the rascal?" Lachlan asked, peeking under the new red couch.

"Probably hiding under the Christmas tree—doubt if he'll show his face until I come back, but you'll know he's here because the food will be eaten and he'll leave a wee gift in the litter box."

Moving inside, Lachlan examined the tree, decked out with a rainbow of flashing lights, every branch adorned with a figurine of some sort. On closer inspection, the figurines were all historical figures—Mary, Queen of Scots, Henry VIII, Robert the Bruce, William Wallace—that statue gave Lachlan pause. After dropping his bag, he strode straight up to the tree and fingered the piece. Perhaps because he was a Wallace, his heart rate always spiked when faced with an image of Scotland's hero. Maybe even because Lachlan had always wanted to be a man like his ancestor—decisive, passionate, strong, committed to right, focused and determined, willing to die for his country. A shiver crept down his arms. "Where'd you find all these?"

Walter hobbled beside him. "Here and there. Collected them over the years."

"But isn't it a little early to put up your tree?"

"Why not? Besides, I like to look at my figurines." He shot a thumb over his shoulder, gesturing toward the kitchen. "You want something to drink?"

"I'm good, thanks." Lachlan followed Walter into the kitchen.

"Do you think you'll have any trouble with the commute from Glasgow to Linlithgow?" The old man hobbled toward the sink.

"As long as there's no strike and the trains keep running, I don't think it'll be a problem for a couple weeks."

"That's what I figured." Walter looked away and drummed his fingers on the counter. "So, have you decided what you're going to do?"

Lachlan's gut turned over. "Just taking it one day at a time at the moment."

"I suppose that's for the best. I'm glad I never married. Saved myself a shipload of strife."

"Yeah." He didn't want to talk to anyone about Angela. If only he didn't have to face divorce crap now that he'd returned to Scotland—but he'd watched mates go through it and it never was pretty—always drew out, ripping them up on the inside. God, if only there was a way to avoid that kind of pain, he'd take his issue in karate kicks every day for the rest of his life.

"Good thing you didn't have any kids," Walter said.

"Isn't that the truth?" Lachlan spotted the cat food feeder beside the refrigerator. It had about two liters of food in a plastic container that fed into a dish below—same with the water beside it. "How often do I need to fill up the food?"

"When it runs out."

"How long does all that last?"

"A couple weeks or so."

"So...you needed me here to take care of a phantom cat that won't need to be fed or watered during the entire time you're away?"

"I suppose you'll need to clean the litter box a time or two." Uncle Walter pointed. "It's in the guest bathroom, so don't forget to leave the door open."

Lachlan snorted. At least he had a quiet place to hang out until he found a flat to let. "Anything else?"

"There's some milk and Weetabix, otherwise you're on your own for meals." Walter meandered back to the living room, toward a suitcase, satchel and an antique-looking cane. "Call my cell if you need anything. I'll be meeting your parents at Heathrow and then we'll fly to Malta from there."

Lachlan hadn't seen his parents since arriving. Mum had yet another speaking engagement in London, so he'd probably passed their flight somewhere over Northumberland. Ah well, he didn't want to be mollycoddled, not that his mother was the type who ever babied him. To be perfectly honest, Lachlan just wanted to be alone. He'd arranged for his partner to take his classes at the dojo for the week and the only commitments he had were kinesiology therapy at the hospital in Linlithgow. He'd earned his degree in kinesiology in the US at the University of Wisconsin, Madison. Mum had encouraged him to study in America, especially since Lachlan's granddad used to be the UK Ambassador to the Unites States. Lachlan had picked Wisconsin because it sounded western and produced fantastic linebackers. His freshman year, he'd hoped to walk on as a linebacker, but a cute blonde had swayed him toward karate. Their romance lasted about a month, but Lachlan found a new love—martial arts, his strength, self-defense and samurai swords—he won nationals and had represented Great Britain in the Olympics where he earned the gold and now he also held three world titles.

But the Olympics had earned him a knighthood. He'd nearly earned a fourth world title in Brussels right before his world had crashed around his ears. Nothing like a vindictive almost-ex-wife to cause a man to lose his edge two minutes before the final fight of the most important match in the world.

Fuck.

"You all right there, sport?" asked Walter, swinging his satchel over his shoulder.

"Sure." Lachlan scratched his head. "My mind wandered for a moment."

"I suppose that's to be expected." The old fella grasped Lachlan's shoulder and squeezed. "Just remember you mean a great deal to your mum and to me."

"Thanks." Lachlan wished he felt like he meant a great deal to anyone at the moment—or anything positive to take away the black chasm filling his chest.

"And remember your history, son. Though you may not realize it, Scotland's history is in your blood."

"Aye, Mum never lets me forget it."

"I'll wager she does not." He pulled up the handle on his suitcase and looked at his watch. "Well, there's a taxi waiting."

Lachlan opened the door. "You need some help?"

"Nay, I'll take the lift." He hobbled through, leaning on the cane in one hand and rolling along the suitcase with the other.

"Very well." Lachlan waved. "Don't worry about anything here. The cat will be fine."

"Crumpet." Walter strode into the hallway and pushed the button for the lift.

"I beg your pardon?"

"Crumpet—it's the furball's name." The doors opened and he stepped inside.

"I suppose that will come in handy—see you in a fortnight?"

The old man regarded him with owlish eyes made enormous by the distortion of his lenses. "Perhaps."

"You always did talk in riddles." Lachlan laughed as he watched the metal doors close until Uncle Walter's careworn, slightly comical face completely disappeared.

With a long sigh, he picked up his duffle and headed back to the guest room. "Hiya, Crumpet," he almost shouted. "Don't even think about sleeping on the bed with me. I'm allergic." Cat dander made his nose itch.

Walter had left a towel on the bed for him and a gift bag with a tag that read "To the champ". He tossed his duffle against the wall, then stripped off his jeans, pulled on a pair of black karate pants and his favorite grey zip-neck sweatshirt with a picture of man's evolution across the chest, ending with modern man performing a classic side kick.

He took in a deep breath and the chasm in his chest stretched, making his head swim. He wished the pain had been caused by his concussion. The sounds of the empty flat intensified his misery—the hum of the refrigerator, the tic-tic of the radiator attached to the far wall.

So this is where I've landed?

Yeah, Lachlan had lost a match or two, but he'd never completely lost everything—at least that's how it felt. His knees gave out as he dropped to the bed. He'd lost his townhouse—only five blocks from the dojo he'd started up with his best friend. He'd lost the only woman he'd ever loved. He'd taken his time dating Angela, getting to know her, learning everything about her, living with her, sleeping with her, waking up every morning beside her.

He tried to hold it in, but his gut erupted making a sob strain through his throat. Curling into a ball, he gnashed his teeth, squeezed his fists and clamped every muscle in his body, but the pain in his heart hurt even more.

What had he done wrong? Yes, he'd noticed she'd grown more distant, but figured it was her work. Being a schoolteacher always had its ups and downs for her, especially at the beginning of a school year.

John?

Fuck.

Lachlan had never wanted to beat the shit out of anyone before, but he just might risk going to jail if only to smash his fist into the turd's face—break the bastard's knee with a kick—cripple him for life.

Shoving the heels of his hands against his temples, he tried to meditate on something good, something warm, something happy—the sun. Lachlan never used karate for vengeance. He taught his students self-control and defensive moves to avoid attack. He preached the need to use peaceful tactics to diffuse arguments and only resort to a fight when there was no other option.

But he'd make an exception.

After the onslaught of toe-curling anguish, Lachlan rolled to his back and stared at the ceiling. If only he could hide in Uncle Walter's flat for the rest of his life, he might survive. He could spend his days in meditation, erasing Angela from his memory, overcoming his deep-seated desire to do harm to the man she'd cheated with.

He hated the sickly pain eating his heart, eating away at himself.

Where had he gone wrong? Had he been such a bad husband? Yes, they'd had their disagreements, but didn't all couples? God dammit, he'd put the woman on a pedestal. He'd done his share of the cooking and cleaning. Hadn't he?

Sitting up, he regarded himself in the mirror. God, he looked like shit. But who wouldn't after spending the night in a foreign hospital, being discharged with a warning to take it easy and see his doctor as soon as he arrived home. The nursing staff had acted so goddamned chipper. How were they to know the rug had been pulled out from under his entire life? Christ, Lachlan didn't care about a wee strike to the head.

He hissed when he touched the bruise at his temple, partially hidden by a mop of shoulder-length brown hair usually secured at the back of his crown with a band the way Angela wanted it. Maybe he should shave his head. Or maybe he should grow it even longer, travel to Alaska and become a mountain man. He certainly looked the part—thick beard, with two days of growth on his cheeks and neck where it shouldn't be—and it itched like a bitch.

His hip knocked the gift bag over.

Lachlan shifted his gaze and stared at it for a moment. It wasn't like Walter to leave a gift. Heaving a sigh, he reached for the bag and pulled out a note.

Dear Champ,

I presumed you would figure out that Crumpet could take care of himself for a week or two. But I also knew you'd be hurting on the inside. Believe it or not, I've suffered a tragedy or two in my lifetime, as well. Right, so go ahead and pull out the medallion inside. This isn't a gift, but a loan. I lent it to your mother before you were born after she'd experienced a tragedy and it turned her life around in a miraculous way.

Go on, now. Hold it in your palm and put it around your neck. Feel the temperature of the metal against your chest.

Lachlan dug inside the bag and pulled out the medallion. It was about the size of a fifty-cent piece but round rather than being a decagon. Heavier than it looked, the worn piece was inscribed in Latin.

Lachlan turned Walter's note over.

As you can see, this old relic is inscribed in Latin. I found it when excavating the Fail Monastery ruins eons ago.

The front reads: "Verum est quasi malis navis in nocte" and means "truth is like a beacon".

Lachlan confirmed Walter's statement, then flipped the medallion to the back.

On the reverse it reads: "Sed pauci volunt sequi", translated: "but few choose to follow".

He rubbed the hunk of bronze between his fingers. *Truth is like a beacon, but few choose to follow.* Indeed, his mother had always drilled into him the importance of the truth. She'd spent most of her life trying to interpret historical facts and take her findings to the world.

Honestly, Lachlan's entire life had been a quest to seek the truth. His dedication to martial arts and kinesiology, to finding the body's balance, energy, peace and healing all centered around the need for a man to be truthful to himself. Otherwise, Zen could not be achieved. Inner peace could not be found.

The problem?

His inner peace had been obliterated with a single phone call.

He slipped the leather thong over his head and plopped back to the pillows, staring at the paint chipping off the ceiling until sleep took the pain in his heart away.

Chapter Two

The Scottish Borders, November, 1314

Lady Christina de Moray's horse stutter-stepped as if the gelding sensed her unease. But who in all of Christendom could remain calm at a time like this? Sitting taller and craning her neck, she searched the ranks of approaching English soldiers for any sign of her son.

She'd waited thirteen years for this day. During the duration of her purgatory, she'd spent endless hours on her knees praying this moment would come. The wind picked up her veil and blew it into her face. Batting the ugly grey wool away, she continued her search while the English rode into formation on the other side of the border. On the Scots side, she sat on the outside of the row of nobles atop a galloway pony that was far smaller than the knights' destrier warhorses. King Robert had allowed her to come because her son was the first of several prisoners for whom they were negotiating a trade in exchange for English prisoners of war as part of the peace terms after the Battle of Bannockburn. Though "peace" might be an exaggeration.

The de Moray army was led by Hamish, her man-at-arms. They were among the ranks behind the row of nobles. This was a diplomatic meeting—an exchange and nothing more.

Though a frigid day, Christina's palms still perspired in her gloves. She prayed she would recognize Andrew, though the last time she'd held him in her arms he was only a bairn of two. With a shiver, she remembered the day the English had breached her castle walls and taken her child from her embrace. Gracious, at five and ten, Andrew would practically be grown—but still not a man.

He had blue eyes and was named for Christina's husband, a nobleman who died from his wounds in the Battle of Stirling Bridge. Aye, Andrew de Moray had fought beside William Wallace. Together, they were named Guardians of Scotland and, shortly thereafter, she had lost him to fever— the only man she would ever love. Eight and ten was far too young to be a widow.

But this day she didn't want to think about how the world had spiraled out of control with Andrew's death. She would soon have her son back on Scottish soil. They had so many things on which to catch up—three and ten years of separation to pack into a few months until King Robert would require Andrew to squire for Sir Boyd. The great knight who had once squired for Wallace now led the procession forward to meet with the English party beside the marker that defined the boundary between the two countries.

What will Andrew be like? Surely he will know his mother. Though a lad of five and ten will not want to be pampered.

At Roxburgh Castle, Christina had a package for the lad— his father's sword, surcoat bearing the de Moray coat of arms, and a leather targe with brass nails, fit for a man of great import. He would be given a Scottish galloway stallion and a royal caparison so that everyone who saw him would know him to be a nobleman—and that one day he would become a knight.

Aye, she had many plans for Andrew and, finally, the day had come. Like a hawk, she watched the English side. Someone towed a line leading a horse bearing a rider with his wrists bound. Merciful father, the prisoner was a lad for certain. His dark locks blew sideways with the wind, but his beard had not yet come in.

"Andrew!" she cried out, then smothered her outward exuberance by pressing a fist to her lips.

The lad glanced her way as if he'd heard his mother call his name. Sir Boyd and the others must have started the parley, because Andrew's attention was quickly drawn back to the proceedings. But Christina's heart leapt. For the first time in three and ten years she was gazing upon her son. At long last, they would be a family again.

A rumble sounded from behind the English ranks. Screeches of swords drawn from their scabbards on both sides of the border hissed through the air. The thundering of horses grew nearer.

Christina's stomach twisted while a sharp jolt shot through her insides. The horse beneath her neighed and sidestepped again. The line of English soldiers opened, giving way to a cavalry of warriors, their faces hidden by bucket helms.

"Andrew!" Christina shouted, spurring her horse forward.

The scene erupted in mayhem. Ahead, her son was swallowed by soldiers behind the enemy line. Men bellowed. Swords clashed.

"No!" She slapped her reins, demanding speed from her gelding. The horse reared while destriers laden with armored knights cut them off. The sound of battle boomed from the ranks while arrows hissed above.

Frantically, Christina searched the mayhem for Andrew. *Where have they taken him?*

Her galloway skittered away from the fight. Wind swirled, blinding her with her veil. A thick hand peppered with black hair grabbed the gelding's bridle. Instinctively, Christina reached inside her sleeve for her dagger. "Release me!"

"So now the bleating Scots have women fighting their battles?" growled the smelly English pikeman. "I'll show them what we do with women the likes of ye."

He reached for her arm.

Recoiling, Christina sliced her dagger and aimed for his shoulder. The fabric of his shirt slit open.

"Bitch!" the man swore, grabbing her wrist and twisting. Hard.

As she was pulled from her mount, Christina's knife fell to the ground. "Do not touch me!" she screamed.

The cur's brutal grip only strengthened as he wrestled her to the ground and pounced atop her. Blood cold as ice pulsed through her veins as she thrashed and kicked, fighting to free herself from the crushing weight driving into her chest. An ugly laugh rumbled from the blackguard's belly while he stuck his tongue out and licked her face. "Once ye've had an Englishman, your Scotsmen will never measure up."

Whipping her head from side to side, she escaped his mouth, but he threw back his hand and slapped her face.

Searing pain stung her cheek. Tears welled in her eyes, blurring her vision.

The varlet's weight shifted, pinning her shoulders while his hand reached between them.

In a blink, Christina knew what he was doing. Fighting for her life, she jerked her shoulders trying to wrest free while she dug her left heel into the ground and threw her right knee to his groin. Missing her mark, she connected with the crack of his bum.

He growled, punishing her with another slap.

But Christina wasn't about to stop fighting—not until she took her last breath. Boring down with her heels, she thrashed. "Get off me, ye brute." She would hold her son in her arms this day if it was the last thing she did. And by the shift of the crushing weight on her chest, she only had moments before her life's breath completely whooshed from her lungs.

The very thought of dying whilst her son was still held captive infused her with strength. With a jab, she slammed the heel of her hand across the man's chin. He flew from her body like a sack of grain. Praises be, had the Lord granted her with superhuman strength? Blinking, Christina sat up.

No, no. Her strike hadn't rescued her from the pillager.

A champion had.

A behemoth of a man pummeled the pikeman's face with his fists. "Never. Ever." His fists moved so fast they blurred. "Harm. A. Woman!"

Bloodied and battered, the varlet dropped to the dirt.

A swordsman attacked her savior from behind.

"Watch out," she cried, but before the words left her lips the warrior spun to his feet. Flinging his arm backward, he grabbed his assailant's wrist, stopped the sword midair and flipped the cur onto his back.

Onward, he fought a rush of English attackers with his bare hands, without armor. Not even William Wallace himself had been so talented. This warrior moved like a cat, anticipating his opponent's moves before they happened.

Five enemy soldiers lay on their backs.

"Quickly," the man shouted, running toward her, his feet bare.

No sooner had she rolled to her knees than his powerful arms clamped around her. The wind whipped beneath her feet. He planted her bum in the saddle.

"Behind!" Christina screamed, every muscle in her body clenching taut.

Throwing back an elbow, the man smacked an enemy soldier in the face resulting in a sickening crack.

She picked up her reins and dug in her heels.

"Whoa!" The big man latched onto the skirt of her saddle and hopped behind her, making her pony's rear end dip. But the frightened galloway didn't need coaxing. He galloped away from the fight like a deer running from a fox.

Christina peered around her shoulder at the mass of fighting men behind them. "My son!"

"Do you see him?" the man asked in the strangest accent she'd ever heard.

She tried to turn back, but the man's steely chest stopped her. "They took him."

"Who?"

"The *English*, of course."

The more they talked, the further from the border the galloway took them.

"Huh?" the man mumbled behind her like he'd been struck in the head by a hammer. Everyone for miles knew the Scots and the English were to exchange a prisoner that day.

The champion's big palm slipped around her waist and held on—it didn't hurt like he was digging in his fingers, but he pressed firm against her. The sensation of such a powerful hand on her body was unnerving. It had been eons since any man had touched her, at least gently. The truth? Aside from the brutish attack moments ago, Christina's life had been nothing but chaste.

White foam leached from the pony's neck and he took in thunderous snorts. He wouldn't be able to keep this pace much longer. Christina steered him through a copse of trees and up the crag where just that morning she'd stood with King Robert and Sir Boyd before they'd led the Scottish battalion into the valley. There, she could gain a good vantage point and try to determine where the backstabbing English were heading with Andrew this time.

At the crest of the outcropping, she pulled the horse to a halt. "The pony cannot keep going at this pace."

The man's eyebrows slanted inward and he gave her a quizzical stare. Good Lord, his tempest-blue eyes pierced straight through her soul. "Are you speaking English?"

Shaking off her solicitude, she thrust her finger toward the ground. "Hop. Down."

Immediately, the warm palm left her waist and the warrior slid off the pony, though with legs the length of a two-handed sword, he didn't have far to go. Christina reached her hands out for a bit of help, but the man strode to the edge of the crag without so much as a backward glance. He planted his fists on his hips and stared out over the battle. "Jesus Christ, that's realistic."

Snapping a hand over her heart, Christina gasped. *Blasphemy.* After sliding down from the horse without assistance, she stood still for a moment—why was there something familiar about this stranger? Could she be in danger?

Nay.

The man had rescued her from certain death. But the more she examined him, the odder he appeared. He wore black trews far looser and longer than any chausses she'd ever seen. And on top, a curious thick grey shirt cinched below the waist—his garb appeared excessively casual. He had no cloak, no surcoat displaying his coat of arms. And as she'd noticed before, his feet were bare, of all oddities.

And 'tis miserably cold.

True, there had been something familiar about his eyes.

And Christina had only seen one man in her entire life who stood as tall as he, and that man had died in the service of his country nine years prior.

But her new protector was the least of her worries. Her son had been no more than fifty paces away and she'd lost him. Her heart sank to her toes.

As if he'd heard her thoughts, the warrior turned and faced Christina, throwing his thumb over his shoulder. "Who are those maniacs?"

For pity's sake, he used unusual speech. "King Robert's army." She eyed him. "Ye speak as if ye've just flown down from the moon."

He batted a hand through the air. "You can stop with the act now—no one's around who cares."

"I beg your pardon? *I* care. Have ye climbed out of some hole in the midst of a bog?" She stamped her foot. Perhaps this man needed things spelled out. "They were supposed to conduct a peaceful exchange—my son for one of theirs—but ye ken ye can never trust an English king. I havena seen my son for three and ten years until this day. And just when Sir Boyd rode forward for the exchange, the evil swine's blackguards attacked."

The man's eyebrows pinched together and he looked at her like she'd grown two heads. "Jesus, I can barely understand you. What is it? Auld Scots?" He paced and gestured out to the battlefield. "What I saw of the fighting was just too goddamned realistic—and the man who was on top of you—I'll tell you right now, that was *no* act. If I hadn't collared him, he would have raped you."

She wrung her hands, trying to make sense of this unusual behemoth. True, he'd acted like a champion, but now he was being nonsensical. "I can tell ye true, that accursed man wasna playacting. Had ye not come to my aid there is every chance I would be laying in a pool of my own blood about now."

"Unbelievable." He again looked to the battlefield, where the two enemies began to head in opposite directions. "Where are the bloody police?"

"Pardon?" How could she make sense of such gibberish?

"They're going to need a bigger jail when they haul all those nutcases in."

Christina didn't understand a word—except jail—it sounded like gaol. "Never mind them." She scanned the horizon. Whoever took Andrew was long gone by now.

Curses.

"As I said, I've waited three and ten years to see my son and I'm finished with standing by helplessly. King Robert released me from being a prisoner in my own castle." She turned back to the horse. Aye, she had the remains of the de Moray army, but no one in her ranks could fight like this stranger. "Please, I cannot ride into England myself and go after him. I need someone like ye. Someone who can fight—who can help me scale castle walls and bring my Andrew home."

He sauntered toward her. "So let me get this straight…The English have your son and you want to break into a maximum security prison to help him escape?"

She scoffed. "Ye make it sound as if Andrew's a felon."

"He's not?"

"Nay, he was abducted from my home and taken from me when he was but a bairn. Finally, after we won at Bannockburn, King Robert negotiated for Andrew's freedom in exchange for an English prisoner."

The man's eyes nearly crossed as he shook his head and waved his hands. "Wait. Let's back up a moment." He scratched his head, looking completely lost. "You said the Battle of Bannockburn?"

"Aye."

"If my memory serves me correctly, Bannockburn was fought in the year thirteen hundred and fourteen."

"At least ye havena been under a rock for so long ye dunna ken the year."

He snorted with a laugh. "So, you're trying to tell me the battle down there is real—that King Robert is *Robert the Bruce*?"

"Aye."

"Shut up."

"I beg your pardon? I merely answered your question."

"No. It's just I am either dreaming or you're feeding me a line of tripe."

"Anyone can plainly see ye are awake." She moved around the horse and regarded the warrior over the galloway's back. "But I'm thinking ye're addled in the head."

"I'm beginning to think I agree with you." He raked his fingers through his thick, shoulder-length locks—his hair was awfully well-groomed for a man. "I have no idea how I ended up here. I can't even remember having a night on the sauce. Do you have a car nearby?"

"I beg your pardon? Are ye speaking in riddles?"

He threw his hands out to his sides and rolled his eyes. "Maybe I should go along with the reenactment thing. So, ah, you said you needed help finding your son?"

"Aye." Had she finally explained the direness of the situation well enough? This crazed warrior didn't seem dumb—though his Scots Inglisch needed work. Perhaps he was from the continent. "I've waited longer than any mother should. 'Tis time to take things into my own hands and now I'm free to do so."

"Do you know where they took him?"

She held up a finger. "That, we must find out." The ride to Roxburgh was a good four hours and doing it alone could invite a world of trouble. Her man-at-arms was nowhere to be seen and she needed a champion like never before— regardless if this warrior was a wee bit touched in the head, he could fight like Goliath. She held out her hand. "My name is Lady Christina de Moray."

The corner of the man's mouth turned up. "Wife of Andrew de Moray—Guardian of Scotland, the same hero who rode with William Wallace?"

"Och, I'm his widow. And how did ye ken all that when ye had no idea Bruce's army is fighting off the English this day?"

"Just a hunch. Forgive me for ignoring my manners." The big man bowed over her hand and gave the back of it a light peck. "I am Lachlan Wallace at your service, m'lady."

Christina's heart nearly stopped when the warrior's dark blue gaze met her own. All she could manage was a gasp.

CHAPTER THREE

After he kissed the back of her hand, the woman blanched. In sharp contrast with her black dress, the whites of her eyes were wide like she'd seen a ghost. Her little gasp made Lachlan's stomach backflip. Had she recognized him? Squinting, he leaned in for a closer look. Oh no, he'd never seen the lady before. He would have remembered a doll face like hers with mahogany curls framing her features from beneath that ridiculously frumpy veil. He would have remembered those wide-set eyebrows arched above incredibly expressive silver-blue eyes. Though the rosy heart-shaped face now regraded him with confusion.

Regardless, stomach squeeze or not, with an ugly divorce in the wings, Lachlan was in no shape to take notice of a zealous reenactment lass gone overboard. And the bit about her son was priceless. Did she even have a son?

Lady Christina hadn't even acknowledged his question about a car and her horse was a scrawny mule that looked like it needed to be on a feeding regimen at an animal sanctuary. Worse, he'd lost his mind. The last thing he remembered was falling asleep on Uncle Walter's spare bed. When he opened his eyes, a barbaric monster was attacking the petite little woman. By God, Lachlan couldn't abide anyone who struck a woman and Lady Christina—*if that was her real name*—was, by far, too small and frail to fend off an ugly mail-clad beast.

Lachlan scratched his head for about the millionth time. "Where did you say we are?"

She beckoned him toward the horse. "We're on the borders." She pointed over her shoulder. "The English came from Kielder Forest to the south. 'Tisn't safe to tarry. Ye can bank on the reivers swarming in soon. They always scavenge the dead, the heathens."

"Right." Strike that up for another quirky detail about this loony female. "So, where do we go from here? I'm not familiar with Kielder Forest. Is it near the motorway?"

She flashed him a look as if to accuse him as being the lunatic. "We must haste to Roxburgh Castle. Bruce's army is stationed there and that's where we agreed to rendezvous should something go awry."

He glanced back to the battlefield. None of the dead reenactors showed any sign of movement. A sickly twinge snaked up the back of his neck. He couldn't fool himself anymore—he'd seen his share of death when flying Black Hawks with the SAS in Afghanistan and those poor souls lying in the grass weren't faking it. Damn. They were good and dead.

Christina grasped the reins and placed a hand on the saddle. "Will ye give me a leg up?"

Lachlan had ridden a horse a time or two—thought it would be fun last year when he went on holiday with Angela. "Sure thing." Stooping, he locked his hands together and let her do the rest. Light as a typical sixth grader in one of his classes, she eased into her sidesaddle like sliding into her favorite chair.

Lachlan stepped back and regarded the horse's hindquarters. Down on the battlefield, he hadn't given much thought to launching himself behind the lady's saddle and hightailing it out of there. He'd needed to move fast and there were no other options available. "Do you think this little guy can hold me?"

"He'll manage." She patted the gelding's neck. "I suggest ye climb aboard. 'Tis at least a four-hour ride. We'll be lucky to arrive afore dark as it is."

Lachlan shoved his foot into the stirrup and swung his leg over the poor beastie. "You said Roxburgh Castle?" His mind rifled through the volumes of information his mother had imparted through the years. An author of historical non-fiction, specializing in Medieval Scotland, Mum had won a Pulitzer, her books had become films, and she'd restored Torwood Castle to such an accurate level of detail, people came from all corners of the earth to visit the historic site.

"Aye," Lady Christina replied to his question about Roxburgh.

Lachlan vaguely recalled something about the fortress on the River Tweed—but the once-great Bruce stronghold wasn't even a relic. About all that stood was a bit of the curtain wall and a gate arch. "Near Kelso Abbey?" He shouldn't have needed to tack on "abbey" to the name of the town, but this woman was playing the medieval role so well, he figured she'd act like she understood him better if he added it. He'd been to Kelso before and the abbey was in ruins, not much more than a single tower looming in the midst of an enormous graveyard.

"Ye've been there?" she asked.

"Not sure." He wasn't about to admit to anything just yet.

As he adjusted his seat, the horse started to amble its way down the hill. Lachlan slid a palm to Christina's waist for stability. That's what he was supposed to do, right? He chewed the inside of his cheek, looking for something else to grab on to. He'd put his hand there before and she hadn't said anything, so he figured it was probably okay…as long as he didn't let it slip too low or too high…or apply too much pressure. He didn't want to give her any ideas—no, not with the mess his life was in at the moment. But dear God, his hand nearly spanned her soft little abdomen.

Down boy, he chastised the appendage that hadn't seen much action of late—in months, truth be told.

Dammit, he was hitching a ride and that was it. *This woman is a nutcase. I do not need someone like Christina de Moray in the fiery mix. A woman like this little spitfire just might kill me.*

At least now they were riding north and he could keep an eye out for the power lines or rows of wind turbines that peppered the landscape. He'd be certain to see something modern soon, then he'd figure a way back to Walter's flat. Unless he was in the midst of the most realistic dream he'd ever had.

Hell, he had no wallet, no shoes—nothing but his jockeys, his karate pants and sweatshirt. And for some insane reason he was sharing a pony with a crazed medieval zealot. Talk about being stranded. Dammit, if Angela had waited a couple more weeks to leave him, he could have called her for help— if he had a phone. Mum was in London with Da—his stepfather, but still the man he admired and respected as his father. He could call Jason, his partner at the dojo. Yeah, that was probably the best idea. Someone ought to let him borrow their cell once they arrived in Kelso.

"Are ye comfortable back there?" Christina asked over her shoulder.

"I'm fine." His stomach growled. "Do you have anything to eat?"

"Unfortunately, we were separated from the pack mule, which is another reason why we need to return to Roxburgh. We wouldn't travel far without supplies."

Jeez, she sounded so convincing. Lachlan looked to the horizon—not a damned power line in sight—no contrails either. He'd keep an eye out for those as well—a plane's contrail could be seen for miles.

Odd, though, Lachlan had never been any place in the borderlands that had so many trees. And Christina drove the horse along a path pummeled with hoof and human prints. "It looks like a lot of people hike this trail."

"Indeed. Especially the armies—'tis a major trade route between Scotland and England."

"Right." Lachlan just rolled his eyes, then leaned closer to her veil and inhaled. Dammit, the peter pinged again. What the hell was messing with his mind? Sure, he had to admit the lass was darned cute. And he couldn't help leaning in to catch another oddly appealing whiff. Her heady perfume had to be infused with a triple issue of feminine hormones. Christ, her floral scent was like a homing device for any male—of *any* species. He couldn't put his finger on the exact fragrance, but it was decidedly female and distracting.

Shaking his head, he cleared his addled mind. He wanted none of it. He wasn't even divorced yet. Becoming tangled up with a history lunatic wasn't a remote possibility. Besides, his mother had immersed him in enough history to last a lifetime.

On and on the horse ambled. The going was tediously slow and Lachlan opted to trot alongside them for about ten miles—which was a help because the pony could move faster without him. He could have run longer, but not without a camel pack of water or a pair of shoes. His feet were raw with about a gazillion nicks and cuts. They'd stopped a couple of times to drink from burns—he figured they were safe enough since the water ran swift and clear.

When the wind brought a pall that stank of sewage and God knew what else, Lachlan snorted. "What's that stench?"

"Humanity." She pointed. "Ye can tell we're nearly there—'tis fortunate there's still some daylight remaining. Your running made the journey pass more quickly for certain."

To the northeast, a black cloud hung low in the sky. They rode into an open lea—a field that looked like it had recently been harvested—in fact, haystacks dotted the landscape. Not bales, but old-fashioned stacks like those depicted in his childhood picture books.

"Is that medieval pollution?" he asked, again looking for power lines, a paved road or a tractor. *Anything?*

"Ye have the most unusual speech. What is this, *pollution?*"

"Smog—particles that make the air hazy and hard to breathe."

"Like smoke?"

"Yeah. Like smoke." He hit his forehead with the heel of his hand. Surely she'd let up.

Through the next copse of trees, an enormous grey fortress sat at the confluence of two rivers. Surrounded by thirty-foot, stone curtain walls, innumerous columns of smoke billowed, funneled to the sky by thick chimneys. As they rode along the southern bailey, Lachlan eyed the guards standing atop the wall-walk dressed in mail and helms with bows and quivers of arrows slung over their shoulders. Behind them, two square towers flanked the wall to the west. Barely visible was another gabled square roof to the north and as they turned the bend and headed up the hill to the giant gatehouse, a circular tower loomed above looking dark and gothic.

Guards were posted everywhere and most of them had their eyes on Lachlan and Christina as they neared.

He gulped. He might be able to fight off a half-dozen men, but they were in the open and totally exposed. If one of the wackos above decided to do some target practice, he and the lady would be dead. "I hope they consider us friends."

"They wouldna expect a woman and one man to ride up and lay siege to a castle as impenetrable as Roxburgh." She chuckled. "Besides, I imagine there might be one or two people within who are anxious for my return."

Why did it not surprise him when the portcullis rose as they rode across the ditch and up the motte? Lachlan stared at the gate's iron teeth pointing downward as they rode beneath. *Piss off the guard who mans the crank and you'd be dead on impact.*

Though most medieval castles in Scotland were in ruins, Lachlan had been to the intact Edinburgh and Stirling Castles and they weren't as functional looking as this. Why hadn't he heard of Roxburgh's restoration before? "Where's the abbey from here?" he asked.

She pointed east. "That way, though ye can get a better view of it from atop the wall-walk."

He glanced over his shoulder as the gate creaked downward behind them. Sure enough, a square tower loomed in the distance with a cloud of smoke hanging above it. But there was no sign of the Kelso he'd driven through a time or two.

"M'lady." A man wearing mail with a sword strapped to his belt rushed forward and grasped the horse's bridle. "We feared ye were captured."

"I nearly was." She let the man help her dismount while another lad took charge of the horse. "If it hadn't been for this warrior, I would have met my end for certain."

Lachlan slid to his feet and the lad led the horse away. "If someone could give us a lend of their cell, I'll call for a ride home."

A crowd had gathered. By God, not only Christina, but everyone stared at him as though he had two heads.

"And where are ye from, stranger?" The burly man craned his neck. He had a grey beard and a deep scar across his cheek—a man who enjoyed fighting with blades for certain.

Lachlan tugged down the hem of his sweatshirt and squared his shoulders. "Linlithgow."

Scarface crossed his arms and stepped forward like he wanted to pick a fight. "Ye dunna sound like any Scot I ken."

"Hamish." Christina grabbed the man's shoulder and pulled him aside. "This champion fought off a half-dozen

English soldiers to rescue me from…" She hid her face in her palms. "I cannot say it."

"What the devil is the commotion about?" A self-assured looking knight with a solid build pushed through the crowd. When he caught sight of Lachlan, the man's face turned white as a ghost. "Jesu." He crossed himself, but his stare did not waver.

Christina stepped beside the bold looking gentleman, dressed in mail and armed to the teeth. "He does have a striking resemblance to William, does he not?" Christina looked to Lachlan and gestured toward the impressive-looking knight. "May I introduce Sir Robert Dominus Boyd—he squired for William Wallace afore his…ah…death."

The medallion warmed against Lachlan's chest. He'd forgotten about the piece until now. And how in God's name did a hunk of bronze suddenly turn up the heat? Was it to blame for this weird state of affairs? What did Walter's note say? Lachlan's mind blanked.

Again, everyone looked at Lachlan expectantly as if he were supposed to do something. He bowed deeply as required when greeting the queen. "Pleased to make your acquaintance. I am Sir Lachlan Wallace." He never used the sir, but had been knighted by the queen after winning the gold in the Olympics for judo.

"A knight?" Boyd eyed him as if he'd lied. "Why is it I ken nothing of ye?"

Lachlan had no answer. For some odd reason, the engraving on the medallion came to mind. *Truth is like a beacon, but few choose to follow.* He opted to tell the goddamned truth. "I just returned from Brussels where I competed in a tournament…" Something in the back of his mind warned him to stop there.

"Ye've been on the tourney circuit have ye? And who were ye champion for?"

Lachlan knew what Sir Boyd meant—and the wrong answer was definitely Great Britain. If these zealots were diehard medievalists, they would know Great Britain hadn't come into existence yet. "Scotland, of course." His answer wasn't a lie.

"Fought for the highest bidder did ye?"

"As long as I agreed with their politics."

"Hmm." Sir Boyd ran his fingers down his beard, a perplexed expression on his face. Then he turned to Christina. "I havena seen a man of his girth since William."

She looked Lachlan from head to toe, her tongue slipping to the corner of her mouth. "I thought the same."

"There's an uncanny resemblance. Made a shiver run up my spine when I first spied him."

"He looks like a pauper," growled Hamish from behind. "And who would wear a picture of a hunchback becoming cured? What is that suspicious mural emblazoned on his chest? My oath, I reckon he's a follower of Satan."

Lachlan glanced down at the picture of evolution on his favorite sweatshirt. There was no use even trying to explain.

"He's a heretic for certain," said another.

"Nay!" Lady Christina stamped her foot. "Satan doesna rescue women from their enemies."

"Excuse me?" Lachlan spread his hands to his sides. "I'm standing right here."

"Aye, ye are." Sir Boyd walked in a circle around him, eyeing him like a piece of meat. "What happened to your weapons? Where is your coat of arms and where are your boots?" He pinched Lachlan's sweatshirt and rubbed it between his fingers. "What is this garb ye wear?"

"Aye, if he speaks true and has returned from the tournaments, he ought to be laden with coin," Hamish added.

"All lost to a woman," Lachlan said. Hell, Angela had taken his townhouse and God knew what else. He hadn't seen what she'd put into storage. For all he knew she'd robbed him blind. Bloody hell, he hadn't even had a chance to check the balance in the bank accounts yet.

Hamish snorted with an exasperated shake of his head. "Ye let a woman take your weapons and your boots?"

Dropping his hands and clenching his fists, Lachlan bit back his urge to land a punch to the old guard's snout. "I haven't had a chance to fetch them as of yet." Christ, the more they talked, the deeper he dug his hole. How the hell had he ended up on a battlefield with nothing? But one thing was for certain, he had to take charge now or else he'd end up with a crowd of fifty zealots lining up to take a swing at him. His gaze shifted to Lady Christina, who wrung her hands with worry furrowing her brow. "What are we going to do to find the lady's son?" Lachlan asked, deflecting the conversation from himself. "The lad was there. She saw him—and then the English attacked."

She grabbed Sir Boyd by the forearm. "We must make haste afore they take him too far into England."

"Ye're right. I've sent out spies already. My guess is they havena gone far. I reckon the bleeding English are hell bent on another invasion."

Christina clasped her hands over her chest and swept her gaze across the crowd. "We must collect our army and ride straight away."

Sir Boyd shook his head. "I dunna recommend it. Let us find out where they've taken Andrew first and then we can plan our attack."

"I agree with Lady Christina." Hamish stepped forward, giving her a nod—one that showed respect and fondness. Did he have a thing for his mistress? "If we dunna ride by the morrow, the trail will grow cold."

Boyd eyed him with a twitch to his jaw. "We shall put it before the king. If he agrees, then we'll ride at dawn."

"My new champion needs to be armed," said Christina.

Hamish coughed out a loud snort. "Champion, m'lady?"

"Sir Lachlan fought off countless blackguards to rescue me." She poked her man-at-arms in the chest with her pointer finger. "Whilst ye were otherwise engaged."

"I was battling the same mob of English rascals."

"Do ye challenge Lady Christina's appointment, Hamish?" asked Sir Boyd.

Scarface puffed out his chest. "Bloody oath, I do."

Lachlan's gut turned over. Fight the old mail-clad, pot-bellied zealot? There'd be no contest.

Boyd pointed. "Do ye put up your sword?"

Hamish drew his weapon and held it aloft. "I do with honor."

The knight gave Lachlan a deprecating once-over. "And what have ye of value?"

Should he back down? No. He'd not only humiliate himself, he'd humiliate Lady Christina. She might be a little hellion, but he kinda liked her. Lachlan tugged the medallion from beneath his sweatshirt. "Just this."

"Jesu." Boyd yanked the leather thong from Lachlan's neck. "Where did ye find this?"

Christina stepped in. "Didna Eva wear such a medallion?"

The knight turned it over in his palm. "I swear this is one and the same—she and William argued about it time and time again."

Prickly heat spread across Lachlan's skin. Surely they didn't mean Eva MacKay, his mother? And his father always referred to himself as Bill—well, his adopted father. Right? "Who are you talking about?"

"Ye dunna ken?" Suspicion filled Boyd's eyes. "She was there at Willy's trial. Father Blair always thought she was a witch—said she disappeared as soon as the sentence was pronounced."

Hamish scooted backward, his eyes bugging out. "Ye reckon he's a sorcerer?"

Sir Boyd pursed his lips as if considering.

"Burn him!" someone shouted from the crowd.

"Aye—stone him."

The dissonant chants grew and swarmed around the courtyard.

"Silence!" bellowed Sir Boyd.

Lachlan stuffed the medallion back into his shirt. "Whoa. I think I've overstayed my welcome. I'll be leaving now."

"Nay. We need ye." Lady Christina slid between Lachlan and the formidable knight. "Please, Sir Boyd, ye will agree with me if ye see this man fight. He is highly skilled—and I only witnessed him fighting with his hands—against armed soldiers at that."

Boyd gave a single nod. "Hamish—does your challenge still hold?"

The man-at-arms looked to Christina before he stepped forward and squared his shoulders. "Indeed."

"Choose your weapons," said the knight.

Lachlan held up his fists. "This is all I have." Though trained with a samurai sword, he preferred to keep things less bloody and opt for hand-to-hand combat.

Hamish drew his sword. "To the death?"

"Are ye out of your mind? I canna bear to lose either one of ye." Christina reached for the stout man's sword, but he jerked it away from her grasp.

Hamish paraded around the circle of onlookers. "Who here is willing to lend a poor beggar a blade?"

"Bloody hell, will we spend this entire eve arguing?" Boyd yanked the sword from his scabbard and handed the hilt to Lachlan. "Do ye ken how to use one of these?"

He took the weapon and balanced it in his hand, making note of the sharpness, the weight. Heavier than a samurai sword, it was honed sharp on both sides—but still a two-handed weapon. With a flick of his wrist, he whipped the blade in an arc, making it hiss through the air. Then he looked

Hamish in the eye. "I'd prefer hand-to-hand, but if the gentleman favors swords, I'll comply."

The crowd moved back, making a circle.

Boyd stepped between the challengers, just like a referee would do in a karate match. "This is sparring only. Ye both heard her ladyship. She needs men who are able bodied, not a pair of bloodied milksops. Ye ken?"

"Aye," said Hamish snarling like a caged baboon.

Lachlan bowed to Sir Boyd, "Yes, sir." Then he bowed to his opponent and crouched in a defensive stance. He'd done this a gazillion times. He'd fought with fists and knives, swords and nunchucks, bow staffs, guns and all manner of weaponry. Even if the man he faced was more skilled with a sword, Lachlan had no doubt he could disarm him.

"Best of three." Boyd sliced his hand through the air and backed into the crowd.

Lachlan reached for his inner peace, listening to his breath rush in his ears. A fight always started like this—in slow motion. He watched the shift of Hamish's eyes, the twitch of his scarred cheek.

Anticipating a thrust to the gut, Lachlan countered with a defensive upward strike. The stout warrior barreled in with a series of hacking strikes—easy to predict and defend, but leaving little room for attack.

But the man wore heavy mail and in a matter of ten seconds, his timing slowed. With a burst of strength, Lachlan defended the next hack with a clanging upward strike. The force of the blow sent Hamish's sword flying from his grasp. Using the momentum, Lachlan released his right hand and circling his fist under, he collided with the man-at-arms' chin. Hamish's head snapped back. With two steps, the medieval nutcase crashed to his back.

Lachlan lunged in for the kill, holding his sword above the big man's heart, waiting for a judge to shout three points awarded.

"First round to Lady Christina's new champion," bellowed Boyd.

That was good enough for Lachlan. He instantly let up and moved back to his starting position, waiting for Hamish to lumber to his feet and collect his sword. Lachlan proved the better fighter in the first two rounds and the contest was over. Honestly, Hamish was as strong as an ox. Though strength was important, Lachlan always taught his students the aggressive and cunning combatant wins.

By the end of the match, Hamish was breathing like he'd run a marathon. He held out the hilt of his sword to Lachlan. "I dunna ken what kind of sorcery ye're using, but I've seen no man fight as fast and crafty as ye."

Holding up his palm, Lachlan shook his head. The sword probably meant a great deal to the man. "I don't want your sword. I just need a lift."

Hamish scowled and readied this weapon like he wanted another ass-kicking.

"Stop." Lady Christina stepped in. "Sir Lachlan is right. This was not a contest to be won or lost, 'twas a demonstration of my new champion's prowess."

The scar on the man-at-arms' face stretched downward as he gave Lachlan a deprecating glare. "I still dunna trust him, m'lady."

"I agree," said Sir Boyd. "I shall advise the king of his presence. We shall allow him sanctuary behind Roxburgh's walls, but he must be kept under lock and key."

"Why?" Lachlan asked. "Haven't I proved enough?"

Sir Boyd snatched back his sword and handed Lachlan his medallion. "Do ye think we would allow a stranger—a possible sorcerer to roam freely about the castle? Ye'll need to do much more than prove your might afore we give ye free reign."

"Are you serious?" Panning his gaze across the hostile faces, Lachlan held up his palms in surrender. "Christ, I just need a phone to call my friend to give me a lift home."

Boyd stepped in. Though he had to raise his chin, they stood nose-to-nose. "Ye see, ye are speaking gibberish, and that makes me verra nervous. Aye, ye can fight like Wallace, God rest his soul—ye look like him, too. But I canna trust ye, not yet. And my word is final until the king speaks differently." He threw his thumb over his shoulder. "We willna throw ye in the pit, but ye will stay behind bars. Lady Christina will see to your needs until the king decides what is to be done."

Lachlan looked sideways. At least a dozen soldiers surrounded him with pikes leveled at his throat. Even if he had a prayer to fend them off, the portcullis was closed. His gaze shot to the top of the curtain walls. If he managed to break away, he'd be an easy target for the archers. The odds weren't good, no matter which way he considered it.

Before they led him away, he searched the faces for Lady Christina. Met with her wide-eyed stare, his jaw clenched and he shook his head.

Stabbed in the back by a woman yet again. Will I ever learn?

CHAPTER FOUR

Christina gulped against her thickening throat. Sir Lachlan's fierce glower before they took him away cut her to the quick. Why did he have to make her feel as if she'd betrayed his trust? Surely he must understand the need to keep everyone in the fortress safe. And though Lachlan hadn't done anything to hurt her or anyone else, he certainly proved himself capable. Goodness, if there ever was a one-man army it was he.

Besides, she would insure her new champion would receive food and hay to sleep upon—far more than a man could expect had he remained outside the castle walls at the mercy of outlaws, the English, or border reivers. Alone, Sir Lachlan would have faced all manner of dangers, especially after dark.

She couldn't worry about her new champion's ill feelings or glowering glares at a time like this, anyway. Now that the prisoner trade had been thwarted, she had dealings with King Robert whether the Bruce liked it or not.

She grasped Sir Boyd by the elbow. "Come, we need to gain an audience with the king."

It had been four months since Robert the Bruce had sent the English back to their lands with their tails tucked between their legs—four months since Christina had been released from being a prisoner in her own fortress, Ormond Castle on the Moray Firth. Since that time, she'd joined her king and the nobles who supported him, her only goal to be reunited with her son, heir to the de Moray barony.

She didn't delude herself into thinking her quest was of utmost importance to Scotland. King Robert had a great many things on his mind, but he still needed the nobles to support him. By freeing Andrew from captivity and bringing him home to Scotland, the Bruce was making an ally of the most powerful clan in the Highlands. There was a reason William Wallace had been successful at Stirling Bridge. The man built loyalty. Fighting beside Wallace, Christina's husband had a significant role in Scotland's success. Had her son's father survived, things might have turned out quite differently for the kingdom and Robert Bruce knew it.

Regardless of how anxious she felt when in the king's presence, she held her head high whilst she followed Sir Boyd through the labyrinth of buildings toward the royal donjon. She was in control of lands needed by the crown and showing the slightest bit of fear would be folly. Thank heavens her father, the late Earl of Atholl, had taught her inner strength. For this was no time for wallflowers. This was a time to stand her ground and make it known that neither she nor her son could be cast aside for another cause deemed more important.

With Sir Boyd, she marched through the donjon doors, across the great hall and up the stairwell to the first landing— straight to the solar King Robert used to direct his affairs. As was proper, the knight addressed the sentries standing guard outside the door. "Sir Boyd and Lady de Moray to see His Grace forthwith."

"I'm afraid ye'll have to wait, sir." The man bowed to Christina. "M'lady. The king is gathering with his ministers."

"Ballocks to that." Boyd pushed past the man and pulled down on the latch. "I *am* one of his bloody ministers."

Christina shuffled inside the solar on the knight's heels, then curtseyed deeply. "Your Grace, what are we to make of this day's events?"

The king grumbled, looking under his thick eyebrows and raking his gaze across the faces of the noblemen seated at the table. "We were discussing that very issue."

She moved closer to King Robert's chair. "We must make haste to follow the men who took Andrew afore they venture too far into England."

"'Tis already done." The king motioned for his squire to fill his tankard. "Sir Boyd sent our best men to track the varlets afore we left the battlefield." His stare grew dark. "This is the last time I place any trust in King Edward. No greater backstabber hath ever walked Christendom."

"Thank ye, sire." Christina bowed her head and curtseyed. "I should have kent ye'd act swiftly. I long to have my son home for Yule, as ye promised."

King Robert's lips thinned and stretched over his teeth. "We will do what we can to see him returned, but as I've said, if Andrew is lost to us, *ye* will have no choice but to choose a husband and set to breeding a new heir."

"Indeed," said the High Steward, licking his lips. He'd made his intentions clear where she was concerned and Christina had not been impressed.

The thought of making a match with the pompous toad made her stomach churn. "Now, let us not grow hasty. I couldna possibly do anything to put my son's inheritance in jeopardy."

"Aye, and we've discussed that many times," agreed the Bruce. "Ye'd best remember your place and set to your duty whilst ye're at court."

Her face burned. Why did the king make a spectacle about her need to be amenable to a suit of marriage whenever she had something unsavory to discuss?

King Robert shifted his gaze to Sir Boyd. "What other news? I had word there was a contest in the courtyard."

Christina looked to the candles alight in the wheel-shaped chandelier overhead. Nothing happened at court without the king gaining knowledge of it straight away.

"A knight has arrived from the continent," said Sir Boyd. "He fought off several Englishmen to rescue Lady Christina from capture."

"Och, I never should have allowed a woman to ride to the border. I should have kent Edward would turn backstabber." The king's gaze softened. "Ye must forgive me, Lady Christina."

She clasped her hands together, ever so grateful for the change in subject. "Oh no, ye wouldna have been able to keep me away. I saw my son today and for that, I would pay all the silver in my coffers."

"And what have ye done with this knight? Is he trustworthy?" The king reached for his goblet and took a swig.

Boyd shook his head. "He must earn his trust. For now, he's behind bars in the gatehouse. His speech is odd—I've only met one other person in my life with such a tongue."

Setting his drink on the board, the king regarded his champion knight intently. "And who might that be?"

"Eva MacKay," Christina answered. A clammy chill spread across her skin as she glanced to Sir Boyd. "She wore a similar medallion as well."

"William Wallace's wife?" asked the king. "I met her briefly. Good woman."

"Aye," said Sir Boyd. "This fella looks like Wallace for certain—every bit as tall as well."

The king scratched his beard. "We could use a man like that."

The High Steward shook his finger. "Agreed, *once* he's proven his loyalty."

Robert again raised his goblet, but this time in toast. "Here, here."

"But he's already done that." Christina took in a deep inhale and stood her ground. "I would have been…ah…*violated* for certain if he hadna fought for my virtue."

After taking a long drink, the king gave Sir Boyd a hardened stare. "Is this true, Robbie?"

Boyd nodded. "Aye, he saw a woman in distress and fought off a half-dozen pikemen."

King Robert leaned in. "And then he challenged a soldier in the courtyard?"

Clapping her hands together and tapping her fingers to her lips, Christina stepped in to set the record straight. "My man-at-arms, Hamish, challenged *him*, Your Grace."

"And he fought fair?" asked the king.

Sir Boyd nodded. "Aye, he stopped precisely after each of two take downs."

"And ye've still decided to keep him under lock and key?"

"Unless ye disagree, Your Grace." Boyd made a hissing sound through his teeth. "He's unusually skilled and—"

"But he uses his skill for good," Christina interrupted.

The knight sliced his hand through the air. "That verra well may be, m'lady, but I wouldna want him wandering the passageways at night until we ken a bit more about him."

"Sir Boyd is right," said the king. "Let us come to ken this knight, Sir…?"

"Lachlan," said Christina. "Lachlan Wallace."

Every man seated at the table gasped and mumbled.

"Dear God, mayhap he is an illegitimate son of our hero?" King Robert rocked back in his chair. "Did he mention anything about his parentage?"

"Nay," said Boyd. "But I wouldna want word spreading that Willy sired a bastard."

Christina had to agree with him there. She had only the greatest respect for William Wallace and his sacrifice for Scotland. Such a black mark would only serve to sully the hero's reputation and she would never want to be a party to that.

***

Lachlan sat with his back to the wall, his legs crossed. There weren't many options for comfort. As a matter of fact, there were no options. The cell they'd caged him in was about three feet wide and only a bit more than five feet high. Fortunately, it extended a good eight feet to the back wall where there sat a bucket—for him to piss, he assumed by the smell of it. Musty hay was strewn across the dirt floor. Some kind of green slime grew on the opposing wall. He could only tell because a bit of light shone in from the barred windows in the door separating his quarters from the guard's tower.

He shivered against the chill in the air.

No one had come past since the guardsmen had locked him inside a couple of hours ago, he reckoned. Damn. Lachlan wasn't wearing a watch, he didn't have his phone and his toes felt like ice.

Next time I relax on a strange bed, I'll keep my socks on—maybe my shoes, too. And I'll never accept another gift from Uncle Walter as long as I bloody live.

While he sat, he tried to make sense of the turn of events. He'd given up pinching himself. Aside from the nicks on his feet, he had a cut on the heel of his hand from his little sparring session with the mail-clad ape Lady Christina seemed to admire so much. The bleeding had stopped, but the throbbing hadn't. No dream could possibly be this vivid. Hell, movies weren't this vivid.

Did I pass through a time warp?

What had they said about Eva? It's a common enough name, but the irony was that there were too many parallels to ignore.

Lachlan looked a lot like his stepfather, Bill Wallace, who never used William because referring to himself as William Wallace was simply too disrespectful of Scotland's hero. Lachlan admired the man. Loved him like a true father. He was a decorated British colonel. His parents had told Lachlan the truth when he graduated from university. Weird, though. Lachlan looked more like Bill than he did his redheaded birthmother, Eva.

What if she'd really time traveled? If she had, why didn't she tell me about it?

Lachlan's mother was a world class expert on medieval history and knew more about William Wallace than anyone on the planet.

Drumming his fingers against his lips, he contemplated his mother's background. She'd taken him on archaeological digs when he was a lad, had filled his head with countless details, but until now he'd never thought much about where she'd gained all that knowledge. Mum had studied historical journalism at university and was sharp as a tack. But now that he was stuck in this hellhole, Lachlan wondered about the vast amount of pure detail she could spew at the drop of a hat. And Walter's note said she'd worn the medallion. Christ, there were too many coincidences.

Not to mention, Robert Boyd, a man who was known to be one of Robert the Bruce's favorites, had said flat out that Lachlan looked like William Wallace.

What the hell?

He tugged the medallion from beneath his sweatshirt and held it to the light. The damned thing had *warmed* against his skin. Why? Was it because Lady Christina had introduced him to Sir Boyd or because she'd mentioned Wallace? And when does a hunk of bronze grow warm without something heating it up?

Lady Christina and Sir Boyd had thought their Eva might be a witch because of her medallion…and she had an odd accent just like Lachlan did, though he could tell anyone who listened that his wee burr was the normal one.

He sighed and turned the medallion over in his palm. Something had to be tied to this relic.

He thought back.

Walter had written a note...

What had it said?

Goosebumps spread down Lachlan's arms as he pictured Walter's scrawling penmanship in his mind's eye.

"*This isn't a gift, but a loan. I lent it to your mother before you were born after she'd experienced a tragedy and it turned her life around in a miraculous way.*"

Fuck—why hadn't he thought of that before?

Because I've been a wee bit occupied.

He'd bet a million bucks the Eva Sir Boyd mentioned and his mother were the same person.

Christ, I'm going to be sick.

Sweat broke out on his forehead.

How the hell do I get home?

He pressed the heels of his hands into his eyes.

Don't jump to conclusions. There have to be answers out there. A person doesn't just fall asleep and wake up hundreds of years in the past...

The door opened and someone stepped inside holding a blinding torch. Lachlan shaded his eyes while footsteps approached. Once the torch had been placed in an iron holder on the wall, he made out Lady Christina, a lad he hadn't seen before, and two guards armed to the teeth with helms shoved low over their brows.

He gave the men a good eye roll. One that said he wasn't interested. The problem with being six-foot-six was that everyone wanted to pick a fight with him to see if they could win. Early in his life, Lachlan had taken a liking to martial arts and teachings of inner peace and self-defense—to gain superb skill and only use it when necessary. But he also learned he could stop a brawl with the minimum of effort. Now it appeared his skill surpassed his inner peace—at least in their minds.

Still wearing a drab black gown and grey veil covering everything but her face, Lady Christina stopped outside the cell door with her arms laden. "I've brought ye a cloak and a basket of food, and Peter has an armload of hay for ye to make a pallet."

Lachlan stared. He should thank her, but with the present circumstances as they were, he felt anything but mannerly.

"Now dunna move," said a guard, working a key into the lock while the other toad stood with his pike at the ready.

Lachlan could take both of them if he wanted to—just might have to if this bullshit kept up, but he'd play along for now until he figured a way out of this mess. "Did you bring any shoes?" he asked none too nicely—to make a point, dammit. It didn't matter how much his mother had drilled in his manners, he was bloody cranky. "Socks? My feet are cold."

The door creaked on its hinges and the lady waved the lad inside. "Apologies. I'll have a cobbler measure ye for a pair of boots on the morrow."

The boy was dressed much like the pictures Lachlan had seen of a squire—a rough-hewn tunic, chausses and leather shoes that looked homemade and a bonnet that was too big for his head. He tossed his armload of hay to the dirt and shuffled backward out the door, the eyes in his dirty face as round as coins.

Lachlan chose to ignore him. "Yeah, well I reckon you don't have any size sixteens lying around anyway."

"I beg your pardon?" She stepped inside and handed him the cloak.

Made of wool, it was surprisingly thick. "A cobbler would be great," he replied. God, these people didn't understand anything he said.

She set the basket beside him, followed by a ewer and a tankard. "I brought ye some ale as well."

Lachlan finally gave in to his mother's voice screeching in his head. Damn, it never hurt to be polite. "Thank you."

"Is there anything else ye need afore we head for our beds?" Dear Lord, she could stand up inside this box without hitting her head.

"You said before you needed someone like me." He took her hand.

"Watch yourself," warned a guard.

His gaze slipping to the maggot, Lachlan tightened his grip, but not too hard. The fine bones in her hand were utterly frail and petite compared to his. "I want to help you find your son." He stared up at her. If she allowed him to help, he'd be released from the cell—might find a way home. "I'll go stir crazy if you keep me in here much longer."

She smiled. Warmly. How was it women could look so winsome when they had a man by the balls? "I want ye to be the de Moray champion—but ye heard Sir Boyd, ye must prove your loyalty."

Lachlan snorted. "How am I supposed to do that when I'm locked in here?"

"The king must decide."

"Please." He tried for the pleading, puppy-dog eyes look. It always worked on women, especially Mum. "I cannot maintain my strength sitting in these cramped quarters. I need to work out."

Shaking her head, Christina gaped at him like he was speaking Martian. "To what?"

"To spar, to run—do things that build muscle and strength."

"Oh, aye." She returned his hand squeeze. "I dunna want ye turning into a tub of lard, either."

Was he cracking the ice? He poured on the puppies. "Look. I'll give you my promise to be on my best behavior, but I need at least four hours per day of exercise."

She drew a finger to her lips as if thinking. "I shall do my best to influence Sir Boyd to allow ye a modicum of freedom."

Lachlan released her hand. "Thank you, m'lady."

She leaned down and patted his shoulder. "I have told the king ye are my champion."

"Then allow me to prove it."

She nodded. "Give me time," she whispered. "I ken ye have a good heart. I feel it in my bones."

Chapter Five

Christina slept fitfully, her mind bouncing between her son and Sir Lachlan. The only thing that had kept her thriving through thirteen years of captivity was the need to free Andrew from the clutches of those English tyrants. Yesterday's failure cut her to the quick, but if anything, it made her more determined. When faced with adversity, she was one to find an open window. She'd been a prisoner herself, constrained to the walls of her castle. Her new freedom infused her with confidence. As she sat up and stretched, a ray of light shone through a wee gap in the window furs.

The fire had ebbed to coals and under most circumstances, Christina would pull her comforter over her head and dream until Ellen came with the bellows. But not this morn.

The light filled her breast with a beam of hope. Sir Lachlan Wallace had come into her life for a reason. To her, he'd already proven his valor. She might be merely a woman, but he had saved her from the humility of rape and, quite possibly, death. Scraping her teeth over her bottom lip, a twinge of guilt needled at the back of her neck. She should not have stood idle while they locked him in the gatehouse cell. True, she'd done what she could to make him comfortable, but her champion deserved better, especially at this time of year. Yule was neigh, for heaven's sake.

She hopped out of bed. The floorboards cold underfoot, she dashed to the hearth and stoked the fire with squares of peat. Then she hopped in place a few times to grow warm before she braved her chilly garderobe.

After dressing, Christina headed for the great hall to break her fast—and, more importantly, to find Sir Boyd.

Fortunately, she found the knight seated alone on the dais.

She climbed the steps and took a seat beside him. "Where are the other nobles, m'lord?"

He plunged his spoon into his porridge. "Still abed, the lazy bast—um—I mean the lazy Scots."

"I woke with the sun." A servant placed a bowl of porridge and spoon in front of her. "And it is fortuitous that I find ye alone."

"Oh? Why is that?" The young knight arched his eyebrow. Though Robbie had grown into a handsome man, she was six years his senior. She had been ten and eight when she'd first met the lad—the same day as the Battle of Stirling Bridge. Robbie had been a sandy-haired, wide-eyed lad of twelve, ever so proud to be William Wallace's squire. At the time she'd come to visit with her husband, she was pregnant. On that very day, Christina had also met Eva MacKay. She'd always remember how Lady Eva had placed her hands on Christina's belly and told her the bairn would be a lad—the lass had the gift of a seer for certain.

Gathering her thoughts, she cleared her throat. There was no use thinking about the past and if there was anyone at Roxburgh Castle in whom she could confide, it was Sir Robert Dominus Boyd. "I think we are treating my new champion unjustly."

He drank down a bit of cider. "How else should I treat such a man, especially when the king is sleeping within Roxburgh's walls?"

"I think Sir Lachlan is the knight I need to help me save Andrew."

"Aye?" Robbie shoveled a bite of oats in his mouth. "I dunna trust him."

Christina picked up her spoon. Regardless of her trust, she needed to tread carefully when it came to Sir Boyd. He had great influence with the king as well as with the men. "I trust him. He saved me the horror of being violated and then shared my horse to Roxburgh, behaving the perfect gentleman throughout the journey."

Sir Boyd wiped his mouth with the back of his hand. "He could have used ye to ferret inside these walls."

Christina's ears grew hot. Goodness, this man could think of every angle to thwart her purpose. "I think not."

"What if he's a sorcerer?"

She slapped her hand on the table. "Then he is but an angel."

"Blasphemy," said the knight in an accusing tone.

Though she, indeed, must tread lightly where Sir Boyd was concerned, it didn't mean she should play the meek widow and allow him to bamboozle her. "Nay—do not think angels only exist in the Bible, good sir. God has sent us angels throughout history."

"Aye," he agreed with sarcasm in his voice. "Like those who destroyed Sodom and Gomorrah."

Little did he know he'd opened a window for Christina to further her purpose. She snatched the opportunity. "Do not tell me ye believe Scotland is filled with unchaste subjects."

He chuckled and reached for his tankard of cider. "Far less than England, at least."

"Is it Sir Lachlan's medallion that's bothering ye?"

He took a drink. "Of sorts, and the way he seemed to materialize from nowhere."

"Aye, well, I believe Eva MacKay—the last person with such a medallion—was an angel of sorts. What say ye? As I recall, ye spent far more time with her than I."

"Jesu." Sir Boyd ran a hand down his face and looked to the rafters. "Willy loved Lady Eva almost as much as he loved Scotland. But she disappeared for eight years—his darkest years." He shook his head and chuckled. "I'll never forget the day she returned. If ye remember, she was taller than most men."

"Indeed I do—she towered over me for certain." Christina leaned forward, encouraging him to continue.

"Aye, well that day she came to us wearing a wee skirt—the length of a tunic. Her legs were bare, except covered by a sheer cloth that clung to her skin—made her flesh shimmer. She wore shoes with tall, pointed heels that looked practical for nothing. If I werena a God fearing man, I would have sworn she'd come from the *future*." Facing her, he pointed his finger under Christina's nose. "Never repeat such words."

She clasped her hands over her thumping heart. Dear Lord, and he thought she was speaking blasphemy? Repeating such words could see her burned at the stake. "Ye ken I willna."

His stern countenance softened a wee bit. "Then their love affair resumed as if they'd never been separated. There was no' a thing she wouldna do for him. And she stayed beside him until the end."

Christina sighed. "Aye, she did."

"She healed him, too."

Gulping, Christina lowered her gaze to her bowl of oats. A familiar and sickly lump swelled in her throat. "Unfortunately, she couldna heal my Andrew," the words slipped from her lips with an icy overtone.

"What happened that day?" Robbie asked. "I've always wondered. It was the verra day Eva disappeared the first time."

"I dunna ken." Her eyes blurring with sudden tears, Christina blinked and swiped her hands across them. "I went to the chapel to pray and the next thing I kent, my husband had died and she was gone. William spent an entire sennight in solitude and I had no choice but to return home alone to birth my bairn at Ormond Castle."

Sir Boyd scratched his head—reminding her of the old Robbie she knew. "Lady Eva was like a mother to me. Though I didna ken much about her, she always kent the right things to say. She was the only woman I could go to with questions." With a gasp, his jaw dropped, eyes growing round as sovereigns. His face grew white and he leaned forward, resting his forehead in the palm of his hand. "My God, the warrior's name is Lachlan."

Christina placed her hand on his shoulder. "Aye—?"

Boyd looked up, pain etched across his face. "Eva was in Scone when my friend took an arrow and died. I wanted to kill Willy that day. I'd never had a friend my age and Willy made me mind the horses whilst the lad joined the ranks of the archers." Sir Boyd's lips trembled. "I bawled like a bairn at the funeral whilst Eva held me in her arms and made the pain go away."

"I'm sorry."

"Nay—ye dunna understand. My friend's name was *Lachlan.*"

"Ye dunna think…?"

Sir Boyd shook his head. "They're not one and the same. Ye canna bring someone back from the dead. Besides, *your* warrior looks too much like Willy."

"Do ye think William and Eva may have had a child?"

The knight smirked. "That makes no sense. Willy died childless nine years ago and the behemoth behind bars in the gatehouse is in his prime."

"Well, I'll be the first to agree there's something odd about people who wear those medallions, but I'll also be the first to testify they are sent to us to perform good deeds." She picked up her spoon and shook it. "I want ye to allow Sir Lachlan to spar with the guard."

Sir Boyd eyed her as if considering. "Have ye any further requests, m'lady?"

"Not this day." She smiled inside. She couldn't have asked for the conversation to have proceeded any better if she had scripted it out.

***

Two-fifty-three, two-fifty-four… Lachlan counted while pumping pushups. The far door screeched open, but he didn't stop to see who it was. So far this morning, they'd brought him a bowl of watery mush and he wasn't at all happy about it. Surely they had eggs and sausages in a place like this. Was that too much for a *champion* to ask, even if he was incarcerated?

"Tiring yourself out, I see?" a deep voice echoed between the stone walls.

Lachlan stopped and rocked back to his knees. "Sir Boyd?" The great knight was flanked by two guards.

"Ye look surprised to see me."

"I admit you weren't the first person I expected."

"Lady Christina convinced me to have ye spar with the men. Are ye up to it?"

"I'd fight an army if it meant getting out of this cage."

One of the guards used an enormous key to open the door. "Mind yourself or ye'll end up right back here."

"I'll keep that in mind." Lachlan crawled through the opening, then stood.

Sir Boyd glanced down to his bare feet. "Still no shoes?"

Lachlan wriggled his toes. "The cobbler visited earlier—made me put my foot through the bars."

"Aye, well, Malcolm is most likely less than half your size—not a fighting man for certain." Boyd examined Lachlan's face, pinching his eyebrows. "Did ye spend time in the Holy Land?"

"No…well, sort of. I went to Malta with my parents when I was young." Lachlan didn't want to let too much out of the bag. He'd vacationed in Malta a few times because his parents kept a timeshare there.

"Parents?"

"Yes. Why do you ask?"

"Just curious." It appeared Boyd was playing with his cards close to his chest as well. Lachlan didn't care one way or the other as long as he figured out a way home. Lady Christina was hell bent on rescuing her son—maybe Lachlan had landed there to help her? Whatever the reason, he'd play along until he figured a way back to his time. He still didn't know if he was in a time warp or among a group of zealots occupying a remote part of the borderlands. Regardless, why couldn't the process that had landed him on the battlefield reverse itself? He was still holding on to the idea these nutcases had cordoned off a patch of the borders and created their own medieval world. Maybe some disappointed fan saw his loss on TV, stole into Uncle Walter's flat, drugged him and hauled him to the battlefield where he awoke?

Strange, but not impossible. Right?

Boyd beckoned him with a wave of his hand. "Come. Today the men will be sparring with their fists. To be able to wield a sword is one thing, but a man who can win with cunning and only the tools which God gave him is truly a champion."

"I agree." Lachlan fell in step behind the knight. "What is your favorite weapon, sir?"

"Horse and pike." Boyd flashed a wry grin over his shoulder. "A man with a sword canna come near ye if ye're riding at a gallop with an eight-foot spear in your hand."

Always one to seek the greater advantage over an opponent, Lachlan chuckled. "I like the way you think."

"Aye, but dunna misunderstand. I'd use a rock to crush a man's skull afore I'd let him run me through."

"Isn't that why we train? To learn how to stay alive, given the worst circumstances imaginable?"

Boyd stopped, turned and jammed his fists into his hips. "I hadna ever heard it put that way, but ye're spot on." He looked over Lachlan from head to toe. "Where did ye learn to fight?"

"Master Amori from Japan."

The knight's face blanked. "From where?"

Lachlan forced himself to hold in a guffaw. "Have you heard of the Orient?"

"An Oriental trainer is here in Scotland?"

How should I respond to that? Lachlan knew of several Asian black belt champions who lived in the UK. *Keep it simple.* "Unfortunately, Master Amori passed away a few years ago."

"I've heard tale of the great army of Genghis Khan—the monks of the Order of Saint John still practice tactics learned when the Oriental general invaded the Holy Land."

Jeez—this guy came up with the weirdest shit. Lachlan rubbed his temple. *Khan—end of the twelfth century, beginning of the thirteenth, I think. About a hundred years ago for Boyd. Not Japanese, but Mongolian.* "Yes. Khan was unsurpassed in his day—but a ruthless tyrant."

Boyd chuckled and started off again. "I've met enough of *them* in my day." Though not a lad, the knight couldn't be any older than Lachlan.

"How old are you, sir?" he asked.

"Eight and twenty." Boyd arched an eyebrow. "And ye?"

"Thirty."

"Hmm. I would have taken ye for younger."

It must be on account of a good diet and exercise. Lachlan snorted.

"Ye find that funny?"

"Yes, I suppose. If a man eats well-rounded meals, he stands the best chance for good health and long life."

"What is this? Well-rounded?"

"Lean meat, plenty of vegetables, whole grain breads, milk, cheese, fruit."

"That's a verra pleasant thought, but in midwinter a man's fortunate if he can find an apple in the cellar that hasna gone bad."

Stepping into the courtyard, Lachlan held up his wrists. "If you're planning to have me spar, you'd better remove these manacles."

Boyd folded his arms across his chest. "They stay."

I could use them as a weapon. "Suit yourself." Lachlan panned his gaze across the faces of the army. "Who wants to be my first victim?"

CHAPTER SIX

Christina's chamber overlooked the courtyard. She hooked the window furs to the side, opened the shutters, then took a seat in the window embrasure to watch Lachlan spar. Aside from his bout with Hamish, she had only seen him fight on the battlefield and she'd been too distraught to give him a fair assessment. At least that's what she told herself as she leaned forward. Of course, at the mature age of four and thirty, she was too old to admire his good looks. Though anyone could find a talented display of brawn fascinating to watch. And if she, indeed, intended to fold him into the de Moray army, she would need an iron-clad opinion of his level of skill.

My interest is purely for the good of my clan. I must remain completely impartial. If he is the right man to fetch Andrew, he will have my support. Once my son is returned to me, God willing, we will spend our Yule with King Robert then return to Ormond Castle and strive to put these years of oppression behind us.

Below, Sir Lachlan strode around the circle of men, his arms outstretched—at least as far as the chain between his manacles would allow. After two turns, Sir Boyd removed his weapons and his mail, handing them to a guard. Raising his fists, the king's greatest knight stepped into the center of the courtyard. Mirroring his stance, Lachlan faced Robert the

Bruce's champion. Christina's stomach squeezed. Lachlan was perhaps a hand taller, but Boyd had squired for William Wallace. There wasn't a man in Scotland who could best him.

In a blur of fists, blocks and kicks, the two men engaged like a pair of wildcats, weaving in and out, deflecting blows with one hand while issuing punches with the other. Lachlan spun with a lightning fast kick aimed at the head. Ducking, Boyd clipped Lachlan's heel. The larger man drew his knee in—Christina had never seen such a move. Then he snapped a forward kick so fast, she didn't realize what he'd done until Sir Boyd's head snapped back and he toppled over.

With a gasp, she covered her mouth.

Lachlan shuffled back, crouched and ready for another bout while he waited for Sir Boyd to recover. Who on earth would be so polite when sparring? When Sir Boyd wiped his nose with his shirt sleeve and was met with a swath of blood, the entire courtyard erupted in mayhem.

As she sprang to her feet, Christina's heart nearly burst from her chest. The men rushed poor Lachlan. Except for a man who jumped on his back, the warrior fended them off with sweeping blocks. The man on his back slipped his arm around Lachlan's throat, choking him. Still fighting off multiple men at once, Lachlan's feet skittered backward until he slammed the choking cur into the wall. With a bone-jarring grunt, the attacker dropped to the ground. Downed guardsmen peppered the courtyard, yet still more ran in to take a swing at her new champion.

"Halt," bellowed Sir Boyd, marching forward and shoving men aside.

"He's a beast!" someone shouted from the back of the ranks.

"I am merely a man." Lachlan held up his arms, stretching the length of chain between his wrists. "I could have used this length of chain as a weapon. I could have strangled the life out of half of you, but I chose not to because I am a man of honor."

Christina's heart hammered so loudly, she practically had to lean out the window to hear what was being said.

Sir Boyd shook Lachlan's hand. "Bloody oath, how did ye manage to kick me after I blocked your spin?"

"Just a countermove I picked up along the way, I guess."

"And then ye fought off the whole mob of soldiers?"

"Not exactly. I was only trying to defend myself."

Boyd grabbed Lachlan's upper arm and squeezed. "Jesu, ye *are* Goliath."

"I'm a warrior. I've dedicated my life to fitness, to toning my body and studying different forms of defense. I've studied how motion can flow from one movement and build to the next, and to the next." Sir Lachlan pointed to Sir Boyd's chest. "May I show you something?"

"Of course."

He held out his hand. "Grab my wrist and wrench it up my back."

"As hard as I can? 'Cause I'm likely to break it."

"Do it as hard as you like."

"Break it," shouted Hamish.

Christina would have a word with her boisterous man-at-arms.

Sir Boyd snatched the wrist and whipped Lachlan around, brutally yanking the poor man's arm up his back.

Instead of crying out with pain, Lachlan rolled out with the force of the move. He slammed his elbow into the side of Sir Boyd's head, spun around, flipped Boyd's arm over and kicked him in the backside.

"What the devil?" the knight shouted as Lachlan forced his wrist downward. Now poor Robbie could do nothing but drop to his knees. "Arraagh."

In the blink of an eye, Lachlan released his hold, took two steps back and bowed. "A continuous flow of motion, sir—

and believe me, I'd be a fair bit more effective without these bloody manacles."

"Aye, that's what I'm afraid of," said Boyd, rubbing his wrist and rising to his feet.

"I can help you. If you are willing to trust me."

Boyd scratched his beard as if considering. "These are trying times and trust comes easy for no man. Especially someone who appeared out of the blue. Why havena I heard tale of ye afore?"

Lachlan's gaze shifted to Christina's window, but he pretended not to see her. "Like I said. I've been away."

"I ken of a woman who claimed the same."

"Was she friend or foe?"

"Friend—for the most part, I'd reckon."

"Did she betray you?"

"Nay."

"Then why did you say 'for the most part'?"

"'Cause she had a way of disappearing that nary a soul could explain—not even Father Blair, God rest his soul."

Lachlan again looked at Christina, but this time, his gaze lingered. "People say I'm a patient man, but I wouldn't recommend pushing me too far—that cell you're locking me in is a bit too cramped for a bloke of my size. I'll stand beside your army. I'll do what I can to help Lady Christina find her son, but if you continue to treat me like a criminal, I'll be like that woman you knew and you'll never set eyes on me again."

"I'll keep that in mind," said Sir Boyd as he snapped his fingers and hailed a pair of guards.

Lachlan continued to stare straight up at Christina's window. His eyes bore through her like a drill. Her heart thumped like she'd been running a footrace.

She had no doubt his words were intended for her ears as well as Sir Boyd's. He turned one palm up, making a bowl and pretended to use a spoon to feed himself with the other.

Goodness, the man was telling her he needed food. Hadn't they given him enough?

Most likely they hadn't.

She nodded and gave him a subtle wave before the guards led him back to his cell.

***

Lachlan sat cross-legged in the center of his cell, his wrists on his knees, his palms turned up and his eyes closed. Focusing on the sun, imagining a cool breeze on his face, he transported himself to a place of peace—a place where the pain from the bruises he'd sustained in the courtyard no longer felt like iron pokers jabbing into his flesh.

He might have grown sick and tired of being treated like a criminal, but Lachlan could still compartmentalize his emotions. Martial arts had taught him many things, the most useful being self-control. Meditation was like a hypnotic drug for him. When things were at their worst, he could transport his body and mind to a place of peace and tranquility.

"Ah-mm, ah-mm," he silently whispered as if the air flowing in and out of his body was the source of wind. With each "ah", he filled his lungs and with each "mm" he slowly let the breath rush through his nose until his air completely dissipated. Over and over, he repeated the meditative sequence while his body transitioned to a place of weightlessness.

When the guardhouse door creaked open, he didn't move. But he did know who was walking toward his cell and that she was alone. Her light footsteps gave her away, as did the swish of her frumpy skirts. Inhaling, Lachlan caught the hint of roasted meat—lamb perhaps—and freshly baked bread. He caught something else with his next inhale. Oiled leather.

"Are ye planning to sit there all night and ignore me?" asked Lady Christina, sounding like a true aristocrat who was by no means accustomed to being snubbed.

A long exhale released from his lungs while Lachlan opened his eyes. "Forgive me, m'lady. I was meditating."

She squinted, drawing her eyebrows inward. "What say ye? *Med-i-tate-ing*?" She pronounced the word clearly like a foreign language teacher would to a class.

"Concentrating," Lachlan revised.

"Ye have an odd way of doing it if ye ask me." She set her basket on the ground. "And what are ye concentrating about?"

"Clearing my mind."

"Why would anyone want to do that?"

"If I didn't do it, I'd be one angry bastard."

She flinched at his course language, but didn't admonish him.

He looked from one claustrophobic wall to the other. "Wouldn't you be angry if you were locked in this miniscule cell after you'd helped someone escape from an attack? After you proved to others that you were not a threat?"

She pursed her lips and glanced sideways. Then she gave him a nod. "Aye. But ye need to hold on to the reins for another day or two. I'm working on Sir Boyd. He's found favor with ye for certain."

"Wonderful."

"Mayhap your meditating is a good idea. If it keeps ye from growing too angry."

"It does." Feeling like a schoolboy sitting cross-legged and craning his neck, he shifted to his knees and grasped the bars.

She gave him a coy look with those pixie doll eyes. "Ye ken we are only trying to win back our freedom."

"Yes. I'm a Scot, too. Remember?"

"A different sort of Scot, but a Scot nonetheless, I suppose."

No use trying to argue with that nutty logic. Lachlan gestured toward the basket. "It smells like you brought my supper."

"Forgive me." Christina swept down and plucked a parcel wrapped in leather. "Ye indicated ye needed more food, so I brought ye a leg of lamb and a loaf of bread." She grinned, plucking something else as well. "And an apple."

The apple was about the size of a plum. A crabapple at best and looked as sour as an unripe lemon. But the lady beamed, incredibly pleased with herself as if she'd climbed a tree and plucked the measly piece of fruit from the highest limb and somehow lived to tell about it.

"I am in your debt, m'lady." Lachlan reached through the bars and took the gifts.

"I hope it is enough. All that food should feed three or four men."

He set the parcel and apple beside him, wishing he could stand straight and give her a proper thank you. "Men as large as me?"

"Nooooo." Her gaze slid down his body while her tongue slipped to the corner of her mouth. "There are not many men about with your—ah—girth."

He laughed, ignoring the quick rush of goosebumps rising on his arms. "It appears not." In his lifetime, Lachlan hadn't met many men his size and fewer who were larger.

"Are ye going to eat?"

He untied the leather thong around the parcel. "Will you join me?"

"I've already had my meal, thank ye."

The bread was half-soaked with juice from the meat and she hadn't exaggerated when she'd said she'd brought him a leg of lamb. She'd given him an entire leg, shank and all. The only problem? There was nothing to cut it with. He ripped off an enormous bite with his teeth while she watched.

Then her dainty mouth formed an "O". After reaching into her basket, she held up a pair of shoes. "The cobbler finished your boots. Goodness, I'd wager both of my feet would fit into one of these."

"Thank you." He pulled them through the bars and kept chewing.

She pointed to the footgear. "Are ye aiming to try them on?"

Gulping down his bite, Lachlan looked them over first. He'd never had a pair of handmade shoes before. They had thick soles of a woven fiber—possibly hemp or thistle. The leather uppers were soft, with two loops stitched into each side and a leather thong to tie them with, crisscrossing over the foot and again at the ankle, making them boot-like.

"Are they not to your liking?" Christina asked.

"They are very nice." He gave her a smile—at least as much as he could. Presently, there wasn't any place on his body that wasn't sore from the gang fight in the courtyard. He slipped his foot into one and tied it. "Perfect fit, though it's unfortunate I can't walk around a bit to test them."

"Mayhap on the morrow." She smiled like she was about to tell him something exciting. "I've talked Sir Boyd into allowing ye a turn or two upon the wall-walk. Ye were asking about the abbey and ye'll be able to see it from there."

That was the best news he'd heard for days. Who knew a turn on the wall-walk of an archaic castle would be thrilling? But it would give him an opportunity to see Kelso Abbey. From his last visit he had a clear picture of the ruin in his mind's eye. Seeing something familiar would be a relief—and with luck, he'd spot a few power lines—a cell tower—a paved road—contrails. Any sign that he hadn't completely lost his mind or his…century.

She clasped her hands—a gesture he'd noticed her often do. "I've a question to ask and I want ye to promise ye'll tell me true."

Finished with tying the second shoe, he held up his hands. "I've told you the truth about everything so far."

"Verra well." Her knuckles turned white. "Are ye a sorcerer?"

Christ, he nearly blew snot out his nose. "I am not, never have been, and do not intend on becoming one, m'lady."

"Then how can ye fight with the strength of five men?"

"I've said I'm a warrior and that is true. I started training at a very young age." He wanted to say he'd joined the armed services and had done a turn in the Holy Land …or Afghanistan. *Did Afghanistan exist in the fourteenth century?* Bloody hell, Lachlan didn't know. His mother was the historian in the family. He gave Christina as sober a look as he could. Who knew how much fighting techniques had improved over the centuries? One only needed to look at boxing pictures from the early 1900s and compare them with modern photos to know mankind had made great strides in understanding physical fitness in the past hundred-plus years. It was one thing to be strong and oafish. It was another to turn a man's natural aptitude into a fighting machine. "I work hard every day to maintain my strength. I eat well, too. A man cannot be at the top of his game unless he has a well-rounded diet."

"Ye mean meat?"

"I mean everything—especially meat, dairy, grains, fruits and vegetables." He'd said the same to Boyd.

"Och, if only all that was in season year round."

"If only." If he ever got out of this cell, he'd find out about their cellars and storage and canning, pickling— whatever they did to keep food through the winter.

"So if Scotland's army ensured they ate hearty, they'd become better warriors?"

"I'd bet on it." He eyed her. "I can help them…and just maybe that's why I'm here."

"Ye dunna ken why ye're here?"

"No—it's as if I've suffered a concussion and awoke in the midst of a battle."

"Ye'd suffered a what?"

"A blow to the head."

"Well, for what 'tis worth, I reckon ye may be right. But I think ye were sent to me to rescue my son." She twisted her lips. "The only question is…"

"What?"

"Will ye do it?"

"Yes," he said without hesitation. If it meant he'd awake the next day back in Uncle Walter's flat, he'd do just about anything as long as it wouldn't land him in jail for the rest of his life. "Unless…"

Her crystal blue eyes grew startled. "Unless?"

"Unless you aim to continue to keep me in here like a criminal." *If that happens, I'll dig my way out of this hellhole.*

"Please. I will bring ye anything ye need and I'll speak to the king again. I give ye my word I'll find a way to see ye released from this cage and those irons removed, mark me."

He tipped up his chin, insuring he didn't appear *too* trusting. "From the hospitality I've seen thus far, I'm not convinced."

"Och, ye dunna understand. We are a kindhearted people."

"Really?" he held out his manacled wrists. "Who knew?"

"Ye'll soon discover we are hospitable once a man proves his worth. Ye must ken, after years of war, we've had no choice but to be suspicious of newcomers—especially folks who appear out of the blue, fight like Goliath and have no kin to speak on their behalf."

She reached through the bars and grasped his hand between her palms.

Lachlan's heart skipped a beat as if her touch thrummed with electricity.

And on the other side of the bars, the lady's lips parted with a wee gasp. Had she felt the sudden zing, too?

Slowly, he raised his eyelids until he met with the intensity of her blue-eyed stare. A pink tongue moistened her lips. "Trust me," she whispered.

His heart squeezed. Hell, she was prettier than a rose in full bloom. Rarely did Lachlan ever do anything without thinking about his action first, but when he raised her hands to his lips, pure emotion seized his sanity. Closing his eyes, he inhaled her scent—the heady fragrance of woman—the same ambrosia he'd noticed when they'd ridden together. Unfortunately, it had the same effect on him now as it had the last time he'd kissed her hand—a scent heady like jasmine, winsome like the sea. A slightly stuttered breath slipped through his lips as he kissed, then again inhaled her delightful fragrance.

The lady opposite politely cleared her throat.

His eyes flashed open. The poor woman turned redder than a ruby as she slipped her hands away and clasped them over her heart. "Until the morrow," she said.

Lachlan nodded. "Tomorrow, m'lady." Christina may have vexed his heart for a moment, but with a blink, he regained his senses. Who said "the morrow" unless they were performing Shakespeare?

A complete and total nut.

No, no. He mustn't let a soft-spoken, blue-eyed woman with a pretty face get under his skin—especially when he was the idiot who'd allowed himself to be locked behind bars.

Chapter Seven

With Hamish's shove in the back, Lachlan stumbled out onto the wall-walk. Tripped over his feet was more like it. Without socks, the new boots Christina had given him needed to be worked in. He swiped a finger through the quarter-inch of snow sitting on top of the wall. "It's November, right?"

"Aye. November three and twenty," said the old guard. "Looks as if we're having an early winter, which leaves me wondering why a man would ask to take a turn around wind-blown ramparts when he should be sitting afore a hearth."

"Sorry. There are no hearths in my *cozy* accommodations." Lachlan craned his neck, looking over the top of the guard's head and closing his new cloak against the chill. "Where is Kelso Abbey from here?"

"Ye'll see it on the other side." Hamish pointed his thumb over his shoulder. "Nary a man could miss the monstrosity."

"Oh?" Lachlan asked, though he didn't elaborate on the true purpose of his question. He himself had seen the monastic ruin that loomed over the small village. He remembered it well—no roof, lots of gravestones. It stood as a testament to the ravages of Father Time assisted by years of border wars between England and Scotland. He jogged around the wall-walk with Hamish huffing on his heels.

"What the devil? Now ye're up here, are ye in a hurry to climb down again?"

"No," Lachlan said over his shoulder, quickening his pace. "I thought you were a warrior?"

"What does that have to do with running?"

"Everything." Lachlan chuckled to himself until he ran past the towers and the abbey came into view. After skidding in the snow, he stopped himself by wrapping his arms around a stone merlon before he slipped through a crenel and broke his neck.

"Holy shit," he mumbled while a clammy chill coursed down the outside of his limbs. Before him emerged no abbey he'd ever seen. There wasn't only a west tower, a twin eastern tower jutted toward the sky looking just as impenetrable, while two crossings cut through the nave in a double cruciform layout. Black smoke spewed from dozens of chimneys. The cathedral's slate roof was fully intact. Not one, but many cloisters surrounded stone buildings with pointed roofs, lightly dusted with the morning's snow.

"What is this, ye say? *Holy shit?*" asked Hamish.

Lachlan stood dumbstruck. "Shite," he corrected while staring at the abbey.

Bloody fucking hell, this isn't possible.

The guard laughed. "Ye do have a sense of humor, aye? Well, I say a man hasna been to the borders if he hasna seen Kelso. 'Tis the grandest of the border abbeys."

"I'll take your word for it." In the past few days, Lachlan had tried to convince himself he was among a mob of zealots and he'd play along with their game until he figured a way home. But this? He surveyed the entire scene. Roxburgh Castle didn't exist in the twenty-first century except for a pile of rubble. Kelso Abbey was but a single-tower relic. When he was a lad, his mother had dragged him to enough old ruins for him to know nothing *this* authentic existed—not even Torwood Castle—restored by his mum—possessed this kind of expansive detail. How the hell could it? Everything Lachlan saw was medieval. He scanned the horizon. Not a bloody power line or wind turbine in sight. No cell towers, no contrails, and no car parks. No cars for that matter. No paved roads he could see either, aside from a stone bridge with three arches.

Hell, that could have been built by the Romans for all I know.

"Well, I reckon ye've had long enough up here. The wind's blowing a gale."

Lachlan blinked. "I've only just begun my workout."

"Your what?"

Ignoring Hamish, he started to run. Jesus, he needed to think. If he truly was in the fourteenth century, how the hell was he going to return to his time? Christ, if he didn't find a way home soon, Angela would end up with everything. And when the hell was this band of medieval Scots planning to give him his freedom? He hadn't even committed a crime. All he'd done was fight off a few barbarians to save Christina and for that they'd been treating him like a dog. He'd thought to go along with them until he figured out a plan. But for the love of God, he was in the fucking fourteenth century.

What the hell was he going to do now? Rounding a corner, he pulled the medallion out from under his sweatshirt and held it in his fist.

Send me home, goddamn you.

He ran a few more laps, concentrating on things from home. Mum. His dojo. His partner, Jason. His car. Uncle Walter's flat. The spare room—the last place he remembered being before he awoke to this nightmare.

He ran past Hamish who'd quit two laps ago, clutching at his chest. "You're not a runner?"

"I'm a cavalry man," the warrior wheezed. "Running's for pikemen."

"I disagree." Lachlan increased his pace. In his estimation, a lap had to be a half-mile or more. He could run around the wall-walk all day. Let Hamish stand there and freeze.

After a couple more laps, the guard gave up and fell into step behind him. "I think ye've lost your mind." Hamish had already started gasping for air.

"Why's that?" Lachlan asked, barely winded.

"'Cause ye push yourself like ye're heading for the Crusades."

"I push myself because if I don't, I'll grow soft and lazy."

"What's wrong with that?"

"I feel better when I'm fit."

"Aye, but isna this a wee bit extreme? I think it looks like the sky's brewing up another snowstorm any moment now."

Lachlan glanced over his shoulder. "Are you cold?"

"Bloody oath, I'm freezing me cods."

"You're already soft, Hamish." Lachlan pointed to the river. "I could swim to the far shore right now if necessary."

"Och, nary a man would make it across the Tweed alive on a day as chilly as this."

"It's only November." Lachlan turned and ran backward, egging the guard to run faster. "I could swim across and run five miles thereafter."

"Ye'll sink for certain. That river has a strong current that will drag ye under and wrap around your legs. The weed alone will trap your calves like a spider's web."

Sir Boyd stepped out from the stairwell and waved them over. "Good morrow. I see ye're enjoying our icy autumn morn."

"Aye, and he reckons he's going for a wee swim next," said Hamish.

"In the Tweed?" Boyd gave Lachlan a once-over. "There's a bit of ice on the shore. Ye'd succumb to the cold afore ye reached the other side."

Looking between the two men, an idea popped in Lachlan's head—probably a bad one, but hell, all he had in the world right now was an old bronze medallion he'd been given on a loan. *Might as well go for broke—as long as I choose my words carefully.* "If a man has the right training, he can control his mind and body."

"Now ye're sounding like a sorcerer," said Hamish.

"Nope, there's nothing underhanded about it." Lachlan jammed his finger into Sir Boyd's chest. "In fact, I could teach you and your men to do the same—make them stronger—give them an edge over those English bastards who keep trying to invade your lands."

Boyd raised his eyebrows as if considering. "Prove it first."

"All right, but I need a couple of assurances from you beforehand."

The knight scowled. "Ye are in no position to be making demands."

"If I'll be staying here, I want your trust." Lachlan held up his wrists. "Remove these manacles and I want my own place to sleep."

"Ye have a place to sleep," said Hamish.

Lachlan eyed Boyd. "Where do the other men bed down? Behind bars?"

"In the hall, of course."

"The hall?" Bloody hell, maybe he was better off in the cell. "Whatever. No more manacles and no more treating me like a criminal—you have no grounds on which to detain me."

"King Robert determines whom he trusts."

"But he listens to the knights and nobles who support him." Lachlan shook his finger under the knight's nose. "Especially you." He watched Boyd's face. The nobleman met him with an unfaltering stare that suggested he was a man of his word. Regardless, if they didn't cut him some slack, he'd take a flying leap from the wall and take his chances in the river, manacles or not.

Sir Boyd ran his fingers down his beard. "I think I'd like to see this feat of mind control."

***

By the time they'd made it to the river, the sun was higher and most of the snow had melted. The area must have had a lot of rain recently, because the river was swollen and the current strong. A crowd of onlookers stood several feet away at the top of the bank.

Shrugging, Lachlan removed his cloak, folded it and placed it on a rock to keep it dry. Then he pulled his sweatshirt over his head and tugged down his karate pants. He stripped down to his jockeys for two reasons. The first was being unencumbered while swimming and the second being to keep his only clothes dry. A swimming contest he could handle. Coming down with pneumonia because he had to sit in wet clothes all afternoon would have been plain stupid.

Glancing over his shoulder, he gave the onlookers a thumbs up. After sucking in a deep breath, he took a running dive into the swift moving torrent. Plunging into the icy Tweed was akin to a whirlpool bath filled with ice. He hadn't become a martial arts expert without injury and the shock of being encased in icy water wasn't a new experience. Though the river's current was angry, the weed reaching up and brushing his legs as he pumped was just as troublesome. Holding his breath as long as he could, he pulled himself toward the surface. When his head broke through, he used a burst of energy to block his mind to the frigid cold and swam.

Lachlan powered through the water with his eye on the shore. At the halfway point, it didn't surprise him to see Sir Boyd standing with his boots and clothing on the other side. Not that Boyd came across as a bleeding heart. The two of them needed to have a private conversation sooner or later.

One that centered around trust and how they would retrieve Lady Christina's son. Now he realized he was stuck, there had to be a reason. There had to be a reason he'd awakened on the battlefield beside Christina de Moray. And she was on the borders to rescue her son. It didn't take a genius to realize his purpose. He might be the only person in Scotland who could actually pull off a successful rescue of her son. Aside from his loss in Brussels, Lachlan was a world champion. Few men on the planet could outfight him and by the looks of Scotland's army, few men even knew how.

When his feet touched the silt, Lachlan filled his lungs with air and stepped out into the icy cold. He clenched his teeth to prevent them from chattering. "You doubted me?"

Boyd handed him a drying cloth and the cloak. "Nay. After your stunt in the courtyard, I kent ye could swim across and back if need be."

After wiping down his skin, Lachlan tossed the cloak around his shoulders. "I am serious about helping her ladyship rescue her son."

"Ye may be." The knight dropped Lachlan's boots in front of him. "But first, I have some questions of my own."

"Fire away." After drying his legs, he slipped his feet inside the chilly boots.

"Where did ye come across that medallion?"

That was one thing Lachlan hadn't removed when he stripped down. The damned thing now warmed against his skin, though it was still close to freezing outside. "My uncle gave it to me."

Boyd's eyes shifted. "Ye ken I've seen a medallion like that afore?"

"I recall you mentioned so, right before the crowd started shouting to burn me."

"We dunna take kindly to people who materialize from nowhere—and in the midst of a battle to boot."

Lachlan had no logical explanation for the man. "I only wish I knew how I ended up here."

"But there's a reason ye are, I'd wager."

"Why is that?" Lachlan wanted to hear Sir Boyd's ideas before he blurted his own hypothesis.

"'Cause there was a reason Eva MacKay came to see Willy."

MacKay? Lachlan's knees nearly gave out. Jesus. MacKay was his mother's maiden name. "Ah…what did this woman look like?"

"Nearly as tall as me. Red hair. Pretty."

"And what was the reason for her visit?"

"I was only a lad the first time she came, but even then 'twas obvious to me she and Willy were meant to be together. Something happened the day she tried to save Andrew de Moray—Christina's husband, and Eva disappeared. Willy refused to tell me what, though—said I wouldna understand on account of my being a wee lad."

Had Mum tried to save him? If she had, she would have altered the past. Hmm. "Then she came back again?"

"Aye—I reckon Willy would have died if she hadna returned to tend him—she didna seem all that happy about it, either."

Lachlan narrowed his eyes, putting the pieces together. Wallace was destined to die by execution, nothing else. No wonder Mum wasn't happy. She would have been mortified. "What was wrong with him?"

"Festering battle wound to the shoulder."

"What year was that?"

"'Twas before he was captured and suffered a mockery of a trial. Must have been thirteen-o-five."

"Jesus." *Mum wouldn't have been mortified, she would have been completely and utterly freaked out.*

Boyd arched an eyebrow. "Ye look just like him, ye ken."

"William Wallace?"

"Aye."

Such a statement made Lachlan uneasy. He'd always held Scotland's hero in high esteem. No one should look like him. In his mind, no one could hold a candle to the common man who took on Edward the Longshanks. "Tell me more about Eva."

"Let's see…" Boyd scratched his beard and looked up to the sky. "I was nine and ten the second time she showed up, with bare legs and dressed in garb I'd never seen afore. Jesu, she appeared in Leglen Wood like she'd flown down from the stars. And she was angrier than a wee badger. But she had some medicine in her satchel that fixed Willy right up." Boyd frowned. "Mayhap it would have been better if he'd died in the cave."

"On account of his death in London?"

"Aye."

"But didn't his death spur the Scots to action?"

Boyd nodded with a deep sigh. "That and Robert the Bruce took up the reins—a solid king of men he has become."

"All right." Lachlan wanted to know more. So, his mother had time traveled before him? Why hadn't she told him? *Probably because I'd think she was nuts.* "Then what happened?"

"She stayed beside him until the end—married him, too."

"Wait. Eva MacKay married William Wallace?" Good lord, his poor mother had been through hell and back.

"Aye."

"What happen to her after Wallace's death?"

"No one kens. She traveled to London with Father Blair and Eddy Little. Went to his trial and after the lord justice gave his address, she started to argue. Blair told me she vanished right then and there."

"Jesus Christ."

Sir Boyd crossed his arms and took a step forward. He didn't smile and he clearly didn't want to shake hands. "I'll ask ye once again. Do ye ken Eva MacKay?"

Lachlan looked the knight in the eye. The man was tough as nails with a battle-hardened glare. He'd said he was only twenty-eight, but he looked ten years older. Then Lachlan looked past him to the horses Boyd had brought across the bridge with him. He knew full well the extent of medieval torture. If he didn't provide the right answer, he could end up in a pot of boiling water or worse.

But Lachlan had a few moves up his sleeve and he wasn't about to let Boyd take him without a fight. Not anymore. He'd had enough of manacles and cages to last him the rest of his life.

Though he exhibited no outward sign of preparing for defense, Lachlan's every muscle twitched, ready for anything. Then he looked Boyd in the eye. "My mother's name is Eva MacKay."

CHAPTER EIGHT

King Robert moved in beside Christina on the wall-walk. "I'm told your champion is making a fool of himself by swimming the Tweed. Doesna he ken it snowed this morn?"

Christina pointed. Sir Lachlan had stripped down to his braies and even from atop the ramparts, she could tell the man was hewn from pure muscle. "Hamish didna think he could swim the Tweed with the current being so strong and Boyd challenged him. Sir Lachlan couldna refuse lest he'd become the court jester for the next year."

The king looked dubious. "I reckon Boyd has another reason for coaxing him out to the river. By the size of him, that man looks like he could swim the length of Loch Lomond in the midst of winter."

She watched Lachlan dive into the water without a moment's hesitation. His head disappeared for a very long moment—too long. Just when she thought to holler for someone to throw him a rope, his head emerged—nearly halfway across already and his arms worked the water with powerful strokes. "He may catch his death."

The king gave her a sidewise look. "I'll wager ye'll see to it he doesna."

"What do ye mean by that?"

"He's your champion, is he not?"

"Aye."

"Then I expect ye to care for him as ye do all the de Moray men."

An exhale of relief slipped through her lips. At least the king couldn't hear her thumping heart. "Indeed, I intend to. And I must prevail upon ye to allow him free movement within Roxburgh walls."

"Perhaps. Once he returns to the castle, bring him to me."

***

At least Lachlan made it back to the castle without being locked in manacles. And he hadn't been sure if he'd agree to return to Roxburgh at all. By some miracle, on the riverbank, Boyd hadn't run him through—or tried to. He'd only threatened to do it and that was if Lachlan did anything to hurt Christina or the king. Sir Boyd had surprised him by admitting he thought Lachlan was Eva's son all along. When the knight probed further, Lachlan explained what he knew about the medallion as well as the year he was born. In the end, Boyd thwacked him on the back and said any kin of Willy's was kin to him—but warned never to utter a word of it to anyone. He reckoned confessing to being a time traveler was worse than practicing witchcraft...and everyone knew what happened to witches and sorcerers.

By God, if Lachlan ever made it home, he'd have a good long chat with his mother and the first question would be, "Who the hell is my father?" William Wallace, Scotland's greatest patriot and martyr?

Shut up.

After Christina met them in the courtyard, he and Boyd obediently followed the de Moray matriarch to Robert the Bruce's lair. It appeared the king had watched his swimming demonstration from the wall-walk.

I suppose entertainment is sparse without televisions.

Climbing the worn wheeled stairs, Lachlan had no choice but to stoop over to keep from hitting his head—again. He'd already knocked it twice and, if you asked him, Scottish sandstone was every bit as hard as basalt.

Fortunately, they exited on the second floor landing, but not before Lachlan knocked his head on the way out. "I swear, these stairwells were made for dwarves."

"Oh, please." Christina glanced at him over her shoulder. "I had no problem, nor would any normal-sized man."

"What is that supposed to mean?"

"Ye are enormous. I'm certain no one needs to remind ye of that fact."

Lachlan rubbed the biggest knot on his head—one of many. "No, especially around here."

She stopped in front of a door that arced up to a point just like anyone would expect to see in a medieval castle. "Ye say the oddest things at times."

Lachlan swiped his hand across his mouth. "I suppose I need to be more careful about that."

"Aye, ye do, especially in front of the king." She shook her dainty finger under his nose. "Pay ye mind. If Robert the Bruce decides he doesna like ye, there'll be hell to face for certain."

"Will it involve torture?"

"Of course." She threw out her hands. "What would ye think? He'd give ye a white stallion and send ye on your way?"

"That would be preferable over being scalded."

"Or flayed."

"Christ." He rubbed his outer arms. Boiling pot be damned, being skinned alive had to be worse. "He'd do that?"

"Aye, the English flayed the Scots in Dunbar and, since, we've taken our own back a time or two." The woman talked about torture like it was a perfectly normal everyday occurrence.

Remind me not to get on her bad side.

Before he could ask more about the torture methods employed by the crown, the door opened and introductions made while Lady Christina stood beside him looking prim and proper and not saying a word. King Robert was an imposing man with a dark beard and eyes that looked like steel balls. Of all the statues and renderings of Bruce that Lachlan had seen, the closest likeness was the one near Bannockburn where he's wearing full mail and mounted on a horse, holding a battleaxe in one hand and his reins in the other. That Bruce, like this man, had chiseled features and hardened lines, eyebrows that angled inward as if the man had a great deal on his mind.

The king sat behind a table in a large wooden chair—one that looked like it housed the Stone of Scone—but that rock had been stolen by Edward the Longshanks and taken to England. As he bowed, Lachlan stole a glance under the table to ensure his recollection was right.

Yep. No stone. Maybe I paid more attention to Mum than she gave me credit for.

"I owe ye thanks for rescuing Lady de Moray," said Robert the Bruce in a deep, commanding voice. "Scotland would have lost a great deal had she been taken in the battle."

"Thank you—ah—Your Majesty."

The Bruce laughed and looked to his surrounding men. "What is this, *Your Majesty?* He is odd, is he not? Though your majesty has a pleasant ring to it."

"Indeed it does, Your Grace," said Christina. At least she was allowed to speak in the king's presence…and she'd advised Lachlan of the king's rightful title without making an obvious correction.

"How old are ye, sir knight?"

Lachlan looked both ways before answering, just to be certain there wasn't a child in the room. *How old am I? People stopped asking me that after my eighteenth birthday.* "Thirty years old, Your Grace."

"Are ye married?"

Dear God. "I was."

The king frowned. "Unfortunate. Death has a sordid way of robbing us of our loved ones."

Lachlan decided it was no use trying to correct the man. Did they even have divorces in the fourteenth century? Unfaithful wives who dumped their husbands before marching into battle were probably dealt with severely. "Indeed," he managed to say while swallowing his urge to chuckle at the image of Angela locked in the stocks for a week.

The Bruce didn't look amused in the slightest. His steely eyes cut through Lachlan like a pair of lasers. "I would have taken ye for a younger man. But a man of thirty? Why did ye not join me for the wars?"

"I've been away for years." That was the truth. He'd been away from medieval Scotland all his life.

"In the Holy Land?" asked the Bruce.

"In Malta—and Rhodes." Indeed, Lachlan had been both places. Fortunately, hotspots for the Crusades.

"A crusader, then?"

"Of sorts."

"Ye didna pledge to an order?"

"No."

"Acted as a mercenary soldier?"

"A student, mostly."

"Och aye." Those steely eyes softened with a look of respect. "Sir Boyd tells me ye've trained with the descendants of Genghis Khan."

Lord, how one misunderstanding could lead to another. Lachlan pushed the medallion aside. The bloody annoying gewgaw heated like someone held it to a flame. "Um...I trained in warfare with a man from the Orient. Whether or not he was related to Khan, I cannot say."

"Hmm. And what is your purpose in my army now?"

I wish I knew. Lachlan scratched his head trying to come up with something truthful that wouldn't get him stretched on the rack.

Lady Christina held up her finger—she proved quite adept with such a small appendage. "I have named him my champion. He will help me find Andrew."

The king glanced her way, but then regarded Lachlan with a critical eye. "What are his motives, m'lady? Riches? Land? Power?"

Not about to let a woman speak on his behalf, Lachlan stepped forward. "As long as I'm here, I want to be treated with the same respect due any man." He gestured to her ladyship. "And serve my lady as she sees fit."

"And your king?"

He bowed. "Of course that goes without saying, Your Grace."

The king almost cracked a smile. "He does learn quickly does he not, m'lady?"

"Aye he—" Christina turned as the door burst open.

"Your Grace." Two mail-clad warriors marched inside, wearing swords at their hips and targes strapped across their backs. They both bowed, then the larger stepped forward. "They've taken Andrew de Moray to Norham Castle."

Clasping her hands together, Christina gasped. "My son."

"He's alive?" asked Bruce.

"We believe so. At least that's what the English bastard told us afore we—" The guard bowed to Christina. "Beg your pardon, m'lady, but we had no choice but to send the poor beggar to his maker."

"This is war. And in war, there are casualties on both sides. No one kens that better than I," said Christina with a hard edge to her voice Lachlan hadn't noticed before. He gave her a look. Though darling and petite, she might not be quite the delicate flower he'd pegged her to be. "Please,

Robert," she even called the king by the familiar. "Norham is so close."

"Aye, and 'tis crawling with English," said the guard.

Sir Boyd leaned back and folded his arms. "That only means we need to attack swiftly."

"Nay." The king sliced his hand through the air. "We'll have better luck against her ramparts when the siege engines arrive from Stirling."

"I'll go in alone," Lachlan heard himself say with conviction. Though he didn't want to die before he managed to make it home, he'd been far better trained than any of the characters in this chamber. In the Special Forces, he'd been trained in covert warfare. He could slip inside and play a ghost until he found the lad.

Boyd snorted. "Ye'd be gutted the moment ye opened your mouth."

"I'm not planning to make any lengthy speeches." He shot a pointed look to Sir Robert Dominus Boyd, a man he was beginning to respect—and the only person in this century who knew the truth. "Tell me I'm wrong. I have no doubt King Robert knows it's expensive to move an army—and to engage them is even more costly with loss of life. Besides, you said you're waiting for catapults to come from Stirling. Why not let me slip inside while you're waiting—one man can be a more powerful weapon than an army given the circumstances."

"But what if ye're caught?" asked Boyd. "They'll move Andrew south for certain."

"I like the crusader's plot." Bruce slapped his palm on the table. "If Wallace is seized we'll attack as soon as the retinue leaves the safety of Norham's ramparts."

Lachlan raked his fingers through his hair. How little value they placed on his life. The king's indifference made him want to withdraw his offer.

Lady Christina wrung her hands. "Do ye honestly think ye can spirit Andrew away without being captured?"

He gave her a nod—at least *she* showed some concern for his welfare. "I think I have as good a chance as any man."

Christina covered her mouth. "Ye will not put Andrew's life in peril?"

Well, it's only natural she would show more concern for kin than for me. "Less than if King Robert's army attacked the English directly."

Lowering her hand, the lady squared her shoulders. "Then I say we do it."

"That's settled, then," said King Robert with a clap of his hands. "Sir Boyd and Sir Lachlan will plan the rescue and, tonight, we shall feast in their honor."

Chapter Nine

Christina allowed herself a modicum of hope as she climbed through the stairwell with an arm full of new clothes. They had discovered Andrew's whereabouts and Sir Lachlan had volunteered to rescue him. Would she hold her son in her arms at last? If only she could allow herself to feel happiness, but it was too soon. If she set her hopes too high and their plan was thwarted, she might wither and die from disappointment.

Exiting on the fourth floor of the west tower, she made her way down the narrow passageway—clear to the back. After they'd agreed on a plan, Sir Boyd had appointed Lachlan with a small chamber to allow him to prepare. Very few men received chambers of their own, not unless they were knights. Lachlan had said he was knighted, though he hadn't mentioned by whom. It didn't matter, really. Christina imagined he'd received his knighthood on the continent while he was on the tourney circuit.

Though her champion was an odd sort, she liked him. Liked his honesty and his strength of character.

Arriving at her destination, she knocked on the door. "Sir Lachlan, are ye within?"

"Yes, m'lady," his deep voice resonated through the timbers.

She slipped a hand to the latch. "May I come in?"

"Ah…" water dribbled. "Sure."

Grinning, she pushed the door wide. Then her heart nearly stopped. "Oh my heavens, why did ye not say ye were bathing?" His hair was wet and slicked back. Rivulets of water trickled through the dark curls on his chest. Merciful saints, it was quite a massive chest at that. It rose and fell with his inhale. Christina had seen him stripped to his braies from a distance, but up close, he was so much more *virile*.

The dark and devilish look in his eyes was enough to stop her breath. The last time a man had stared at her with such hunger, she'd been but a young bride at the age of eight and ten. Ill equipped was she to control the swarm of tingles spreading across her skin. Heaven help her, this man was sculpted from granite. Merely the definition of the braw beneath the flesh on his arms was enough to make her legs unsteady.

Slightly parting her lips, she forgot to breathe as her gaze meandered down, down until she met with the waterline. Goodness, with his knees over the edge of the tub, his feet hung to the floorboards.

He glanced down into the bath. "I'm covered—more or less." He did look a wee bit silly with his feet dangling over the side of the wooden half-barrel with a fire crackling in the hearth behind him. "Come in and shut the door—you're letting out all the warm air."

"Pardon me." Peeking over her shoulder, she checked to ensure no saw her, then slipped inside. She still needed to give the man his new clothes. Besides, she was a widow and completely impervious to the wiles of the flesh. She held up her armload. "I'll only be a moment. I ordered these made for ye the same day I ordered your boots."

He glanced at the pile. "You did? Clothes?"

"Aye, ye wouldna want to continue looking like a shabby tinker. If ye'll be staying on with us, ye'll need to dress like a proper knight else ye'll never look like ye belong."

"Uh…I guess you're right, thank you." He threw a thumb over his shoulder. "I rinsed out my things before I climbed in the bath."

Christina peered around him. Sure enough, his trews and shirt hung from the mantel. "I'll just set these on the bed and then be on my way."

"All right…but…" He looked away, a wee blush making the cheeks above his beard turn red.

"Is something ailing ye?"

Glancing to the pile of clothes, he cringed, looking rather uncertain for a braw warrior. "Would you mind helping me with those?"

Now Christina's cheeks burned—blushing for certain. "Ah, ye have no squire?"

"No."

Of course he didn't. She knew that. Lachlan had been alone with nothing when he'd rescued her. Drumming her fingers against her lips, she glanced to the door. Heavens, she shouldn't be in a chamber with a man whilst he was bathing in the first place. "I used to help my husband, though I canna say 'tis proper for me to remain here with the likes of ye."

"What if I promise to keep my hands to myself?" He swathed the cloth across his chest. Merciful mercy, must he make everything look sensuous? "I'm about done here anyway."

"Have ye washed your back?" Christina drew her hand over her mouth. Gracious, where had that remark come from? Aye, she must remain impartial, but offering to wash the man's back? She wouldn't have offered to do that for Hamish or any of the guardsmen in her service. Why this man?

Unfortunately, he wrung out the cloth and held it up. "Would you mind?"

Her fingers trembled as she reached for it. After dipping his hand between his thighs and fishing in the water, he handed her a bar of soap—rosemary soap. Then he had to go off and grin—a wicked, devilish grin. Why on earth was such a man blessed with perfectly straight, white teeth and eyes that shone like sapphires? Dear lord, everything about Lachlan Wallace was ridiculously unnerving. With a gulp, she moved behind him, working the soap to a lather with trembling hands. "Ye told the king ye'd been married. May I ask what happened?"

He tugged on the medallion that still hung around his neck. "My wife left me for another man."

"A cuckold?" Christina spat out, her eyes popping. "Holy saints, what woman in her right mind would opt to be unfaithful to a man as braw and gifted as ye?"

His shoulders shook with his laugh. "I wish I knew." Then he dropped his chin to his chest.

Christina swirled the cloth over his back, a powerful back banded and sculpted, just like the front. She worked the lather in, pressing firmly to soothe his muscles. "I'm sorry."

"I suppose it was my fault. I must have been too focused on winning tournaments."

"Aye, being a knight is a verra demanding vocation."

"Huh. I guess you're right." He didn't sound convinced, however.

Christina dunked the cloth in the water and then swirled a bit more, the scent of rosemary making her swoon a bit. Her lightheadedness had to be caused by the soap, because she was impervious to the dark, shoulder-length hair sending droplets of water down his flesh or the fact that he'd trimmed his beard. Good heavens, simply the neatly groomed facial hair made her jaw drop when she'd entered.

"Mm," he moaned, making a spike of heat swirl low in her belly. "That feels so good."

He leaned a bit further forward as if he wanted her to massage lower. Christina glanced down. Merciful fae, his back tapered to a sturdy waist, supported by incredibly well-sculpted buttocks. Her entire body took on the heat from the hearth. Her heart hammered as if it would leap from her chest. After forcing herself to close her eyes and clear her mind of all she'd seen, she splashed water over his skin, quickly rinsed the soap away and gave him a firm pat. "That ought to set ye to rights."

He regarded her over his shoulder. "Thank you. After spending the past few days in the bowels of this hellhole, your talented fingers helped soothe away the knots from sleeping on a bed of rocks."

"'Twas nothing." Standing, she brushed her hands off and held them toward the fire. "I shall keep my back turned whilst ye dry yourself and put on your braies."

"Braies?"

Holy snapdragons, must she explain everything? She pointed behind her, not daring to turn. Who knew what he was doing at the moment. "The linen undergarments on the top of the pile."

"Right." The water rushed with the sound of him standing. A cloth rustled like he was rubbing himself dry.

Peering over her shoulder, she nearly swooned. Perhaps she mightn't be as impervious as she thought. Water glistened over a virile bottom that could only have been forged by a divine hand. Buttocks sculpted like a prized stallion. With a wee gasp, she snapped her head back and clapped a hand to her chest, trying to steady her breath. Christina's heart thrummed with the frantic rhythm of a battlefield drum. She pressed her face into her palms.

I am being utterly ridiculous. He is but a man and a younger one at that.

The floorboards creaked with Lachlan's footsteps.

Peeking through her fingers, Christina regarded the braies he'd been wearing earlier that day hanging from the mantel hook. They were a dark blue—an odd color for undergarments. She took a step closer and ran her finger over the damp material. In a bold move, she plucked them from the hook and held them up. Goodness, she'd never seen anything the like. They even had a compartment for easy urination. She tugged the waistband. It pulled out and snapped back into place as if by magic.

Heaven's stars.

"How do you keep these boxers up?" Lachlan's deep voice rumbled from behind.

Before she caught herself, she turned. Lord, help her, Christina's knees wobbled. How much more could she endure? The blue garment dropped to the floorboards as her mouth went dry. Lachlan faced her, holding the waist of the linen braies to his hips. But she could see *everything*. Every chiseled muscle in his abdomen, the deep cut of sinew at his hip, the dark line of hair trailing from his navel and beneath the linen. Before Christina could stop herself, her gaze dipped lower. Holy saints, the outline of his manhood stretched the cloth taut. She'd never seen a man so well endowed. Taking a deep breath, she pressed her hand against her forehead and tried not to swoon while she forced herself to snap her gaze to his face. "They're braies, not box-ers." She bent down, picked up his blue ones and held them up. "Ye ken?"

"Right, bra-ie-s," he said as if it were a new word for him. "How do you keep them up?"

"There should be a bit of rope in the pile. I told the tailor ye needed everything." She hung his wet blues on the hook, pattered past the tub and found the rope. "Here it is."

He tied it around his hips and looked down. "They don't look very secure to me."

"That's because ye need to roll them down around the rope. Have ye not worn them afore?"

"No, ma'am."

Huffing, she stepped in and made quick work of untying, rolling and retying. "Ye see. 'Tis simple."

"Once you know how." He gestured to the pile. "What's next?"

"My heavens, they surely do things differently on the continent." She snatched up the tunic-length shirt. "Then your shirt, chausses, jerkin…do ye have a set of mail?"

"Chainmail?"

"Aye."

"Can't say I do." He took the shirt and pulled it over his head.

"All fighting men need to wear mail lest they be cut to the quick."

"That stuff is awfully heavy—really hinders a fighter's ability to move fast." He scratched his neatly cropped beard. "What about a leather couton?"

"I havena seen one of those for years."

"I would prefer a coat of arms like that…you know, made from layers of compressed leather. My mother has one on display in her castle."

"Your mother has a castle?"

"Yes."

"Why havena ye mentioned her afore?"

His eyes shifted like he harbored a secret. "You didn't ask." He reached for the set of chausses and pulled the legs apart. "Hmm…I'll need a little help with these, too."

She pointed to the ties on the sides of his braies. "Ye affix them with those."

He gave her the blankest expression she'd ever seen in her life. "But where's the crotch?"

She snatched them from his grasp. "That's why ye wear braies, silly. The linens are for your top bit and the chausses

are for your legs." Heaven help him if he were to travel to the
north by Ormond Castle and attempt to belt on a plaid.

He fingered a woolen leg of the chausses. "It's a lot easier
if they're all one piece."

"Aye? Well, that's just not how 'tis done." She handed
him one leg. "Step into these and I'll help ye tie them."

He complied. "Do you know of anyone who could make
me a couton?"

She bit her lip. "We could ask the tanner."

"Of course." He smacked the heel of his hand to his
forehead. "Why didn't I think of that?"

She laughed. Though as big as an ox, the man could tickle
her insides like no one she'd ever met. Fortunately, he needed
no help with the thigh-length jerkin and tied it closed.

She gestured to the last garment. "I had a surcoat made
with the de Moray coat of arms. I hope ye dunna mind
wearing my colors." She'd paid handsomely for the swift
embroidery of a blue shield with three stars and the de Moray
motto.

He held it up. "Wow. This is cool."

She glanced back to the hearth. "Truly? I thought it was
rather warm."

"No, I meant it's nice." He pulled the surcoat over his
head and pointed to the lettering. "What does Tout Prêt
mean?"

"The short version is, *finish everything*." She waggled her
eyebrows. "But to a de Moray, it means, *go forth against your
enemies, have good fortune and return with captives*."

He chuckled, running his fingers over the embroidery.
"Wow, all that in two words. But I hope to return with a
liberated captive."

"God willing." Christina's stomach flitted with excitement
at the thought of seeing her son. "Dressed like a proper
knight, I pray ye will be successful." She stepped back and

allowed herself to admire him. "Do ye like your new suit of clothes?"

He shook a leg and took a couple of steps. "I love it. Aside from the braies, it's a lot more comfortable than I thought it'd be."

"That does make me happy. If only Sir Boyd had seen fit to give ye a coat of mail."

Lachlan gestured to the corner. "He gave me a few weapons and a leather strop for sharpening."

She followed his line of sight and guffawed. "My word, those things look rusted beyond repair."

"I had a close look at them and they'll be fine once I've had a chance to buff out a polish."

"But I dunna want my champion bumbling around the countryside with a rusty old sword and dirk."

"I'll have them fixed up in no time." Lachlan stepped closer and twirled a lock of her hair around his finger—one that had slipped from her veil. "Is your hair naturally curly?" he asked, his voice decidedly deeper.

"Aye—the mop hangs in ringlets."

"I'd like to see it without the veil." He reached up, but she clapped her hands to her crown. "May I please? Just a wee peek?" His eyes looked so shiny and trusting, how could she possibly refuse a stare such as his?

With a nod, she slowly lowered her hands. Lachlan removed her bronze circlet and pulled the silk veil away, his eyes growing darker. Unable to bear the embarrassment, she spun away and drew her fingers to her lips. "'Tis an unruly tangle of tresses. When I was young, my mother feared she would never see me married."

He gathered her hair in his hands and ran his fingers down the length of it until the ends dropped back to her hips. "I think it's gorgeous," he said, his voice soft, deep and ever so raspy.

Good gracious, she suddenly felt as nervous as a finch and those blasted flutterings in the pit of her stomach started again. Sir Lachlan was so barbaric, yet he made her feel like a young woman for the first time in more years than she could remember. She mustn't allow him to flummox her sensibilities. Taking a deep breath and casting aside those accursed tingles, she crossed her arms. "Please, sir. I must tell ye I am a matron of four and thirty. Not a maid to be trifled with."

Touching her shoulder, he encouraged her to face him. "Thirty-four?" His brows arched over intelligent eyes. "You are still a beautiful young woman with a lot of life left. And I reckon every man in Roxburgh is quite aware of your allure."

Her tongue slipped across her bottom lip. "Sir, ye mustn't."

"I know." He took her hand and kissed it. Though he'd done it before, this time, he watched her eyes. Christina could have sworn the warmth of his tongue caressed her flesh. Her head swooned with her wee gasp.

"Am I being too bold?" he asked.

"Ye toy with me." She drew the kissed hand to her nose and caught his scent—rosemary with a healthy dose of raw male. Before her knees turned to boneless mollusks, she snapped her hand away. "I'd best go. And ye'd best remember to attend the feast after the compline bell."

He walked her to the door. "Yes, m'lady."

Before he pulled down on the latch, Christina stopped and regarded his face—presently the safest place to look. The question had been needling her ever since he'd told her about his ma's castle. "Your mother—who was she?"

A long whistle slipped through his lips as he hesitated and shifted his gaze to the ceiling. "I cannot lie to you, m'lady, as I couldn't to Sir Boyd earlier today. My mother's name is Eva MacKay. I think you may have met her."

Chapter Ten

Lachlan sat on the floor with a pot of whale oil and sharpened his weapons. Christina had been right when she said they were in poor condition, but he didn't want her to worry. Dear Lord, all color had fled from the poor woman's face when he'd told her his mother was Eva MacKay. He could practically see the cogs in her head spinning, trying to pull the logic from his mind-blowing admission. Finally, she'd blurted, *"That makes no sense at all."*

She could say that again. Nothing made sense to Lachlan, either, but he had no choice but to roll with it. Christina had followed her comment with a question, *"How can Lady Eva be your ma? Ye are a grown man of thirty."*

To that he had no reply, except for to say there were a great many things he didn't understand, either. He just opened the door and let her walk away, shaking her head in bewilderment. He couldn't explain why he was there. He couldn't say how long he would be visiting the fourteenth century. And God knew, he couldn't stay. At some time, he'd find some portal leading home—his mother obviously had, so there must be every chance he would. And he damned well couldn't explain what happened to his mother. By God, Mum had a lot of explaining to do when he got home. What if his father really was William Wallace?

Jesus.

It was for the best if Christina didn't get too close. From the moment she entered his chamber, his mind had raced with all the ways he could coax her to kiss him. Dear God, he wanted to do a hell of a lot more than that. And heaven knew, he'd been about two blinks from wrapping her in his arms and showing her how a twenty-first century man could turn a woman to molten honey with a kiss. Not a peck on the back of the hand, but a lush meeting with those ripe, bow-shaped lips. How long had it been since the woman had been properly kissed? *Too long.* She'd been a prisoner for thirteen years and he doubted she'd entertained a lover.

Thank God his erection hadn't shot through the top of the bath water after she came in, her lips pursed like she was trying not to notice he was naked. Did she have any idea how erotic it was to have a gorgeous, fully-clad woman raking her gaze over his body? Suddenly, he'd been reminded of exactly how long he'd gone without sex. Christina couldn't have hit him with the fact any harder if she'd smacked him between the eyes with a mallet. He wanted the woman with a need driving so hard, he couldn't remember feeling that kind of desire since he was dating Angela.

Dammit.

Lachlan had hidden his unwarranted attraction by kissing the back of Christina's hand, but it took a fair bit more control than he'd like to admit *not* to pull the lady—seven hundred years his senior—in his arms and give her a real kiss. Washed up at the age of thirty-four? Given other circumstances, Lachlan would have enjoyed showing her exactly how alluring she was. He hadn't stretched the truth when he'd said every man in Roxburgh knew it. They all looked at Christina with desire in their eyes. Who wouldn't? She was adorable even with the frumpy veil.

Running his fingers through her hair had been a mistake—and she smelled too damn good. His first thought was to bury his face in her neck and lose himself in the thick tangle of chocolatey curls. He couldn't remember the last time he'd seen a woman with natural ringlets hanging all the way down to her hips—shapely hips at that.

Mercy.

The more Lachlan thought about Christina's allure, the harder he worked on the task at hand, honing the iron blade with every pass down the leather strop. By the time the compline bell rang, he had the dirk looking like new. The sword wasn't half bad, though it didn't yet shine like the dirk. He slid the knife into his belt, slung his cloak over one shoulder like he'd seen Boyd do, and headed to the great hall.

Thanks to his ma, he even knew what a great hall was.

After ducking out of the stairwell, Lachlan followed the noise and found the crowd toward the back of the fortress. It appeared he might be a little late because all the tables were already full. Sir Boyd sat on the dais with the king and the other nobles Lachlan had seen in the king's solar earlier that day, but there weren't any women up there.

"Sir?" a man dressed like a pauper tugged his sleeve.

"Yes?"

"Lady Christina wishes for ye to sit at her table."

He glanced to the hounds corralled at the far end of the chamber, looking half-starved and anxious to be served their portions. "At least I won't have to keep company with the dogs."

"She said ye were funny. Even I dunna have to eat with those mangy mutts."

"What is it you do, ah…"

"Glen," The man said over his shoulder as he led Lachlan toward the dais. "I'm one of her ladyship's servants. Came down with the de Moray army from Ormond Castle, I did," he said as if being a part of Christina's entourage had boosted his importance considerably.

"There ye are," Christina called, waving. She sat at a table close to the dais and patted the bench beside her.

Lachlan grinned. "I'm impressed. You're seated at one of the highest tables in the hall."

"Of course I am. I'm the widow of Sir Andrew de Moray, and lady of one of the greatest baronies in all Scotland."

And Lachlan thought she'd be impressed because he recognized she was sitting at a high table. He climbed over the bench and looked down. Things had certainly come a long way from the wooden trencher in front of him to the royal place setting complete with seafood fork he'd experienced when he was knighted by the queen. In fact, there were no eating utensils whatsoever. No serviettes, either.

However, there was a tankard and a big ewer of ale. It hadn't taken Lachlan long to acquire a taste for medieval ale. He lifted the ewer and offered it to the lady. "Can I pour for you?"

"My thanks." Christina gestured to the couple across the table. "Allow me to introduce Sir Semple and his wife, Lady Semple."

Lachlan bowed his head politely. "Pleased to meet you."

The knight didn't look amused. "'Tisna often ye see a man go from being locked in the gaol to sitting one table down from the king."

"He's my guest. And he saved my life. If ye ask me, my champion should never have been locked in the guardhouse," Christina said before Lachlan had a chance to tell the man exactly what he thought of Semple's high-and-mighty hogwash. She patted Lachlan's thigh and gave him a smile that indicated she was pleased with herself.

Except she left her hand there a few seconds longer than necessary. The gesture made Lachlan's heart thrum and his blood run hot. Just when he moved to cover her hand with his, she drew hers away.

Glancing aside, he picked up his tankard and took a long drink.

Shit.

Beginning to feel like a high schooler in the lunchroom sitting beside a girl he liked, Lachlan breathed a sigh of relief when the servants placed enormous wooden trenchers filled with meat and bread on the table. Then everyone pulled knives from their sleeves—about the size of steak knives but sharp on both sides. With no other choice, Lachlan pulled out his dirk, near twelve inches longer.

"What? Where?" Christina looked baffled. "Is that the dirk from the pile of rust I saw earlier this day?"

"Yep." Lachlan held it up and turned his wrist to display both sides. "Shined up pretty well, didn't it?"

"Verra well, I'd say, but ye canna eat with a dirk." Christina hailed Glen over. "Let Sir Lachlan borrow your eating knife."

He shoved the dirk back into his belt. "Oh no, I can use my fingers."

Christina gave the back of his hand a thwack. "Not at the king's feast ye canna. It would be barbaric."

Marveling at the irony, Lachlan watched Sir Semple spear a piece of meat and rip off a bite with his teeth. He then accepted the eating knife from the servant. "I guess I'll have to add that to the list of things I'll be needing."

The rest of the meal progressed without incident until the musicians came out onto the gallery. Suddenly, everyone had to get up and push the tables and benches against the walls to make room for dancing.

Christina clapped, her eyes filled with excitement. "King Robert has brought minstrels from Edinburgh Castle and he aims to keep them at Roxburgh for the entire Yuletide season. And he's asked me to oversee the greening of the castle in a fortnight."

Lachlan blinked and remembered the Christmas tree in Uncle Walter's drawing room. At the time, he'd thought the holidays were a long way off, but now he wondered if he'd be back home in time to share Christmas dinner with his family.

"Are ye all right?" Christina asked.

"Huh?"

"Ye look as if ye are miles away." She grasped his hand. "Ye simply must dance with me."

Not budging, he stood like a rock. "No. I'm sorry, but I don't dance."

"Dunna be absurd. All men dance."

Not in my era. "No, sorry, I never learned."

"Och, ye sound just like your mother." The lady clapped a hand over her mouth and took a step back, her eyes popping wide. "Nay, nay, nay…I dunna believe it," she said, shaking her head as if she were on the verge of growing hysterical.

"Me neither at the moment." He held out his palm—the last thing he wanted was for Christina to freak out because of what he'd told her. Maybe he should have kept his mouth shut. "I'm game if you're willing to see a grown man trip and fall on his face."

She took in a deep breath and accepted his hand. "I think we both could do with a bit o' merriment, picking our feet up. Ye have a difficult task ahead of ye and I've been beside myself for years pining for my son—and now, he's so close it makes the worry all the more difficult to bear."

"I'm sure it does, m'lady." He bent down and moved his lips near her ear. "Now quickly, tell me what I have to do."

A bit of mischief flashed in her silvery-blue eyes. "Most likely it will be a country dance and ye just do what I do, except the opposite."

"Right." He rolled his eyes to the ceiling. "That's clearer than mud."

They stood in lines across from each other with the women on one side and the men on the other. Once the music started, it wasn't until Lachlan plowed into the man beside him that he realized what Christina had meant by doing the opposite—he was supposed to mirror her. Though years of karate had made him lithe on his feet, he still figured he looked like the ogre Shrek trying to attempt ballet.

At least a drummer kept up a quick tempo while a fiddler scratched his bow jauntily beside a flamboyant lutenist. Lachlan wanted to examine their instruments for authenticity, but every time he took his eyes off Christina's feet, which kept disappearing beneath her skirts, he stumbled. Then the direction of the dance changed and he nearly fell into the poor lady. Wrapping her in his arms to keep from plowing over the petite woman, he lifted Christina and twirled her in place.

"Oh, my goodness," she squealed, clapping a hand to her veil to keep it on. "This isna part of the dance."

He chuckled. "I should have been more adamant, it's dangerous to dance with me." He set her down.

Thankfully, the music stopped. "I though ye were catching on quite nicely until ye whisked me off my feet."

"I thought it was a much better option than falling on top of you."

She blushed like a fairy maiden. "Well, when ye put it like that…"

"Beg your pardon, Lady Christina, but would ye care for another turn?" Stepping beside them, Hamish shot Lachlan a smug glare. "With someone who isna likely to trample ye?"

"Och, the poor man didna hurt me." She patted Lachlan's shoulder. "But aye, since there are not enough women partners for the half of ye, I'll take another turn—Though dunna forget I'll be in mourning until Andrew is returned to me."

Lachlan bowed and removed himself from the dance floor. No wonder Lady Christina always wore black and grey. She did so because she was a widow and because her son was still an English prisoner of war. Once he found himself a bench and another tankard of ale, he regarded the other women in the hall. They dressed in all sorts of colors, mostly prime colors like red, green and blue. Once her son was returned to her, perhaps Christina would wear yellow. Lachlan imagined an ice-blue dress with a yellow veil—if she had to wear a veil at all, it would be sheer enough to see through. No one should ever cover up such gorgeous hair. Ever.

He leaned back against the table and watched the dancing from behind his tankard. Hamish sure could pick up his feet—the bastard didn't miss a step. And yet he wheezed when running. The only problem was the man stuck out his ass like his hamstrings were too tight. They probably were. Lachlan hadn't seen any of the guardsmen do any stretching since he'd been there. Working part-time as a kinesiology therapist to support his true love, the dojo, he'd seen his share of tight hamstring muscles. The thing was that everyone had their Achilles heel. Lachlan knew how to work with his patients and his students to make them stronger—to make them at one with their bodies. He called it finding their center. Everyone needed a self-tailored set of exercises to bring out their best.

Hamish seemed like a good enough soldier. Clearly he adored his boss—her ladyship. Christ, Lachlan adored her ladyship, too, and watching Hamish try to dazzle her while he danced in a circle with Christina on his arm was almost too much to bear. In fact, Lachlan didn't like Hamish so much at the moment. As the dance progressed, the man-at-arms leaned in nearer, grasped her hand in his grubby mitts, smiling like a scar-faced simpleton. He probably had bad breath to boot.

By the time the music ended, Lachlan had drained his tankard. Thank heavens the musicians stopped for a break and the dancers dispersed. He hopped to his feet and met

Christina before Hamish could offer his arm. "Are you thirsty, m'lady?"

She fanned her face. "A tad overwarm."

"I could fetch ye a goblet of wine if it pleases m'lady," offered Hamish, the wretch.

She shook her head. "I think I'll step outside for a quick moment."

"Aye, that'll cool ye right down." Hamish nodded like a bobbing woodpecker.

Lachlan quickly offered his elbow. "May I accompany you? I wouldn't want you to go out alone with so many soldiers milling about."

"Thank ye." She wrapped her fingers around his arm and gave her man-at-arms a pointed look—one that clearly meant he was supposed to move along. "And thank ye for the lively dance, Hamish. It was most invigorating."

Lachlan chuckled to himself. It appeared Christina's assessment of Hamish as a dancing partner was much the same as his.

A blast of frigid air hit them hard as they pushed outside. "My 'tis chilly," she said.

"Would you prefer to go back inside?"

She rubbed her outer arms. "Not just yet."

He removed his cloak. "Perhaps you'll be a bit more comfortable with this around your shoulders."

"But ye need it."

He wrapped it around her. "Me? Nah. I'm a walking furnace."

She laughed and shook her head. He did, too. He probably said all kinds of things that didn't make much sense to her. Maybe he should try to be a bit more careful? Especially if he stayed in the fourteenth century much longer. With luck, however, he'd find a way to pull Christina's son out of Norham Castle, witness her happiness, and fly away home.

She started strolling along a quiet, cobbled path that led toward the south wall. "Ye ken, I glimpsed Andrew when we met the English at the border."

"Really? You didn't tell me you saw him."

"I did. I even called out his name and he looked straight at me."

"Does he look like you?"

"I reckon he looks more like his da, though he has a mop of dark locks, like me for certain. And though he was sitting a horse, he seemed lanky."

"How old did you say he is?"

"Five and ten."

"Ah, at fifteen, most lads are lanky. I certainly was."

"Ye? 'Tis difficult to imagine ye as skin and bones."

"Oh yes. It took a lot of work to build my strength. And it takes work on a daily basis to keep in shape." But Lachlan had so many questions, he didn't want the conversation to turn toward him. "What happened on the battlefield that day?" he asked while they strolled further away from the great hall.

"Ye were there."

"I only arrived after the fighting started." In truth, he'd awakened on the battlefield feeling like he'd been drugged.

"Well, ye ken it was supposed to be a peaceful exchange—my Andrew for one of theirs—'tis why King Robert allowed me to ride with them."

"Was King Edward there?"

"Nay, at least I didna see him. 'Twas the Earl of Northumberland who conducted the exchange."

"Do you think the earl planned for battle all along?"

"I'm no soldier, but I wouldna be surprised if he did— they made it look like a band of rebels flanked us, but King Robert doesna think that makes any sense. That combined with the fact they havena tried to set up another exchange makes him suspicious."

"Didn't they want their man returned—who is he? Someone important?"

"We thought he was—a land baron from Essex." She reached for his hand. "Your fingers are cold."

"A bit." He closed his fingers around hers while his heart leapt like a teenager's on his first date.

"Are ye nervous about the mission?" she asked, seemingly content to stroll along holding his hand.

"Not really. I'm anxious to see this Norham Castle, find out where they're holding Andrew and then come up with a plan to slip him out without causing World War Three."

"World War?" she asked, her breath forming frigid puffs of air.

He looked to the sky. "Forgive me. I meant to say I'd like to take Andrew out of there without bloodshed."

"Och, that is a lofty goal."

"Well, I always say shoot for the stars." He shivered involuntarily. Jeez, going without his daily workout routine was beginning to take its toll.

"Ye're cold." She released his hand and started to remove his cloak.

He stilled her fingers. "I'll be all right."

"Mayhap we can coax Master Tailor for a warm drink afore we head back. His workshop is ahead." She led him to a door and opened it. "Hello? Is anyone here?"

Lachlan followed her inside, though there was no answer. Someone must have been there recently because it was warm and the remains of a fire crackled in the hearth.

"Master Tailor?" Christina called, peering through the dim light. She turned around and smacked into Lachlan's chest. "Oh my goodness, forgive me."

Instinctively, he gripped her shoulders. "It looks as if we're alone."

Nodding, her gaze slid up until it connected with his. Holy Christ, his mouth went completely dry. Crystal blue eyes sparkling with the amber hues from the firelight made her look like an angel.

"I'm glad," he managed to utter while his head tilted downward as if being pulled by a magnetic force.

Her rosebud lips parted with her wee gasp. Lachlan tipped up her chin with the crook of his finger and with his next blink, his lips met an invitingly soft mouth. His skin smoldered with hot desire, crackling into goosebumps as he slid his hand beneath her veil and threaded his fingers through her hair. God he loved her hair. Soft, silken, thick and wild, he wanted nothing more than to lose himself in her mane of curls.

On a sigh, she turned to butter in his arms. Her fingers slipped to his waist and pulled him flush to her body. Soft breasts molded into his chest. With a blast of desire, Lachlan slid a hand down her back and cupped her buttock, pulling her hips flush against his lengthening erection. Unable to think, he thrust his tongue into her mouth while he ground his cock against her abdomen. Christ, where was a bed when he needed one?

To hell with the bed, the wall would do.

With a guttural groan, he deepened his kiss, his hands grasping at those damned thick, black skirts. Ever so gradually, he eased her to the wall, rubbing into her softness, imagining how soft she'd be once he slipped inside her core. His one hand slipped to her breast while his other continued to inch up her skirts.

Hot and hard, he wanted to be inside her with every fiber of his body. Christina's wee gasps as she matched his kisses made him harder than a stick shift. The hand working her skirts met with soft, warm skin as he slid his palm to her tight little bum. God save him, he'd wanted to bed her since she'd thrust her fists to those sassy hips when they were looking out over the battlefield.

"God, you're beautiful," he growled while his cock throbbed with need.

"Ye keep telling me that and ye'll have me believing it," she said with the sexiest, most breathless voice he'd ever heard.

His fingers sank into her supple flesh. Her breasts were so full, so pliable, he craved to have his mouth on them, craved to suckle her nipples and listen to every soft moan. "You'd best believe me, because whenever you're near, I feel like a caveman."

"A wild beast?"

He nearly roared. "The wildest imaginable."

His lips trailed down her neck as he cupped her breast and kneaded.

"Ahhhh," she sighed like a goddess.

Something banged outside, as if a door shut across the close.

With a sharp gasp, Christina pulled away and slipped from Lachlan's arms. "My heavens. What is this power ye have over me?"

He dropped the skirts bunched in his hand. "Uh, I think it's the other way around. I can't seem to form a rational thought when I'm in the same room with you."

Her face flushed and flustered, she hastened for the door. "The last thing either of us needs is a scandal. And to be caught kissing in the tailor's shop?" With another gasp, she clapped her hand against her chest. "Heaven forbid."

Lachlan had a lot more on his mind than a mere kiss. Christ. He'd had the woman's skirts up around her thighs. Worse, he'd need another dip in the icy Tweed just to cool the fire burning in his cock.

Chapter Eleven

Lachlan stood beside Robert Boyd on the shore of the tiny islet that split the River Tweed directly across from Norham Castle. Wearing only his braies and his new boots, Boyd's squire had wiped Lachlan down with whale oil. Bloody hell, they used whale oil for everything. How times had changed. The entire United Kingdom would be in an uproar with so much illegal oil everywhere.

"Once ye dive in, ye'll be on English soil," said Boyd, handing Lachlan the leather satchel containing rope with a grappling hook, leather thongs, a couple of spare daggers and a few things Lachlan had collected for his survival kit. Under the circumstances, he would have preferred to have a few sets of zip tie handcuffs, if only he could figure out how to pop in and out of his century. He chuckled. A barrage of oddball thoughts like that had swarmed through his head as they'd ridden from Roxburgh to Norham while keeping to the Scottish side of the border.

Under cover of trees over the past couple of days, they'd watched the comings and goings at the English stronghold. Another thing Lachlan would have brought with him was a set of binoculars, not to mention night vision goggles, a canteen with cutlery, a good set of hiking boots, a glock and a bazillion magazines of ammunition, and most of all, a dozen pairs of jockeys. Holy hell, the braies Christina had given him were scratchy and roughhewn, and the fabric had relaxed so much, the family jewels didn't feel secure at all. Nothing like setting out on a dangerous mission with your unit wagging to and fro.

Lachlan tied the satchel around his waist, careful to pull it secure under the sword he had strapped to his back. "You sure you don't want to come with me?"

Sir Boyd chuckled with a wink. "Say the word and I'll strip down."

Lachlan thought about it for a moment. Under most circumstances, having Boyd with him would be the way to go, but they hadn't trained together and they didn't know each other's signals. "Maybe next time. Right now my best chance is to go in alone."

"Then go with God." Boyd slapped his shoulder.

Lachlan gave the man a nod. "Go with God" wasn't common lingo for a military sendoff, either. He'd prefer something like "kick some ass", but the words didn't matter. Robert Boyd was beginning to grow on him. If he'd been a real fourteenth century knight, Lachlan would have liked to call the man a friend. Instead, he dove into the fast moving torrent and pumped his legs and arms with every shred of strength he could muster while the current pulled him downriver. Holy shit, the icy cold sapped a man's strength like nothing else.

When Lachlan reached the shore, he looked back to Boyd and gave him a wave. It was difficult to make him out through the darkness. Caching the moonlight, the alabaster of the knight's face shone slightly through the trees, but if Lachlan didn't know he was there, it would have been difficult to spot him.

Shivering in the freezing air, Lachlan climbed the hill wearing nothing but his wet underwear. Reminded of night ops in Afghanistan, it could get cold there, too, though there were nowhere near as many trees. Fortunately, Lachlan aimed to use the tree line for cover. They'd watched enough of the English guard to know the river side of the ramparts was patrolled by only one sentry. It was also the furthest wall away from the big tower house, which would be an advantage.

But he didn't fool himself. Something always went wrong on a mission like this. Always.

Though he wanted to scale the wall and spirit inside as fast as possible, he waited in the trees, rubbing his arms to stave off the cold and watching until the guard made his pass. The bastard stopped and stared out over the top of Lachlan's head for what seemed like an eternity. Had the guard seen him? Did the man sense he was being watched? Whatever the reason, Lachlan didn't move, taking shallow breaths through his mouth, praying the chump didn't have a bow and quiver of arrows slung over his shoulder.

When the guard finally moved on, Lachlan crept to the edge of the trees and listened until the footsteps faded. Then he dashed across the narrow path between the trees and the stone wall, the hasty movement making him warm.

It took him three tries with the grappling hook. Each time the iron tines scraped the stone above like the sound of a lorry in need of a brake job. Letting the rope hang, Lachlan stepped back and surveyed the length of the wall.

No Sassenach bastards in sight.

Perhaps the screeching had only been loud to his ears?

After testing the rope for soundness, he hefted himself up the wall—up a good thirty feet or so. Hand over hand he pulled himself higher while his feet stepped up the vertical wall. The cold forgotten, Lachlan's psyche shifted to covert mode. He was on the mission of his life and nothing would stand in his way. Nothing.

His arms shook when he peered through the open gap of the crenel—just as he met with the deadly sharp point of a blade leveled only an inch away from his eye.

"Thought ye would come in and help yourself to some of our stores did ye, thief?" asked the guard, his English burr rolled with a hint of Liverpool.

Holding onto the rope, the balls of his feet digging into the craggy stone wall, Lachlan used his peripherals to verify no one else was standing nearby. The thickness of the stone prevented him from gaining a clear line of sight, but no one stood beside or behind the Sassenach. "Aye," he growled, watching the man's eyes.

"Then climb over like a good thief and we'll see what his lordship has to say about ye." He chuckled. "The last blighter we caught left here short one hand."

Lachlan tightened his grip, thinking of all the ways he could take down the blighter right now. With a twist he could impale the bastard with his own sword. If he dropped a bit, he could use the rope to swing to the next crenel. But he needed a bit of information first and the best way to do that was to play nice. "I canna believe ye caught me." He poured on the auld Scots burr.

"Now come on, nice and slow. And don't think about dropping, else I tell ye true, the Norham guard will hunt ye down and run ye through."

"I wouldna want that," Lachlan said as he pulled himself through the crenel, watching the bastard's blade for the slightest flicker of movement.

"Bluidy hell. Ye haven't a stitch of clothing aside from your braies?"

Lachlan didn't answer. Now with his feet planted firmly in the crenel, he had a better scope of the scene and this trickster had no idea what was coming.

Holding his sword in one hand, the guard beckoned with the other. "Now give us your weapons."

"Verra well." Lachlan pretended to reach back for his sword, but with the motion, he snatched the man's sword-wielding wrist, twisting and bending it forward so far, he had no choice but to drop the weapon. Skittering backward, his opponent led with his left. Lachlan blocked and dove forward, taking the man to the stony wall-walk floor. The sentry's helm flew from his head while sinew crunched. The thug cried out in pain. Moving like an asp, Lachlan trapped the guard with his body and slammed his hand across the man's mouth. "Shut up."

Kicking his feet, the bastard tried to fight.

"Stop struggling." Lachlan jammed his thumb in the nerve in the guard's neck where it would cause excruciating pain. "Don't make me kill you."

The thug showed some sense and his body went slack, though he was still breathing like a rabid dog.

"Where is the prisoner, Andrew de Moray?"

Eyes shifted to the east for a split second, but he didn't talk, didn't move.

"Where?" As soon as Lachlan moved his hand, the bastard spat in Lachlan's face, then started bellowing like a mad bull.

Lachlan slammed his fist into the bastard's temple, knocking him out. "You had to go and make me do that, didn't you?"

"Ye there?" a shout came from down below. "Are ye well?"

Lachlan shoved the man's helm over his head and rose to his knees. "Aye. Dropped me sword on me toe. Hurts like holy hellfire, it does." He prayed he sounded remotely similar to a local.

"Bluidy clumsy maggot," came the reply, but the sentry headed off, thank God.

On his knees, Lachlan peered over the courtyard to the east. The stone building looked just like the stable at Roxburgh. *A barn? That makes no sense. But the guy looked over there. I'm certain of it.*

He had no time to be wrong and less time to argue with himself. He untied the guard's cloak and slung it around his shoulders. After tying and gagging the unconscious goon, Lachlan dragged him to the corner tower and shut him in a small pie-shaped room. He doubted the Sassenach would be blowing the whistle before morning and by that time, he planned to be long gone.

It took him no time to slip down the winding stairwell. Keeping to the shadows, he made his way to the barn and stole inside. Shit, if he needed night vision goggles before, he needed a goddamn blowtorch now. He stood against the wall and waited for his eyes to adjust—long enough to see his breath. Christ, standing still made his toes feel like ice cubes. Lachlan jogged in place, closing the cloak taut. Dammit, the last thing he wanted was to leave a trail of bodies on his quest to locate the lad. But he hadn't expected to find a congenial guard on the wall-walk to give him explicit directions, either.

The muffled sounds of horses came through the alleyway. Something creaked on the floor above. Lachlan's gaze darted to the right, catching the outline of a ladder that led to the loft. Through the opening came a faint glow.

Someone was up there for certain.

Eyes rarely ever lie.

Swiftly, he climbed up the ladder, stopping when his gaze was level with the floorboards.

Shit.

Four forms slept in the hay. The good news was that above them glowed a copper overhead lamp. It didn't cast much light, but enough for him to see more than a few feet in front of his nose.

The next problem? Which one of the sleeping bodies wrapped in blankets was Andrew?

While Lachlan crawled out of the hatch to his knees, he took a closer look. The man snoring the loudest was too big for a fifteen-year-old boy. The one on the far end looked like he might be older as well, which left the two in the center sleeping side-by-side. Hell, this would be a lot easier if he had a glock in his hand rather than a sword. With a gun, he could wake them all up, have Andrew tie and gag the others and then slip out easy peasy.

Tiptoeing around to the heads of the row of dreamers, he got a better glimpse of the lads. One had lighter hair and the other had a thick mop of dark waves—that had to be Christina's son for certain.

Lachlan hesitated. He could speak the lad's name, tap him awake, or just heft him over his shoulder and make a run for it. Years of training told him the last choice would be the most reckless and the most likely to cause mayhem. He glanced to the others, not liking the prospect of rousing Andrew, either. No matter what he did, the kid would be startled.

And why wasn't the lad locked in a cell? He slept on his side with his head tucked atop his arm like he was in dream heaven. Were all these boys prisoners? Was the snoring hulk their jailor?

The most dangerous is the burly giant sawing logs. Where are my zip cuffs when I need them, dammit?

Stealthy as a ghost, Lachlan slipped a length of rope from the satchel and made a noose. Without a sound, he placed it over the man's head, making a snare. The jailor's snores stuttered like he might be coming awake. Lachlan snapped his fingers away and rocked back into the shadows. Once the man's breathing returned to normal, he tied the end of the rope to a post. The noose would stop him and if the man woke with a start, he'd end up with a nasty whiplash. At least it wouldn't kill him.

A floorboard creaked when Lachlan slipped over to Andrew's head. The boy mumbled restlessly. Lachlan placed his hand on the lad's shoulder. "Andrew," he whispered.

Eyes flashing open, the whelp gasped like he was being murdered. "Help!" he shouted.

Lachlan motioned with his finger to his lips. "Wheesht. I'm here to take you home."

Snarling like an angry wolverine, blankets fell away as the teen leapt to his feet and sliced a dagger across Lachlan's chest.

Dumbstruck, he snatched the boy's wrist and disarmed him. Christ, he didn't even see the knife coming—nor did he expect it. And it stung like a son of a bitch. "Do you not understand? I'm taking you to your ma."

What the hell? Is the lad sleepwalking?

"Huh?" With an angry gnash of his teeth, Andrew took a swing at Lachlan's temple. "I do not even know my mother," he shouted, sounding like he was an adolescent King Richard in Shakespeare's *Richard III*. Throwing aimless punches, the boy obviously wasn't going to go without a fight.

The big man with the noose struggled against his bonds, bellowing garbled curses, only to make his ropes tighten.

Before Lachlan could subdue Christina's son, the other two teens charged. The sandy-haired lad yelled like a banshee wielding a pike and the other with a spiked mace. Ducking, Lachlan shoved Andrew out of harm's way. The pikeman charged. Lachlan rolled to the side, reaching for the weapon. Clamping his fingers around the shaft, he flipped his attacker, slamming his back to the floorboards. The lad didn't move.

The mace came at Lachlan's temple with a whop. Blindly, he bobbed and twisted. The young man teetered with his miss. Lachlan walloped him in the back with the staff of the pike, sending him sputtering to his face.

Andrew raced for the ladder.

Diving, Lachlan tackled him as they fell through the hatch onto a haystack. Wrestling the lad's arms behind his back, he quickly bound a thong around his wrists while he growled in the boy's ear, "It's about time you met your mother. She's been pining for you for thirteen years and the least you can do is come along with me without a fight."

Without another word, Lachlan threw Andrew over his shoulder and raced for the stable door. Shouts from the battlements echoed throughout the inner bailey. Against the moonlit sky, soldiers ran along the wall-walk, their blades glistening in the icy moonlight.

Blood soaked through Lachlan's braies, but he couldn't think about stopping the bleeding now. "Is there a gate to the river?"

"Put me down! I refuse to leave with an outlaw."

Lachlan stood the boy on his feet, grabbed his collar and shoved him against the wall. "I'm hauling your ass out of here whether you like it or not. You will meet your ma and then the two of you can sort out what happens next."

Andrew bucked.

Lachlan stopped the whelp by crushing his forearm against his windpipe. "We have about two seconds until I'll have no choice but to use *you* as a human shield. If you want to live, you'll tell me how the hell to slip out of here."

Andrew sputtered and gasped, his eyes round with terror. If the boy didn't want to be saved, Lachlan needed him to be scared shitless, else they'd never escape alive. "The moat," he gasped. "There's a sluice gate."

Finally.

"On the river side?" Lachlan flung the cloak from his shoulders.

"Aye. But ye will not make it. I'll holler."

"The hell you will." Before the boy could raise his voice further, Lachlan shoved his hand over his mouth, pulled a rag from his satchel and gagged him. For the second time, he hefted the backstabbing little turd over his shoulder and headed for the shadows at a run, wishing he could wring the pipsqueak's neck.

An arch leading to an abyss stood thirty yards ahead.

That has to be it.

"There!" someone yelled from the top of the ramparts.

An arrow hissed just over Lachlan's head.

Andrew squirmed—about a hundred and thirty pounds of flopping juvenile delinquent.

Lachlan ran faster.

Another arrow shot through the air, spearing the turf in front of them.

Two paces ahead, the ground dipped toward the water.

Lachlan skidded downward through the mud until his feet completely lost their purchase. Flying through the air, he clutched the boy's legs hard against his chest. Arrows hissed as, together, they hit the moat with thundering dunks. Looping his arm between Andrew's bound wrists, Lachlan kicked with his legs and swam with one arm, pulling their bodies through the water as fast as he could. The rear archway was too goddamned far away.

Guards swarmed above them everywhere. The deafening sound of iron creaking screeched through the air.

They're lowering the gate!

Andrew sucked sharp gasps through his nose, his jerky fighting worse than dead weight.

"Kick with both your legs!" Lachlan shouted.

The gate dropped rapidly, now only a foot above the waterline.

Lachlan swam with every fiber of strength, his muscles burning, the cut in his chest searing.

Six inches to clear.

Lachlan pushed Andrew's head beneath the water. Holding his breath, he kicked and swam, demanding power from the sinews in his body now punishing him with hot, burning pain. Submerged in pitch black water, he held on to the lad and surged ahead with the outflowing current.

His feet cleared the arch in the nick of time. The gate clipped his toe as it sliced through the water and boomed closed with an enormous wave pushing them down the far hillside. Tumbling over and over, Lachlan clamped his arms around the boy and gave in to the force, careening with their bodies and hurling down to the river in a muddy torrent.

They hit the Tweed hard, immediately swept downriver by the current. Lachlan fought for the surface, pulling them both skyward until their heads broke the surface. Pain throbbed across his chest with every stroke. His head spun as he searched for the far shore.

I'm losing too much blood.

But he couldn't stop, he couldn't think of himself. Christina was relying on him, regardless of whether the sack of lard in his arms wanted to be rescued or not. She deserved to see her son and, like it or not, Andrew deserved to know about his roots. Grinding his teeth, Lachlan persevered until his feet hit the silty bottom.

He dragged the boy out of the river while the sound of an army trampled down from Norham Castle's ramparts. Hefting Andrew over his shoulder, Lachlan staggered to the tree line. Once protected by the forest, someone grabbed his arm.

"Why in God's name did ye tie the lad?" growled Boyd's voice.

"He wasn't exactly willing to be rescued," Lachlan huffed as he made his way toward the horses with Boyd running beside him.

"With all that ruckus, there's no time to change into dry clothes. Dear God, it sounded like the Battle of Stirling Bridge in there."

Lachlan focused on pumping his legs, moving toward the waiting men. "Cloaks will do until we reach Roxburgh."

"Can the lad ride?"

"Not if he doesn't want to go."

"Then throw him over the horse and we'll tie him on."

Lachlan did as Boyd suggested, a grunt belting from his gut with the release of the weight.

"Jesu, ye're wounded," said the knight, handing him his cloak.

"No shit—thanks to the young whelp here." Lachlan pointed to a soldier. "Someone throw a blanket over Andrew's back and tie him on."

Shivering, he staggered to his horse and fastened his cloak around his shoulders.

"Are ye good to ride?" asked Boyd.

"Let's go." Lachlan mounted. Christ, what in God's name was he doing? Riding a horse on the medieval border between Scotland and England? Soaking wet and in the midst of winter? It was only due to pure determination he could manage to stay mounted on the mule and urge him forward. He drove a goddamned car, not a smelly beast.

But right now, he picked up the reins and dug in his heels. Smelly or not, this horse was his only ticket to survival.

Chapter Twelve

Wrapped in a fur-lined cloak, Christina paced in the guard tower above the main gate of Roxburgh Castle. For two days she had maintained her vigil. But this night, not even Ellen, her chambermaid, could coax her to retire to her bedchamber.

White clouds of her breath swirled in the air as she paced, then stopped and stared out the narrow window used for dropping hot oil and the like on the tops of attackers' heads. Over and over, she maintained the combination of pacing and staring while the guard occasionally brought in peat to stoke the brazier that smoldered in the center of the stone floor. Though it had burned to all but coals now.

Awhile later, a guard entered with an armload of fuel. "'Twill be dawn in a couple of hours, m'lady. Ye really ought to try to sleep."

"Nay, not when I could see my son any moment."

"They could be another day, mayhap two." He placed a square of peat onto the coals.

She held her hands out to the warmth. "What are two days out of three and ten years?"

The man bowed. "I shall leave ye to your vigil then."

"My thanks."

Clutching her cloak closed, she returned her attention to the path leading from the castle gates. She could see the river, thanks to the moonlight dancing across the swift current. With her next blink, movement came from the tree line. Gasping, she leaned forward as far as the thick walls would allow. Her heart fluttered as the entourage became clearer. Indeed, they'd returned. But someone was hurt, no two men were injured—one was draped across his horse's back and another hunched over his horse's withers.

Please, lord, it cannot be Andrew.

Christina headed for the stairwell at a run. By the time she reached the bottom, the retinue had ridden into the outer courtyard, lit by torches.

Frantically, she searched the faces for Andrew and saw not a young face. Lachlan lolled over his horse's neck, his face white as snow. Her gaze shot to the man tied across the horse's back. His thick, brown locks hung in waves. Instantly, her stomach clamped into a rock. "What is the meaning of this?" she demanded.

Lachlan slid from his horse, took one step and collapsed to the cobbles.

"My God." Torn between the urgent need to help the faltering knight and to finally embrace her son, she looked from Andrew to the man who was supposed to have saved him.

"It appears the lad didna take kindly to being rescued." Sir Boyd dismounted and moved beside her.

Christina clutched her hands to her chest—she must have misheard. "I beg your pardon?"

With a grim scowl, Boyd drew a dirk from its scabbard. "Andrew slashed a dagger across Sir Lachlan's chest."

"No." She vehemently shook her head, her face growing hot. "Merciful heavens, no. Not my son."

Still shifting her gaze between Andrew, wet, gagged and hogtied to the horse, and Lachlan, wet and unconscious on the cobbles, she wanted to scream. How could this be? Her son attacked the man she'd sent to rescue him? Christina thrust her finger toward the west tower. "Carry Sir Lachlan to my chamber and fetch Ellen—tell her there's a wounded man who needs tending."

"Your chamber, m'lady?" asked Hamish.

"Do it, I say." She then dashed to Andrew's horse. "Untie him. Now!"

Boyd complied as she removed the lad's gag. Holy Moses, he was wet and shivering to the bone. She shot Robbie a heated glare. "This is not how I envisaged greeting my son."

They set Andrew on his feet and she opened her arms. But the lad glowered and scooted away. "I do not know ye, madam."

Dear God, he sounded like one of *them*. A *Sassenach*. She dropped her arms in disbelief. "Young man, ye are Andrew de Moray, chieftain of Clan de Moray and *I* am your mother."

"He canna be trusted," said Sir Boyd. "He'll run."

The lad's teeth chattered.

She stamped her foot. Deciding against wrapping Andrew in her embrace, she grasped his shoulders firmly. "Then put a guard on him at all hours." She shook her finger at Robbie. "I make it your responsibility to see to his safety and see to it he has a change of clothes forthwith."

"Aye, m'lady."

She slid her palm to the small of Andrew's back. "Can ye walk?"

The lad nodded. Goodness, he had her eyes.

"I'm taking him to Sir Lachlan's chamber. Post a guard. I do not want there to be a moment when he isna watched. For pity's sake, he could verra well catch his death." She started leading the shivering child toward the tower. Heaven's stars, he was taller than she by two hands, but that did nothing to allay the ire burning in her breast. "Ye men are disgraceful. How long did he ride with wet clothing? 'Tis *freezing*!"

Not waiting for an answer, she hurried her son up the four flights of stairs, hastening to Lachlan's small chamber. A guard had already gone ahead and set to lighting the fire and the mantel candles, bless him. She ushered Andrew to the bed. "We shall have ye warm in no time."

The poor child's teeth still chattered. But he gaped at her with distrust in his eyes. "When can I go back to Norham? Lord de Vere promised to make me his squire as soon as I broke his new stallion."

"de Vere?" Christina took a step back. She'd heard of de Vere, the Earl of Oxford, and none of it was good. "He is not your father."

"But the horse is ready." Andrew scowled with an angry face. "I planned to show him on the morrow."

"Do not think of that evil man for another moment. I have saved your father's sword and ye will become a knight of King Robert the Bruce."

The lad slid away from her, crossing his arms against the cold. "No, no, no. Bruce is a usurper—not a king." Andrew shook his head adamantly. "I'm to become a great knight and ride for Lord de Vere."

Was he delirious? Why on earth would he be talking such drivel? It was all Christina could do to bite her knuckle and not take the lad by the shoulders and shake him. Instead, she tottered across the chamber and rubbed his hands between her palms to warm them. "I ken ye've gone through a terrible ordeal. But hear me true, ye will become a knight and ye will be lord of your castle. But first we need to make ye warm."

She reached for a blanket and wrapped it over him as heat from the fire swirled through the chamber. A guard brought in a fresh shirt and chausses. Christina turned her back as her son changed. He spoke not a word when she draped his wet garments over a chair, then sat with him until he drifted off to sleep.

***

Daylight shone through the castle's arrow slits as Christina made her way to her chamber. For years, she'd pined for this day and now that it had come, she was more confused than ever. Through her entire life, fleeting moments of happiness always turned to complete despair in a heartbeat. Why must it continue to be so?

Arriving at her bedchamber, Christina found Ellen rinsing a cloth in the bowl. "How is Andrew, m'lady?"

"He's sleeping. Pray he doesn't catch his death." Exhausted, Christina glanced to the bed. "And Sir Lachlan?"

"He's asleep as well." Ellen folded the cloth and draped it over the rod affixed to the table. "What happened?"

Christina explained the whole mess—at least what she knew of it.

Ellen's brow furrowed as she wrung her hands. "I canna believe the lad would run a blade across Sir Lachlan's chest when he was trying to rescue him."

"Aye, well, Andrew thinks he's an Englishman and now I must do everything in my power to ensure he kens he's a Scot."

"And an important Scot at that, m'lady."

Her stomach sank to her toes. "He willna be if Robert the Bruce hears the same words Andrew spewed above stairs a few moments ago. Our lands will be forfeit and my hand will be given to whomever the king deems worthy."

"Och," Ellen lamented. "When I was a wee lassie, I always wanted to be a princess. But after watching all your trials, I'm glad I'm but a commoner."

Christina tried to smile. "Life is never easy, no matter your lot. Look at King Robert. He's still trying to negotiate with the English for the release of his queen."

Across the chamber, Sir Lachlan shuddered.

Ellen hastened to the bedside, placing the back of her hand on his forehead. "He's ever so cold. I havena been able to warm him."

Christina stepped up to the bed and rubbed her champion's icy fingers between her palms. "We need more blankets and add more peat to the fire."

"Verra well, m'lady."

Ellen brought two woolen blankets from the garderobe and Christina helped her spread them atop the shivering man. Then Ellen moved to the hearth and reached for a square of peat. "Ye shouldna had the guards bring him here. Ye need your sleep, m'lady."

"And so do ye." Christina smoothed her hand over Lachlan's forehead. "Set up a pallet for me and then head to your quarters. 'Tis almost daylight already."

Once Christina was alone with Lachlan, she leaned forward and kissed his forehead. "I do not wish for ye to suffer on my account."

"Not to worry," he whispered through clenched teeth. "The wound is not too deep."

She straightened. "Ye're awake?"

"I've been in and out. I'm freezing."

"I have some wine. That might warm your insides."

"Any whisky?"

"A lady doesna keep whisky in her chamber, sir."

"Of course." He shivered. "How could I have been so lamebrained?"

Chuckling at his funny word, she moved to the sideboard, poured Lachlan a cup of wine and returned. "After watching ye spar, I'm surprised a lad of five and ten could cut ye so."

"It was dark and I wasn't expecting him to be sleeping with a knife—after all, I thought he was a prisoner." Lachlan pulled himself up and the bedclothes dropped to his waist, exposing the blood-soaked bandage Ellen had wrapped around his chest. "It was my fault. I should have expected that they'd brainwash him."

"They did what?" She gave him the cup.

He took a wee sip then tugged a plaid about his shoulders. "They made him believe he's an Englishman."

Exhausted, Christina leaned her legs against the side of the bed. "I still canna believe how he speaks. He sounds like King Edward's ward."

"Unfortunately, he does." Lachlan shifted his seat and grimaced. "Damn."

A bit of fresh blood seeped into the bandage. "My heavens. Do ye need to be stitched?"

He pulled the cloth away and looked beneath. "I don't think so. It has nearly stopped bleeding." He shivered again.

Christina pointed to the cup. "Drink some more, 'twill make ye feel better."

Nodding, he drank down the rest. Gooseflesh rose across his skin as he handed it back to her with chattering teeth. "Thank you."

"Ye'd best slide back down beneath the bedclothes and wait whilst the spirit warms your insides."

He did as she asked and rolled to his side. "Do you know what the best thing is for hypothermia—I mean for someone who is having trouble warming up?"

"There's more we can do?"

"In fact, there is. It helps immensely to have someone lie beside the patient and impart their body heat."

Christina gave him a sobering blink. He wanted her to warm him with her body at a time like this? "Where did ye learn that?"

He patted the mattress. "At university."

"Honestly?" Goodness, this man continued to surprise her at every turn. He'd attended university? *No wonder he's so smart.*

"It works best when they lay skin to skin—the heat from the warm person meets with the skin of the cold person much faster that way."

Her cheeks burned like someone had held her face to a brazier. "Mayhap I should call the physician for ye?"

He chuckled—a deep, low rumble. "Not in this century."

Christina wasn't overly fond of physicians, either. They had done nothing to save her husband. In fact, deep down, she believed their bleeding him may have caused his early death.

Lachlan grasped her hand with icy fingers. "Please, m'lady. You need to sleep and I need your warmth."

She bit her lip. "But it would be so improper."

He heaved a tired sigh. "Bolt the door. I won't tell anyone and, Lord knows, I'm in no shape to take advantage."

"Are ye certain something as trivial as my heat will set ye to rights?"

"It will surely help me a great deal." He opened his eyes and gave her a forlorn-looking stare, one she surmised wasn't as innocent as it appeared.

"Verra well." She slid the bolt across the door, then turned with her arms folded. "I'll strip down to my shift but no further."

"That'll be better than nothing."

Her hands trembled as she removed her circlet and veil. Then her kirtle overdress and her underdress and, lastly, her slippers. Shaking out her shift, she eyed him. He watched her intently. Heavens, it had only been a few nights since they'd both lost their senses in the tailor's shop, groping for each other like starved lovers.

"Don't you wear a corset?" he asked.

"A what?"

"Never mind—corsets mustn't have been invented yet if a refined lady such as yourself hasn't heard of them."

"Whatever do ye mean?"

He closed his eyes and sighed. "Forgive me. I must be light in the head."

She tiptoed toward him. "Now are ye certain ye dunna want me to sleep on the pallet?"

He lifted the bedclothes, welcoming her in. "Positive."

"Verra well, but I must have your word that ye willna try to ravish me."

"Only if it pleases your ladyship," he said in a deep burr. He flapped the linens. "Now come here."

She crawled beside him and lay on her back staring wide eyed at the canopy above. How on earth was she supposed to sleep when in a bed with a braw warrior? The mere scent of him sent her senses into a frenzy. Merciful snapdragons, even her heart was hammering fast as a dog chasing fleas.

He pressed his body flush against hers and draped an arm over her waist. "It works best if the two people spoon."

Had his voice always been so deep? "Spoon?" she squeaked.

"Roll to your side."

Ah yes, she realized what he meant. Goodness, sometimes it was as if he were speaking a foreign tongue. Christina usually slept on her side anyway, but when Lachlan placed his palm on her tummy and spooned into her body, her eyes popped open. Indeed, his skin was cool, but she was anything but. Oh, for the love of everything holy, she would give her eye teeth to have all well with Andrew so she could be free to enjoy the comforts of Lachlan's arms. But life had dealt her another blow—one she must find a way to fix afore Robert the Bruce decided it was time to meddle.

A long sigh slipped through her lips. "What am I to do about Andrew?"

Lachlan pulled her even closer with a wee hum. "Take it one day at a time. Show him who his family is and what he means to Scotland."

She clutched his hand and held it over her heart. For the first time in years, she enjoyed the comfort of a caring soul. "I'm so afraid he willna want me."

"The lad will come around. It may take time, but he won't be able to stop himself from loving his mother."

"I hope ye're speaking true."

"I am."

She lay in Lachlan's arms for a time listening to his breathing. The rhythmic sound of it soothed her, until she remembered his reward. "Sir Lachlan?"

"Mm," his deep voice lulled as if he were nearly asleep.

"I've a purse for ye in reward for bringing Andrew home."

"Hmm." It almost sounded like he chuckled. "Is it a leather purse?"

"Aye."

"Good. Now go to sleep…unless you *want* me to ravish you."

CHAPTER THIRTEEN

Lachlan awoke warm and more comfortable than he'd been in days. Better, he was surrounded by the most erotic scent he'd ever imagined. It reminded him of lying in a field of lavender on a sultry summer's day. Wavy long hair surrounded him and his cock thrummed with the most heavenly morning erection. Swirling his palm around Christina's tummy, he pushed himself between her buttocks.

Mm, oh, yeah, did that feel good. He thrust his hips forward, allowing himself a moment to revel in pleasure.

If it weren't for the pain searing across his chest he would already have the woman on her back, begging for her share of morning love making. As he closed his eyes, he drew on years of meditation to block the sting. Once the throbbing in his chest stopped, he felt like hell on wheels—on top of the world.

He nuzzled into her neck and trailed kisses up the lady's nape.

"Mm," she said, coming awake.

Gradually he inched up her shift, higher and higher. When his fingers found the hem, he slid his hand up between her thighs.

"Dear lord," she gasped, trying to pull away.

"Stay," he growled into her ear, slipping his finger between the woman's moist softness.

Christina tugged against his hold, though her effort wasn't exactly herculean. "We canna. We must not."

He swirled his hips against her buttocks. She was right—partly. But this woman had suffered for so long. Years. Her husband died, what? Fifteen years ago? And then her son had been taken from her and she was imprisoned in her own home. And now the lad had shunned her. No, Christina de Moray hadn't known love in years. A tragedy. Lachlan couldn't think about himself when she needed affection so much more. "Let me give you pleasure."

"But—"

"Let it be my gift to you—only for you." Pushing through her thighs, he found the nub that would drive her mad. With a light touch, he swirled his finger. "I promise not to ravish you." He grinned, burying his face into her mass of curly locks.

"Ye...what?"

"Sh." Though lying down, he could feel the tension in her body ease as he worked his magic. Pushing his finger further, he slid into her entrance. "Will you open for me?"

She relaxed enough for him to slide his finger all the way inside. In and out he stroked her. In and out. Then he returned to her clitoris and used her moisture to increase the friction. "Close your eyes and imagine me inside you."

She gasped, as if the thought were too sinful to consider.

Lachlan rocked his hips in the same lazy rhythm as before, her feminine scent driving him to the edge. All he needed to do was incline his cock a bit and he would be inside her. He would be thrusting his hips like a cowboy riding a bull. He'd feel that warm, tight sleeve squeeze around him, giving him blessed release.

But he needed to do this for Christina. He needed to show her that she was alive and sensuous and utterly desirable. That she was a vivacious flesh-and-blood woman and that she could feel passion again.

Her breath caught when his finger brushed lighter than before. She liked it—feathery touches. Letting her wee gasps and moans guide him, Lachlan worked his finger until a sharp gasp caught in the back of her throat. Then he rose up on his elbow and captured her mouth in his, muffling her cry of elation.

Panting, she opened her crystal blue eyes and stared at him. "Now I ken ye're a sorcerer."

He grinned and waggled his brows. "There's nothing magic about making a woman come."

She brushed a strand of his hair away. "Nay. There is everything magical about it."

He nuzzled into her silken hair. "I wish it weren't morning already. There's nothing I'd like more than to spend the day right here."

With a sigh, she glanced toward the door. "I must rise and meet the day face on. And Andrew needs to ken he has a mother who cares for him, whether or not he wants me."

"He wants you. He just might be twenty-five before he realizes it."

She sat up. "Five and twenty?"

"Adolescents tend to think they don't need their parents. It's not until they graduate from university and head out on their own that they realize their parents were smarter than they gave them credit for."

"Well, for all that is holy, I do not have ten years to wait around for Andrew to realize I am a good mother." She hopped out of bed and strode to her pile of clothes.

Lachlan combed his fingers through his hair with a cringe. "Sorry. That was a careless thing to say."

"Aye, it was."

He almost slipped out of bed, but then rethought. If Christina was angry, she wouldn't want to see exactly how much he wanted her right now. He watched her dress. When she dashed out the door without a backward glance, he dropped to the pillows and stared at the canopy overhead.

What the hell am I doing here? I spirited her kid out of Norham Castle. Why hasn't the medallion sent me home?

He held up the hunk of bronze and studied the inscription. "You need to take me home now, dammit."

When nothing happened, he dropped the damned thing and closed his eyes. What the hell was he missing?

Lachlan?

His eyes flashed open. Holy Christ, he could have sworn he'd heard his mother's voice as plain as if she were in the same room. He pushed himself up. "Mum?"

I'm here. Not here, but using psychic traveling to contact you.

What the heck? That sounded like something he'd hear in the fortuneteller's tent at a fair.

"You're in my head?" he asked aloud.

Of sorts. I've only done this a couple of times and the connection doesn't last long. So tell me, are you okay?

He replied with his thoughts... *Yes, except for a knife wound across my chest.*

Oh, no. Damn Walter Tennant for giving you the medallion without telling me! Is it deep?

Maybe in a couple of places where it's bleeding a lot. Otherwise, not too bad.

Have you stitched it?

No.

Stitches will help you heal faster. And keep it clean.

I'd rather go home and have it stitched in a hospital with antiseptic...What the hell am I doing here? My life is a shambles and I'm stuck in the frigging fourteenth century.

What is the year?

Thirteen-fourteen. But I need some answers. I've met Christina de Moray and Sir Boyd. They say they know you. Boyd says I look just like—

*William Wallace…*Mother hesitated as if letting the news sink in.

A chill raced across Lachlan's skin. Holy fuck, the conviction in Mum's thoughts was palpable. *Yeah—William Wallace. What about that?*

Um…He's your father.

Lachlan's gut turned over while he spread his enormous palms across his lap. *What the hell, Mum? Why didn't you tell me this before?*

Oh, right, I can see it now. My boy heads to primary school telling everyone his father is the greatest hero and martyr that Scotland has ever known? Not to mention he was seven hundred years my senior. If that news was ever leaked to the media, it would have had me committed for life.

But what about the medallion? I rescued Christina's son. Wasn't that what I was supposed to do? Why haven't I been whisked back to the twenty-first century?

There came no reply.

Lachlan's gaze darted around the room. "Mum?"

Still no answer.

The door opened. "How are ye today, Sir Lachlan?" asked Ellen. The maid wore a white coif atop her mousy brown hair. She averted her eyes as if embarrassed.

He looked at the chambermaid, half-expecting her to be carrying a message from his mother. When she stood there waiting for him to answer her question, his gaze snapped down to the bedclothes—at least he was covered to his waist. "Can you sew, Miss Ellen?"

"Och, Lady Christina is better with needlepoint than I." She started backing out the door. "I'll just give ye a moment to dress."

That figured. Who would have thought a chambermaid in the fourteenth century couldn't sew? "Would you please bring me some whisky and tell Lady Christina I need her help when she has a moment?"

"Straight away, sir." Ellen slipped all the way out and disappeared.

Lachlan stared at the door—carved in an arc to fit in the stone medieval jamb, complete with blackened iron reinforcement nails. His skin went clammy as the reality of his predicament set in.

I'm stuck in a goddamned nightmare.

For how long?

How long was Mum here?

Christ, long enough to end up pregnant.

She slept with William Wallace? I. Mean. The. William bloody Wallace?

He dragged his fingers through his hair. *Shut up!*

Sliding out of bed stretched the wound on his chest. A stream of blood trickled down his abs and he sopped it up with the cloth beside the washbasin. Still shaking his head, he donned his braies, rolling the linen with the rope as if he'd been wearing medieval boxers all his life.

Fuck!

He needed to go home, even just to confront his mother. Moreover, he needed some normalcy in his life. True, he had a divorce to face, but if he let Angela keep everything, she ought to leave him alone—go off with her lover and, hopefully, never bother him again.

No, Lachlan didn't want to face the ugly side of divorce, but he needed the routineness of the dojo. God, he loved teaching, he loved the kids, loved seeing them improve. There was nothing better than watching a young person's face the first time he broke a board with his or her bare hand. There was nothing better than pushing young people to their limits and seeing them reach goals they never thought possible.

Lachlan stared into the polished brass mirror—or was it bronze? Hell, he didn't know. But the image before him distorted as if gazing through water rather than a mirror. Everything around him was strange. Sure, he'd had some exposure to medieval history, but that wasn't his passion like it was his mother's. He needed health food drinks, his gym equipment, good running shoes and a goddamned coat. He needed coffee and his cellphone and his Fitbit. Most of all? He needed those kids. When things were going haywire around him, he could pour his heart and soul into the dojo. God dammit, Lachlan would rather help solve the problems of an adolescent school kid than face his own.

He stepped up to the mirror and ran his hand over his beard. It needed trimming again. Christ, his hair looked like he'd scrubbed it with a brillo pad.

Was my father as hairy as me?

Lachlan shuddered. He'd just thought about William Wallace as if he bought in to his mother's story.

But he was tall like me…and Boyd said he looked like me…Holy fucking shit!

***

It was almost a relief when Ellen found Christina and told her Lachlan needed some stitching done. Andrew had broken his fast in silence. After, he'd consented to take a stroll with her on the wall-walk, but the lad said all of two words. It was painful to take a turn with someone who held her in such poor esteem. He didn't need to say anything. The anger oozing from his very flesh was enough to tell her it would be a very long time before Andrew developed any sort of affection for her at all—if he ever did.

The blasted English had ruined her son—had turned him against her and his country. Never in her life had she seen anyone, let alone a child of noble birth, so confused as to his identity.

Her shoulders sagged as she opened the door to her chamber. Lachlan immediately stood, wearing only his braies and chausses. He must have found her comb, because his hair shone, brushed away from his face, emphasizing his chiseled features. Though Lachlan, too, seemed agitated.

"Are ye well, sir?" she asked, trying not to allow her internal turmoil to boil to the surface.

"Yes, thank you." He pointed to the blood-seeped bandage wrapped around his chest. "Would you mind making a few stitches? My mother thinks wounds heal faster if they're stitched."

Shocked, Christina's gaze panned the chamber. "Is your mother here?"

"No." Lachlan didn't explain further. He moved to the bed grasped a flagon from the table. "If I lie down, would you cleanse the wound?"

"Is that whisky?"

"Yes." He tugged the end of the bandage and began unraveling.

"Merciful heavens, the spirit will burn ye like hell's fire."

He gave her a cocky wink. "That's why I'm planning to lie on the bed. I might be tough, but I doubt my knees will hold up if I try to stand."

"Ye're serious? Why would someone ask for such torture?"

"It's the only thing in this time I know of that will clean the cut and prevent infection."

"Good Lord." She gave him a once-over, the wheels churning in her mind. If only she had the nerve to ask him what he meant by "in this time", but she didn't want to know the answer. Not now. Not with Andrew being a total disaster. Christina could only handle one catastrophe at a time. "Verra well, if Eva believes in the spirits' healing powers, I certainly am not one to question such an odd request." The sooner she poured the whisky, the sooner the abominable torture would be over. Besides, she'd seen far worse torture in her days. Pouring on a wee bit of spirit shouldn't kill him.

At least, I dunna think it will.

Lachlan handed her the flagon and reclined against the pillows.

"Are ye certain ye dunna just want me to stitch ye up?"

"It'll be all right. Come now, do it quickly before I change my mind." His jaw tensed beneath his dark beard.

"Ye look nice with your hair groomed back," she said, taking the flagon and pouring a line of whisky across the six-inch wound as fast as she could.

Nearly bucking off the bed, a strained and agonizing bellow pealed from Lachlan's throat. His entire body shuddered as if he were fighting the devil. His eyes blinked in rapid succession while he bared his teeth and panted, followed by a high-pitched hiss.

Christina clutched the flagon to her chest and took a step back. "Are ye dying?"

Arching his back, Lachlan pressed the heels of his hands into his eyes. "Nnnn-o."

"I didna think pouring pure spirit on your wound would be smart. Blast, Eva MacKay."

As his breathing returned to normal, Lachlan lowered his hands and regarded her. "Why do you say that? I thought you were friends."

"She was there the day my Andrew died, my son's father. I dunna ken exactly what happened that day 'cause she sent me to the chapel to pray. The priest found me on my knees when he came to give me the news that Andrew has passed. And Eva disappeared for eight years after. It was as if she'd flown away like a hummingbird."

Lachlan grimaced. "Do you blame her for Andrew's death?"

Christina shook her head. "Nay, he was already too sick. The physicians had tried everything. Andrew was unconscious and barely breathing when Eva came into the chamber with Willy, asking for clean rags and boiling water..." Tingles spread down Christina's arms. "As a matter of fact, she called for whisky then as well."

"He was wounded by an arrow?"

"Aye, from a crossbow."

"With a lead arrowhead?"

She nodded. "Most likely."

"Mum said he died of lead poisoning."

"Pardon?" Christina's head spun. The whisky must have seeped through Lachlan's skin and caused him to be inebriated. "I must have poured too much spirit on your wound." She retrieved her sewing basket and busied herself threading a needle—the finest, thinnest bone needle she owned.

"How did you meet her?" Lachlan continued to persist in pursuing this bizarre line of conversation.

"Lady Eva?" Christina still couldn't believe that he'd continued to refer to the woman as his mother. He was too old to be Eva MacKay's son.

"Yes."

Pulling the silk thread through, she let out a huff. "The first time I met Eva was right after the Battle of Stirling Bridge—William had sent for me." Gooseflesh again rose across her skin. "Because Eva had told him to—they said she was a seer—she even placed her hands on my belly and told me my unborn would be a lad."

Lachlan nodded as if the news didn't surprise him in the slightest. "So, Sir Andrew had already been wounded?"

"Aye, but it took months for him to succumb to his wounds. He was a verra strong man." Christina held up the needle. "Are ye ready for this?"

"Yeah." He watched her as she leaned over and studied the gash.

When she pushed in the needle, the big warrior didn't flinch. That's when Christina knew without the slightest doubt how much pouring whisky on raw flesh had hurt him. "Eva was tall, lithe and lovely with green eyes the color of spring grass." Christina chuckled with her next stitch. "She always used the oddest twists of phrase—much like—." She stopped mid-stitch and met Lachlan's midnight blue-eyed stare. Merciful stars, his dark gaze was too much like William's. It just wasn't natural.

"She used speech that seemed odd?" Lachlan clarified, rolling his hand.

"Aye, as if she hailed from a faraway land." She wasn't about to admit that Eva's burr was much like Lachlan's.

"Would you believe the future?" he asked.

"Och, if wee fairies would make my bed in the morning and keep my porridge warm on the coldest day of winter I might be inclined to believe it."

His Adam's apple bobbed as he pointed to the other side of his chest. "I think I need a few more stitches over there."

"I dunna recall saying I was finished." Christina returned her attention to the task, biting the corner of her mouth. She hoped Lachlan would come sober soon, for he was suggesting the unthinkable. His words bordered on heresy.

"So then," he continued, blast him. "You said Eva disappeared for eight years. Did you see her after she returned?"

Thinning her lips, Christina nodded. "She came to visit me when I was being held prisoner at Ormond Castle—asked me to help William raise an army of Highlanders."

He sucked in a shallow breath with the next plunge of the needle. "How could you do that if you were a prisoner?"

"That's exactly what I told her. But I did help—I sent a messenger throughout the Highlands asking for men to join William." Chills again tingled down Christina's arms. "Willy did train those men, though they didn't march with him— they fought for Robert the Bruce." She tied off another stich.

Shaking his head, he clapped a hand to his forehead. "Holy shit." Even his skin had grown clammy.

Christina pulled back, trying to hold the needle steady. "Did I hurt ye?"

"No." Lachlan flicked her veil behind her back, giving her a better view of him from the corner of her eye. "What else can you tell me about Eva?" he asked.

At least this time he hadn't used that godawful term "mum". Christina thought back while she pushed in the needle for the last suture. "We called her Miss Eva until she married William—"

"Wait." Lachlan grabbed Christina's wrist. Practically crushed it under his powerful grip. "Were you at my mother's wedding?"

"Nay." Her shoulders tenser than a pouncing cat, she met his wild stare. "Goodness, Lachlan, it canna be. Ye are far too old to be Eva's son, even if ye do look like Willy."

His hand shook as he released his grip and held up the medallion. "You'd best start believing in fairies, m'lady, because I'm here on account of the powers behind this wee chunk of bronze."

Shrinking from the medal, Christina snipped the thread. "I'm afraid ye're in your cups, sir. Ye're making no sense at all, which is no way for a lady's champion to behave."

"Listen to me." Lachlan sat up and grasped her shoulders. "I'm as sober as a rock and I'm telling you Eva MacKay is from the future, and so am I."

Chapter Fourteen

Christina ran up the wheeled staircase as fast as she could. Her entire world was shattering around her and Lachlan had the gall to tell her he was from the future? Heaven help her, how much more could she take? She had Andrew to worry about. Now her champion was spewing rubbish about the future and insisting he was Eva MacKay's son? Worse, she could hardly be in the same chamber with Lachlan Wallace and keep her heart from thrumming out of her chest.

The man was braw and handsome and smart. He had a gentle nature, yet could crush her with his fist. She'd poured raw spirit on a six-inch gash across his chest and he'd shown few outward signs of the agony. She'd stitched him up and he hadn't so much as grimaced. Dear Lord, not even her husband was as rugged as Lachlan—yet the poor man was touched in the head. He'd been benumbed by the fairies for certain.

Tears stung her eyes as she dashed out onto the wall-walk, sucking in deep breaths. It was cold and the wind blew bitter, but Christina didn't care. If she could, she'd mount her horse and ride for miles. If only it were safe to be alone. If only she could run away from her problems and hide.

Curses, curses, curses. Why must thoughts of Lachlan continually plague my mind?

The man knew she was beside herself with worry about Andrew. Why did he have to become a pain in the backside now? Holy crosses, if she didn't persuade her son to support King Robert, the de Moray lands would be forfeit. Lachlan knew she was in no state to receive such disturbing news about his mother. Aye, there had been something uncannily odd about Eva, regardless of the fact that Christina liked her. But being from the future? Holy Moses, Sir Boyd had said he thought the same only sennights ago. And Christina had defended Lachlan to the knight as if he was an angel from God.

Is the medallion the work of Satan? If it is, then why does Lachlan perform good deeds?

His magic from this morn could very well be evil. Though she'd been married, she had little experience with such things. And how did he make her body respond with such rapture, yet with such coveting?

I should be entirely focused on Andrew and, yet, my body aches with desire for Lachlan. This is not a normal state of affairs.

This very morn when she'd accused him of being a sorcerer what had Lachlan said? *"There's nothing magical about making a woman come."*

Come?

Is that what happened?

Why hadn't it happened when I was with Andrew?

"Lady Christina—are ye unwell?" Sir Boyd marched toward her from the opposite direction.

She could have melted on the spot. The last thing she needed was another knight brining bad news or worse. "Nay, I just needed a walk and fresh air."

"Ye look as if ye've seen a ghost."

"Perhaps I have."

He eyed her, moving his fists to his hips. "Whatever do ye mean?"

She let out a long sigh. "Remember when ye said ye thought Eva was from the future?"

"Shhh." Robbie glanced around all sides to ensure they hadn't been overheard. "'Twas only the thoughts of a verra young man."

"Nothing makes sense." She threw up her hands and started walking west—where they would encounter fewer guards. "Lachlan is a man of thirty. And Eva was older than I, but not so old she could possibly have a son the age of my new champion."

"I ken, 'tis why I tried to put the whole foolishness out of my mind when he told me Eva was his mother." Boyd gave her a sidewise glance. "Except..."

"Except?"

"The resemblance between Willy and Lachlan is too similar. I lay abed at night thinking about it, trying to make sense of it all. But in my estimation, their child should have only attained the age of nine."

"Unless your suspicions about the medallion are true."

He stopped, looking over his shoulder. "What are ye saying?"

Shaking her head, Christina covered her mouth with her hand. "I'm making no sense at all."

"No, ye arna and those thoughts could see ye burned if the bishop at Kelso Abbey heard such sacrilege." Sir Boyd then snorted as if he thought the whole conversation amusing.

She backhanded the knight's arm. "Ye are to tell no one."

"Ye ken I've shared my own suspicions, so I'd be every bit as guilty." He gave her a bow. "Your secrets are safe with me, m'lady."

"And I thank ye...else I wouldna have opened up to ye the way I did."

"'Tis good to ken ye are comfortable coming to me with your woes."

Christina chewed on her lip. Whom could she ask? Sir Boyd was an attractive knight, though far too young for her. But he was popular with the ladies. He might know. "May I ask ye a—um—rather sensitive question?"

"Ye should feel free to ask me anything, m'lady. There are not many of us around who rode with Willy, who kent what it was like in the early days living in caves."

"This is personal in nature." She cringed, doubting herself.

"Aye? The same holds true, I'd reckon."

"And ye are popular with the women folk."

Again he stopped walking and eyed her. "Tell me what's on your mind afore ye make me blush to my toes."

"Um." It was her turn to look over her shoulder to be absolutely certain she wasn't being overheard, though she doubted with the gale blowing like a rushing torrent in their ears that anyone outside of three feet away would be able to hear a thing. "Have ye ever heard of making a woman *come*?"

Dear Lord, no man hath ever turned such a brilliant shade of red. The corners of Sir Boyd's lips pulled down, his face growing even redder until he turned and looked out over the River Tweed and ran his hand down his face. "Aye, m'lady. 'Tis one of the few pleasures known to man...or woman. I think 'tis God's greatest gift."

Christina's cheeks burned as she let out a long breath. Now that Sir Boyd knew what she'd been thinking she should be more than a bit embarrassed. But it was embarrassment mixed with relief. At least Sir Lachlan hadn't put a hex on her—right?

"Have ye slept with him?" Sir Boyd asked.

Aside from keeping him warm last eve? "Not slept as in *lain*..."

The knight donned a battle hardened scowl. "Has he said inappropriate things to ye?"

"Nay. He has been a gentleman, as I would expect."

"Then where did ye hear such crude talk, may I ask?"

She squared her shoulders. "Ye may not."

"Verra well, but if your virtue should need defending, ye must call upon me at once." Sir Boyd snapped his fingers. "Goodness, with all this talk, I nearly forgot why I came up here."

"Is it Andrew? I dunna ken if we can turn him around afore he meets with the king."

"We canna. 'Cause the Bruce is already speaking to him at this verra moment."

Christina's heart nearly pounded out of her chest. "Pardon? Why in heavens name did ye not tell me this as soon as ye saw me?"

Chapter Fifteen

Andrew de Moray stood straight, his lips pursed, every muscle in his body tense right down to the fists clenched at his sides. If only he had a dagger hidden up his sleeve, he'd end Robert Bruce's reign here and now. It didn't surprise him that his capture was as Lord de Vere had proclaimed. *"Scots are devious, filthy savages"*. After the earl had told Andrew he could become a knight, the youth had done everything to ensure he wasn't mistaken for a heathen Scot. Hell's bells, he'd been teased by every boy in England, including the servant's children until he'd declared his fealty to King Edward. True, Andrew may have been born to Scottish parents, but his father was dead and his mother had never been a part of his life. He didn't even recognize the woman. He didn't even look like her—not too much, anyway. Nearly a man, Andrew's choice had been made ages ago. Who had fed and clothed him? Who had allowed him to work with horses—his only true love? Not the matron who claimed to be his mother.

And now the usurper, the self-proclaimed king, sat across the chamber glowering like the tyrant Andrew knew him to be. The Bruce's eyes drilled through him with the gaze of a falcon. Just what Andrew expected from a ruthless murderer of innocents, an imposter, a *backstabber*.

"Ye do not bow before your king?" said the imposter sitting on the throne.

Andrew's gut twisted. "I will not be intimidated by a puppet king."

The Bruce threw back his head with a belly laugh. "I believe ye have me confused with John Balliol." Then he leaned forward and jammed his finger into the armrest, his look penetrating, as if he could read all the vile thoughts swirling in Andrew's head. "I assure ye, I am no puppet, and I *am* your king. After years of tyranny and bloodshed caused by the English, I have united the Kingdom of Scotland, lands rich with black soil and fat cattle, and nobles who pay me fealty."

Andrew's fingernails bit into his clenched palms. "Ye are but a pustule on the face of the great King Edward."

The man scoffed. "Ye are awfully certain of yourself for a whelp."

"I am a squire for Sir Robert de Vere. He will make me a knight—"

"Is that so?" The king stood and walked around Andrew. Though Robert Bruce was a good hand or two taller, the young man refused to be intimidated. "Ye ken ye were born into one of the most powerful Scottish families in the kingdom?"

Andrew focused his gaze on the hearth. "That is what I'm told."

"Where have the bleating swine kept ye all these years?"

"My care has been entrusted to de Vere, the Earl of Oxford."

"Did he turn ye into a man? Did he feed and clothe ye? Give ye a bed to sleep in and books to read?"

"I was given ample food and my clothing is adequate for a squire." A memory of being dressed in rags and bone-thin from hunger flashed through Andrew's mind. Though he'd received little in the way of comforts, his poor treatment as a young child had only served to make him stronger. Andrew's knees buckled a bit and he curled his toes. Once he'd grown taller, everything had changed for the better. He was on the road to greatness before being captured. And now, the Scots would try to break him—they had no idea how tough he'd become. "I was given a tutor when I was ten."

"So ye can read?"

"Yes." Andrew wasn't about to give this false king the courtesy of answering with "Your Grace" or even a "yes, sir".

"What other skills did de Vere teach ye?"

"I'm good with horses—the best. I can break them and ride like hellfire. I'm to join the tourneys when I reach my majority."

"Are ye now?" The Bruce arched an eyebrow with his patronizing smirk. "And de Vere has treated ye like a son, took ye under his wing and given ye the highest quality instruction in all of Christendom?"

Andrew gulped. Blast it all, why must his mouth grow dry at a time like this? "Yes." Of course, de Vere didn't treat him like a son...the great earl was teaching Andrew how to be a warrior. Andrew had rarely been inside the enormous castle, apart from the kitchens. Even the two years he'd endured with the tutor were in the kitchens. He slept in the barn with the stable hands and learned his trade from de Vere's guardsmen—not the man-at-arms, but good, rugged warriors all the same.

I will be a knight for de Vere.

"And King Edward will grant ye lands and riches?" the Bruce persisted.

"In time, he will." *Why doesn't he understand?*

"Are ye certain of yourself?"

"Ah...Yes." Andrew now clenched his fists so hard his knuckles burned.

"So ye would give up your lands and riches in Scotland to follow a tyrant king?"

Bloody hell! Andrew felt like he was about to burst. The evilest despot in all of Christendom was calling Edward II, a man with impeccable lineage, a tyrant? "Edward is benevolent, and k-kind, and steadfast, and—"

"Ruthless?" bellowed the king, his eyes turning charcoal black.

"No! He is strong." Blast it all, Andrew's voice cracked.

"Ye have a great deal to learn afore I recognize ye as a nobleman in this realm. Do ye ken what it means to be a Scot?"

Andrew ticked up his chin in a show of defiance. "Ye mean a backstabber?"

Before he could blink, Robert the Bruce backhanded him across the face. "Insolence!" the man boomed.

The iron taste of blood spread across Andrew's tongue. But the sting radiating on his cheek infused him with confidence. He'd taken a strike and still stood his ground. Puffing out his chest, Andrew stood taller.

"Scotland is a land of lush moors and mountains that touch the sky." The Bruce spread his arms wide. "Scotland is a land skirted by tempestuous seas and sculpted by the rush of the north wind. Her people are hardy and hard working. They fiercely protect clan and kin, and hold dear their honor. But do ye ken what a Scotsman holds dearest in his breast?"

Andrew shook his head, the palms of his hands clammy.

"Freedom." The Bruce stopped and stared, his gaze penetrating to Andrew's soul. "Freedom, lad. We'll not be bowing to a ruthless overlord—a man who murders and rapes pregnant women and impales hard-working farmers on wooden spikes."

Andrew gasped. "He would nev—"

"Silence!" The Scottish king slammed his fist into his palm. "Ye are but a whelp and ye have nay seen the atrocities carried out in the name of England. Ye have been mollycoddled and protected by a villain who claims he will make ye a champion."

"He will!"

"Aye? But he canna make ye a great man—a nobleman who will take his seat beside a king, paying fealty, and, in return, given leave to gain riches off his lands and to lead his clan. A young noble could gain honor, could rise to be a *legendary* knight, could lead his people to become the greatest clan in the north."

Andrew gasped when the Bruce's gaze again met his. Even gooseflesh rose across his skin.

"But such honor is reserved for the best of men. Not for lovers of tyrant English kings and definitely not for young pups who ken no manners." The king sauntered so close, his breath rushed through Andrew's hair. "Ye didna bow to me and ye didna use my proper address. Not once."

Andrew looked to his toes and tried to swallow. His skin pricked, his face felt too damn hot. If only he had a knife, he'd plunge it—

The self-proclaimed king lowered his voice. "The next time ye come before me I will make my decision as to how I will dispatch your lands. I hope ye've grown a pair of cods by then."

***

Christina stepped from the stairwell just as six heavily-armed guards escorted Andrew from King Robert's solar.

"What is the meaning of this?" She looked from one to the next. "My son is no criminal!"

"Lady Christina," bellowed the king from within. "Come here and shut the door. I need a word."

She swept into the solar with a fire igniting in her belly. Her son might be a bit misguided, but that was not his fault. It was the fault of the English despots. Treating Andrew like a criminal would only serve to distance him further from his country and kin. "For the love of honor, Your Grace. Six guards?"

King Robert glowered, standing naught but a foot away. "The lad needs to learn a modicum of respect."

"He is confused."

"That is an understatement. He is unhinged. I have no doubt if Andrew had the use of a weapon he wouldna have hesitated to use it, just like he did on your champion."

The walls closed in around her. "He doesna ken what he's doing. The English have brainwashed—I mean, they have filled his mind with falsehoods and hogwash."

"I think ye are not being truthful with yourself." King Robert threw up his palms. "This situation is dire. The lad may never come around."

Wringing her hands, Christina's heart hurt so badly, it nearly burst. "Please. I've waited three and ten years to have my son home. He needs time—time in the country away from court and away from this bloody border for certain. Ye ken as well as I we could fall under attack at any moment." She steepled her fingers and pressed them to her lips in a praying motion—praying that God would place the right words in her mouth. Words that would buy precious time. "Please, my king. I had hoped to spend Yule at court afore we returned to Ormond Castle, but now I see we must haste away from here at once. Two or three years growing to love his clan and kin will set my son to rights. Of that, I swear to ye."

The Bruce sat in his chair and scowled. "I havena three years. By God, a year stretches me to my limits."

Christina's heart fluttered. Could there be a chance? She kept her fingers touching her lips while she listened.

"Ye ken I need a strong leader at Ormond Castle. I need a *man*—a warrior who can defend our northern shores from attack be it from English or Norse. I need a man like your late husband, God rest his soul."

Christina wanted to wail and crumple into a heap. What she wouldn't do to turn back the tides of time so that Sir Andrew Senior would have lived, so that her son would have been raised with a father who was a strong example. So that her son would have no doubt as so who he was and learn to hold dear the clan he was born to protect.

Slowly she lowered her hands to her side, stretching tall and showing nothing of the quivering nerves making her heart race. "I give ye my word. Allow me to take my son home. To show him the beauty and grandeur of his lands. To prove to him how deeply a mother's love runs. Please, please, please, for Andrew is still only a child."

"A child who should be well on his way to becoming a man."

Christina gave a single nod. "A child who has been held captive for so long he kens nothing else." She would not back down, not when she was so close to purchasing time.

The king drummed his fingers—still eyeing her with intelligence and cunning. "I give ye until Christmas next. Ye will come to court and bring the lad before me. If he has not accepted his lot by then, I shall have nay other choice but to grant the lands north of the Moray Firth to a trustworthy and stalwart nobleman."

Blinking back tears, she bowed her head. "Thank ye, Your Grace."

"Make no bones about it, Lady Christina. I will also grant *your hand* to that same nobleman. Ye have royal blood running through your veins, a lineage more important to the kingdom than any one subject. Do ye understand?"

She curtseyed, keeping her head bowed. "My service shall always be for my king and for Scotland."

He thumped his fist on the armrest. "Aye, then ye'd best make certain your son believes the same in short order."

"It will be done, Your Grace. With so much at stake, given your leave, the de Moray guard and I shall depart at dawn."

Chapter Sixteen

Lachlan was totally convinced the obstreperous horse Hamish had given him couldn't walk a straight line if there were walls encroaching on either side. And Lachlan had no doubt the bull-headed guard leading this medieval diamond formation was chuckling right down to his toes. The more Lachlan pulled on the reins, the stroppier the nag became. If he squeezed his knees, the damned mule-brained gelding reared.

Is the beast even broke?

The horse must have had some training, because Lachlan managed to mount without much difficulty. It wasn't until he tapped his heels that the mangy, bird-brained donkey decided to be a shit. He hadn't had this much trouble riding to Norham. At least the horse he'd borrowed from Boyd had been reasonably well-behaved.

They'd been riding for five hours with nine or so to go until they reached Leith where Christina said the de Moray *birlinn* was moored, which would save them weeks of riding, according to her ladyship. When given the choice of riding or sailing, Lachlan decided he'd rather sail. He'd be comfortable manning an oar, though he didn't know much about sails.

Doubtless I'll learn.

"Ease up on the poor bugger's mouth," said Andrew, riding alongside Lachlan, with Christina on his other side. The lady had decided that, as her champion, Lachlan should be responsible for riding with her and the lad. She wanted to make Andrew feel an important part of the twenty-man retinue, but kept him in the center of the formation partially for safety, though mostly to ensure he didn't try to run.

"Huh?" Lachlan asked, rubbing his fingers over the annoying stitches in his chest.

Andrew gave him an adolescent guffaw. "The harder ye pull on the reins, the more your mount will try to resist ye."

Lachlan dropped his hands to the horse's withers and the gelding immediately lowered his head and began to amble like the others. "You seem to know a thing or two about horses."

"Indeed, I do." Andrew almost smiled as he patted his mount's neck. "A squire would not be worth his salt if he wasn't sure of his seat."

"Where did you learn?"

"From Lord de Vere's stable hands—he hires the best horsemen and owns the best destriers in England."

"Destriers?" Lachlan asked.

"Do ye not know anything?" Andrew rolled his eyes like a typical teenager. "Destriers are the best warhorses in all of Christendom."

"Aye, I'll agree to that," said Christina.

Lachlan gave Andrew an appreciative nod, an idea forming in his head. He knew kids and they all craved respect. *Hmm.*

Riding across a burn that cut through a picturesque lea nestled between rolling green hills, Lady Christina cupped a hand to the side of her mouth. "Hamish," she hollered. "We shall take our nooning here."

"Verra well, m'lady."

Lachlan had never been so glad to have a break. He had to pee, the stitches in his healing chest itched like he'd been bitten by a hundred mosquitoes, and he was so hungry, he could eat half a cow—not that he wasn't accustomed to pain, it just he'd been afflicted with one too many complaints at the moment. "What's on the menu?" he asked, dismounting his horse and adding sore thighs to his litany. Good God, now he knew why cowboys walked like they were bowlegged.

"Cheese and oatcakes," Christina said, holding out her hands, waiting for someone to act gentlemanly since her son had already dismounted and was ladling water into his mouth from the swiftly running burn.

Lachlan hobbled over and helped her, his fingers closing around her waist. His heart hammered at the friction of her soft breasts sliding down his chest. Why on earth did his errant male instincts have to hone every time he touched the woman? Christ, they were surrounded by an army and his cock gave a hearty ping.

Down big fella.

"Ye dunna look too happy about the fare," she said, pushing a mahogany curl beneath her hood—black, of course.

He took a step back to distance himself from her wicked, mind-consuming scent. In the future if he wanted to bamboozle an opponent in the karate ring, all he had to do was splash on some eau de Christina. Two feet of distance and the cold air helped to cool his lust. No, Lachlan wasn't one to let the weather bother him—but he didn't have a proper coat or winter boots or a hat. A motorcar with a heater would come in handy about now—especially if he could drive to Uncle Walter's flat and give him hell for this charade. Fourteen hours to travel from Kelso to Edinburgh? He could do it by car in an hour.

"The food's fine…for a bird," he answered, giving her a grin. He looked around. Teasing her ladyship was probably not expected from her champion, but protecting her from possible attack was. Remembering his purpose, he turned full circle, before choosing his vantage point. "I'm climbing to the top of the crag. It should give me a good look to ensure all is well."

She smiled as if pleased with his suggestion. "I'll save a portion for ye, then."

"Thank you."

Working his legs in a brisk climb was exactly what Lachlan needed to stretch out his saddle soreness. In no time, he was breathing deeply, taking longer and longer strides. In fact, he was feeling more like himself. He wasn't a goddamned complainer and he didn't like the way his attitude had dipped over the past few hours.

At the top, he inspected the horizon with a critical eye. Once certain they weren't being followed, he stepped behind the brush and relieved himself. Indeed, the view was magnificent. Far more forested than in modern times, the land below was speckled with farmlets and crofter's shielings. Harvest had come and gone. There were still a few haystacks that hadn't been stowed for the winter, but it looked like winter nonetheless—bare tree limbs stretching like brown skeletons flanked by the odd evergreen. Between it all were verdant grasslands carpeting the lowland hills—nowhere in his travels had Lachlan ever seen such a brilliant green, green that could only be found in Scotland.

He turned and watched one of the guards doling out the oatcakes and cheese while Christina perched on a log, having been served first as was the custom. Yesterday, she'd come to him to tell him they were riding in the morning. She hadn't asked him to go, she'd just assumed that as her newly proclaimed champion, he would drop everything and take up the old sword he'd been issued for Andrew's rescue. She'd given him a leather pouch, a "purse" to reward him for the return of her son. He'd nearly tried to give it back, then thought twice. There was only one thing worse than being stuck in a century where you could end up with your head, or any other appendage chopped off for the slightest misdemeanor and that was to be stranded without a mere pence in his pocket. At least now he could buy a pint of ale or an eating knife and not have to rely on the charity of others. Off to the side, Andrew slowly moved away from his mother, looking like he'd done something naughty.

When he'd slipped a good ten yards away, he broke into a run, dashing straight for the horses.

The lad untied his mount and leapt on its back. The crack of the reins reverberated all the way up the hill as if the boy had slapped the leathers right beside Lachlan's ear. Down below, Christina shouted orders while Hamish and the others scrambled to their feet, but Andrew was already a hundred yards ahead and gaining, taking the path around the outcropping.

Lachlan's legs took over, pumping down the other side of the crag, his knees absorbing the shock of the steep decline. Clamping his teeth, he eyed the spot where Andrew must traverse before hitting the open lea. Gripping his fingers into tight fists, Lachlan demanded more speed from his thighs, ignoring the searing pain in his chest, ignoring the jagged rocks beneath his thin-soled boots. The little schemer wasn't about to escape. Not on Lachlan's watch.

Thunderous hoofbeats pummeled the ground. Dear God, the boy hadn't exaggerated when he boasted about being a horseman. The little shit could ride like a jockey at Ascot.

A flash of brown zipped behind the trees. Lachlan focused on his path.

Two steps to impact.

His blood thrummed through his veins like jet fuel. He had this. Christina would not be disappointed. Not today.

Leaping through the air, Lachlan focused on one thing. Andrew's back.

When he hit, his fingers latched on to the boy's shoulders. Andrew shrieked.

The horse reared with the impact.

The boy held on, slapping his reins. "Get up!"

Lachlan clamped his wrists in a gable grip and fought to stay on. "Stop the beast," he growled in Andrew's ear. He steadied his seat before forcing his hands down to the leather reins.

"Let go," Andrew shouted, his voice cracking.

"No. Bloody. Chance." Using brute force, Lachlan pinned Andrew's hands down with his wrists while tugging the reins hard. The horse skidded, dipping its hindquarter, his forelegs rising off the ground as he reared and twisted his head against the tug of the iron bit. Lachlan squeezed his knees to stay on but the horse responded by rearing so high, both Lachlan and Andrew flew backward.

Midair, the young lad squirmed to break free. Keeping his arms wrapped around the boy, Lachlan held tighter. "You're not going anywhere."

They hit with a bone-jarring thud that made Lachlan's teeth rattle, his ribs crushing beneath the weight of the sturdy fifteen-year-old squire, the stitches in his chest tearing his flesh.

Thrashing and kicking, Andrew wrenched an arm free and threw an elbow to Lachlan's jaw.

"God dammit."

"Ye cannot make me stay."

"Oh yeah?" In one move, Lachlan rolled the boy to his back and pressed the full weight of his body atop him. "I've known you for all of two days and I already want to wring your neck."

The boy squirmed like a true fighter. "Let me go and I'll be out of your hair forever."

"Right. If I let you go, do you honestly think you'd make it to the border alive?" He chuckled. "Not in this century."

Andrew stopped and glared. "I can take care of myself."

"Right again. And who has the upper hand now?"

"But ye are a champion—I can handle myself with an average man." Andrew thrashed his legs. "Remove yourself. I cannot breathe."

"Not a chance." Lachlan took a fraction of his weight onto his elbows. "I'll tell you what. I can teach you to fight like me—take down a man my size."

The squirming stopped. "Ye would do that?"

"Maybe."

Andrew smirked. "But ye want something in return."

"More than one thing." Lachlan nodded his head toward the camp and the sound of approaching horses. "First of all, your mother has done nothing but worry about you for the last thirteen years."

"But she allowed the English to take me—then never came after me until after the war."

"Do you think she could help that? Until the Battle of Bannockburn was won, the English imprisoned her in her own castle. Once the Bruce took back the north, she did everything in her power to negotiate your return."

"But—"

"Look, Hamish and the others will be here any second, so I'm going to make this fast. First, I want you to give your mother a chance. Go to Avoch and see where you were born—see your legacy—discover what kind of man your father was."

"Will ye let me go back to de Vere after?"

"The Bruce said a year. Christmas next. That's the deal." Lachlan didn't have any grounds on which to make a deal, but if he could earn a commitment from Andrew, the child might not be in such a hurry to run.

Andrew pursed his lips. "And secondly?"

"You teach me how to ride a horse."

"Truly? A knight such as ye would learn from the likes of me?"

"Why not? From your display today, I'd wager you're the best horseman in your mother's retinue."

"Honestly?"

Lachlan waggled his eyebrows and grinned. "I wouldn't have said it if I didn't mean it."

Hamish and the other guards rode in and surrounded them. But Lachlan didn't budge, keeping his gaze locked with Andrew's. "Do we have a deal—a bargain?"

"A year. And I learn to fight as well as ye, sir?"

"That's my promise."

"But that will take forever." The lad huffed. Whether that was for show or he truly was an idiot, Lachlan wasn't quite certain. Yet.

He tried one more angle before he released his weight. "Are you afraid to face the truth?"

CHAPTER SEVENTEEN

The trip up Scotland's eastern shore sailing a genuine, handmade Gaelic *birlinn* would have been perfect except for the brooding teenager who sat scowling with his arms crossed at the stern. Lachlan wanted to tell Andrew how lucky he was to have escaped the English and to now be on an adventure to discover his roots, but his experience with his students— especially the difficult ones—had taught him that telling the lad anything would only earn his scorn and Andrew would be all the more difficult to reach.

Regardless, Lachlan decided to enjoy the heck out of the voyage. He wasn't much help with the sailing part, but he paid attention and did whatever he was told. Christina watched him from beneath her cloak's hood. She, too, sat astern near her son. They didn't talk much, but though Andrew scowled like a grumblebum, Christina was equally pinched in her expression. Lachlan's heart squeezed for her, knowing how much she wanted to make a bond and how futile her attempts had been. Hell, it wouldn't have mattered if she'd been a queen, Andrew would have rejected her all the same. Until the lad figured out who the good guys were, she didn't have a chance, and that was going to take some time, if it happened at all.

Merry bloody Christmas.

During the voyage, Lachlan's thoughts shifted to the medallion and his own plight. Somehow, there had to be more to the forces behind the medallion. It didn't just dump him there forever, did it? He would go home eventually. Right? If his mother had been transported to be Wallace's companion and healer, then there had to be something more for Lachlan to do.

Obviously.

And tackling Andrew when he tried to escape hadn't been an accident, either. Oh, no. He'd been sent to ensure that Andrew de Moray, named for his father, was going to accept that he was a Scot.

Lachlan stared across the North Sea; dark blue, icy water stretched to the horizon. He'd had his share of difficult students, but never a child deprived of affection. It didn't take a psychologist to determine that after the lad had been captured, he hadn't received much nurturing, if any. Fortunately, he'd been in his mother's arms for his first two years, which gave Lachlan a thread of hope. Though that didn't allay the fact Andrew was going to be a tough kid to win over. The boy thought he hated Scotland. What was so bloody great about England? Andrew was promised a knighthood by an earl? And then he'd turned around and scoffed at the promise of lands and riches by a king? Was it the idealism and stubbornness of youth or something deeper?

Lachlan intended to find out. He doubted a portal to home would open until Andrew's about-face was finished. The *birlinn* tacked west and entered a firth.

"Where are we now," asked Lachlan.

Hamish stood at the bow and pointed. "Entering Moray Firth. We'll be mooring within the hour."

Being an inexperienced sailor, Lachlan did what he was told and stood out of the way near Hamish while the de Moray men set to their mooring. The first thing he saw was the grey curtain walls looming on a hilltop. At each of the four corners was a turret and rising above it all stood a square donjon, or keep. It reminded him a little of Torwood Castle that his mother had renovated. This one was a motte and bailey fortress, built to defend the northern waters. Lachlan looked west. "Where is Inverness from here?"

Hamish pointed to a hazy cloud in the distance—smoke from many hearths no doubt. "It's twelve miles if ye ride around the firth. Which I recommend for the likes of ye." The old man-at-arms quirked his eyebrow. "Ye'd set to sail and sink me *birlinn* afore ye hit deep water."

"'Tis my ship, Hamish, and I think Lachlan has contributed splendidly considering he's had no seafaring experience." Lady Christina stood and regarded her son. "Ye can see Ormond Castle on the shore. Would ye not like to set eyes on your home?"

Andrew folded his arms and didn't budge. "This is not *my* home."

A pained expression of hurt stretched the lady's features before she turned on the pretense of looking to the shore. Lachlan's gut twisted in a knot. If he didn't have to jump over nine rowing benches and jockey around twenty guardsmen, running the risk of being hit in the head by a swinging boom, he'd march over there and introduce the whelp to a knuckle sandwich. He groaned. Though deep down he wanted to slap the lad until he begged for mercy, Lachlan's training forbade it. Aye, he could defend himself, but he couldn't be the aggressor. Sooner or later, Andrew would snap. He had to, because Lachlan was too bloody close to snapping himself. If the little shit didn't learn a modicum of respect, Lachlan couldn't be held accountable for his actions.

The breeze pushed back Christina's hood, picked up her dreary veil and whisked it from her head. By some miracle, it sailed directly into Lachlan's hands. He turned to Hamish and held it up. But before the guard could say anything, her ladyship's voice rang out. "Please, I cannot possibly arrive at the castle with my tresses flapping in the wind like a young maid."

Hamish nodded. "Just keep your head down." Then he motioned to the sailor controlling the sail ropes. "Tack north."

No one on the planet could have convinced Lachlan that Hamish hadn't ordered the boom to swing just as he was about to cross the hull. He'd already taken two whacks to the head and he wasn't about to take another.

"Jibe-ho," shouted the man with the ropes.

How the hell was Lachlan supposed to know what jibe-ho meant? Well, he did now, and he crouched as low as he could while he crawled over the benches. He was rewarded with a smile from Christina, strained as it might be. Even when she was stressed to her limits, the woman looked cuter than a pixie covered with morning dew. She draped the grey veil over her head and tried to cover her hair, but it wasn't playing nice. Ringlets of dark chocolate curls danced with the wind. Lachlan clasped his hands together to keep from cupping her face between his palms and planting a very inappropriate kiss on her lips. Such an outward display of affection would be frowned upon by everyone, especially Andrew.

No, Lachlan needed to keep his distance. The slip the other day wouldn't happen again. Christ, he could never, ever crawl into the woman's bed, not ever again. It didn't matter that he'd passed out and someone had carried him there. Nope. He shouldn't have ended up in her goddamned bed. Admiring Christina de Moray from afar must suffice. Eventually, this nightmare, or whatever it was, would be over and he'd go home to clean up the shambles of his life. This wasn't his time. He had a job to do in mentoring Andrew and once the lad figured out who really loved him, Lachlan knew without a shadow of a doubt he'd be whisked back to the future just like his mum had been.

As they sailed onto the beach, clansmen, women and children lined the shore, all shouting their welcomes and waving their arms. They all looked like hearty stock, stout and rosy cheeked. The women wore muted kirtles with plaid arisaids pinned around their shoulders or draped over their heads. The men dressed in all manner of colorful plaid. Some wore trews, many in furs and others with woolen plaids belted around their waists. Cavemen came to mind.

Perhaps that's a bit harsh.

After the men had pulled the boat onto the shore, Christina stood on a rowing bench and held up her hands. "I am elated to tell ye my son, Andrew, has been returned to us."

The crowd erupted with boisterous shouts and applause.

She waited with her hands folded until the noise ebbed. "I also want to introduce Sir Lachlan Wallace, my new champion."

When she gestured to him, Lachlan bowed his head, though his welcome came more in the form of murmurs and curious stares.

But that didn't dissuade Christina. She clapped, pasting on a brilliant smile. "Thank ye all so much for your warm welcome. Your greeting means the world to me and to celebrate the heir's return to Ormond, we will have a grand feast!"

***

Christina sat at the high table and looked out over the noisy hall. It had been a long time since she'd had family sit with her. Aye, there had been guests and Hamish always joined her even though he wasn't of noble birth. But tonight, he joined his family at the table close to the dais. Andrew sat to Christina's right. One day he would take up his mantle and occupy her chair—the chieftain's seat—though not yet. Sir Lachlan sat on Andrew's other side. They all faced the clan, as was traditional. Before her husband's death, there had been many feasts where both sides of the table had been filled with happy and boisterous kin. Honestly, before King Robert liberated Ormond Castle, there had been few visitors aside from the clansmen and women under de Moray protection who lived and worked on the surrounding crofts or held positions in the castle. A prisoner in her own home with an English retinue of rude and obnoxious English sentries patrolling her curtain walls, her son held captive beyond the border, there was no reason to celebrate anything.

Now that she was home among the happy faces of her clan, she wanted to sing of joy and dance all night. If only Andrew were content to be among his kin again. If only those conniving English brutes had left him alone. But they had filled him with false hope and lies. With no one to show him the truth, why wouldn't a child believe his captors? Why wouldn't he try to impress them and better his station in life? Andrew was a de Moray. He naturally would rise above his lot and work to earn respect and honor, even if he wasn't entirely certain what those words meant.

Yet.

And I aim to make this a Yule celebration my son will never forget.

When the doors from the kitchen opened, children ran and squealed in anticipation of a hearty feast of roast pork and applesauce. Christina couldn't help her chuckle, though Andrew grumbled beside her. She gave him a nudge. "We have fifty breeding sows, a thousand head of sheep and two-thousand head of stocky Highland cattle."

"Have ye counted them lately?" asked Andrew.

"I haven't. We employ herdsmen to the task."

Andrew held up his palms and scoffed like a highbrowed snob. "I wouldn't trust a one of them."

Fortunately, Tearlach offered her first pick from the trencher of meat. Pointing, she forced a smile. "The end piece with all the spices baked into the rind for me, thank ye."

"And some applesauce?"

"Of course."

Christina waited while Andrew was served, but her son started eating before Lachlan had selected his. "'Tis proper manners to wait until everyone at the table is served afore ye start in."

Andrew looked up. "Only in Scotland."

"Actually, if Lord de Vere had given ye proper training, ye would have found manners much the same throughout Christendom." Christina leaned forward. "Do ye not agree, Sir Lachlan?"

The knight held up his new eating knife. "Wholeheartedly. Manners were drilled into me from a young age."

Andrew shook his head and shoveled food into his mouth.

Christina cringed, watching him from the corner of her eye while she cut her meat and carefully pulled each bite from her knife. Perhaps she shouldn't say anything about etiquette until Andrew had a chance to settle in.

"Our crops are extensive as well," she said. "Wheat, oats, barley and hops, and all manner of vegetables."

"Lots of things to dry and can for winter." Lachlan swirled a bite of pork in applesauce. "And an apple orchard, I'd guess."

"Indeed," Christina said, thrilled someone was engaging. Even if Andrew sat there like a lump, he still had ears. "We have apple trees, hazelnuts, walnuts, plums, and my favorite, raspberries." She held up her tankard of ale. "And Angus is our brewer and winemaker." She took a long drink. "He can work miracles."

Andrew picked up his tankard and guzzled. "Hmm. If ye drink it fast, ye cannot taste the piss."

Christina drew her hand to her chest, her tongue growing dry with her revulsion.

"Enough of your disrespectful rubbish." Lachlan used his fingers to flick the back of Andrew's head—nothing that would hurt, but a gesture clearly expressing disapproval. "This woman's your mother and you'll pay her due respect or we don't have a deal."

Andrew clamped his lips shut, shooting Christina the most hateful glare she'd seen since the English were booted out of her castle. She ate in silence for a time, until someone came into the hall and announced snow had begun to fall. Truly, she couldn't stay upset for long, not with Yule around the corner. Taking advantage of the welcome news, she clapped. "We must make a Yule log and green the castle. It will be Christmas in a fortnight."

The lad beside her snorted. "Why bother? This crumbling old keep is so dank and cold, nothing could make it inviting."

"Where the hell did you come up with that line of tripe?" Lachlan grabbed Andrew's wrist and bent it downward until the lad grew red in the face and began to pant. "I'm not going to say it again. You treat your mother disrespectfully and I'll treat you ten times worse. Do you understand?"

"Y-y-y-y-yes," the lad said, his face redder than the scarlet comforter on Christina's bed. "Let. Go."

"Stop," she whispered. "People are beginning to stare. Dunna make a show in front of the clan."

"This is only temporary pain." Lachlan gave her a glare of his own and didn't let up. "But are you suggesting I can kick his bony bum when no one is looking?"

Gasping, Andrew practically fell under the table, bending downward in the direction of his wrist.

Christina pursed her lips. "No," she clipped.

Releasing his grip, Lachlan nudged the lad in the shoulder. "Don't grow too confident. Your ass is mine for an entire year."

Andrew rubbed his wrist. "And I'll put ye on the meanest stallion in my mother's stable."

Lachlan raised his hands and beckoned with his fingers. "Bring it on."

Christina sighed and rolled her gaze to the rafters. Sir Lachlan had been awfully brash with the lad since he'd stopped him from running away. They'd struck up some sort of agreement where Andrew would teach Lachlan to ride and he, in turn, would train Andrew how to be a knight. She approved for the most part. She even liked the fact that the man had demanded respect from her son, but must he do it so forcefully?

Fortunately, Christina was spared from having to answer or further ponder his question when Kenneth, the clan bard asked to climb the steps to the dais.

"Please do," she beckoned him. "And what story will ye tell us this eve?"

Kenneth looked to Andrew. "I believe 'tis time for the heir to hear how his father took Urquhart Castle from the English overlord, Edward the Longshanks."

The hall erupted in applause while Andrew now turned a shade of white.

Impressed with Kenneth's choice, Christina joined in the applause and motioned for him to continue. Andrew needed to hear the true tale of his father's heroics by someone other than herself and this was a fine place to begin.

A short man with wild eyes and furry all over, Kenneth stepped forward and spread his arms wide. "The death of King Alexander III in the year of our Lord twelve-eighty-six marked the opportunity England had been waiting for to invade Scotland. Licking his chops, Edward the Longshanks rode his black steed across the border and claimed he was rightful suzerain over our kingdom.

"With no forthright heir to the throne of Scotland, the tyrant king took it upon himself to appoint the weaker John Balliol, Lord of Galloway, to rule our lands. Balliol was considered the least likely to pose a threat to England, though everyone knew the better candidate was the powerful, Lord Bruce of Annandale, grandfather of King Robert the Bruce."

"Here, here," came bellows from the clan.

"Immediately, Longshanks began his humiliation of Balliol, issuing personal insults and demanding public demonstrations of fealty. Adding to the outrage, the Scots were used like pawns and forced to fight England's battles on the continent. When Balliol tried to fight back, the evil English king sent his army to sack Berwick."

Kenneth eyed Andrew with a ferocious glare. "No mercy was shown and the English took no prisoners. The slaughter continued for three days. The atrocity of Edward's barbarism is still remembered to this day."

With an enormous sigh, Kenneth faced the crowd. "After Balliol abdicated, Edward marched his army northward, killing and pillaging as they laid waste to the land. In the north they took Urquhart Castle, gateway of trade with the south. He nearly starved us out of existence."

The bard continued the tale, "He imprisoned the great Sir Andrew de Moray in Chester Castle, but he couldn't hold our leader for long. Sir Andrew dug his way beneath the curtain walls, stole away north on a farmer's hay wagon. After weeks of running and hiding, the great knight pounded on Ormond Castle's gates."

The clanspeople cheered.

"Wasting no time, he brought together the de Moray army and marched to Urquhart Castle. For days, he laid siege to the fortress, with nothing but bowmen and a single trebuchet catapult. Sir Andrew and his warriors drove the English south, liberating Scottish keeps and villages in their wake until they met up with William Wallace in Scone."

Kenneth peered over at Andrew as he continued, "Together they formed an alliance and beat Longshanks in Stirling. That's when our great and powerful chieftain took an arrow for his kingdom and lovely Lady Christina laid him to rest three months hence."

The bard did not flinch while Andrew sat upright, his expression unreadable. "Your da was a warrior of great repute, respected by the hero, William Wallace. Together they fought the most powerful army in Christendom and won. It wasn't the end of the dark times for the kingdom, but their victory was a call to arms throughout the land. And now that the Bruce was victorious at Bannockburn, we are free men once again."

Kenneth gave Christina a wink and bowed.

The hall erupted with applause. Christina grinned as wide as she could. The two men dining with her this eve could not have been more different. Andrew was again red in the face and Lachlan was slapping his hands together and whistling for more.

Andrew slammed his fist on the table, making the hall go suddenly quiet. "Ye are all wrong. My father was a traitor and my mother a whore. Lord de Vere said Scottish varlets shag their mothers and know no honor."

Lachlan sprang to his feet, grasping Andrew by the shoulder. "That's enough. You do not go into someone's house and tell them they're cheats and liars."

Andrew jerked his shoulder from the knight's grasp. "But 'tis true. Everyone wants me to be happy to be here. But this is not my home. These are not my people and she is no mother to me—and ye—ye are nothing but a charlatan."

Lachlan's face grew dark, his mouth in a hard line. "You want to become a knight?"

"I will become a knight. Lord de Vere promised."

"Well then your training starts here and now." Lachlan grabbed Andrew's wrist and pulled him toward the steps. "Clear the tables!"

Christina clasped her hands over her heart. "Please, do not hurt him!"

Glancing back, Lachlan met her gaze. "I'll make sure he lives."

Christina wanted to scream—tell the man he was overreacting to an adolescent's outburst. "But—"

"M'lady," Hamish bellowed from the floor. "May I have permission to join ye?"

Sinking back into her seat, she nodded.

"The only reason I haven't planted my boot in the lad's arse is on account he's your son." Her old man-at-arms approached.

"He's awful, is he not?"

"He's foolish." Hamish took the seat to her left. "And I dunna envy the task to bring him around."

Down below, Lachlan held up his fists to his face, circling her poor son. "Come now, show me what you've got."

The lad clenched his fists, but too low to protect his face from a strike. Clearly he had little training. "I could *kill* ye." Though he lacked nothing in insolence.

"I doubt that." Lachlan nodded. "Give me your best."

Roaring like a braying bull, Andrew lunged in with a jab to the jaw. The big man caught Andrew's fist midair and flipped the lad on his back, the floorboards thudding with a bang. Clutching his chest, the child gasped like he couldn't breathe.

"Get up," Lachlan demanded, pacing back and forth.

"I c-can't," Andrew shouted between gasps.

"No?" Lachlan bent down, grabbed the boy by the shoulders and stood him on his feet. "I'll give you until the count of ten to catch your breath, then we go again."

Christina sat clutching her arms across her midriff. "I canna bear this."

Hamish placed his hand on her shoulder. "Whatever ye feel inside, do not interfere. This is for the lad's own good."

Clenching every muscle in her body, her stomach roiled while she watched Andrew rush toward Lachlan with attack after attack, only to be thwarted every time.

"I hate ye, ye *evil* tyrant." Andrew yanked a dirk from Kenneth's belt, raised it over his head and charged.

Stepping to the side, Lachlan swept the dirk into his hand as if by magic and spun Andrew into a strangle hold, inclining the knife to the lad's neck. "Apologize to your mother."

The boy shook his head vehemently. "I cannot."

"Do it now," growled the knight. "Or I'll cut out your tongue and make sure you never speak another word."

"Damn ye." Andrew struggled, glaring at her. "I'm sorry for calling ye a whore."

Lachlan tightened his grip. "Not good enough."

Tears streamed from Christina's eyes. "Please, stop."

Lachlan ignored her. "Apologize!" he bellowed so loudly the chandeliers overhead seemed to shudder.

"Please!" Christina pleaded.

"Do it!" Lachlan didn't give an inch.

Christina stood.

"Hold your wheesht," Hamish growled and snatched her hand, pulling her back. "Ye mustna interfere, m'lady."

She clamped her teeth so hard, her jaw hurt.

Please son, please. Bend just a wee bit.

"Forgive my impertinence," Andrew sobbed, a tear streaming down his face.

Lachlan immediately drew the knife away, but continued to hold his grip. "Here are the rules: You will be respectful of your mother while enjoying her hospitality. You will be respectful of Clan de Moray at all times. Please and thank you will become your favorite words. You will report to me for lessons every morning. You will call me sir…is that clear?"

"Yes," Andrew whispered.

"Yes, what?"

"Yes, sir."

"You will do your mother's bidding come afternoon and if there is time after that, I will allow you to impart your *vast* knowledge of horsemanship." Lachlan said vast with a mocking edge in his voice. "Do you understand?"

Andrew shook his head.

"I can't hear you."

"Yes, sir."

Lachlan beckoned Andrew's guard. "Kiss your mother goodnight and head for your bed because come morning you're going to need your rest." Finally, he released his grip.

Andrew stood and looked up the dais steps.

Lachlan gave him a pat on the shoulder "Go on, then."

"Come on, come on," Hamish whispered.

Everyone in the hall stood motionless, as if they were all willing the lad to move forward.

Hanging his head, Andrew climbed the stairs and gave Christina a wee peck on the cheek.

She brushed his mop of hair away from his face. "Sleep well, my son." Then she focused a heated gaze upon Lachlan.

Chapter Eighteen

"I will meet with ye in my solar forthwith," Christina said as she swished past Lachlan in a whoosh of skirts.

He gulped. He should have known she'd be madder than a badger. But the boy needed a lesson. Ducking his head, Lachlan followed the lady up the narrow stairwell. He'd already hit his head three times and he hadn't even slept at Ormond yet. He wondered what his father would have done. Not Bill Wallace, decorated war hero of the twenty-first century, but William Wallace, the man supposedly his father. Scotland's hero had been every bit as tall. He must have had difficulty negotiating doorways and narrow stairwells. If only Lachlan could have traveled back a bit further in time, he might have been able to see William in action.

That would have been unbelievable.

But the forces behind the medallion saw fit to send him to Lady Christina to help her son...now Lachlan needed to figure out how to convince the woman that his tactics had been a necessary step. After he followed her into the solar, she faced him, her blue eyes blazing like hellfire.

Something wobbled in Lachlan's knees. Dear God, now was no time for his heart to race. He had a goddamned argument to make. He set his jaw and gave her a defiant stare of his own.

"That was my son down there ye made to look like a fool. Bless it, he could have been hurt."

"Okay. I'll admit I caused him mild pain, but never once did I allow him to be injured."

"Ye threatened to carve out his tongue!"

"Well, there's that, I suppose, but isn't that the type of thing that's done in the Middle Ages?" Honestly, he'd been afraid the tongue carving part was over the top, but she'd told him about flaying people alive. Jesus Christ, that had to be far worse.

Christina threw up her hands. "Och, ye are insufferable. It's bad enough the lad sounds like an Englishman. And now ye've gone and humiliated him in front of the clan."

"Not before he insulted you, the entire clan and me. Tell me, what did you expect next? The entire clan to run up to the dais and give him hugs?"

"I wanted him to realize how ridiculous he sounded."

"Right. It's kinda hard to prove that to a teenager who, since he was an infant, was taught to hate everything about his heritage. He thinks he knows good from bad, right from wrong. He thinks he's smarter than we are. Worse, he's adopted the insidious English snobbery that irritates the heck out of me even in my century."

She regarded him for a moment, her features softening. She had to know he was right, she couldn't be *that* blind.

"The clansmen and women needed to know that no matter what we will not—" Lachlan held up his palms. "Let me rephrase—you will not allow a child to run roughshod over you."

Groaning, she looked to the ceiling with its white relief swirling like damask. "What's done is done. But I doubt Andrew will be able to weather many scenes like the shame ye presented him with this eve."

Lachlan nodded. "I agree."

Her eyes brightened. "Ye do?"

The corners of his mouth turned up. "Of course I do." Reaching out, he placed his hand on her shoulder with a reassuring squeeze. "You call the shots for the most part— aside from a few things."

"Such as?"

"I have complete say over his physical training—weapons, fists, self-defense and exercise regime."

"Can ye promise me he willna be injured?"

"I can promise I will do everything to see to his safety, though a man can't climb down your stairwell without risking his neck."

"Verra well." She didn't laugh at his jibe. "And I want his full attention in the afternoon. Afore the meal, I spoke to a cleric who has agreed to give him lessons in Latin."

"Excellent."

She grinned. "And I want him to enjoy Christmas ever so much."

Lachlan huffed a sigh—jeez, he didn't want her to get her hopes up too high. "That could be stretching things a bit."

She traced her finger around the crest embroidered on Lachlan's surcoat. The sensation made electricity fire across his skin. Then she had to meet his gaze with a set of hypnotic blues—blues the color of the aqua water surrounding Iona's white-sand beaches. "I will make this a Christmas to remember, no matter what Andrew thinks. He might even pooh-pooh the whole ordeal, but the spirit will touch his heart. And once touched, it will worm its way around and around until Andrew sees the truth."

Her fingers continued to lightly brush over the de Moray coat of arms on his chest until Lachlan could take no more. He grasped her hand and brought it to his lips but only for a brief peck. "Let's continue these talks. I'm now convinced I am here to help your son realize his place."

As her eyes shifted, disappointment flashed through them. "Are ye certain?"

"Nearly. Why else didn't I end up back in my own century after I rescued him from Norham?"

"Do ye not like it here?"

Lachlan twisted his mouth. Never in his life had he considered traveling through time, but now that he was there, he'd begun to find his way, adapt a bit more—at least for now. "Unfortunately, I left my life in a shambles and I need to go home to put the pieces back together."

Christina's eyebrows drew together. "Go back to the woman who left ye?"

"Well, go back to ensure Angela doesn't take everything I own."

"A cuckold has the power to do that in your time?"

His shoulders sagged. "Divorce can get ugly and, yes, she's entitled to half of everything I own."

"That is so strange. Such a woman should be stoned or hanged or tortured, or—"

"And you're upset that I showed Andrew exactly how much he has to learn?" A low chuckle rumbled in Lachlan's chest as he pulled Christina into his embrace and kissed the top of her head. "We're not so different you and I."

"Dunna say that."

"Why?"

"'Cause the longer ye stay, the more difficult it will be to see ye go." She pulled out of his arms, blinking rapidly, a quivering smile plastered in place. "Besides, I need a champion like ye. Hamish is too old."

Lachlan's heart sank. Something in his alpha-male heart wanted to hear her ask him to stay—not because he could be her champion, but because she wanted, she needed him as a man. He clenched his fists to keep himself from reaching out to her. Who was he fooling anyway? Did he have any control over the medallion? It had sent him to her without any forethought on Lachlan's part. Even if he chose to stay, would he be allowed to do so?

Ironically, he was a lost soul with ties in both centuries, now he knew the truth. Not even his mother had a claim to that kind of birthright. And how had she contacted him? He had so many damned questions and no place to find the answers.

Turning, Christina strode toward the hearth. "I still canna believe it."

"What?"

"That ye came to me from a different time."

He stepped toward her. "Even though I don't talk like you? Even though I can fight like a banshee, yet am hopeless on the back of a horse?"

"That is rather odd, I will admit." She reached up and tugged on the medallion's thong, until she held the bronze disk in her hand. Thoughtfully, she studied the front and back. "Are ye following the beacon of truth?"

"I like to think I am. My mum always taught that the truth will set you free."

"Did she now?"

"Mm hmm." Lachlan brushed the pad of his pointer finger over her cheek's silken skin. "But she kept one truth hidden from me until very recently."

"What was that?"

He gulped. "You know the truth thing on the medallion?"

"Aye."

"Well, if that's my rallying cry, then it will mean the world to me if you trust that I'm not lying."

She let the disk drop back to his chest. "Ye can tell me anything, I'd reckon."

He needed to tell her the truth. "My father is—was William Wallace."

She took in a sharp breath. "I kent it."

"You did?"

"Aye, Sir Boyd and I both agreed neither of us had seen a man fight with your valor since William passed. And ye look more like him than ye do Eva." She started for the door. "Dunna think for a moment ye dunna belong in this time, 'cause ye do."

Lachlan grabbed her wrist and stopped her. Her lips sparkled ruby with the flames from the hearth. God, he wanted to kiss them, to pull her into his arms and crush her pillow-soft breasts against his chest and devour her. If only he could run his hands up and down her spine, sink his fingers into her sexy bum—but it wouldn't be fair. To either of them.

He watched her slip out the door.

***

The days passed so quickly, Christina hardly had a moment to herself. And her son tested her at every turn. On top of that, every time she turned around, she saw Lachlan. Lachlan teaching Andrew to spar. Lachlan in the hall during meals. Lachlan singing with the minstrels—dear Lord, his bass voice sent a lively sparkle throughout her insides. How that man could continually turn her head, she couldn't fathom. Of course, she knew he wasn't a sorcerer, but he may as well have been one because he'd vexed her so.

When she and Ellen returned from clipping evergreens with two guardsmen wheeling barrows behind them, Lachlan and Andrew were in the exercise arena practicing horsemanship. She would have missed them if she hadn't looked through a gap in the hedge.

Aye that man has me vexed for certain.

Christina stopped and grasped Ellen by the arm.

"What is it, m'lady?"

"Wheesht." From their vantage point, they wouldn't be noticed. Christina lowered her voice. "Ye and the guards take the clippings into the hall. I want to watch my son.

"Aye?" whispered Ellen, waggling her eyebrows. "I reckon watching his student would be far more entertaining."

Christina feigned a gasp. "Ye are shameless."

"Nay, I am observant." Ellen beckoned the guardsmen. "Come along and leave her ladyship to her spying."

Christina painted on her most matronly smile while Ellen led the men and the barrows away. "I'll follow shortly to direct the greening." Then she turned her attention to the exercise arena. Lachlan cantered the gelding through the center of the arena with the right front forward.

"Change," Andrew shouted and Lachlan switched position of his stirrups with quite a bit of effort, but managed to get the horse to change to a left lead.

Imagine that. A valiant knight who is a novice equestrian. He didna lie about that, now did he?

The more she came to know Lachlan, the more curious he became.

How could such an accomplished man know so little about horses? Truly?

After riding around the arena using the right lead, then back the other way, using the left, Andrew bade Lachlan to stop, walked straight up to the gelding and probed the beast in the flank with his crop. Andrew skittered out of the way just as the poor animal kicked and bucked, vaulting down the paddock until he unseated his mount.

"Whoooooooa," Lachlan bellowed, landing in the dirt on his bum. He sat there a moment and shook his head. "What the hell happened?"

Her son merely shrugged.

Clenching her fists, Christina started toward them. Blast it all, the lad had best assume some respect before she completely lost her composure.

Lachlan hopped to his feet and brushed off his backside. Sauntering toward the trickster, he shook his finger. "You poked him. I saw it out of the corner of my eye."

"Ha." Andrew took a step back. "Ye must be able to bring a wily beast under control. When in battle or in the midst of the crowd, your mount could be frightened by any manner of things."

Christina stopped in her tracks. The lad actually made sense.

"All right." Lachlan swatted him on the shoulder. "So tell me, what should I have done in that situation?"

"Allow me to show ye." Andrew took the reins and climbed onto the gelding. "A horse is not much use when his hindquarter is disengaged." He moved his heel back. "Do not kick your mount in the flank. If ye do, ye shall end up on your backside every time. Still, ye must take charge."

Crossing his arms, Lachlan nodded.

"Slide one hand down the rein and pull the gelding's head toward your knee." He demonstrated by bringing the horse's head to the side. "Remember, if ye control the head, ye control the beast." Then he made the horse walk in circles by maintaining his grip on the rein and tapping his heels.

Christina wanted to applaud. For the first time in her life, she watched her son actually be helpful—he was an accomplished horseman and he could impart his knowledge to her champion. Lachlan was absolutely right. He had been sent to her to help bring the lad around. Thank heavens for Lachlan and horses. And thank heavens for Christmas. Without a moment's hesitation, she raced for the keep. Andrew may be acting like a malcontented youth, but he would be shown love and respect this Yule, whether he desired it or not.

CHAPTER NINETEEN

After stabling the horse, Lachlan walked across the courtyard with Andrew. Over the past few days, they hadn't exactly built up comradery, but at least they were on civil speaking terms. Earlier, he'd shrugged off the stunt Andrew had pulled with poking the horse in the flank. Still, he didn't know if he could trust the kid. And he had to keep reminding himself not to rush things.

"So what's your favorite breed of horse?" Lachlan asked. It was always safe to talk about horses or weapons with Andrew. Anything else was a crapshoot.

"Ye mean a type?" The lad grinned—holy hell, that was a first. "A destrier for certain."

Lachlan noted that medieval folk didn't yet use the term "breed" for a horse type. "Not a galloway like your mum rides?" Lachlan hardly knew modern breeds or types like thoroughbreds and quarter horses, but a destrier? *What the hell?*

"No chance. I'd not allow myself to be seen on a pony if I had my druthers. A destrier is a knight's horse, but…" The lad hung his head and kicked a stone.

"But?"

"They are dear. A squire could never afford one—even a knight must earn many a purse afore he can hope to buy such a mount."

"A destrier, you say?" Lachlan tapped his chin with his forefinger. "They must be big-boned to support a knight in full mail."

Andrew looked truly interested. His posture even straightened. "They are—the largest warhorses of the lot."

"So when a knight can't afford a destrier, what sort of horse does he ride?"

"A palfrey would me my second choice."

"A palfrey?" Lachlan pulled open the door to the great hall. He had heard nothing of these *types*.

Andrew stepped through. "Of course," he said as if it were the most obvious thing in the world.

Hit with the pleasant aroma of freshly cut pine, Lachlan stopped in the entryway of the great hall. "Smells like Christmas."

Lady Christina turned from where she was directing a man up a ladder. "How was the riding lesson?"

Lachlan rubbed his backside. "Only got thrown once."

Taking on a sudden case of disinterest, Andrew headed for the stairwell.

"A moment." Christina hastened toward him. "I've arranged for your Latin lessons to commence on the morrow."

"Latin?"

"Aye, all noblemen should be familiar with Latin at the very least."

Lachlan didn't miss Andrew's eye-rolling look of disgust. "But why? I hate books. I hate reading and writing."

"Noblemen oft write in Latin," Christina explained. "If their missives are stolen by outlaws, it is less likely for them to understand the contents."

Lachlan moved in, holding up a finger. "Your mother has a good point."

Andrew glared at him as if he'd suddenly grown two heads. "Why do ye always have to take her side?"

"I what?" Lachlan moved his hands to his hips. "Sure, you love horses and weapons, but there's a whole lot more to life."

"Well, it's not in books."

Jeez, the kid couldn't be more mistaken.

"There must be a million poverty-stricken children out there who would do anything to learn to read, let alone learn Latin."

"Well then find some street urchin to take my place." Andrew whipped around and dashed up the stairwell, his footsteps echoing.

Christina's shoulders sagged. "I thought he'd be thrilled."

Fed up, Lachlan returned his attention to the greening—goodness, Christina took her Christmas decorations seriously. "I don't think Andrew has the capacity to be thrilled about anything. If you'd like I could take the lessons with him."

"Ye could, but I'd prefer to see him give Father Sinclair a chance. Ye're already doing far more for the lad than anyone should ask."

"I don't mind. He's growing on me."

"Are ye serious?"

"Well, if he'd learn to smile and stop being a priggish bastard toward you, I might enjoy being around him."

She chuckled, drawing her hand to her forehead. "I have no idea how we shall endure the next year."

"As I said, take it one day at a time." Lachlan looked from the walls to the rafters. "Holy smokes, when you said you were planning to green the castle, you decided to go all out."

"'Tis our way of bringing spring inside until the end of winter."

"I like it." He grinned. "And where are you planning to put the tree?"

Her eyebrows knit together. "I beg your pardon?"

"The Christmas tree."

Her ladyship gave him a panicked stare as if she'd never heard of such a thing.

She probably never has.

"In my time everyone greens their homes, but the centerpiece is a tree that is decorated with garlands." Lachlan tried to describe it in terms she would understand. "We trim it with ornaments like balls and ribbons and bows."

"Oooo." She drummed her fingers against her lips. "That sounds lovely."

"I think so. And we put gifts under the tree."

"Gifts?"

"Yes, we wrap them in paper and then open them on Christmas morn."

"For the entire clan?"

He chuckled—jeez, that would be pricey to say the least. "Well, people pretty much live in their own homes and gift giving is restricted to the immediate family and maybe a few close friends."

She smacked her lips as if considering. "I see. The de Moray clan partakes in a grand feast and we give our people nutmeats and bread baked with sweet fruits. 'Tis everyone's favorite feast day."

"Mm, I can smell the baking already." He flicked the pine branch in her hand. "If you could have anything you wanted what would you like for Christmas, m'lady?"

She heaved a big sigh. "My son to be content."

"Unfortunately, that's something *I* can't give."

"Hmm." She waved her branch toward the dais. "Mayhap introducing a new tradition might be worthwhile. I think the hall would look grand with a festooned tree."

"And the presents?"

"Perhaps we could do something for Andrew above stairs in my chamber. 'Tis quite homey up there."

Lachlan gave her a wink. "I think I know the perfect gift for him."

She shook her bough, her eyes shining with her mischievous grin. "Oh please, do tell."

"Have you heard of a destrier horse?"

She dropped her hands to her sides. "He wants a warhorse?"

"Well, he does want to become a knight."

"Holy snapdragons. We have plenty of garrons and galloways, but a destrier?" She bit her thumbnail. "Let me put some thought into it. Heavens, a warhorse? Perhaps I should rethink gift giving in my chamber. We'll have to take him outside whilst it's still light—afore the feast."

***

Andrew relished the feel of the iron weave in his hand as he sparred with Sir Lachlan. The big man had taught him a great deal already and he reckoned the squires back at de Vere's castle would be impressed. When he returned, he'd be promoted to the top of the ranks and made a knight as soon as he reached his majority.

He might have to endure a year of hell at this dank outpost, but at least he would gain in strength and skill. Watching Sir Lachlan spar with the other guards had made Andrew realize the knight's true talent, though how he could have ridden in the tourney circuit on the continent was a quandary. He couldn't handle a horse worth beans. Regardless, the man could fight with the strength of ten warriors and Andrew wanted to learn everything he could. If he could match that kind of prowess with his horse skills, he'd be unbeatable, and invaluable to Lord de Vere.

Just when Andrew thought he was gaining the upper hand with a thrust to Sir Lachlan's right hip, his damned mother came into the courtyard.

"Father Sinclair his waiting in the solar for your lesson."

Why did she always have to make things miserable? "Can ye not see I'm still in the midst of my lesson with Sir Lachlan?"

"No." The big knight grabbed Andrew's wrist and disarmed him faster than he could blink. Dammit, how did he do that so quickly? Andrew didn't even have a chance to set up a counter maneuver.

He looked at Lachlan and gritted his teeth. "I said I do not want to learn Latin."

"How do you know if you haven't tried?"

"I just do."

"Not an answer. Until you can provide me with a rational explanation of why learning Latin would not behoove a young man of your stature, you have no choice but to comply with your mother's desires."

Taking mother's side again. "What if I refuse to learn?"

"Then you are more foolish than I initially thought."

"Blast it all. Ye are as horrible as she!" With that, he made a show of stomping off toward the second floor solar.

Mother's footsteps clapped the stone steps behind, but Andrew didn't wait for her. The sooner he got this damned Latin lesson over, the sooner he'd be free to take Sir Lachlan to the riding arena and put him on an untrained colt.

Bursting through the door, Andrew came to an immediate stop.

"Hello," said a cleric with grey streaks through his brown hair. But Andrew wasn't looking at him. A redheaded lass with striking blue eyes smiled from across the board. Holy smokes, she was lovely.

The cleric pushed himself to his feet. "I hope ye dunna mind I brought my ward, Aileen. She's been awfully keen to learn Latin and I hoped ye would enjoy having a study partner."

Aileen waved, her smile lighting up the entire chamber. "Good afternoon."

"Ah…" Andrew wanted to turn and run, but his legs wouldn't move.

"There ye are," said Ma, coming up from behind. "Has Father Sinclair already made the introductions?"

For the first time, Andrew didn't resent his mother's presence. He gave her a sharp nod and slid into the chair beside the lass. "Yes, thank ye." The corner of his mouth quirked as he looked Aileen in the eye. "So why do ye want to learn Latin?"

"'Cause 'tis the language of our Lord." Then she turned a brilliant shade of pink and lowered her gaze. "Besides, nary a lass like me would gain a chance to learn reading and languages if it werena for the kindness of Father Sinclair."

The tutor shook out his black robes and resumed his seat. "Shall we begin? I'd like to start by scribing the alphabet." He slid two pieces of vellum toward them, the inkwell was already set in the center of the table with three quills.

Aileen snatched one. "This is going to be so fun."

Andrew took a quill of his own. "Perhaps it will be."

Thankfully, Mother quietly slipped out the door, closing it behind her.

Chapter Twenty

A good four inches of snow had fallen last night. The slushy stuff seeped into his boots while Lachlan led Andrew through the wood, searching for the perfect tree. He'd seen men rubbing their boots with whale oil. Now he knew why.

The boy followed with a two-man saw tucked under his elbow. They both wore their sword belts because Hamish had warned them the only place anyone was safe was behind the curtain walls. Lachlan was growing used to being armed to the teeth at all times. He even liked the danger. Sure, he could be attacked at any time back home, but the likelihood was far slimmer and men generally didn't walk around laden with dirks, swords and knives. Here, the de Moray guard patrolled the curtain walls around the clock and twice daily a retinue rode out to patrol the grounds, especially now that Andrew was there. Christina feared invasion. She'd been a prisoner too long not to constantly worry about another attack by the English.

Lachlan wished he'd spent more time listening to his mother's stories. He'd like to reassure Christina, but couldn't remember anything about the de Moray family, except they eventually earn an earldom and a dukedom, and the name changes with some taking Moray and others Murray…he thought.

A lot of good it would do to tell her.

"Have ye not found a good enough tree yet?" Andrew asked.

Lachlan hadn't been looking very hard, but he glanced back at the lad. "We want a symmetrical one that will look nice festooned with decorations."

"Sounds daft to me."

"It will smell marvelous and the lassies will think it's beautiful."

"Truly?" the lad asked with a bit of interest in his voice.

"Indeed. All women love to decorate things for the holidays."

"Hmm." Tapping him on the shoulder, Andrew pointed. "What about that one?"

Lachlan followed the finger's direction and grinned. He thwacked the boy on the shoulder. "I knew you were the right person for this task. That Scots pine is perfect." At least it was as close as they were going to get. Most of the evergreens were tall and spindly. This young arbor stood about six feet and was mostly A-shaped. It was thick with long needles, as well.

"We need to cut it off at the base," Lachlan said.

"Then we'd best sit."

Having never used a two-man saw, Lachlan followed suit. Ice cold, wet snow immediately soaked through his chausses—a pair of snow pants would have come in handy for certain. "What should we give your mother for Christmas?"

"Huh?" Andrew asked, leaning back and drawing the saw toward him. "What are ye jabbering about now?"

"We should give her a present."

"Right, give the woman who is forcing me to remain in this frigid wilderness and study Latin a gift."

"She loves you and this frigid wilderness will all be yours one day." *Unless the boy throws it away on a pipedream.* Lachlan worked the saw faster with the increase of his irritation. "Now, I want the next thing to come out of your mouth to be positive. What. Shall. We. Give. Your. Mother?"

Andrew knitted his eyebrows. "Bloody hell, ye do not have to sound so angry about it."

"That wasn't positive."

"Very well, go to the smithy. Blacksmiths always have fancy bobbles tucked away to bring in a few crowns here and there."

A blacksmith? Who would have known? "Do you want to go with me?"

Andrew smirked. "Latin lesson."

"Okay, then you'll have to trust my judgement."

"Select whatever ye want. I do not care."

"That's sad, because your mum cares very much about you."

***

Christina inspected the table, laid out with ribbons and baubles she and Ellen had collected for the tree. With her duties of running the keep and Lachlan's seemingly endless training, there hadn't been much time to ask questions, so she'd done her best to find suitable trinkets. Goodness, she was excited to bring a new Yule tradition into the castle and thrilled that Andrew had gone with Lachlan to select the pine. It would look magnificent on the dais behind the high table for all the clan to enjoy. She just knew it.

Even with Andrew's reluctance to take his place in the clan, Christina couldn't help but be excited. For the first time in thirteen years, she would no longer be a prisoner during Yuletide. She prayed every day Andrew would grow to love her or at least grow to love the castle and clan. When he wasn't trying to be a curmudgeon, she saw such strength in the lad.

And the Christmas feast was only three days away.

Ellen stepped beside her and rubbed her hands. "I think all we need now is the tree."

Christina glanced toward the door. "I hope the snow didna hamper the lads."

"Och, they're hewn of Highland stock the pair of them."

The words had barely escaped Ellen's lips when Sir Lachlan and Andrew burst though the hall doors carrying a glorious pine. Grinning like an excited young maiden, Christina gestured to the stand the smithy had fashioned. "Put it there, lads."

Lachlan led the way. "Andrew selected a fine tree for you, m'lady."

They set it into the stand and Lachlan tightened the bolts. Stepping back, he whistled. "She's a beauty."

"Oh my," said Ellen. "'Tis so tall, it is like bringing the forest into the hall."

Christina gestured to the decorations. "I hope we've collected enough to trim the tree like ye said."

"Look there, Andrew. Your mum thought of everything." The big knight drummed his fingers against his lips. "Except we need a star or an angel for the top."

Gasping, Christina shot a panicked look to Ellen. "A star or an angel for the top? Will it not fall?"

"We'll trim the top bough just enough so it stays in place."

"We could use the angel trumpeter figurine from your mantel, m'lady," said Ellen. "Shall I go fetch it?"

"Aye." Christina clapped. "Please do."

Clifton, the clan's Celtic harpist, began to play lyrical music to help set the scene.

She surveyed the collection of decorations. "This is your idea, Sir Lachlan. How should we proceed?"

"First, we string the garlands and ribbons, then we hang the baubles and ornaments from the branches." He looked to Andrew. "What should we start with?"

With his typical shrug, the lad selected a string of brass beads. "Will these work?"

"Sure. Just wrap them around like this." Picking up a red ribbon, Lachlan demonstrated unrolling it around the upper branches of the pine—up where only he'd be able to reach. Then he glanced to the lad. "Ready to give it a try?"

Rolling his eyes, Andrew complied while Christina selected another roll of ribbon. If only her son could find some enjoyment in doing anything with her. She'd endured so many of his eye-rolls and shrugs, she could scream. But such an outburst was inappropriate behavior for the lady of the keep and she refused to allow herself to fly off on a tirade. Besides, a temper tantrum on her part would only serve to further distance her from Andrew.

And 'tis Yuletide for heaven's sake.

Lachlan reached out to her to draw the ribbon around the tree, while he hummed with the harp music. She couldn't help but chuckle the way he made the music flit around her insides like happy butterflies.

She glanced at Andrew who was looking over the selection on the table. "Have ye learned to play any instruments?"

His lips thinned and his eyes narrowed. "As ye haven't allowed me to forget, I was a prisoner. I rarely took my meals in the hall, let alone was offered tutoring in anything but English."

"Ah, but anyone can sing," said Lachlan, draping a gold ribbon over a branch, then handing the reel to Christina.

"I do not care for singing."

Of course, he doesn't care to do anything that will bring him joy.

Things went quiet while the air grew tense. All three of them worked, mechanically adding ornaments as Christina's mind raced for something she could say to make Andrew happy. Then an idea sparked. "Would ye like to learn to play the bagpipes? The king has decided pipers will play during all battles and royal gatherings."

A glass ball dropped from Andrew's fingers and smashed to pieces on the floorboards. "Robert Bruce is not a real king. Lord de Vere will lead an army into Scotland and he'll kill anyone who does not bow to King Edward."

It was as if she'd been slapped in the face. If Christina had heard such treasonous words uttered from one of her clansmen, she would not hesitate to throw them into the pit and arrange their hanging. "Please." She reached out to him. "Do ye want de Vere to come to your home and lay siege? To imprison ye for another three and ten years?"

He batted her hand away. "This is not my home. Can ye not understand? I have no memory of this place." Turning, he ran for the stairwell.

"Andrew!" Christina started after him, tears welling in her eyes.

Lachlan gripped her shoulder. "Let him go."

Her throat closed. The room spun. Whipping around, she slammed her fists into the wall of Lachlan's chest. "He hates me." Dammit, she could hold in her anguish no longer. With a shrill cry, Christina crumpled. Her entire life had been for naught. For so many years, the only thing that had kept her going was the hope that her son would one day be returned to her. Clan de Moray had fought beside Robert the Bruce and incurred heavy losses to bring Andrew back to Ormond, but nothing she did would ever amount to enough for the lad to realize where he belonged. She could shower him with kind words, tutors and gifts, but he would hate her all the same.

She wilted into a pathetic heap, wailing as forlornly as she had at her husband's graveside when Andrew was but a wee bairn in her belly. All hope fled. Her spirits sank to the depths of hell.

Somewhere during her collapse, before she hit the floor, Lachlan gathered her into his arms and hastened to take her into the small antechamber behind the dais. The door closed behind them.

"Easy, sweetheart," he whispered into her veil. "Easy now. I have you."

His gentle words only made the pain in her heart stretch and ache all the more. Why must she be attracted to a man she could never have? A man who planned to leave her. A man who had a life in another century for pity's sake. "My life is nothing but complete misery," she cried.

"Oh, no, how can you say that?"

"My son hates me, ye are chomping at the bit to go back to your time, and nothing I do is ever good enough."

"No, no, no. You knew bringing Andrew home would be difficult. You knew he'd challenge you at every turn."

"But I dinna ken he'd tear out my heart and chew it to bits." Christina curled against Lachlan's chest, unable to stop the flow of tears.

He sat in an overstuffed chair and rocked her gently. Over and over, he repeated calming words. "That's right, let it out…Let it all out…Things will improve, I know it…You and Andrew will be a family again."

His warm lips caressed her forehead while she wiped her eyes. "Blast it all. Here it is Yule and I'm supposed to be the stalwart matriarch of the clan, and here I sit bawling like a bairn."

Lachlan brushed warm lips against her temple. "Everyone needs to let go now and again. It is healthy for the soul."

She nodded and nestled her head against his protective chest. "I dunna ken what I would do without ye here."

He nuzzled against her temple. "Believe it or not, being with you has been my salvation. It has given me purpose in life again."

A flutter rippled through her heart. "I wish ye would stay forever," she whispered, shifting her eyes up to meet his fathomless, expressive blues. She took in a sharp inhale, as he smoothed the rough pads of his fingers along her cheek. Ever so slowly, his lips neared while long, feathery lashes shuttered his eyes.

When their lips finally met, all the pent up emotion within Christina's breast surged, funneling into a whirlwind of heat. Pushing away all thoughts, she allowed herself only to feel. Lachlan could be so physical, so powerful, so brutal, but when he wrapped his arms around her, Christina felt invincible. Be it true or nay, she felt loved, and cherished, and valued. Reaching up, she slid her fingers through his locks. Soft waves of thick tresses contrasted with hardened male.

She wanted Lachlan Wallace almost as much as she wanted her son to take up his mantle. If only she could have them both, but there she stood, on the precipice of losing each man—Andrew to the enemy and Lachlan to a life so alien to her, she couldn't conceptualize.

As his kiss eased, he cupped her cheek in the palm of his hand. "I wish I could hold you in my arms forever, too."

"Ye do?"

"Aye," he said, sounding more like a Highlander.

"When…" She closed her eyes and forced herself to be strong. "When will ye go back?"

"Honestly, I have no idea."

She tugged the medallion out from under his shirt. "And all this mentions is following the truth. It is so strange."

"It is."

"But why canna ye have control over it?"

"Maybe I can." He kissed her fingers and then tucked the medallion back down his shirt. "Let's do our best to enjoy the holidays. My mother always said enjoy every moment, because you can never count on tomorrow."

"I'm beginning to think your mother was quite a wise woman."

"She was…I mean, she is." Lachlan set Christina on her feet. "Are you ready to face the clan?"

"One more thing." Taking Lachlan's face between her hands, she kissed him—lips to lips, tongue to tongue. As bone melting as it might be, Christina put everything she had behind her ardor. If she must live for today, then she would no longer hide the desire burning deep inside her core. She kissed him because every fiber of her being wanted him, appreciated him, pined for him. If there was a thread of hope he'd decide to stay, she would prove to him how much she desired for him to do so.

When she straightened, he leaned back in the chair, his eyelids heavy. "My God, woman, you know how to make a man melt."

CHAPTER TWENTY-ONE

The following morning, Lachlan headed to the blacksmith shack. It was hard to miss, located near the stables, the ring of a hammer striking iron clanged all day long. He chuckled to himself. Two months ago, he never would have dreamed that he'd be living in a medieval castle, but for some odd reason, it suited him. Be it his mother's love of history or the fact his father had walked this very ground not so long ago, he'd begun to grow comfortable with his surroundings. The sharp smells no longer turned his stomach, but they told him where he was and what was happening around him. Indeed, his sense of smell had become more acute. He could tell a horse from a cow or a sheep. He knew when he was close to the chicken coop or the swine's bog, or the middens. True, he stayed as far away from the middens as possible.

He loved it when the kitchen's bread ovens were baking the morning's bread or when the lads were turning a mule deer on spit in the massive kitchen hearth. He loved to walk through the castle grounds and see the clansmen and women hard at work doing everything from washing clothes to tanning leather and making shoes or saddles by hand. Everything in this era pulsed with a harmony that had been lost to his generation—probably lost for eons.

Ducking inside the shop, Lachlan cleared his throat. Though open to the frigid air, the warmth from the fire radiated around him.

The blacksmith glanced up, his arms thick from years of working iron. "Ah, Sir Lachlan, how can I help ye this morrow?"

"I'd like to purchase a Christmas gift for her ladyship."

"Och, are ye certain ye are in the right place? Ye might want to visit Morag up the way and buy one of her nice mince pies."

"No. I want something a tad more personal—a keepsake. A necklace or a brooch or the like."

"Oh, I see. Ye've grown fond of Lady Christina then?"

Why not admit it? "I have."

"Do ye aim to marry her?"

Maybe Lachlan should have kept he mouth shut. "Let's not be too hasty." He pointed to a wooden lockbox on the shelf. "Do you make jewelry?"

"Dabble in it, aye." The stout man pulled the strongbox down and fished a key out of the leather pouch he wore at his hip. "Mayhap I have just the thing." After opening the box, he reached inside and pulled out a square cross stamped with a Celtic pattern. In the center, an amethyst sparkled. Good heavens, the stone was the size of a penny. The piece would sell for at least five-hundred pounds in a jewelry store in Edinburgh.

Lachlan held the cross in his palm. "Is this bronze?"

"Aye and I pilfered that wee stone from a dead Englishman's purse after our victory at the Battle of Stirling Bridge."

Though disgusted by the idea of rifling through a dead man's effects, his heart jumped. "You were at Stirling Bridge?"

The man stuck out his chest with pride. "I was."

"What was it like?"

"Pure masterful strategy by William Wallace and Sir Andrew de Moray, God rest their souls." The man crossed himself. "Due to our leaders' patience and refusal to give up their ground advantage, the English didna have a chance. Killed one and twenty myself."

Lachlan shouldn't have been impressed with such a vile admittance, but he was awed. These were brutal times and Scotland's people had been ruthlessly oppressed. Had Lachlan been at Stirling Bridge, he would have been honored to take up arms. "What did William Wallace look like?"

"An enormous man—shoulders wider than a stallion's hindquarter." The smithy squeezed Lachlan's shoulder. "Why, ye are nearly as powerful as he, the same coloring, too." He leaned closer. "Bloody hell, even his eyes were piercing like yours."

Though the smithy's fire was still burning hot, a chill made Lachlan's hairs stand on end. "What else do you have in that box?"

"A few trinkets—a ruby ring—at least I think 'tis a ruby." The contents clinked as he pushed around with his pointer finger until he held up a brooch. "Always wondered what I'd do with this, though."

Lachlan plucked the piece with his fingers. It was a bronze shield with a lion rampant. "Isn't this royal?"

"Indeed. 'Tis the likeness of King Robert's signet ring, though five times the size."

"How many people would recognize it as the king's?"

The smithy shrugged. "Not certain. The Bruce wears his family coat of arms on his brooch. I just was toying around to see if I could make the lion."

"You did a fine job."

"My thanks, but I think her ladyship would prefer the cross."

"How much for both?" The ruby ring caught Lachlan's eye with a sparkle. "And the ring, too?"

The beefy man scratched his thick beard. "A shilling for the necklace—I've got to charge for that, the amethyst is a keepsake. Ah…and five pence for the brooch, but I do like the ring."

"How about two shillings for the lot?"

"Two, aye?" The big man grinned, his teeth crooked and stained. "I reckon, I couldna pass an offer as generous as that."

Lachlan dug in the leather purse Christina had given him, paid for the items and thanked the blacksmith. "Next time anyone needs a fine piece of jewelry, I'll ken where to send them."

His next stop was the tailor shop to purchase a yellow silk veil for Andrew to give Christina because the lad had his head too far up his arse to think of pleasing his mother. Besides, it was about time for the woman to wear colors other than black or grey.

If I have anything to do with it, she's going to enjoy this Christmas, dammit.

***

When Christmas morn finally came, Christina scooped a spoonful of porridge, intently staring at the stairwell. "Where is he?"

Lachlan reached for a pitcher of cider. "You kidding? He's a teenager. I wouldn't be surprised if he sleeps until noon."

"Oh heavens, that willna do at all." She pushed back her chair. "I must send someone to wake him."

Lachlan dipped his spoon in his porridge and stirred. "Does he have any idea?"

She grinned, her insides practically bubbling over. "None whatsoever. Hamish went to collect the destrier from the Foster's croft at dawn."

Lachlan took an enormous bite. "Nothing like a bribe to help Andrew change alliances."

Thwacking him on the arm, Christina shook her spoon beneath his nose. "It is not a bribe, 'tis a gift, and dunna forget it was your idea."

"And I think it's a great one. How much did the horse cost?"

"That is not something ye ask a lady."

He chuckled before he shoveled in his next bite. "At least some things haven't changed in the past seven hundred years."

"Wheesht, someone could hear ye." Christina glanced over both shoulders right before Andrew came stumbling through the stairwell, his hair mussed, he's eyes still half-closed.

Lachlan beckoned him to the table. "Come break your fast, lad."

"I'm starved," he said, sauntering toward the dais.

Christina stood and held out her arms. "Happy Yule, son."

Andrew grabbed a slice of bread from the table and shoved it in his mouth. "Happy Yule," he garbled and took a seat, ignoring her invitation for an embrace.

She slid back into her chair, refusing to let his oversight dissuade her excitement. At least the lad had responded with some civility, though with his mouth crammed full. Manners could come later. Right now, all she hoped for was acceptance. She poured him a cup of cider. "There will be a big feast tonight and I've arranged for an ensemble of minstrels to play country dances."

After guzzling his drink, Andrew set his tankard down and looked to Lachlan. "Will Father Sinclair and Aileen be there?"

"Don't ask me, ask your mother," said the big knight.

Though he frowned, ever so slowly, Andrew shifted his gaze to Christina and arched his brow.

"Of course, the father will bring his ward. She's quite a special young lady learning to read and a commoner at that."

"I think everyone should learn to read," said Lachlan.

"So do I," Andrew agreed, taking a bowl of porridge from the servant. "Can they sit at the high table with us?"

"Hmm. I think that would be a splendid idea." Christina busied herself by scooping the dregs of her oats from her bowl. Only a fortnight ago, the lad had emphatically denied liking studies at all. Was it the cleric who'd changed his opinion or the cleric's ward? It didn't take a seer to divine that the bonny wee orphan who Father Sinclair had brought along to be Andrew's study partner had something to do with it.

Christina chuckled to herself. Her son needn't know she and the cleric were in cahoots. After all, she was the daughter of the Earl of Atholl. She'd been raised to be shrewd and to run a keep in the best interests of her family and her clan. Besides, what youth didn't enjoy flirting with a lass near his age?

When Andrew finished eating, she placed her palms on the table and sat very tall. "We must go to the stables at once."

Andrew looked to Lachlan—a maddening habit he was forming. "Will we not spar this morn?"

"It's Christmas. No one works on a holiday as important as this." Lachlan stood and gestured toward the door. "Come, I'll think you'll like what you see."

The lad didn't budge. "What? Have ye been practicing your lead changes without me?"

"Have I had that kind of time?" Lachlan strode over and pulled out Andrew's chair with a loud scrape on the floorboards. "Are you going to follow or do I need to throw you over my shoulder?"

Groaning, Andrew stood as if it took a great deal of effort. "The pair of ye are always pushing me to do things I'd rather not."

"Aye," said Christina, leading the way down the dais steps. "Just like learning Latin."

Freshly fallen snow crunched underfoot as they made their way across the courtyard and out the postern gate.

After they stepped inside the stable, Hamish met them. "Are ye ready, m'lady?"

She tried not to look too happy, though her insides were about to bubble over. "The question is, is Andrew ready?"

Andrew narrowed his eyes. "What is this?"

Christina clasped her hands to steady them. Dear Lord, if this ploy didn't work, she'd never win him. "I've decided that since ye will become a great knight, 'tis time for ye to have a knight's horse."

With her words, hoofbeats clattered as Hamish led a heavy-boned gelding into the alley and walked him toward them. The horse shook his head and snorted, his chestnut mane flapping to and fro.

Andrew's eyes grew round. "A destrier?"

"Go on," said Lachlan. "He's all yours."

In two strides, the lad reached out his hand. With a nicker, the horse pushed his muzzle into Andrew's palm.

"I think he likes ye," Christina said as a tear spilled down her cheek. She quickly swiped it away before anyone could see.

Andrew glanced back with excitement in his eyes for the first time since he was but a bairn. "May I ride him?"

She stepped aside and gestured toward the arena. "Of course ye can."

As he mounted and rode through the gates, Lachlan gave her warm wink. "This is perfect."

Together, horse and rider started out with a slow warmup while the breath of each one puffed in misty billows. Christina covered her mouth and bade herself to hold back tears. "He looks so grown up on that big fella."

"Aye he does," Hamish agreed from behind. "He looks regal as well, if ye dunna mind me saying so."

"Like a knight." Lachlan leaned his elbows on the fence rail. "All he needs now is his armor and a surcoat with the de Moray crest."

She gave him a look. "One thing at a time. When he's ready he'll have all that as well as his father's sword, dirk and targe. I just willna give those things to him until he takes an oath of fealty to the de Moray clan."

"It's best if you don't shower him with too many gifts at once," said Lachlan. "Make him earn his place. He's turned a corner, but still has a long way to go before his head is screwed on straight."

Christina laughed. "Ye do have the oddest phrases at times, I'll say."

Though the snow chilled her toes to the bone, she would be no other place right now. Andrew put the horse through his paces, walking, trotting, then taking him to a canter and changing leads. He weaved him in a serpentine pattern and leapt him over a log. Stopping the destrier in the center of the arena, he faced them before making the horse spin right then left.

Lachlan batted his hand through the air. "Now you're showing off."

Andrew smiled and trotted his mount toward them. "With some practice, I'll make Jupiter bow just like a knight would do in a tournament."

"Jupiter?" asked Christina.

"That's what I've decided to call him—after the Roman God of the sky. Father Sinclair taught us about him."

She connected gazes with Lachlan. Heaven be praised, this day was more joyous than she'd dreamed possible. "Then Jupiter it is."

After riding another turn, Hamish beckoned the lad to the gate. "The big fella has already had a long day—brought him from Inverness whilst ye were still in your bed."

"Verra well, but I want to ride again first thing on the morrow." Andrew dismounted and brushed off his chausses.

Christina pulled her cloak tighter about her shoulders. "I say we go back to the keep and enjoy a tankard of warm cider in front of the fire."

Andrew scrunched his face in the old scowl she'd seen far too often. "Ye gave me the destrier to secure my loyalty."

Christina squared her shoulders and met his unpleasant stare. "Nay, he is my Yuletide gift to ye. I'll have ye ken Sir Lachlan suggested a destrier and I simply agreed."

He dropped his gaze and kicked the snow. "Well then, thank ye."

Holy saints, had Christina just heard her son utter words of thanks? She glanced to the sky as a snowflake softly dropped upon her eyelid. "Ye are welcome." If nothing else happened this day, she would go to sleep filled with happiness.

"That's better." Lachlan gave the boy a nudge, handing him a bronze brooch. "This is from me. I thought you might be able to find a use for it."

"A lion rampant?"

Christina leaned in to better see it, then drew her hand over her mouth. She wasn't about to say the lion was a sign of Scottish royalty. Besides, it was a sole lion in relief across a shield and not adorned with anything else.

"'Tis not the de Moray coat of arms," Andrew said.

"Nope," said Lachlan. "I figured your mum should give you a brooch as important as that. But until you've earned the de Moray crest, I thought this one might serve you well."

CÞAPTER TWENTY-TWO

Andrew pinned his cloak around his neck and regarded his reflection in the polished copper mirror. This had to be the best day since he'd come to Ormond. True, no matter how hard they tried, the clan folk couldn't fool him, nor could they shower Andrew with gifts to make him forget he'd been left alone for so many years. He'd been abandoned. Especially when he needed his kin the most. De Vere had only paid him a bit of notice once he'd grown and proved to be sturdy enough for battle. The earl had been anything but nurturing, but Andrew was no longer a bairn who needed to be coddled. He'd grown past needing a mother ages ago. He didn't want to be cossetted by anyone.

That's why he tolerated Sir Lachlan. The big knight might support his mother, but Sir Lachlan gave him room to be himself, not to mention he was a damned good fighting man. A man Andrew could admire. Every day he learned more from Lachlan and, in time, he'd be as skilled in the sparring ring. No, he probably wouldn't grow as tall, but Sir Lachlan always stressed the importance of using cunning and the opponent's leverage to knock him off balance no matter his girth. It was helpful to have size and strength, but even a woman could defend herself if she knew how.

He also had to admit Ormond Castle wasn't as miserable as he'd initially thought. In fact, he'd never had a chamber of his own before. Not that de Vere allowed Andrew to sleep in the donjon at the earl's Hedingham Castle.

Still, Andrew had finally felt like he had earned his place when de Vere told him he would become a squire. For the first time in his life, he meant something to somebody. Did Ma have any idea what it was like to spend years locked in a chamber? Did she have any inkling what it was like to grow up without anyone ever giving him a word of encouragement? When de Vere told Andrew he'd one day become a knight, it was as if someone pulled a black shroud from his soul and lit a torch as bright as the sun.

Perhaps things would have been different if his mother and Robert the Bruce had shown any interest in freeing him when he was a child. But so many lonely years had passed. Lonely years where he had nothing to do but think about abandonment and pray for rescue. No one ever came for him. No one ever fought for him. As the years passed, Andrew couldn't remember his mother anymore. He had never known his kin, his clan or this frigid land in which he'd been born. He'd been forsaken by everyone, left to fend for himself throughout his childhood. So many times he'd gone to sleep in the hay loft wondering if any of his kin still remembered him. He'd finally stopped yearning for a family of his own when de Vere promoted him to squire, saying one day he would be a knight who fought for right and good and honor.

But being a knight for King Edward and being a knight who supported Robert Bruce were two very different things. Ever since Andrew could remember, no one had a good word to say about the usurper and murderer, Bruce. What was he supposed to do? Accept the horse and brooch and kiss the false king's arse?

No bloody chance.

Though he would take the gifts. They owed him that and more. He had agreed to spend a year at Ormond Castle and a year it would be. Sir Lachlan was right, if Andrew tried to escape, he wouldn't make it to the border alive, not alone. Not that he'd been presented with any chances to escape. A de Moray guard accompanied him at all times unless he was with Sir Lachlan.

A knock came at his chamber door. "Are ye ready for the feast?" the guard's voice carried through the timbers.

Andrew let out a sigh. No use keeping everyone waiting and no use wallowing in misery. At least Aileen would be there this eve. She made Latin lessons so much more palatable and everyone was right on one thing, anyway. If he was going to be a knight, it would behoove him to know the language.

Straightening his doublet, Andrew regarded his reflection, wondering if Aileen would see fit to dance with him. He'd told his mother he didn't care to dance, but that was with *her*. Dancing with Aileen was completely different, even though he'd never tried it before. The lass was his age and she batted her eyelashes at him from time to time—surely she wouldn't laugh at him. No, not a girl who was more adorable than a kitten.

Mayhap I'll even be able to steal a kiss?

When Andrew arrived at the bottom of the stairwell, the great hall was already full of merrymakers. Smells of roast beef, freshly baked bread, and mince pies wafted from the kitchen. Servants swarmed through the hall, laden with ewers of ale and wine. Andrew grinned. Aileen waved from the dais, patting the seat beside her. Music swirled through the hall—similar to the fetes he'd attended at de Vere's castle, at least when he was allowed. Though Andrew never got to sit at the high table.

Mother clapped, looking happy as she always did. Hell, the woman was happy to a fault.

"Your new brooch looks quite handsome," she said.

Andrew opened his mouth to tell her he wasn't about to don a plaid as Lachlan across the table had, but Aileen clapped and beamed just like Ma. "Indeed. Your brooch looks stately."

He clamped his lips together and slid into his seat—right on top of a leather parcel with "Mother" written on it. Lachlan told him about the gift earlier, but Andrew felt awkward. What was he supposed to do? Hand it over and say happy Yule?

"Lachlan gave the brooch to him this morn," said Ma. Though she was smiling, Andrew could see through her ruse. She tried too hard to be the mother he'd never had.

"Did he?" asked Aileen, turning with a radiant smile. "The entire clan is agog with news of your new destrier."

Andrew puffed out his chest and gave the lass a wink. "I'm in training to become a knight."

"Oh, that's so romantic." She clasped her hands over her heart. "Will ye give me a ride on your horse?" Holy hellfire, she was bonny.

Andrew grinned. "Certainly. I named him Jupiter."

"After the Roman god?" asked Father Sinclair.

"I did," Andrew said, wishing his mother didn't have to look so pleased. He was bloody going along with her terms…though it didn't hurt that he'd asked Aileen to sit with them. No way in hell would de Vere allow a commoner, let alone a *girl* to sit at the high table. But a wee lassie with red tresses and a smile happier than a kitten?

Might as well enjoy the festivities. Playing the role of Mother's grumpy antagonist can wait for a day.

Lachlan kicked him under the table and nodded his head toward Andrew's seat.

Feeling like a curmudgeon, he reluctantly reached under his bum and pulled out the parcel. Bloody figs, his palms perspired. "Uh…" He shoved the parcel toward his mother. "This is for ye, Ma."

Good God, did she have to look so rapt? It was as if he'd given her a pot of gold and she hadn't even seen what was inside. Hell, Andrew hadn't seen what was inside and that made him feel even more like a boob.

And then she had to go on making a show of slowly opening the gift. Gasping, she held up something made of yellow silk. "Oh my, that is lovely." The look in her eyes was so deeply appreciative, Andrew could watch no longer.

"It's the perfect color for you," Sir Lachlan said, giving Andrew's shoulder a firm pat.

"I love it. Thank ye, Andrew." She clapped her hands and beckoned Ellen. "Will ye please do me the honor."

"Of course, m'lady."

In no time, the entire hall was agog with Mother's new veil. Perhaps he should have gone shopping with Sir Lachlan. At least he wouldn't have felt like such a charlatan. After wiping his hand across his mouth, Andrew reached under the table and grasped Aileen's hand. "Will ye dance with me after the meal?" he asked in a whisper.

A lovely shade of pink blossomed in her cheek while she nodded. "I hoped ye would ask."

"Do ye know how?"

"To dance?"

"Yes."

"Of course." She giggled some more. "Doesna everyone?"

Andrew clenched his fists so she couldn't hurt his heart. "Not me…but I'll give it a try if ye'll show me."

She patted his arm. "Then I'd be even happier to dance with ye. Besides, any chieftain of Clan Moray needs to ken how to kick up his heels."

Andrew froze for a moment. Chieftain? Aileen considered him a chieftain? It sounded so different when she'd said it than it had when his mother had yammered about his birthright. He didn't understand why. Perhaps the admiration in the young girl's voice?

Can I be a chieftain under a tyrant king?

Throughout the meal, Andrew pondered his question with no resolve. Things had been so clear when he'd been a mere squire for de Vere. Now his head buzzed with questions—things that made him uneasy inside.

But he didn't want to think about such troublesome matters this eve. With music and ale and a lovely lass sitting beside him, he pushed his worries away. And when the meal ended, Aileen took his hand and pulled him onto the floor along with the boisterous crowd of merrymakers all anxious to kick up their heels in a circle dance. These were not murderers and thieves as his English comrades had called them. They were families, people who were born in the Highlands who farmed the lands and raised their children with little care to who sat on the throne and governed them.

Though the men would take up arms against England in a heartbeat.

Once the minstrels started playing, Andrew discovered he liked dancing. The steps were lively and he couldn't help but laugh with Aileen smiling at him as they locked arms and skipped together.

After the fifth circle dance, Aileen patted her chest, breathing heavily. "Oh my, I canna remember ever dancing so vigorously. I can scarcely catch me breath."

Andrew brushed her tresses away from her face. "Would ye care to take a turn in the courtyard? The cold air might do ye good."

Her lips formed an "O". "'Twould be scandalous."

Nodding, he waggled his eyebrows. "Mm hmm."

He didn't need to ask again. She took up his hand and skipped toward the door. Pushing through, Andrew took the lead, both of them laughing. He glanced over his shoulder and saw not a single guard. Oh, blessed be the stars above, it invigorated him to be free to run outside with a maiden's hand grasped in his. Her giggles served to make him laugh harder as he led her to the stables while snow crunched under foot.

"I think Christmas is my favorite holiday," he said, feeling giddy inside.

"I ken 'tis mine."

She stumbled a bit and Andrew slowed his pace. "Do ye want to see my new destrier?"

"Oh, yes," she dashed ahead.

Darker than the depths of the sea, Andrew felt his way toward the lantern affixed to the stone wall. Striking the flint, he lit the wick and a muted glow spread across the barn. "Jupiter," he called, wishing he'd had time to train the horse so he would pop his head out of his stall door at the sound of his voice.

One day soon.

"Jupiter," Aileen giggled, tiptoeing down the alley. "Which one is his stall?"

"Second from the end." Andrew grabbed a scoop of oats and hastened to catch up to her.

She grinned at him, her teeth chattering.

"Are ye cold?"

"Aye. I was so warm I forgot to collect my cloak afore we stepped out."

He draped his over her shoulder, pulling her close. "I'll keep ye warm."

She leaned into him, looking up with shiny eyes. He liked Aileen a great deal. She made him feel important.

Together they stopped at the stall.

"Jupiter?" Andrew called, peering into the total darkness inside.

With a snort the horse thrust his head out above the gate.

Throwing her arms around Andrew's waist, Aileen squealed. "He frightened me half to death."

Andrew tightened his grip around her shoulder. "He will not hurt ye." He held up the oats. "Give him a taste of this."

She did and the horse's lips gathered the grain from the scoop in a matter of seconds. Andrew reached in and smoothed his hand along the destrier's mane. "There's a good boy."

Aileen traced her finger down the white blaze on Jupiter's nose. "He's beautiful."

"He is." Andrew's chest filled with pride while he inclined his nose toward the girl's tresses—tresses that smelled like roses. "So are ye."

With a tiny gasp she shifted her wide-eyed gaze his way.

Every fiber in his body stirred to life. His heart thrummed and a fire churned low in his loins, hotter than anything he'd ever felt before.

Parting her lips, Aileen lifted her chin. Holy Moses, she looked more enticing than a plum tart.

Everything around him faded into oblivion as he focused on her bow-shaped mouth. The moist lips beckoned him like a thirsty man to water. Andrew licked his lips. Could he kiss her? Would she kiss him back? Something pulled him closer. What if she recoiled?

All of his thoughts shattered and dissipated as if with a boiling explosion of steam when his lips touched hers. Small hands slipped to his waist. Soft breasts melted into his chest. Oh Lordy, Lordy, Lordy, who knew kissing a girl would feel this good? He cupped her face in his hands and brushed her lips with his tongue, just like his mates had described back at the stable loft in England.

Then Aileen did the miraculous and parted her lips for him. God's bones, his heart nearly burst out of his chest when her tongue brushed his ever so gently.

"Ahem," a rumbling throat cleared behind them.

Before he could blink, Andrew dropped his hands and jolted away from the lass. "Hamish?" his voice cracked while his heart practically flew out his chest.

"Aye, lad." The man-at-arms gave him a one-eyed scowl. "Came out to see why there was a light coming from the stable on Christmas."

Regaining a modicum of composure, Andrew gestured toward Jupiter. "Just showing Aileen my new destrier."

"He's a fine specimen—picked him up from Inverness myself, but ye'd better haste back to the hall afore your mother sends out the guard to search for ye—that could spoil everyone's fun."

"Sorry," said Aileen, looking down and rubbing her arms against the cold.

"Ye wouldna want that, would ye, lad?"

Andrew wanted to put his arm around her, but he felt like such a damned fool. Why did Hamish have to go and spoil his fun? "No, sir."

"Well then I suggest ye make haste afore this lassie catches her death."

That was it? No shouting? No lashings? No threats? Andrew raised his arm and opened his cloak. "Come, Aileen. I'll keep ye warm on the way back."

Thank heavens she complied with his bidding, else he would have run for the wood and never looked back.

As they left the stable, Hamish's chuckle resounded between the stone walls. But Andrew didn't care anymore. With Aileen nestled beneath his arm, being caught was worth a modicum of humiliation. He'd just been blessed with the most amazing kiss ever.

CHAPTER TWENTY-THREE

Wearing a plaid belted around his waist and pulled across his shoulder, Lachlan paced outside Christina's chamber. In truth, he liked wearing a plaid far more than chausses. Maybe because he wore a dress kilt from time to time back home. Anyway, it was damned comfortable and he'd be wearing the plaid a whole lot more in the future.

He glanced down at the parcel in his hand, wrapped in grungy leather. Maybe he should have tried to find some ribbon with which to tie it, make it look prettier. After all, Christina was prettier than a rose blossom. But frills were hard to come by around these parts and they'd used most of the lady's ribbon on the tree. Nope, not a single sheet of Christmas wrapping paper was to be found in the fourteenth century. In truth, he liked the simplicity of the times. He liked not seeing flashing Christmas lights and Santa Claus or hearing jingle bells while he pushed a trolley around the grocery store. He enjoyed the greening of the castle, filling the passageways with pine scent. He loved the wood smoke and amber candle light, and the dusting of snow he awoke to most mornings.

But none of his thoughts allayed his need to give the cross he'd purchased to Christina. He wanted her to have it, wondered how often she received bonny gifts. All through the gathering, he'd waited for the perfect opportunity to give it to her. Surrounded by the crowd, dancing, food and drink, there hadn't been a single chance. Besides, he didn't want to upstage Andrew's gift to Christina. The lad mightn't have been appreciative of it, but the gesture meant a great deal to his mother. And the color suited her.

Lachlan raised his fist to knock on her door. Surely she would allow him a moment or two.

Ellen answered, a look of surprise making her eyes grow wide. "Sir Lachlan? 'Tis late."

"I was about to say the same to you." He hadn't expected the chambermaid at this hour—would he never find Christina alone? "I'd like to speak to her ladyship for a moment if I may."

Ellen shook her head. "I dunna think—"

"He may enter," Christina's voice came from within.

"Verra well." Pursing her lips, the chambermaid opened the door wider and stepped aside.

"I need to have a word with Sir Lachlan in confidence, if ye'll excuse us." The lady placed her hand on Ellen's shoulder and kissed her on the cheek. "Ye may retire for the eve. Happy Yule."

"Happy Yule, m'lady." Ellen looked to Lachlan with a discerning eye. "Are ye certain ye dunna need me to stay?"

Lachlan crossed his heart. "I promise to protect her ladyship's virtue."

The chambermaid blushed scarlet. "Yes, sir." Then she curtseyed and hastened out the door.

With the click of the latch, tension fled from Lachlan's shoulders. Finally alone, he ushered Christina to the settee in front of the hearth. "I must commend you, m'lady. The gathering was the best I've ever seen."

Her wavy chestnut hair, devoid of a veil, shimmered in the candlelight as she took her seat. "My thanks, and I must say everyone admired the Christmas tree." She could smile more radiantly than any woman on the planet and she did so as he slid down beside her. "And I think taking Andrew with ye made him feel more a part of the clan."

"Perhaps." Lachlan draped his arm over the back of the settee. "Though I'd imagine Miss Aileen had more to do with Andrew's good spirits than the tree."

She chuckled. "Ye could be right. The lad did seem smitten."

"Anything to encourage him, I say."

"Agreed. Though King Robert willna approve of a marriage between the pair."

Now that was so farfetched, it made Lachlan snort. "Who's talking about marriage? The lad's only fifteen. He'll probably have a host of girlfriends before he ties the knot."

Her fine-boned shoulders shook with her laugh. "I hope ye are right."

Turning over his hand, he revealed the parcel in his palm. "I've been waiting all night to give this to you."

Her ruby lips formed a delightful "O". "A gift?"

"Yes. Why wouldn't I want to give you a gift, m'lady? After all, you've taken me in, made me your champion, given me meaningful work helping Andrew to change his paradigms."

She scooted away a bit. "Yes, of course." She offered a sad smile, her gaze drifting to the fire.

Bloody hell, Lachlan bit his tongue. Did he have to screw everything up? He liked this woman, was incredibly attracted to this woman, and had her alone in her chamber with an actual bed for the first time since they'd arrived at Ormond Castle and he was yammering about meaningful bloody work? Holy hell, how much further could he shove his foot into his mouth? He didn't want to talk about an employer-employee relationship.

Changing his tack, He placed the parcel in her hand and took a deep breath. "Aside from all that, you brought a ray of sunshine into my heart when I thought no hope remained. You have shown me a way of life I thought had been lost forever."

"'Tis very kind of ye to say," she said as if they'd suddenly grown distant.

But Lachlan wasn't about to give up. Not only his foot, he'd put his entire leg in his mouth, and he wouldn't leave this night until she was good and sure he'd taken it out. "Go on, open it."

Christina's fingers trembled a bit as she pulled the leather thong. "Oh my." She held the cross nearer and inclined it toward the candlelight. "'Tis exquisite. Where ever did ye find it?"

He took the chain and clasped it around her neck. "It seems your smithy is good for more than hammering iron and pulling teeth."

"Malcolm made this himself?"

"Yep." Lachlan admired how the amethyst sparkled against her alabaster skin. "Said he found the amethyst on the battlefield at Stirling Bridge."

"Imagine that. He never told me he dabbled with jewelry."

"Do you like it?"

"I absolutely adore it." She grasped his hands between her palms. "Thank ye."

He grinned, his gaze falling to her lips. A little pink tongue slipped out the corner of her mouth before she snatched her hands away. "Och, I'm glad ye stopped by this eve, else I would have had to wait until the morrow to give ye your gift. The tanner only finished it this day."

"Excuse me?" Lachlan twisted his mouth. "It surprised you that I gave you a present, but you had something made for me?"

She held up a finger. "Something most practical for a champion."

He looked around the chamber, seeing nothing but tapestries, lace and feminine things—no size sixteen boots, no horse saddles. *The tanner?* "What is it?"

"A moment." She rose to her feet and headed for the garderobe.

Craning his neck, he tried to peer around her. "Should I come with you?"

"Nay."

After a bit of rustling, Christina came out holding up a leather couton and grinning like she'd just earned her first karate belt.

"Wow." Lachlan stood and crossed the floor.

"Ye said ye wanted leather armor and I asked the tanner to fashion a coat that couldna be run through."

He ran his gaze down the fine tooling. "My God. This is a work of art." The strips of leather had been stamped with a bold star pattern he'd seen on the de Moray crest over the hearth in the great hall. The stitching was so exact it could have been from a machine, though Lachlan had never seen seams so strong. He worked the thick, reinforced leather panels between his fingers. "It's perfect."

Christina beamed, her eyes sparkling. "Try it on."

After unfastening the plaid at his shoulder, he slipped his arms through and she stepped in and fastened the buckles. "I still think mail would afford ye more protection, but this couton is the next best thing." She placed her palm in the center of his chest. "And I had the tanner fashion it to protect your legs and...um." Her gaze dipped with her blush.

Lachlan's heart thrummed a rapid rhythm beneath her fingertips. "You are a wise woman. And I like the slits over my thighs. They'll make it easier to walk." He tilted up her chin with the crook of his finger. "How did the tanner manage to make it fit so perfectly?"

"I remembered your measurements from Roxburgh."

"You remembered. My word, you are amazing."

She giggled, but still shook her head. "Who would have kent? Give a man a coat of armor and he'll think the world of ye."

He brushed her hair away from her face. It hung down her back in thick waves, the curls around her cheeks making ringlets. "I want you," he whispered.

As if hesitant, her gaze slipped down his new couton and back up, meeting his eyes. "Do ye remember that morn in Roxburgh?"

How could he forget? Simply the mention of it made the fire in his loins rage into an inferno. What had he been waiting for? They were both adults, she a widow, and he…well, he imagined Angela would have secured a divorce in his absence by now. In truth, he was a single man standing in a single woman's bedchamber and he didn't give a frig what century he was in.

"Yes," he replied hoarsely, unable to stop himself from running his fingers through the pure silk of her hair.

She cringed as if a bit embarrassed. "I havena been able to push it from my mind."

With his next blink, his cock shot up like a rocket, hard and throbbing and impossible to ignore. Dear God, how long had it been? A man could only act like a monk for so long. Christ, he'd been afraid Christina had pushed his advances from her mind—done everything to forget her one fleeting moment of passion. It hadn't escaped his notice every single day that she'd done nothing further to encourage him. In fact, the few times they'd kissed since, he'd been the initiator. She'd kissed him back, caressed him a wee bit, but it seemed she made every effort to suppress any smoldering desire that lurked deep inside.

He tugged her arm and pulled her into his embrace. "Are you afraid?"

"Nay." Giving a nod, she lowered her gaze. "Aye."

"Are you afraid…ah?" He needed to word it delicately. "Afraid I'll get you with child?"

She gave one slow nod. "That and of what King Robert might do."

"King Robert?" His brow furrowed. "What does he have to do with *us*?"

She took a step away and turned her back, hiding her face in her hands. "If Andrew refuses to take up arms for the king, the de Moray lands will be forfeit along with *my hand*."

Cold sweat broke out along Lachlan's skin. Jesus Christ, what she'd just revealed was every bit as awful as being held captive. "Can he do that?"

"I can refuse him, aye. But then I would be cast out of my home and left with nothing."

Lachlan gulped. "I could *never* allow that to happen."

"Nay?" She faced him, a combination of defiance and anguish contorted her features as she thrust her finger at his chest. "What about *that* medallion? Ye said ye were from the future. And ye said ye'd be returning home after your work with Andrew was done."

Dumbfounded, his mouth dropped open. "I—I did say that, didn't I?" he mumbled, buying time. Why did dating have to be so much more difficult in this century—especially for an accidental time traveler? Christ, in his time, if a woman wanted to sleep with a man without complications, she asked him to use a condom and did as she pleased. But Christina had so many worries hanging over her head. She could lose everything. Her son, her lands, and worse, herself. How could Lachlan promise to take care of her when his own future was completely unknown?

Raking his hands through his hair, he was the one to look away this time. The medallion warmed against his skin like it was trying to give him a warning. But what did the damned thing want him to do? And why was he worrying about a lump of stupid bronze? He'd asked the miserable medal to send him home enough times with no response. Clapping his hand over it, he took a deep breath.

"I honestly cannot tell you what will happen in the future. But I know what I want right now." The medallion cooled, making him care about it even less. "Right now, I want *you*. We can do things to avoid pregnancy." He reached for her hand. "You are a flesh and blood woman and you deserve to be happy."

Her lips trembled. "But what will the clan say?"

"Why should they know?"

"They always ken everyone's business."

"My guess is they already suspect there's something between us." He drew her hand to his lips and kissed her knuckles. "And I also have a hunch they want you to be happy as well. Your clan stood beside you while you gave birth to a bairn after your husband was killed. They stood beside you for thirteen years while you were held prisoner, unable to hold your son in your arms, unable to raise him as you intended."

She took in a stuttered breath as she grazed her teeth over her bottom lip, her eyes welling.

God, he wanted her more than life itself. He wanted to show her happiness, wanted her to know that not everyone would take from her giving nothing in return. "Not a soul will judge you. I am certain of it."

"Holy saints, I pray not." Snapping her hands to his cheeks in a bold move, a tear slipped down her cheek as she raised her lips and kissed him. Raw passion flowed through her lips as she plied him with the most fervent kiss he'd ever experienced. Christina sighed into his mouth—her response far more aggressive than ever before. The fire from her hunger fed his need to have her. His hands slid around her waist and up her back, pulling her soft, feminine body against his hard, masculine one. He pressed the length of his torso against her, but it wasn't enough. Thrusting his tongue deep into her mouth, Lachlan moved his hands down to her buttocks and tugged her hips flush with his unignorably, mind-consuming erection.

The damned couton proved to be too thick a barrier for his driving need. Pulling away, he unfastened the top buckle while Christina started with the bottom, God bless her. When their fingers met, he couldn't pull it off his shoulders fast enough, though he carefully rested the new armor on the table.

"Dear Lord." She pressed praying fingers to her lips. "I hate that I have brought ye into the mess of my life, but I could withhold the truth from ye no longer."

"I'm glad you told me. I would not have you suffer alone." He raked his gaze down her body and unfastened the brooch holding her arisaid around her shoulders. Dear God, even through the thick wool of her kirtle, the roundness of her breasts enticed him. Then his breath caught as a revelation donned. "There is no place on earth I'd rather be." He pushed the arisaid to the floor and with a trembling hand, he covered her breast. "I said it before and I meant it. I want you. I cannot make promises about the future, but in this moment and every moment I'm with you, I'll do anything to see to your happiness."

A stuttering breath slipped through her lips.

"Please do not refuse me," he growled. Moving even closer and slipping an arm around her shoulder, his fingers slid lower, past her abdomen and down to her tender flesh. Through the layers of fabric, he caressed her.

Gasping and throwing her head back, Christina rocked against his hand. "My God, I am powerless to resist."

"Then trust me," he growled, sweeping her into his arms and carrying her to the four-poster bed that had been beckoning him since he'd entered her chamber. Ever so gently, Lachlan rested her atop the soft mattress. "On this

Christmas night, I aim to show you exactly how much I want you, m'lady."

***

Christina shuddered right down to her toes. Not with fear, but shudders of want, shudders of pure desire, the likes of which she'd never experienced in her lifetime. Never before had she tremored with want while gooseflesh rose across her arms. Even the deep rumble of Lachlan's voice made her insides swarm with flutters of desire.

Gazing into his eyes, she pulled loose the bow securing her kirtle laces. "I do trust ye. I've trusted ye with my son and I will trust ye now." Dear Lord in heaven, the words she'd been longing to say finally passed through her lips. Every night since Roxburgh, she'd lain awake longing to feel Lachlan's touch, longing to be with him, skin to skin.

While he watched her, he unfastened his belt and let his plaid cascade to the floor. Had Christina not been lying on the bed, she would have swooned for certain, for he wore no braies this eve. With a chuckle, he pulled off his shirt and dropped it.

"Perfection." She wasn't sure if she'd spoken aloud, but it didn't matter. Lachlan's nude body was a sight to behold. He stood naked as God made him, virile and powerful, and every inch desirable. No words could describe Lachlan's magnificence. Head to toe and halfway back up again, Christina drank him in…all of him. He stepped closer to the bed, his thick erection jutting proudly from a triangle of auburn curls—*auburn*—much redder than his hair.

Trying to breathe, Christina reached out and touched him.

Arching his back, he moaned with such a rumble, she almost thought she'd hurt him until his manhood throbbed beneath her fingers. "I'm already on the ragged edge," his hoarse voice growled.

She drew her hand away and scooted over to allow him room beside her. She patted the mattress. "Come here."

Needing no more encouragement, he slid down beside her, running kisses along her neck while his fingers worked magic. With a few deft flicks, her bodice was unlaced, her shift as well, and his hand slipped beneath the linen while his thick column pressed against her hip.

His lips worked magic, exposing her breasts and suckling one and then the other. Pushing into him, she feared she might explode as his fingers slipped between her quivering thighs. But she wanted more. She didn't want to come like this, partially dressed. She wanted to join with him. Feel him fill her and take her on a ride to heaven.

Frantic with need, she helped him strip off her kirtle and shift. Rolling into his arms, Christina craved his warmth, craved his hardness. As they kissed, his hard column slipped between her thighs, heightening her need until she was certain she was about to shatter. The heat swirling in her nether parts, the intoxicating scent of spicy male, the gentle caressing of his manhood growing slick with her own wetness made shudders of joy fire across her skin and her breath come in short gasps. "I canna hold back any longer."

"Me, neither." Lachlan's eyes grew darker and a devilish grin turned up the corners of his mouth while he climbed between her thighs. "Are you sure you're ready for me?"

Prone to him, her knees wide, all she could do was nod while the column of his erection teased her. Only inches from her quivering flesh, she brazenly reached down and guided him toward her. She felt naughty and wonderful and ever so aroused. Never in her life had she done something this daring before, but Lachlan had a way of fleshing out her insecurities. He made her feel emboldened and beautiful and wanted. She placed him at her entrance and he slid in ever so slightly.

A wispy gasp sucked through her throat.

"God, you are so wet, I could come right now."

"Please," she begged, sliding her hands to his buttocks and forcing him deeper.

"You drive me insane, woman." He took his weight onto his elbows and lay atop her without crushing. Thrusting his hips forward, he slid deeper inside while covering her mouth and entwining her tongue with his. Completely and utterly alive, Christina gave in to the most thrilling experience of her life. Unabashedly, she matched him, thrust for thrust, digging her fingers into his thick bands of muscle.

Together, their breathing sped as they united in a glorious dance between a man and a woman who'd spent too much time suppressing their affection for one another.

Christina closed her eyes and experienced the amazing merging her body and soul with the only man she had met in fifteen years who had made her crave to be loved again. Her years of oppression only served to make their lovemaking all the more pleasurable. Just when she thought the thrill could not grow higher, her body shuddered on a pinnacle of pure ecstasy. Losing complete control, she cried out, bursting like a shower precipitated by lightning.

With her moans of rapture, Lachlan continued to thrust deep and fast. With a basal, shuddering bellow, he pulled away and released his seed on her belly—protecting her from embarrassment just as he'd promised, then collapsed beside her.

As their breathing slowed to a whispered hum, Christina smoothed her fingers along his closely cropped beard. Her need rose again as gradually, he moved his lips toward her. This time, his kiss was slow, deliberate and all-consuming.

Christina's heart squeezed tight while a tear moistened the corner of her eye. "I had no idea it could be like this."

Chapter Twenty-Four

After the Christmas season, winter passed in a maelstrom of passionate nights and days too short with the absence of sunlight. Christina managed to survive through every cold and dreary day knowing Lachlan would come to her at night. Unfortunately, after the holiday, Andrew had reverted to his unpleasantness, though he seemed to be respectful of everyone except his mother. But she wasn't about to give up. She still had several months to win him over before they must travel south to present themselves before King Robert.

She blocked thoughts of the future from her mind and thanked the stars for bringing her Sir Lachlan. He'd become her redeemer, her salvation. She shuddered, forcing her mind away from the future. She couldn't allow herself thoughts of what might come. Every night she clung to Lachlan, their lovemaking indescribably fantastic. He filled her with his strength enabling her to face every day anew.

March had come and with it the wind and driving rain like it always did, but to Christina it was a new season. Daylight grew longer. The ground thawed and the Moray Firth rose with the melt and rain. Tomorrow marked April first and, today, Ormond Castle had been blessed with sunshine.

After listening to supplications in the great hall, Christina donned her cloak and headed for the courtyard. No one would be able to keep her inside, not after so many consecutive days of rain. Heading for the garden, she stopped short when she rounded a corner and found Lachlan and Andrew sparring. They had done most of their practicing with the de Moray guard through the winter and this was the first time she'd seen the pair working alone for sennights.

Goodness, Andrew has improved.

Afraid she'd interfere, she slipped into the shadows of an archway leading to the chapel.

The partners swung their blades with sharp precision, the iron clanging with each two-handed stroke. Andrew bared his teeth, moving his feet constantly while Lachlan met his every attack, growling orders and giving praise when warranted. At once, their blades met, screeching together until their cross guards met.

"A stalemate is the most critical point of a fight," said Lachlan, his face growing red. "It shows both combatants are skilled. It marks a turning point when you *must* take charge or submit. What are you going to do, lad?"

"I'll bloody show ye," Andrew hollered, twisting his sword over Lachlan's.

For a moment, Christina thought her son had won the upper hand, until the big man moved so fast he blurred while Andrew's weapon clattered to the ground.

Lachlan immediately stopped, stepped back and thrust his fist onto his hip. "What the hell have I been teaching you all this time?"

Andrew's shoulders sagged. "'Tis best to run."

"But before that?"

"Take out their knee, their groin or hit them in the head."

"Right."

The lad threw up his hands. "But what if I can run my opponent through?"

"Why would you want to kill a man when there's a way to avoid it, instead?"

"So he does not come back and kill me in my sleep."

Lachlan heaved a sigh. "Only resort to killing when there is no other alternative."

"Or when ye're in a war."

Christina tapped her fingers against her lips. Was Andrew losing his English accent or was it her imagination? Nonetheless, he was putting up a good argument.

"But that's not today's lesson," Lachlan continued. "If you are attacked in Inverness, you might be arrested for murder if you killed the man and there were no witnesses."

"Who would go against my word? Would I not have the de Moray Clan to stand in my defense?"

Christina's heart leapt. Did Andrew realize what he'd just said? He would have his clan's protection.

"That is up to you." Lachlan eyed him. "Are you ready to take your place beside your mother?"

It was all she could do not to run across the grass and enfold her son in her embrace.

Andrew stooped to retrieve his sword, then straightened with a scowl. "We must go again."

Dropping her jaw, Christina stood there while a hollow chasm filled her chest. Why couldn't Andrew agree? He was so close. Why must he be so obstinate? Would he ever accept his birthright?

Clenching her fists in front of her mouth, Christina stood and watched, her mind racing. What more could she do to encourage the lad? What must she do to win his acceptance? Should she step aside? Doing so could put the entire clan in jeopardy if he turned backstabber and invited de Vere north for an English coup.

Perhaps she wasn't giving Andrew enough encouragement?

But he hates me.

The next time the guards on their swords slid together in a battle of strength, Andrew stepped back. He swung his arms to use his opponent's power and sent Lachlan stumbling while the lad ran the other way.

Applauding, Christina stepped from the shadows. "Well done!"

Andrew lowered his sword. "Aye?" he said in a Scottish brogue. "Ye would applaud a yellow-bellied manure pile?"

Christina's face went from happy to stricken in a mere second. "No. Y-ye performed well. I'm merely stating what I witnessed."

"I do not need praise from the likes of ye." Andrew threw his sword to the ground and started off.

"Just a minute!" Lachlan shouted as he headed after the boy. But he stopped midstride and grasped Christina by the shoulders. "Are you all right?"

"I…What…He…" Shaking her head, she covered her face with her palms. "I can do nothing right."

Pulling her into his arms he squeezed with passion. "Everything you have done is right and that little snot-nosed brat needs to learn a lesson. I'm sick and tired of watching him treat you like thresh on the floor."

She pounded her fist on his chest. "But ye could turn him away from me for good."

"He's already been turned away. It's time he became a man and to do that, I need to take him on a pilgrimage."

She nearly swooned at the thought. "To the Holy Land?"

"No. I call it a Boy Scout trip—a time of challenges in the wild where a young man must learn to live or die. I was met with the same training when I was his age and he needs it now more than anything."

Oh, no, she didn't like the sound of that at all. "Ye say he might die?"

Steeping back, he grasped her shoulders firmly. "I'll be there to ensure he doesn't, but I'll also make sure he knows he's a man and where he comes from and who the bloody hell cares about him."

***

Lachlan planned everything without sharing the details with Andrew. He even knew the site—a place where he and Hamish had hunted mule deer in deep snow. A week after his tantrum in the courtyard, Lachlan approached the lad while he ate breakfast. "Happy Saints Day." He'd tried to use more archaic language to be better understood. As soon as he'd learned some proficiency, people started trusting him a bit more.

Andrew beamed—probably because his mother hadn't come below stairs yet. "My thanks. In two years I'll reach my majority and I'll be knighted by..." Looking away, Andrew didn't finish, but Lachlan knew well enough he wanted to say Lord de Vere.

Fuck de Vere. Good God, if I ever wanted to fight a man, it would be that vindictive bastard.

Lachlan cast aside his own internal resentment. It could wait—hopefully forever. "That may be true, but today I'm taking you on a pilgrimage."

Andrew rested his spoon beside the bowl. "I beg your pardon?"

"You heard me." Planting his fists on his hips, Lachlan continued, "The law might say you become a man at eight and ten, but I say it is time to prove it now, and I aim to put you to the test."

The boy didn't look so smug as his gaze shifted. "Can ye do that?"

"I can and I will. Now pack a bed roll and meet me in the stables in an hour."

Lachlan had every detail worked out. And they'd be roughing it. Thanks to Andrew's lessons and his own practice, he'd learned to handle a horse as well as any other man at Ormond Castle. The kitchen had prepared bully beef and oatcakes, and loaded parcels of food onto a pack mule along with their bedrolls. He'd gone on such a pilgrimage with Bill

Wallace, the twenty-first century man who had acted as his father, who had been his role model throughout Lachlan's life. It didn't matter if Bill Wallace hadn't conceived him, Bill was the greatest man Lachlan had ever known. Bill had encouraged him to join the Special Air Service after he'd graduated from college. Though he'd only served four years, the basic training he'd learned had enhanced his martial arts training and had formed him into the man he was today.

No one at Ormond Castle had any idea of the extent of Lachlan's fighting skills. True, he'd taken over training the guard, but being a seventh level black belt took years, and he'd only scratched the surface.

Andrew de Moray showed more promise than any of the others, but his attitude was in the middens. And now, Lachlan knew what was at stake for Christina. He must do something drastic. Sixteen was a bit young, but these Highlanders lived hard lives, fast lives, and if they didn't grow up in a hurry, they'd most likely be dead.

The bottom line? If Lachlan couldn't cure the boy of his habit of insulting his mother, he just might wring Andrew's neck and face the consequences. He was done with doing things Christina's way and, by God, he wouldn't tolerate listening to another insult from the lad. In Lachlan's century, it wasn't okay to kick the shit out of a youth, but the boy pushed him to the edge. If this didn't work, they might end up facing off. That's why Lachlan wasn't even close to teaching Andrew everything he knew. If the lad turned traitor and fled to England, he didn't want de Moray riding against and murdering Scots.

I pray that never happens.

Once they were mounted, Lachlan had Andrew lead the pack mule beside his destrier. Lachlan chose to ride a stout garron pony. Andrew scoffed, but Hamish had shown Lachlan the benefits of the Highland-bred horse. They were tougher and more agile in the rocky terrain.

They headed south and west avoiding any brushes with humanity, riding around the few towns sprouting through the wilderness between Avoch and Loch Monar. Taking his time, Lachlan rode in circles, making sure Andrew was good and lost. It was dusk when they led the horses through the craggy hills that surrounded the loch and a cave just above the frigid water. Fortunately, the hills were still capped with snow—exactly what Lachlan had wanted. That meant the loch was no more than 40 degrees Fahrenheit. Maybe colder.

"This is where we'll make camp."

"Good, 'cause I'm starving," said Andrew.

"Hobble the horses, then we need to collect wood for the fire."

"Yes, sir." Andrew had taken well to the idea of a rite of passage. At least so far.

Lachlan watched the lad as he made a fire pit by placing boulders in a circle and in no time they'd gathered enough tow, sticks and wood to build a fire, which Andrew lighted with ease.

"You passed your first test with flying colors."

The boy smirked. "Give me something challenging."

Lachlan eyed him. "I don't know if you can handle the next test."

"What is it?"

"Hypothermia."

"Hypo—what?"

He pointed. "Cold water immersion."

"I can handle a dip in a chilly pond."

"Not just a dip, but you must stay in until I say you can come out." Lachlan watched him over the crackling fire. "You will feel like you're going to die, but if you can't handle it you will fail and everyone at Ormond Castle will know you're not ready to be a man."

Andrew rubbed his outer arms like a ghost had just walked over his soul. "I don't want to fail."

"That's what I needed to hear." Lachlan gestured toward the loch. "Strip down to your braies."

"Now? Can we not eat first?"

"Eating is the reward—it will give you something to think about when your balls feel like they're about to freeze off."

Andrew did as instructed and stood shivering with his arms crossed.

"Are you ready?"

"It feels like it's about to snow."

Lachlan looked up to the stars—only a few wispy clouds sailed past the moon. "You'll be fine. Go on. The sooner you get this over with, the sooner you'll be able to eat."

Andrew hobbled over the stony shore and waded in up to his knees. Turning, he faced Lachlan, his teeth chattering. "T-this i-sna so bad."

"Yeah? Go on—up to your neck."

Andrew managed to wade to his waist. "God's teeth, ye cannot expect me to immerse myself further."

"Want me to dive in with you and hold you down?"

"N-n-n-o."

He almost wished the boy agreed. "Up to your neck." Lachlan knew the numbers. There wasn't a bit of ice showing on the shore, which meant Andrew could last a half hour or more—maybe a little less because he was so damned skinny.

It actually surprised him when Andrew finally looked to the shore with only his head poking out the water. "There. My cods are about to freeze into stones. May I come out now?"

"Not yet. Try treading water or swimming if you're cold." Lachlan moved the bedrolls into the cave.

"But I c-c-canna move."

Grinning to himself, he couldn't help but notice how Andrew's accent was gradually changing. The boy probably didn't even notice when a bit of a brogue slipped out and

Lachlan wasn't about to say anything. The sooner Andrew ditched the English accent, the better.

Andrew moved around a bit, his gasps growing sharper. Even from the shore Lachlan heard his teeth chattering.

"Please," the lad pleaded. "I can no longer feel my toes or my fingers."

"A bit longer." Lachlan took his time collecting a bit more wood and tossed it on the fire. "Because the night is cold, I'll let you come out early."

Shivering like a wet dog, Andrew hunched over as he made his way to the shore. He clutched his arms against his body and hobbled toward the cave, his head shaking out of control as his teeth chattered.

"Stop."

"What? I need a blanket afore I catch me death."

"Stand by the fire."

"Why are ye doing this to me? 'Tis cruel." Andrew crouched over the fire and held out his hands.

"We are not done yet." Lachlan stood across the blaze with his hands on his hips. "Stand straight, soldier."

"B-but I'm freeeeeezing."

"Stop whingeing. Are you in this to become a man or do you want to head home to your ma?"

Andrew looked up with a hateful, determined glare in his eyes. Christ, Lachlan almost would have preferred it if the boy had asked to go home. Instead, he dropped his arms and clamped his mouth shut while he straightened to his full height—probably five-foot nine. He'd grown a good three inches since November.

"Have you ever had to survive alone in the wild?"

Andrew's arms crossed again with his shivers. "Nay."

"How would you feed yourself if you were lost and starving?"

"I'd kill a deer."

"What if you had no weapons?"

"I'd set a s-snare."

"What if you didn't catch anything?"

"I'd eat berries—a-a-and dandelion leaves."

"Not very substantive, but it's a start." Lachlan paced, moving his hands and grasping them behind his back. "What about eating grubs and insects?"

"Eeeew. Who would do such a thing?"

"A man trying to survive would do a great many things he normally wouldn't do otherwise."

Andrew swayed on his feet.

"Are you feeling tired?"

"No, sir."

Lie.

"Tell me, why are you always so angry?" Lachlan demanded. "What's eating at your insides?"

"I am not always angry."

Lie number two.

"I beg to differ…and the sooner you start revealing the truth, you'll be able to wrap yourself in a warm blanket." Lachlan stopped pacing and stared across the fire. "Everyone knows you were abducted at the age of two, you were a captive of two kings of England before you came home, and yet you remain loyal to those who would oppress you. Tell me why, Andrew."

"I-I…They made promises—they made me feel important."

"And you do not feel important in Scotland?" Lachlan, held up his hand, stopping the boy's response. "Tell me again, what's eating at your insides? What wakes you up at night? What makes you want to tear your clothes and scream?"

Andrew's shoulders dropped. "They left me," he whispered.

"Who left you?"

"No one came to fetch me. They locked me in a chamber and no one ever played with me."

"You were abandoned?" Lachlan egged him on.

"She abandoned me. She doesna really love me. And now she thinks she can make up for all the years I spent locked in that room."

Dear God, Lachlan wanted to throw up. "She didn't lock you up, Lord de Vere did. He doesn't care about you."

"He did it because he doesn't like to be near children until they can work. But it's all *her* fault."

Stretching his fingers, Lachlan forced himself not to strangle the whelp. "Why do you say that?"

"Because she let them take me."

"You know that's not true."

Andrew rubbed his upper arms and hopped in place. "Lord de Vere told me so—everyone told me so."

"When was the last time someone said that?"

"Right after Lord de Vere thwarted the prisoner exchange on the borders."

So de Vere had been the culprit to cause the battle— Christ, Christina had been attacked, nearly killed. "I see." Lachlan scratched his head. "Do you think your mother loves you?"

Looking to the dirt, Andrew shook his head. "Not really."

"How else would you have her show her love?"

"I dunna ken."

Damn. He wasn't making any bloody progress. He needed to go deeper. "How would you feel if she died?"

"I would hold a gathering and celebrate my good fortune."

If only Lachlan could knock some sense into that adolescent head. "Honestly? She is your only living relative. Your mother, you may recall, was held hostage throughout the duration of your captivity, and she worked with Robert the Bruce to bring you home as soon as it could be arranged."

Bouncing stay warm, Andrew's gaze shifted to the flames. "I dunna like it when ye touch her."

Well, there was something new. An open window, perhaps? "That I can understand far better than your hatred for a woman who wants only for your happiness and freedom." When the lad didn't respond, Lachlan continued with his questioning, "Do you think your mother deserves to be loved?"

"No."

"Why not?"

"I dunna ken."

Wrong answer.

"It seems there's a lot you do not know, lad. But that's okay. The wisest of men realize there will always be things they do not understand." Lachlan pressed his fingers to his lips. "Over the next three days, I want you to think about family and who you are projecting your anger upon. Think about who that person or those people are in their *hearts*. See them as God's children. What does God want from them?"

Andrew gave a shaking nod. "Verra well. Can I fetch my blanket now?"

"Not yet." Lachlan sliced his hand through the air. "Tell me, who is important to you?"

"This is daft—*I'm* important to me, for God's sake."

"There's nothing wrong with putting yourself at the top, but you must care about others."

The boy raised his chin.

He must be growing indignant or testing the water.

"Lord de Vere," Andrew said.

"Honestly?" Lachlan challenged. "A man who locked you in a chamber alone for how many years?"

"Six…b-b-but once I proved I could become a squire, he sent me to live in the stables—even sent a cleric to teach me to read."

"And he promised you would one day be a knight." Lachlan purposely filled his voice with scorn.

Andrew stamped his foot. "Yes, dammit. Why can you not see how important being a true knight is to me?"

"A true knight?"

"Aye, a man dubbed a knight of the order by the King of England."

"And a Scottish knight is lesser? Is his training inferior?"

"Scottish knights are pillagers and thieves. They have no honor."

Lachlan crossed his arms and spoke softly, "Do you believe me to be a pillager and a thief? Am I lacking in honor?"

"Ye are different."

"No. I am but a loyal Scottish subject." Lachlan took in a deep breath. "Tell me, where do you see yourself in two years?"

"I will reach my majority and I will earn my knighthood riding with Lord de Vere."

"All right, so you ride with de Vere for five years, killing Scots and French and supporting King Edward. In five years' time, you will be one and twenty. Where will you be then?"

"I'll be on a crusade with de Vere, fighting the Ottomans and sailing the seas."

Bloody hell, the boy's mind is full of rubbish.

"What if you're injured?"

"Not me."

"And when you're thirty, what then?"

"I'll ride with the Knights Hospitallers and fight for right."

Lachlan cringed. Fighting for a monastic order during the Crusades would lead the lad to a life of misery. "So you want to be a warrior monk? No children?"

"Of course I'll have children. I want to leave a legacy."

"Doesn't a monk take a vow of chastity, poverty and obedience?"

Andrew rubbed his arms again. "I'm bloody cold."

"What would you do if you lost a leg in battle?"

He stamped his foot. "I'd die."

"What if you survived?"

"I'd have a mate slit my throat, dammit."

Lachlan took a deep breath to calm his own internal turmoil. "Tell me five things a one-legged man could do."

"Turn beggar."

"Let me rephrase. What are five things a one-legged man could do to make a contribution to society?"

Biting his bottom lip, Andrew held his hands to the fire and rubbed them. "He could write. And if he used a crutch, he could move around…mayhap be a cleric or a tutor or do some work sitting down."

"What kind of work?"

"Whittling wood. Blowing glass." Andrew looked up, the anger gone from his face for the first time since they'd started out. "I turned the spit in de Vere's kitchen—sat on a stool, too. A one-legged man could do that."

"Excellent." Lachlan stepped in. "So, do you still think you'd want to die if you lost your leg?"

"Aye…but what if I was married? Do ye think my wife would still like me?"

"I have some experience with love. When a person truly loves another, he or she will be willing to work through many obstacles to stay together. If your wife really loved you, she would help you through the difficult times and stand by your side no matter what." Lachlan pointed his thumb toward the cave. "Go on, fetch your blanket and put on your clothes. I'll set out the food."

Chapter Twenty~Five

When Andrew awoke, the sound of dripping water near the back of the cave lulled him. He wanted to sleep, but Lachlan would probably force him awake soon. His hearing growing more acute, he listened for sounds, but heard nothing but the drip, drip, drip.

Sitting up, he stretched. "Sir Lachlan?"

With his next blink, he shifted his gaze to Lachlan's pallet. The damned blanket was gone. Their satchels of food, gone. Abandoned? Andrew's heart nearly beat out of his chest. Ignoring the roll of parchment beside him, he sprang to his feet and ran out of the cave. "Sir Lachlan!"

He raced to where the horses had been tied. Gone. His destrier gone.

God's teeth, he should have known Lachlan would stab him in the back. The bastard was woven from the same cloth as his mother. And he'd frozen him within an inch of his life.

Kicking a rock, he bellowed at the top of his lungs. "Laaaaaaachlaaaaan!"

Damnation, he was angry. When that backstabber returned, Andrew would challenge him to a duel of swords and demand no quarter. He stomped back into the cave to retrieve this boots. That's when he noticed the bit of vellum beside his bedroll. Groaning, he plopped to his arse and opened the damned thing. God's bones, the prose scrawled across the page in the oddest hand he'd ever seen:

Dear Andrew,

First of all, you have not been abandoned. I say it again and give you my promise that I have not left you. Though you will not see me, I will be watching out for your safety. But make no bones about it, you are on your own and must survive for the next three days. You have no weapons but your dirk and your wits. Do not waste your time trying to look for me. This is your pilgrimage. During your time alone, I want you to search deep inside your soul to find the true answers to these five questions:

1. *Who are you?*
2. *Who are your kin?*
3. *Who do you love?*
4. *Who truly loves you? When pondering this, ask yourself who would die for you.*
5. *What kind of man do you want to become? Do you see yourself as a brutal tyrant whose heart is filled with anger or a man who understands his heart and fights for right with every fiber of his being?*

You said you love yourself most of all. Now is the time to enjoy your own company and cast aside your anger. Be brutally honest with yourself, for no one else but you can answer these questions.

I shall see you in three days.

Respectfully,

Sir Lachlan.

Andrew tossed the parchment aside and huffed, looking out through the cave's mouth. He'd been abandoned again, no question about it. He didn't care what Lachlan's note said, leaving a lad in the midst of the wild with nothing but a dirk was abandonment. He was alone. His chest ached. Who loved him? No one, that's who. This must have been his mother's plan—do something dire to make him see right. Andrew's stomach turned over.

Be brutally honest.

While he sat staring out at the loch, those three words played over and over in his mind no matter how much he tried to think of something else. He picked up a rock and threw it as hard as he could.

Dammit, in truth, his mother would be irate if she knew Lachlan had left him in a cave to fend for himself. And for three bloody, miserable days.

***

Lachlan set up camp on a crag across the loch from Andrew, far enough away to give the boy space, but close enough to reach him swiftly if he met with danger. He knew his tactics were a bit radical, but his work with kids in his time had given him enough experience to know something drastic had to happen in order for Andrew to see the light.

Deep down, the boy knew the truth. But he needed some soul searching to realize it. Of course, it didn't matter who told him his mother loved him or his clan supported him or that King Robert was the right king for Scotland at this point in history. Andrew had to recognize and accept the truth himself.

His years living with de Vere had messed with his mind big time. He'd been ignored and treated as a prisoner as a young child. And when he'd finally been given the opportunity to join with society, to learn and to achieve some status, he was so overjoyed, he had to have been blinded...and brainwashed. Somewhere in the depths of his mind, Andrew had pushed aside the horrible years and cast the blame on his mother so that the man who offered him a life did not appear to be a tyrant, but a liberator.

Lachlan wasn't a praying man, but while he watched Andrew, he fell to his knees and prayed the boy would dig deep enough to discover the truth.

For three days, he watched while Andrew set snares and skipped rocks in the loch. He tried to fish with his dirk. He cupped his hands and drank water. Often he hiked around the cave, never venturing far, just as Lachlan had instructed.

Andrew set fourteen snares in all, none catching a thing.

On the third afternoon, Lachlan watched while Andrew dug for grubs. He didn't slide them down his gullet, but he put them in a bit of cloth, took them to the loch and washed them. Leaving the parcel by the fire pit, he collected wood and built up the fire before he made a bowl of rocks and set the worms inside to roast.

Lachlan timed it perfectly, arriving with the horses and the mule just as Andrew opened his mouth to drop in his first bite. "I reckon a feast of bully beef and oatcakes would go down a mite easier than a handful of grubs." He tossed down the satchel of food along with a flask of watered wine.

"Too right." Laughing, Andrew dove for the food, his hands shaking while he opened the buckles.

Dismounting, Lachlan hobbled the horses and took a seat while he watched Andrew gorge himself. "Go easy, or you'll bring it all back up."

"I'm starving."

"I can see that."

"Did ye sabotage my traps?"

"Nope."

The boy drank greedily. "How did ye ken I'd be driven to eat grubs?"

"Because I had to eat them during my test of manhood."

"Ye did?"

Lachlan nodded. "But my test lasted an entire week." He didn't say that he had a tent and a sleeping bag. That didn't matter. Everything he'd tried from fishing to setting snares, to hunting with his knife was unsuccessful and he'd ended up frying grubs in his cook set rather than with hot boulders. "I have to say you were pretty smart making a bowl out of rocks."

Andrew shoved an entire oatcake in his mouth. "I wasna going to eat them raw," he mumbled through the partially chewed food.

When the boy finished and drank his fill, Lachlan sat, crossed his legs and faced him. "You know I have questions to ask of you?"

Andrew nodded.

"Have you thought about how you'll answer?"

"Aye...but...can I fail?"

"Only you will know if you fail or not, because only you know the truth in your heart."

Andrew set the flagon beside him and mirrored Lachlan's position.

"First, I want you to close your eyes and focus on your breathing. Think of the rush of the ocean and the warmth of the sun. Think how it warms your skin on a summer's day. Imagine that warmth radiating through your chest. Breathe in. Breathe out." He encouraged deep breathing for a good five minutes, taking the boy into a meditative state. Lachlan also sought his own inner peace before he was ready to begin.

Completely relaxed, he opened his eyes. "Who are you?"

"I am Andrew de Moray. I am a squire. I am a son. I am a master horseman and a student of martial arts."

"Martial arts? I like that something I've taught you has stuck." Lachlan cleared his throat. He didn't want this to be about him at all. It had to be about Andrew, his mother and his clan. "Who is your kin?"

"My father was Andrew de Moray, rebel who fought with William Wallace and I am named for him. My mother is Christina Strathbogie, daughter of the Earl of Atholl, and she is my father's widow. The de Moray Clan is my kin."

"Did your mother tell you this?"

Andrew nodded. "But it is what I've always known in my heart. And your missive told me to seek what is in my heart."

At least the boy understood his roots, but what about the harder questions?

Lachlan kept his expression deadpan. "Who do you love?"

The lad blushed red, shifting his gaze to the fire. "Honestly, I think Aileen is bonny."

"The lass is cute for certain." Lachlan pursed his lips and waited. This wasn't a time for joking around.

Andrew traced his finger through the dirt. "Do not tell anyone."

"What?"

"I-I do love my mother even though she abandoned me."

He held up his palm. "Let's stop here for a moment." Lachlan's stomach clamped. No matter how much he wanted to put words in the lad's mouth he mustn't do it. He could only ask questions. "Who kept you locked in a tower room for six years?"

Andrew's shoulders slumped while a tear slipped from the corner of his eye. "de Vere," he whispered.

Thank God he got that right. "Who truly loves you?"

"My clan…"

Lachlan clenched his fists and waited. After a long and uncomfortable pause, he continued, "My guess is you thought about this question the most. What does your heart tell you? Who would *die* for you?"

Andrew slapped at the tears shimmering on his cheeks. "Mother." The word came out like an eerie whisper as if Andrew were in the midst of an inner struggle between good and evil.

Closing his eyes, Lachlan forced himself not to show the relief now making his every nerve tingle. "Last question… What kind of man do you want to be?"

Andrew pushed himself to his feet. "I want to be a good man, a man of honor. I want people to respect me."

Following Andrew's lead, Lachlan stepped to the side of the fire and held out his arms. "Well, son, with responses as solid as those you've just given me, you are on your way to being a knight for right." He pulled the sobbing boy into his arms and held him to his breast. By God, this whole thing could have blown up in his face. But he'd gone with his gut. He knew the lad had it in him, he just feared pushing him like this may be premature.

"I-I-I thought you might have left me forever," Andrew blurted as he caught his breath.

"I promise I will never do that." The medallion heated against Lachlan's chest, almost too hot to bear. "Not until you no longer need me." With his second phrase the medallion cooled. What did it mean? Would he be returning home sometime soon? Moreover, did he want to?

Chapter Twenty-Six

Sitting at the high table wearing the yellow veil Andrew had given her at the Yule feast, Christina watched while the servant poured her wine when the ram's horn sounded. Her heart took flight as she sprang to her feet. "'Tis them!"

Not waiting for a reply, she hastened down the dais steps, running all the way to the courtyard. Lachlan and Andrew strode through the archway, looking like a pair of grizzly Highlanders who hadn't seen a bath for a month.

Lachlan's teeth looked white as bed linen when he smiled beneath his dark whiskers. "I hope you've saved us some food, 'cause between the pair of us, we could eat an entire side of beef."

"Speak for yourself." Andrew nudged him in the ribs. "After starving me for three days, I'll hoard the entire steer for myself."

Christina's mouth when dry as she regarded her son. Did she actually see him smile—not a strained smile, but a relaxed and friendly grin? How should she respond? If she made note of her observation, would he reject her?

I canna risk it.

She clasped her hands together and painted on the aristocratic smile her mother had taught. "Ye are in luck. Ye've arrived in time for the evening meal."

"Excellent," said Lachlan. He reached out almost like he intended to embrace her in public, but caught himself in time and grasped her hand. Bowing over it, he plied her with a brief kiss, then straightened. "And how are you, m'lady?"

"Happier now I ken ye are safe." She chanced a timid glance at Andrew. "And ye, young sir? I hope ye enjoyed your scouting journey."

His brow pinched, Andrew stared at her for an awkward moment. Before he answered, he looked to Lachlan. "Uh…" He reached for her hand, bowed and gave it a light peck. "'Tis good to see ye, Mother."

She could have died and gone to heaven right there. In a blink, her eyes stung and her nose itched and dribbled. "Come, let us retire to the hall. I canna wait to hear about your adventure."

Lachlan cleared his throat. "I believe Andrew has something to say in private." He motioned to the onlookers. "Go on, everyone, back inside. We'll follow directly."

The lad twisted his mouth and looked like he'd been asked to make a speech in front of the king or something equally as terrifying.

Lachlan stood behind him and held up his palm—a gesture telling her to be patient.

Patience?

It was all she could do not to throw her arms around her son and tell him how much she'd worried about him, about how much she wanted him to be successful, about how much she loved him.

"I-I-I am sorry."

Christina's jaw dropped. Dear God, save her, she couldn't hold back if she were blocked by a hundred pikemen. Wrapping her arms around her only son, she pulled him into a tight embrace. "My son, my son, ye dunna need to apologize to me for anything. Ye were torn from your home as a wee bairn, and anyone, no matter how strong, would suffer greatly after enduring such abominable atrocities." She moved her hands to his cheeks and gazed into the lad's eyes. "I love ye, I love ye, I love ye, no matter what. I am your mother and I will always love ye."

Andrew nodded while a tear spilled onto her fingers. Shaking his head, he pulled away. "I shan't cry."

"Nay, not here." Clutching a fist to her mouth, Christina forced her own tears at bay. "Come. We shall share a meal together." Once alone in her chamber, she could allow her tears to flow. But now they must put on a display of strength for the clan. Her son had uttered three words she'd longed to hear. With God's help, she was positive Lachlan had put Andrew on the path toward his destiny. The path he was born to follow.

Once inside, she listened to Andrew tell how he'd been left alone for three whole days. Gracious, if Lachlan had told her what he intended to do, she would have tried to put a stop to it for certain. But the experience must have been remarkable. The lad had never spoken so animatedly and while simultaneously shoving his mouth full of food.

All the while, Lachlan ate, drank and listened. Though quiet, the braw warrior's gaze fixated on Christina throughout the meal. What was he thinking? For a moment, perspiration sprang across her skin. If he'd come to help Andrew, was his work nearly done?

She raised a shaking hand to her forehead.

"Are ye all right?" asked Andrew.

Blinking, she forced a smile. "Merely a wee swoon. It must be the excitement of having ye home."

Her champion pushed his trencher away and rose to his feet. "I'm off for a bath. I can barely stand myself."

"Will we see ye on the morrow?" she asked.

"Of course we will," said Andrew. "Sir Lachlan said he'd teach me how to defend myself against a sword using only my fists."

Lachlan met her gaze and gave a smile. Though Christina should rest assured, she still couldn't shake the idea of the medallion and the fact that Lachlan's purpose had been achieved. *Had it not?*

"He's smarter than any man I've ever met," Andrew said as he watched Lachlan retreat into the stairwell.

"I do believe ye are right." She unabashedly patted her son's shoulder for the first time since his rescue. Truly, she didn't want to push the lad, but there were still many unanswered questions and Christmas would be upon them faster than anyone realized. "So, are ye ready to accept your father's mantle?"

Andrew's lips thinned. "To be honest, I dunna ken."

"What's troubling ye the most?" she asked, folding her hands in her lap to steady her jumping nerves.

"When...er...*if* I take up my father's sword, I will be pledging for Robert the Bruce. All my life, I've been told he's a murderer and a usurper. How can I take up arms for a man I canna trust?"

"Hmm, I think ye've touched on a topic any man would have difficulty answering." She reached for the ewer and poured for them both. "Let us first take a step back. Let us consider, for a moment, the death of King Alexander. Do ye ken what happened ever so long ago?"

"Aye, he died whilst riding his horse and he had no forthright heir. Then King Edward was invited by the Scottish bishops to appoint a Scottish king."

"Indeed. It would have been all right if Edward had come to help, but he immediately pronounced himself overlord and began a litany of atrocities meant to humiliate the Scots people."

"But they undermined him."

She arched an eyebrow. "Only after Edward began to murder innocents, lad."

Andrew sat for a while and sipped his watered wine. They chatted a bit more about all that had transpired during King Edward's oppression of the Scots. They discussed the war led by William Wallace and Andrew's father and the reasons behind their patriotism.

Andrew was still puzzled, his brow etched with a furrow far deeper than it should be for a lad of six and ten. "But Robert Bruce killed the Earl of Badenoch in a chapel, a holy place."

"A dark day for Scotland." Christina nodded. "But the earl stood between King Robert and the throne. Moreover, Badenoch openly proclaimed his support for Edward. After the massacre at Berwick, no honorable Scotsman could stand idle and allow a tyrant to murder and torture our people, though the Earl of Badenoch bade us to lay down our arms."

"Tyrant," Andrew said contemplatively. He picked up his goblet and sipped. "'Tis what the English call the Bruce."

"That doesna surprise me. Many people have died on both sides of the border." She patted his hand. "War is never black and white, or good against evil. Both sides always believe in their own virtue. And ye will never agree on everything, especially when it comes to a king. What ye must decide is if ye believe in your clan and kin. Then your heart will lead ye toward the right path."

***

It always seemed to take too long to fill the enormous tub Lachlan had moved into his chamber, but given a couple kettles of boiling water followed by a few buckets of cold, the preparation was always worth it. Indeed, there were not many conveniences about this life. No lights to switch on, no water, hot or cold, from a tap, no cell phones or televisions. No internet, no cars or planes. He could write all night and not exhaust the list of differences. Still, he wasn't ready to go home.

After sinking into the glorious water and letting out a long sigh, he removed the medallion and turned it over in his palm. He'd been gone nearly six months now. What had changed back home? Where was his stuff? Jason surely hired someone to cover for Lachlan's classes at the dojo. Mother must have made his excuses. Angela had been lost to him even before he'd time traveled.

What if I chose to stay?

When no answer came to him, he tossed the medallion on his pile of clothes. Reclining, he closed his eyes and focused on the color yellow, focused on the thrum of his heart and willed his mind to clear. Breathing deeply, the feeling of weightlessness encircled his muscles as if a field of antigravity surrounded him. In and out he continued to breathe, allowing the warmth from the color yellow to infuse his flesh. Nowhere on earth had Lachlan ever delved to this level of inner peace. Yet he was in the midst of unrest, in the midst of one of the most brutal eras in man's history.

He slid under the water, listening to the liquid slosh in his ears. And when he opened his eyes, he imagined only Christina. His thrumming heart squeezed into a knot. She was not yet out of trouble. In about six months, she had no choice but to take Andrew south and present him before King Robert. Not only would Andrew's fate be determined, the king held her life in the palm of his hand.

Snapping out of his meditative trance, Lachlan sat bolt upright.

I cannot sit idle and allow her to be used as a pawn for the benefit of Robert's kingdom. For the love of God, the woman deserves to be happy. Life is so goddamned short. Christina can't just obey without standing up for herself.

Lachlan's stomach turned over.

And I cannot stand idly by while she is forced to marry a stranger.

He glanced to the medallion.

Do not take me away now, you son of a bitch. I'm not ready.

He had no sooner sunk back into the warm water when Christina cracked open the door. "May I come in?"

"Please do." He beckoned her with a wave of his hand.

Her grin brightened the chamber. Though she always had a bonny smile, this time, it seemed happier. "I canna believe the change in Andrew."

Lachlan grasped the soap and rubbed it under his arm. "He's not out of the woods yet, but I think I finally got through."

She pulled a stool beside the bath and sat. "Do ye think he'll fall back?"

"I'm certain of it, but it's up to us to watch and control how far. Teenagers are built to rebel by their very nature. It's what equips them for adulthood."

"Ye have no children. How do ye ken all this?"

"I studied Psychology—um—how people think and I spent years teaching them."

"Well I thank ye." She picked up the medallion and rubbed it between her fingers. When she looked up, her expression of happiness turned to worry. "When?"

He snatched the bronze from her fingers and slung it across the floorboards. "Do you think for a moment that I'll stand idle while King Robert holds your future in his hands?"

Her gaze intensified. "Ye mean to stay?"

"I do." He grasped her hand and clutched it over his heart and squeezed his eyes shut. "Dammit, I wish I had more control, I wish I could look at my own destiny, but I cannot. I can only offer you my sword and my love until I vanish into dust."

Leaning over, she caressed his forehead with her lips. "But isna that all any man can give?"

A weight lifted from his shoulders. Did it matter that his life hung on a precipice?

Hell, yes.

But what more could he do about it?

Love her.

"Take off your clothes," he said.

She giggled—a darling sound that made her crystal blue eyes dance with mischief. "Isna the water turning cold?"

"Not yet. I start with it near scalding." He flicked a splash onto her hand. "I want you naked."

She rubbed her outer arms. "Ye make it sound naughty."

He raised his hips up enough to give her a good look at his lengthening erection. "Good. Now untie your kirtle laces."

Standing before him, she watched his eyes as she removed her veil and ran her fingers through her glorious hair. She tortured him by slowly untying her kirtle and slipping each arm out, then gradually letting the wool cascade to the floor. Stepping out of her slippers, she pulled the lace on her shift. "Ye turn me wanton."

His tongue shot to the corner of his mouth as he watched the pebbles of her nipples strain against the fine linen. "If that's a bad thing, I never want to be good."

In one graceful move, she pulled the linen over her head and took a step nearer. Pert breasts tipped by rose stood proud, ready to be suckled. Simply walking up and down the stairwells and taking care of the keep kept her body toned. Her creamy flesh had never seen the light of day and her curling, hip-length locks caressed her skin in striking contrast. Lachlan rose to his knees and wrapped his fingers around her tiny waist. "You smell like a field of wildflowers."

"And ye smell clean and crisp like fresh rain."

Sitting back, he guided her into the tub, straddling him. "I missed you," he whispered.

"Me as well." She rocked her hips forward as her soft flesh connected with his cock.

Lachlan shuddered with the friction. "I'll never grow tired of your beauty." He sank his fingers into her soft bum and encouraged her to rub up and down his length. Sliding his hand to her breast, he cupped her as he trailed kisses along her flesh until his tongue found her nipple.

Christina threw her head back and writhed in tandem with his kisses. "Can we come together like this?"

A deep chuckle rumbled through his throat. "After all this time, you ought to know we can make love in any position we can imagine."

CHAPTER TWENTY-SEVEN

As Christina predicted, the remainder of the year flew past. And as Lachlan predicted, Andrew had his ups and downs, though by and by, the lad molded into clan life and grew more accepting of his birthright. He'd spent the summer riding horses with Aileen, which worried Christina, though Lachlan told her to turn a blind eye. Playing the father figure, he'd given her son the appropriate talk to ensure Andrew didn't do something daft and end up with a bastard.

With both happiness and impending dread, autumn came and, with it, arrived Sir Boyd. Christina and Lachlan met the great knight in the courtyard.

"My heavens, ye're the last person I'd expect to come to call." She offered her hand, which the knight politely kissed. "What brings ye to the far north?"

"At the moment, a good tot of whisky." Sir Boyd grinned and looked to Lachlan. "I'm surprised to see ye're still here, Wallace."

"Walking through time as my mother did." Lachlan waggled his eyebrows at both of them.

"Ye are incorrigible," Christina whispered, swatting his arm.

Lachlan led the way into the keep. "The pair of you are the only people who know the truth." He gestured toward the stairwell. "Shall we chat in the privacy of the solar?"

"Indeed," Boyd said, following them up the wheeled steps.

Once inside, Lachlan moved to the sideboard and poured three tots of spirit. Christina smiled inwardly. No man she'd ever met would have even thought to offer her a dram, but Lachlan had a way of treating her like a queen and an equal all at the same time.

She slipped into a chair, gesturing for Sir Boyd to do the same. "Tell us, what is the nature of your visit?"

"I'm on a mission for King Robert. I've been visiting the northern nobles. We need more conscripts for the borders."

"More unrest?" Christina accepted a cup from Lachlan. "Will it never cease?"

"Unfortunately, things grew worse after the king negotiated the prisoner exchange for his queen."

"Elizabeth has been reunited with him?"

"Aye, but at a cost. Word is the English are planning another invasion."

After giving Sir Boyd a dram, Lachlan pulled out a chair for himself. "Really?"

"I tell ye true," said Boyd. "Spies loyal to King Edward have infiltrated every corner of the kingdom."

Christina leaned forward on her elbows. "Spies?"

"Aye, ye recall the nobles loyal to England afore the Bruce took charge…and afore that, practically the lot of them walked away from William Wallace—bought by offers of land and riches from Longshanks."

"Will it never end?" Christina heaved a long sigh.

"Only if we strengthen our forces and protect our borders."

Lachlan raised his cup. "And insure the greedy nobles remain loyal."

Christina met his toast and sipped, waiting until the wee burn in her throat passed. "What do ye need us to do?"

Boyd gestured his arms wide. "The de Moray presence in the Moray Firth is of utmost importance. But ye are still required to present your son before the king during the Yuletide feasts."

"I havena forgotten my promise, not for one minute."

"Then I suggest ye make your way to Stirling Castle forthwith."

"Stirling?" she asked.

"Aye, King Robert aims to keep Queen Elizabeth far away from the borders."

"I don't blame him." Lachlan gave a nod.

"Me neither," Christina agreed. "Is it safe to travel with all the spies about? Or should I leave the de Moray army here to guard the fortress?"

Boyd picked up his cup. "'Tis never safe to travel without a regiment of men. I say leave a henchman here to lead a good fighting force. Ride south with a contingent of twenty men as well as Sir Lachlan—keep him with ye and the lad at all times."

"And ye?" Christina asked. "Will ye ride with us?"

"Unfortunately nay. I have business at Dunnottar Castle afore I can join ye in Stirling." Boyd threw back the remainder of his whisky and eyed her. "Now tell me true, is the lad ready to pledge fealty to the king?"

Christina's fingers began to tremble. "He is."

"I agree," said Lachlan with unfaltering confidence. "I do not believe there is more we can do between now and Christmas."

Biting the corner of her lip, she knew he was right. If only she could purchase another year.

***

Days later, Lachlan didn't know why unease prickled his nape as they prepared to leave Ormond Castle. Maybe it was the wagon with a multitude of Christina's gowns and other supplies pulled by two enormous oxen. Perhaps the five pack mules laden with tarps, cooking pots and candlesticks. But in all likelihood, the reason for his angst was probably a compilation of everything. Bottom line, he just didn't feel right. The fact that he was armed with sword, dirk and daggers up his sleeves and in his boots didn't make him any more comfortable, either.

Lachlan took up the rear while Hamish led the retinue. The best man for the job, the old guard knew nearly every byway between Avoch and Stirling. If anyone could lead them across the Cairngorms, it was he.

After they set out, Andrew raced ahead and doubled back several times.

"We're nearly to Inverness," Christina said. "Please stay near me."

The lad rolled his eyes. "Ye talk to me like I'm a wee bairn."

"Oh? How are ye to protect your mother racing your horse around like ye're on a picnic?"

"Lady Christina's right," Hamish barked from his place in the lead. "Stay near your mother. Ye never ken when outlaws are lurking in the shadows until they're upon ye."

Lachlan further didn't like it when Hamish led them straight into the town of Inverness, leading the horses into a yard alongside an alehouse. He spurred his mount straight up to the bumbling man-at-arms. "Why the hell are we stopping?"

"Supplies, ye maggot." Hamish hopped down and loosened his horse's girth strap. "Besides, we always call into Inverness to wet our whistles."

Wonderful. They had at least five days of riding ahead of them and they were planning to mosey into an alehouse and inebriate themselves?

Christina stopped her mount alongside Lachlan's. "My guess is ye still are not accustomed to these times," she whispered so no one else could hear.

"You've got that right." He helped her down and inclined his lips to her ear. "In my time, it takes no more than three hours to drive from Inverness to Stirling."

Her mouth and eyes gaped in disbelief. "Ye're jesting."

"Nope. A lot of progress happens in seven hundred years. You'd be blown away."

"I'd be what?"

"Amazed." He pressed his hand in the small of her back. "Let us wet our whistles quickly so we can ride out of here. The hairs on the back of my neck have been standing on end since we left Ormond Castle."

"I hope 'tis not a sign from the medallion."

"Me as well."

"Come along, Andrew," she called over her shoulder.

Lachlan kept his hand in the small of Christina's back while they walked through the oak door. Like most sturdy buildings he'd seen, the alehouse's stone walls were at least two-feet thick. Inside, oil lamps hung from the rafters. And it stank like a locker room with too many male bodies packed together. As a matter of fact, Lachlan only saw two other women. Buxom and nearly spilling out of their low-necked kirtles, he was certain they did more for the establishment than serve beer.

It also seemed that every traveler in northern Scotland picked this alehouse and this time to call in for a bowl of pottage and a tankard. "It's too crowded," Lachlan grumbled as he led Christina to a table near the rear.

"I'm going to sit up at the bar with Douglas," said Andrew, already heading for the rowdy mob up by the barmaids.

"Be ready to ride at any moment," said Lachlan, holding a seat for Christina.

She slid down and patted his hand. "Ye must calm yourself. There'll be enough time for caution after we cross into the mountains. But near everyone kens the de Morays in Inverness. We're still amongst kin."

Planting his ass in a seat with its back to the wall, Lachlan nodded and held up two fingers to a barmaid and made a spooning motion to indicate they wanted pottage as well. He'd been around long enough to know what to expect in a place like this; ale, a bowl of stew that had been hanging above the hearth's fire for a week, and a crust of bread if they were lucky.

"What supplies is Hamish buying? Didn't we pack enough food?"

"We need a spare wheel for the wagon and Malcolm didna have time to make one." Her shoulder ticked up. "Besides, we always buy hazelnuts and a half-barrel of whisky for the journey. It keeps the clansmen happy."

"I'd be a lot happier if the men stuck to weak ale. The last thing we need is a retinue of soldiers pissed out of their minds."

"That word is horrible."

"I beg your pardon," Lachlan apologized. "Perhaps I should have said in their cups."

"Och." Christina accepted her ale and a bowl from the barmaid. "Ye still surprise me with your utterances."

Lachlan picked up his tankard and took a long swig. If nothing else, the bubbly beer served to quench his thirst. Over the rim of the cup, he watched as a big knight dressed in heavy mail and armed to the teeth pushed through the door, flanked by two burly guards.

"Holy hell," Lachlan mumbled.

Christina looked back. Clapping her hand over her mouth, she sucked in a gasp. "My God," she blurted. "That's Robert de Vere, the Earl of Oxford."

"What the hell is—"

"Andrew de Moray," the knight bellowed in a deep bass.

From his place at the bar, Andrew turned, his face blanching.

"Nay!" Christina sprang to her feet.

Lachlan lunged for her, but she slipped beyond his reach.

In a flash, she stood before de Vere with her dainty fists on her hips. "Ye willna take my son. Ye will not!"

"And I'll not stand for a woman's tongue lashing." The brute raised his palm and gnashed his teeth.

Anticipating de Vere's downward strike, Lachlan caught the bastard by the wrist and twisted his arm up his spine. "Move away," he hollered, to keep Christina from being hit.

De Vere drew his sword with his free hand and hacked it in a backward arc. "I only want the boy."

Lachlan ducked. His grip firmly twisting the knight's arm, he reached up with one lightning-fast countermove and forced the blade from de Vere's grip. The weapon clattered to the floorboards. Gritting his teeth and lunging to the side, he took the earl down.

The sound of swords hissing through their scabbards shot through his ears. An uproar of bellows filled the alehouse as an all-out brawl erupted.

Pouncing on top of his quarry, Lachlan slammed his fist across de Vere's jaw. "Andrew will take his place beside King Robert."

"Nay." The man threw a brutal fist with gauntleted fingers. Lachlan pulled back, but the iron cut through the flesh on his jaw like he'd been hit with a set of brass knuckles.

Lachlan threw another punch and pinned the man to the floor while bodies careened around him. "You've fucked with that lad's head long enough. You'll take him over my dead body."

"That can be arranged." De Vere bucked.

Lachlan flicked his wrist, letting a dagger slip into his palm. He pressed the razor-sharp blade right on the man's jugular. "Call off your men. Andrew's staying with us."

The man bucked and squirmed.

Lachlan pushed the knife hard enough to draw blood. "I'm a hair's breadth away from sending you to hell. *Call the bastards off.*"

The man stopped struggling while his black eyes squinted. "Will ye grant me quarter?"

"Aye."

"Enough," de Vere bellowed loud enough to be heard by the entire burgh.

"Halt," Lachlan ordered, his tone every bit as commanding. If only he could look for Christina, but doing so would seal their fates. He twisted the knife a bit more. "Why are you here?"

De Vere snarled. "'Tis time for the lad to present before the Bruce."

"Ye kent that?" Christina's voice rang out as her slippers pattered the floorboards. Thank God, she was all right.

"Word came Christmas last," said the English knight.

"Spies," she uttered. "But why come for him now?"

"The lad is *my* squire. I am a goddamned earl, for Christ's sake. It makes sense." He tried to jerk free, but Lachlan kept him pinned. "Think on it, my lady. Andrew could marry my daughter—it would strengthen the bond between England and Scotland."

Christina shot a wary look toward Lachlan. "It would give ye access to northern lands."

"I've heard enough." Lachlan pushed the knife like he might make good on his threat. "Andrew de Moray is my squire now. You have no claim over the lad. You kept him alone in a chamber for *six* years and then forced him into indentured servitude—a lad who is a baron in his own right."

The earl snorted. "I was only teaching the boy respect, seeing if he'd turn out any good."

Liar.

Christina gasped, slipping a hand over her mouth. "What would ye have done if he were sickly?"

De Vere's eyes grew darker. "Unhand me. Ye vowed ye would show quarter."

Lachlan pressed down hard, making sure the man knew not to try anything. "Walk out of here and do not look back. You have no claim on Andrew de Moray, nor do you have any claim to his lands." Easing to his feet, he stared at de Vere, though he could see everything through the periphery of his vision.

De Vere made a show of wiping his neck and looking at the blood smeared across his fingertips before he stood and beckoned his men. As he strode out the door, he stopped and turned. "Ye have not seen the last of me."

The door slammed shut.

Christina grasped Lachlan's arm. "Why in God's name did ye allow that blackguard to live?"

"I gave him my word." He looked to Andrew and met the lad's gaze. Right now, being true to his honor and his word was more important than killing a bully. True, de Vere was a powerful man, but he hadn't had the benefit of learning to fight in the twenty-first century. Lachlan had overcome the knight because of technique and because he wore a leather couton rather than an eighty-pound hauberk. He might not be able to convince any medieval man of his reasoning, but he'd just saved lives and, moreover, kept Andrew from being captured, yet again.

"From now on I'm in charge of this retinue and we stop when I say stop." He thrust his finger toward Andrew. "And you will keep your horse in formation. Am I understood?"

"Aye, sir." Andrew rubbed his palms on his chausses. "Did ye ken de Vere's daughter is only eleven?"

"Jesus Christ." Lachlan threw up his hands.

"But what he said makes sense in a way. Would it help to bring peace on the border if I…if I?"

"No." Lachlan sliced his hand through the air.

"Absolutely not," Christina agreed. "There are many Scottish noblewomen for ye to wed and ye shouldna be thinking about marrying anyone until ye are a grown man of five and twenty at the youngest."

Chapter Twenty-Eight

When Christina opened her eyes, it was still dark. As usual when she traveled with her retinue, she slept beneath the wagon covered by a tarpaulin. So many things warred through her mind, sleep had been slow to come. She'd heard the guard change a few times and slept some, but still, she worried.

Holy saints, they were so much safer behind Ormond Castle's walls. As soon as she'd left the fortress, something awful had happened. De Vere knew she and Andrew would be traveling to Stirling. He even knew that King Robert had given her a year to turn the boy into a Highlander. That meant there must be spies at even the highest levels of the kingdom. Did she have a spy in Avoch? If so, who could it be?

Nothing bad had happened since she'd gone home. Lachlan had even taken Andrew into the mountains without attack. Had anyone at that time been aware that Andrew was not behind Ormond Castle's bailey, they would have attacked, God forbid. Indeed, with only the two of them, the pilgrimage would have been an ideal time to kidnap the lad. Something must have changed over the course of the summer. Did Boyd's visit tip the earl off? Though she trusted Sir Boyd, his movements around Scotland would be news everywhere he went. How long had de Vere been in Inverness and how determined was the earl to place his hands on her son and her land?

The man would risk his life. King Edward must be offering an enticing reward for certain. Why did Lachlan not run his blade across the blackguard's throat when he had the chance? I do love that man, but he is far too generous. His benevolence borders on heedlessness.

Christina rolled to her back and pressed her hands over her eyes. Though she didn't understand Lachlan all the time, for the most part she'd been overjoyed with his compassionate generosity. The first time she'd seen him, he saved her from ruination without a weapon. He used his fists and she doubted he had killed a single one of those English varlets.

But I do not agree with his leniency toward the Earl of Oxford.

She did, however, agree with his decision to take command. She had underestimated the danger they were in and Lachlan had sensed it all along.

When something rustled beyond the wagon, she sat up and parted the canvas. Dawn cast dark blue shadows over the clearing and her gaze immediately shifted to where Andrew had bedded down for the night. Her heart flew to her throat as she burst through the shroud. "Andrew!"

Before she reached the empty bedroll, the entire camp stirred to life. Lachlan dashed ahead of her, dropped to his knees and flung back the plaid. "The bed is cold." His gaze shot around the clearing. "Everyone had a turn at guard, who saw him?"

The men stood around as if dazed, scratching their heads.

"Come on. I do not have time to interrogate you one by one. I took the first watch and he was sleeping like a bairn when I was relieved." Lachlan pointed. "Grant, you followed me. What happened on your watch?"

"The same, sir. Andrew was there when I unrolled my blanket."

"Oh, Jesus," said Alexander, barely older than Andrew. "He passed me during my watch. Said he needed to take a piss."

Christina covered her mouth with her palm, her entire body numb. "Did he return?"

"I dunna recall. The next thing I remember, Hamish shook my shoulder and said it was his turn."

"Fuck!" Lachlan swore, batting at a tree branch. "Hamish—check for tracks. Now. Alexander, how long ago was your watch?"

"Must have been after the witching hour, but with the clouds, I couldna see the moon."

"Jesus Christ, where's a goddamn clock when a man needs one?" Lachlan threw up his hands. "Break camp. We ride before we eat."

"His horse is gone," said Hamish returning from the wood. "And the tracks are too thick to make hide nor hair of them. The only thing I can read for certain is he wasna alone."

Christina wrung her hands. "No, Hamish. Ye're one of the best trackers in the Highlands—ye must make out something."

"Nay, we're camped in the drovers' pass." The man-at-arms shook his head. "A herd must have gone through yesterday, 'cause the tracks are thick and muddy. Even a seer couldna read them."

Lachlan threw his tied bedroll over his shoulder. "Can you tell anything? Where are they heading?"

"The same direction we are at the moment."

"That's it." Lachlan pointed to Alexander and another of the younger men. "You two take this godforsaken wagon back to Avoch. We're riding and we're riding hard. Every man tie a parcel of food to his saddle. Hamish—how many miles to Stirling?"

"Over a hundred, give or take."

"What are ye thinking?" asked Christina after she fetched an enormous leather-wrapped roll stuffed full of God knew what.

Lachlan looked her in the eye. "De Vere aims to grow richer. I'm convinced his plan all along was to use Andrew to get his hands on your lands."

"Ye dunna think Andrew…" her voice trailed off. Surely Andrew hadn't willfully gone with them. She cast her mind back to the alehouse. He'd sat at the bar with Douglas. But the place was packed full. Did a de Vere man slip a message to her son?

Lachlan's face turned ashen. "He said marrying de Vere's daughter made sense."

Christina's stomach sank to her toes. "I dunna believe it. By the saints, I will never believe it."

***

For four days they rode hard through the drovers' glens. Lachlan had never been so frustrated in his life. The *highway*, as everyone called it, was nothing more than rutted tracks pummeled by hooves and wagon wheels. Thank God he'd made the decision not to bring the wagon. With winter coming on, the cart could have slowed them down by days. They'd even weathered a snowstorm. True, he'd spent a few miserable months when fighting in Afghanistan, but that was nothing compared to the hardship of crossing the Cairngorms in December.

A muscle in his neck needled him with such an annoying knot, it felt someone had stabbed it with a sharp rock. He hadn't had a chance to inspect his toes for frostbite, but medieval shoes had nothing on a pair of mountain climbing boots. They were thin and handmade. Every one of them could have frostbite. Bloody hell, the soles of his ankle boots were made from nothing but woven hemp. He needed a hot shower and a soft bed. So did Christina, dammit. All the while, she'd ridden along without a word of complaint, aside from her concern for her son.

How much more could she be expected to take? And honestly, Lachlan couldn't be sure if the boy had willfully joined de Vere or if he'd been kidnapped. If he went with his gut, he'd say Andrew hadn't jumped ship, but there had been no cries for help, no signs of struggle.

It was late afternoon when Hamish approached in the distance. During their march, the old guard had been scouting ahead for signs of horses with larger prints than the Highland garron ponies. He'd found many along the way, which meant de Vere was heading toward Stirling. What they all feared was he'd veer off course and head for the eastern seaboard— according to Hamish, the only place they could manage to do that in the middle of the mountains was after they'd crossed through the glens.

This time, the man-at-arms cantered his horse with a bit more urgency than usual. Lachlan and Christina spurred their horses and met him ahead of the retinue. "Finally, they've veered off the path."

Tugging on her reins, Christina slowed her horse to a walk. "Just as ye expected."

"Not quite." Hamish rounded his mount between them. "I thought they'd turn and head toward Montrose, but they're taking the shortcut to Stirling."

"Shortcut?" Lachlan asked.

"Aye, 'tis steep with hairpin turns, but it cuts a half-day off the drovers' path."

Christina ran her reins through her fingers. "Why would he be heading to Stirling? He has what he wanted."

Lachlan looked up the mountain. "Not everything. Boyd said a truce was declared upon the exchange of prisoners for Queen Elizabeth. I reckon de Vere is going in for the kill."

"My God. Do ye think he'll try to assassinate the king?"

"No—sorry, that was a figure of speech. The earl said himself he's after the de Moray lands. My guess is he has a plan he thinks is foolproof." Lachlan glanced to Hamish. "Can you take Lady Christina and the guard into Stirling?"

"Of course I can."

"I dunna think I like the sound of that," said the lady. "What are ye planning?"

"I aim to make sure they don't arrive at the castle before you."

"And Andrew?"

"He's my number one concern." Lachlan motioned to Grant to ride in beside him. "Look, I reckon they have someone doubling back to keep an eye on our progress. If you continue on to Stirling as planned, they'll think we missed their diversion. I want you to ride by Lady Christina in my place. Anything happens to her and you'll answer for it. Understood?"

"Aye, sir."

He steered his horse near enough to grasp Christina's hand and ply it with a kiss. "Stay the course. I'll see you in Stirling." Then he tipped his chin toward Hamish. "Come, show me this trail and draw me a wee map."

***

The days were too bloody short this time of year and it was almost dark when Lachlan gazed down on de Vere's camp. The earl had a relatively small retinue. Lachlan counted sixteen, but that didn't surprise him. He hobbled his horse before slipping down the hill on foot, careful to step lightly and avoid snapping twigs.

By the time he reached them, daylight had all but gone. They mustn't have been too concerned about attack because a bonfire raged. Blades clanged and men hollered like they were casting bets on a sparring match.

"Ye've been taught well," de Vere's deep voice boomed through the forest.

Not but fifty feet from the camp, Lachlan crouched behind a boulder and peered around. Andrew wielded his sword against the larger knight like a pro. He had been trained well, but he would be no match for a knight like de Vere, a man in his prime who had been fighting for king and country his whole life. No, Andrew wasn't yet ready to be dubbed a knight, but he was a hell of a lot closer now than he'd been a year ago.

"What will ye trade for that horse?" de Vere asked spinning and slapping Andrew in the ass with the flat side of his blade. Now he was just toying.

Andrew leapt aside, circling his sword above his head and taking a defensive stance. "He's mine."

"A gift from your mother, was it?"

"Aye."

"The shrew is trying to win ye over to her side, is she?" De Vere paced, his sword lowered.

Andrew didn't take the bait, good lad. "Why wouldn't my mother want to give her only son a gift?" His accent sounded a bit more English. Lachlan didn't like that one bit.

Bellowing, de Vere swung as if he intended to cleave the boy in two.

Andrew blocked with an upward thrust, but the bigger man spun, trapping the lad in a stranglehold.

Lachlan clenched his fists. *What did I teach you?*

Seconds passed. The lad's eyes were wide and he appeared to be scared.

Come on.

Lachlan rustled the brush above his head. Andrew looked. Lachlan gave a single nod before slipping back into the shadows where he wouldn't be seen. In the next blink of an eye, Andrew used his heel to stomp on de Vere's instep. Spinning toward the knight's wrist, Andrew slammed his elbow into de Vere's unprotected throat. Lachlan wanted to stand up and cheer, but settled for a fist pump.

"Bloody insolent whelp." The knight hopped in place. "Tie him!"

Guards immediately followed orders and bound Andrew's hands and legs.

De Vere meandered in and walloped the boy with a slap across the chops.

Bloody coward.

"When we arrive in Stirling, ye will support my cause."

"Marry your daughter?" Andrew spat. "She's a child."

"She will not be a child for long."

"And then what?"

"And then ye sit back and enjoy the spoils." De Vere pulled his dagger and pretended to run it across Andrew's neck. "If ye cross me I'll slit your throat myself."

Andrew's lips thinned as his gaze shifted to Lachlan's hiding place. Slightly shaking the brush, he gave a sign to let the boy know he wasn't alone. Then he waited until the camp was asleep, crept around the perimeter and quietly released the tie line holding de Vere's horses in a row. Several followed as he continued on his way toward Stirling without Andrew. But he had a plan.

Chapter Twenty-Nine

Christina's fingers started to tremble when she finally saw Stirling Castle as the Highland hills parted, giving way to the vast lea cut by the winding River Forth. Since Lachlan had ridden off to fetch Andrew from de Vere's clutches, her nerves had been on the ragged edge. She'd done nothing but clutch her reins, dig in her heels and pray.

Too many emotions coursed through her blood. Seeing Stirling was like going back in time six and ten years. The last time she'd been there, her husband had taken an arrow to the shoulder in the Battle of Stirling Bridge. The wound didn't seem mortal at first, but three months later, the Lord took him.

On that triumphant day, Andrew's father rode beneath the portcullis beside his comrade, William Wallace. Christina had followed at the end of the procession, riding her horse alongside Eva. She still could not grasp the truth. Eva was Lachlan's mother. After William's death, the redheaded lass had returned to her time and given birth to a boy. By Robbie's calculation, if Eva had birthed Lachlan in her time, he'd be a lad of nine. But something behind the medallion was magical for certain. He'd grown into a man afore the powers that be sent him through the centuries to be her champion.

And, oh, so much more.

Indeed, a maelstrom of emotions coursed through her blood as she and her retinue spurred their horses to a canter. Was Lachlan waiting at the castle as he'd promised? She couldn't wait to see Andrew and hold him in her arms again. She wouldn't blubber over him, but she would ensure the lad kent how much she'd worried and how very important he was to her.

At the town gate, they were stopped by the guard—a sign Robert Bruce was holding court. "What is your business?" asked the sentry.

"Lady Christina de Moray and her army here to present to King Robert as commanded by Sir Boyd," said Hamish. It would have been improper for her to announce herself.

Allowed to enter, up the cobblestoned road they climbed to the royal palace. Christina had seen many castles and Stirling was one of the grandest. Still, her gaze swept to and fro. *Where are they?*

Before they reached the inner castle gates, grooms met them to stable the horses. As soon as her feet touched the blessed ground, Lachlan hastened toward them, thank heavens.

Smiling, she craned her neck to look beyond him. "Where is Andrew?"

"On his way."

"Did he see us riding down from the Highlands?"

"No."

"What is it?" Pursing her lips, she squinted. "I sense ye're not telling me something."

Lachlan grasped her elbow. "Come. They've appointed you with a chamber in the white tower."

She jerked her arm away. "Nay. I want to ken where my son is or I'll not take another step."

"He's on his way, I said."

"From where? The moon?"

Lachlan stooped and lowered his lips to her ear. "First of all, I'm counting on you to keep your calm. He's still with de Vere. By my estimation they should be here by the end of the day. Now walk with me to your chamber so we can avoid a scene. I wouldn't put it past the bastard to have spies swarming around this place."

A raging fire burned in her belly. By God, she would have answers. And if Lachlan weren't right about the fact that they were probably being watched, she would have slapped him right across the face. How dare he leave Andrew with that despicable blackguard?

Her lips thinned, her fists clenched as they made their way past merchants' shacks to the tower. She wanted to scream, she wanted to run back to the stables, mount her horse and gallop for her son. It seemed to take forever to reach her chamber, but once the door closed behind them, she faced Lachlan, jamming her fists onto her hips. "Do ye have any idea how awfully harrowing it is for a mother to have her son taken from her arms? Do ye have any idea how much agony I endured during those three and ten years?"

"I—"

"Ye couldna possibly, 'cause if ye did, my son would have met me at Stirling's gates."

"It would have been—"

She slapped him across his insolent face. "I want to shake ye until your teeth rattle! Ye left him with that backstabbing cur and there ye stand like ye havena care in the world, ye *bastard*."

"Stop." Lachlan grasped her shoulders like an iron vise. "Listen to me before you fly off on a rampage. Andrew would have been in greater danger if I'd tried to rescue him."

She twisted from beneath his fingers. "Ye shouldna have gone alone. If we'd taken the de Moray army, we could have laid an ambush and finished the Earl of Oxford."

Lachlan grew red in the face. "That may be, but when I heard de Vere say he was riding for Stirling, I made my decision."

"Och aye, did ye now? Ye're not only toying with my life, ye're toying with Andrew's, and I'll not abide it. For the life of me if—"

"Would you hear me out, dammit?" Lachlan threw up his hands. "I was close enough to the camp to hear his plans. He intends on approaching King Robert to propose a marriage between Andrew and his daughter, just as he told us. He wants the de Moray lands—could care less about our boy."

"I kent it all along—he's a blackguard of the worst sort."

"While I was there I made eye contact with Andrew. The lad is on our side."

"Ye could tell by giving him a look?" She stamped her foot at the absurdity.

"De Vere was talking big, making threats. He even had the lad bound. He's using fear and coercion to bend Andrew to his will. Don't you see? We never did that to him. Andrew was shown respect and love at Ormond Castle—something he'd never had with de Vere."

"Aye, but it's only been mere months since the lad has swayed to our way of thinking. He's vulnerable."

Lachlan's lips thinned.

Christina didn't like that one bit—because there was a hole in his thinking. Crossing her arms, she took a step in. "Are ye certain beyond all doubt that Andrew will support the de Moray Clan, that he will stand tall beside his mother, upon whom he focused his anger and resentment for years?"

"I'm certain enough."

"Enough?" She shoved him in the shoulder. "Blast ye. How can ye toy with my life like this? If I lose my son and my home to that evil knight, I shall *never* forgive ye."

***

Lachlan paced atop the battlements. He'd been damned confident with his plan until Christina's tongue lashing. Now, doubt had his gut twisted in knots and the more he paced, the more he doubted everything. Had he grown too overconfident? Had he misunderstood the whole thing with the medallion? And, for Christ's sake, he'd been in this century for over a year and still had no clue how he'd make his way home.

He stopped for a moment and stared out over the River Forth, snaking its way to the firth.

The bridge has been rebuilt since the battle.

He didn't know why he knew it, but the English had destroyed the bridge trapping their own men to prevent complete annihilation by Wallace—his father. Across the carse of flat, fertile land, a wooded hill rose in the distance, Abbey Wood. Lachlan remembered standing in that very spot on the Stirling Castle battlements with his mother and looking out toward the Wallace Monument, a grand tower that wouldn't be built until the nineteenth century. Mother had pointed out the details of the battle while he'd listened—one of the few times he'd paid attention to her historical prattle. Lachlan did, however, always listen when Mum talked about William Wallace.

The medallion warmed. He closed his eyes and tried to focus on his mother. But it was a man's voice he heard, a deep, resonant voice: *"Be careful what ye wish for, son. Ye have been blessed with experiencing life in two centuries. Where are ye needed most and where are ye most content? Follow your heart, for ye may never have a chance to do so again."*

"Who are you?" Lachlan asked before the spirit could leave him. When there was no reply, he opened his eyes, the scene still the same. Abbey Wood quiet in the distance devoid of the Wallace Monument.

Raking his fingers through his hair, the past year played out in Lachlan's mind. He'd been so wrapped up in daily life, he hadn't thought much about the long term. Did he have a choice? If only there were someone to talk to, someone who knew about time travel and the medallion. God, he was such a damned romantic. He'd gone and fallen in love with Christina. He'd fallen in love with her doll-shaped face and her strength of character. He'd fallen in love with the role of Andrew's mentor. He'd fallen in love with horses and castles and simple fare, and a slower, yet more brutal way of life.

And now he'd gone and screwed it up. Christina was ready to boot his arse across Scotland. And if Andrew made one misstep, the lad would either have his throat cut now or give his lands away to a tyrant and, most likely, end up with his throat cut later.

A guard approached at a run. "'Tis the Earl of Oxford at the gate, demanding an audience with the king."

Lachlan's gut squeezed. De Vere had made better time than he'd given him credit for.

"Are they meeting?" he asked.

"All men-at-arms have been ordered to the great hall forthwith."

I've got one shot to make things right.

Taking off, Lachlan sprinted to Christina's chamber and pounded on the door. "Hurry. De Vere is headed into a meeting with the Bruce."

The lady flung open the door, her light blue veil pinned perfectly in place. She'd changed into a dark blue velvet gown and with the determination in her eyes, she looked more commanding than a queen. "Then what the devil are ye standing there for? Escort me to the hall this instant."

Unfortunately, by the time they'd crossed the courtyard, guards blocked the enormous hall doors with pikes and battleaxes. No matter how they tried to explain, the guards refused to budge. "No one enters until King Robert gives the word."

Lachlan pulled Christina by the wrist. "Come with me."

She resisted his tug. "Where the devil are ye taking me? What if de Vere comes past with Andrew?"

He slid a hand to her waist. "You want inside?"

"Aye."

"After crawling around ruined castles with my mother for years, I've learned a few things. Now come." He led her around the back of the great hall—back where the nobles never ventured. Where it stank and rotting debris filled the gutters. The pathway curved around a steep decline, leading to a dark archway.

"Hold up your skirts," Lachlan warned. "You wouldn't want your hem to drag through some of the ooze we'll be walking through."

True, Christina had been in many kitchens, but he doubted she'd been in one so vast. As long as a footy field, Lachlan had spent some time in Stirling's basement kitchens when he was a lad. True enough, they'd been altered over the years, but he was banking on one thing being the same as it was in all medieval castles. The kitchen that fed the masses had a direct passageway to the great hall.

His memory didn't fail. As soon as they stepped through the archway, they were blasted by heat from the bread ovens. The smell of baking bread overpowered scents he knew lurked from beyond.

A man covered with flour blocked the entrance to the main kitchen. "M'lord, m'lady, what is your business here? Ye shouldna be down in the galley with the common folk."

"We need your help." Lachlan gestured to Christina. "This is Lady Christina de Moray, wife of the patriot, Andrew de Moray—comrade of William Wallace."

The man gasped, hitting his cheek with a flour-covered hand. "Forgive my impertinence, m'lady." Sputtering like a fool, he dipped into a bow. "Ye said ye needed my help?"

"We do." Christina grasped the man's hand as if he were as important as a dignitary. "Ye may have heard the Earl of Oxford has demanded an audience with King Robert?"

"Aye, we've been asked to make extra loaves for his army, and yours, m'lady."

"Excellent," she said. "But make no bones about it, de Vere is ruthless. He's holding my son hostage and intends to demand terms from the king. I must spirit inside afore the blackguard states his case."

"Can you lead us through the kitchens?" Lachlan asked.

"I can and there's only one way in that's no' blocked." He pointed toward the main kitchen that Lachlan knew. "Ye canna go that way until the evening meal is served. Follow me."

The man pulled a torch from the wall and took them down the dankest, dirtiest passageway that stank like rotten fish. Water trickled down the stone walls and slapped underfoot. Just as Lachlan was about to call a halt, the man used a key to open a door and lit a torch secured to the stone wall. "Go up the stairwell. The first door opens onto the dais."

"Thank you." Lachlan placed a coin into the man's palm before they continued up through the dim stairwell, completely devoid of sunlight. At the first landing, he reached for the latch.

Christina stilled his hand. "If a guard sees us, they may try to force us to leave."

"Good thinking." Very slowly, Lachlan raised the lever and only opened the door wide enough to peer inside. "The dais is blocked by a screen," he whispered.

She pressed against his back. "Perfect."

No sooner had they stepped through the door when a voice boomed across the hall, "The right honorable, the Earl of Oxford."

"Ye've relieved him of his weapons?" came the king's commanding bass.

"Aye, Your Grace."

"Then allow him to enter."

More than one set of footsteps approached.

"Oxford," said the king. "I'm surprised to see ye with young de Moray."

Christina grasped Lachlan's hand. "He's here."

Nodding, Lachlan touched a finger to his lips. He wanted to hear what was being said before he leapt from their hiding place and challenged the braggart to a fight to the death.

"I have a proposition for ye," said de Vere.

Odd, the earl didn't use a courtesy title. Did he consider the Bruce to be an equal?

"Do ye need to be reminded ye're on Scottish soil? Ye'll refer to me as Your Grace, else I'll toss your proposition out with your arse."

Lachlan pulled the corners of his mouth down to keep from laughing.

"I beg your pardon *Your Grace*. I must have been thinking fondly of the years we spent together when ye were the Earl of Carrick."

"What have ye come to propose?"

"Ye need a strong army in the north. Ye ken there's none better trained than the de Vere men."

"I beg to differ," replied the king. "I've received word the de Moray army is growing in strength and numbers."

"Do ye honestly think they can best me? My army is King Edward's hammer. But if we made an alliance, I would pledge my fealty to Scotland's throne."

A yawn came from the dais. "I grow tired of empty alliances. And what of your lands south of the border? Are ye not bound by a blood oath to Edward?"

"Ye know as well as I all great men hold land on either side of the border—yourself included. Let the de Moray lad marry my daughter—build the bond between our two great nations."

"And if Edward attacked—which the bastard oft threatens—what then? Would I have an army of traitors infiltrating my kingdom from the north?"

Christina lunged forward.

Lachlan caught her by the waist.

She twisted, a heated whisper spewing from her lips, "I must—"

"I believe ye are right, Your Grace," Andrew's young voice resounded across the hall. "This nobleman is holding me against my will and if I had use of a sword, I would challenge him to a fight to the death right here and now."

Tension fled from Lachlan's shoulders like a cascading waterfall. *Thank God.* He released his grasp and followed Christina to King Robert's throne.

"Seize de Vere," Christina shouted. "He is a venomed asp who spews nothing but lies."

Guards immediately moved in, subduing the earl with a dozen or more pikes trained on his heart.

"My lady?" The king glanced between her and Lachlan. "What the devil?"

"We were traveling from Ormond Castle to make good on our promise to present Andrew to ye this Yule. To present my son, the true heir to the de Moray lands so that he could pledge his fealty to the one true king of Scotland. The earl stole into our camp in the dead of night and captured Andrew from where he lay sleeping."

"Please, Mother, it is I who should be relaying this story." Andrew boldly climbed the dais stairs. "De Vere threatened to hunt me down and murder me if I didna go along with his charade, but I canna in good conscience allow him to ruin our lives, as well as the life of his insipid eleven-year-old daughter."

"Have ye thought this through, lad?" asked the Bruce. "Such an alliance might benefit the kingdom if drawn with the appropriate language to ensure fealty."

"Exactly," de Vere boomed from the floor.

King Robert regarded the backstabber. "Ye no longer have leave to speak, m'lord."

"The Earl of Oxford has no honor," Andrew continued. "He would do as ye suspected. Sign anything ye asked and then take my family lands. When I was his prisoner in England, he only kept me alive to use me as a pawn. He planned to take Ormond Castle for himself as soon as the war ended. Once ye negotiated for my exchange, his plans were thwarted—'tis why he staged the battle on the borders. Now he wants me to marry his daughter? Aside from the fact she's as cruel as her father, de Vere aims to give away her hand when she is not yet a woman?"

The king scratched his beard thoughtfully. "But many highborn marriages are sealed afore the bride sees her first menses."

"That might be, but if I took an oath of marriage, I wouldn't sleep with de Vere under the same roof. He'd slit my throat for certain, and if not he, that wicked imp he calls a daughter would."

"I've heard enough." King Robert sliced his hand through the air. "Take the earl away."

Christina clasped her hands in front of her heart. "Oh, praises be. Thank ye, Your Grace."

The Bruce held up his hand. "This young man has made quite a remarkable turnaround in a short time. I must ask him what changed his mind."

Andrew looked to Lachlan and took a deep breath. "'Tis true, I was angry, and I blamed my mother for my captivity, and my anger was fueled by words of hate from de Vere. I do not ken if I ever would have seen how much I had been persuaded to the English side if it weren't for Mother's champion, Sir Lachlan Wallace. He not only made me reach deep inside and discover who I am and where I'm from, but he made me believe in myself."

"The tournament knight did all that?" asked the king.

"Aye." Andrew bowed to Lachlan. "He told me he was a master of martial arts and that his life's purpose was to train lads to become men. At first I thought he was full of shite."

The king chuckled.

"Andrew," Christina said. She quickly covered her mouth with her fingers. Indeed, her son was proving himself a man and she must allow him to continue.

Andrew looked her way only for a moment, then his gaze returned to Robert the Bruce. "I am Andrew de Moray, named for and son of the great knight who fought beside William Wallace in the triumphant Battle of Stirling Bridge. I was born a Scot and I will be a Scot until I take my last breath." Andrew dropped to his knee. "Ye are my only sovereign, the only man in all of Christendom who can call me to arms, and I pledge ye my undying fealty, Your Grace."

Lachlan managed to close his mouth and swipe a hand over his eyes. Christina's cheeks shimmered with her tears as the hall grew completely silent.

Robert the Bruce stood and drew his sword. "How old are ye, lad?"

"Six and ten."

"Though ye havena reached your majority, I deem ye are a man. There are knights in this kingdom who are not as gifted an orator as ye. I do believe ye are your father's son." The king dubbed Andrew's left shoulder, then his right. "And I knight ye into the Royal Order of Scotland, to be a member of my parliament. May ye carry this great honor in your heart and never turn your back on your duty."

"Ye honor me, Your Grace. I shall endeavor to make ye proud."

Lachlan slipped his arm around Christina's shoulder and squeezed her tight, pressing his lips to her forehead. Dear God, this was the most rewarding moment of his life.

But when King Robert turned and gaped, she hopped away from Lachlan like a frightened doe.

"Ahem." The king eyed them with a frown. "I shall meet with ye in my antechamber alone, m'lady. Precisely when the vespers bell rings and not a moment later."

CHAPTER THIRTY

Christina paced across her chamber floor while Lachlan watched her from his place, standing with his elbow on the hearth's mantel. "How can ye possibly appear calm at a moment like this? Do ye realize the king saw ye with your arm around my shoulders?"

"I've put my arm around your shoulders plenty of times and you never complained before."

"But the king needs to give his blessing first…and ye…ye." She turned her back and pressed her face into her palms. Must she spell it out for him? He was a man who could make no commitments. He was a man who should be a lad of nine, not a man of one and thirty.

Lachlan moved behind her and placed his hand on her shoulder. "Tell me what's upsetting you."

"Too many things." She spun and faced him. "First of all, why are ye still here?"

A look of hurt filled his midnight blue eyes. "You don't want me here?"

"Nay, that isna it at all. 'Tis just Andrew couldna have impressed the king more this day. I dunna understand why ye havena vanished like Eva did—twice!"

"Oh." His teeth grazed over his bottom lip.

Rubbing her hands, Christina started pacing. "King Robert doesna understand ye as I do."

Lachlan brushed one of her wily curls away from her face. "Why can't you just tell him we're a couple?"

She stamped her foot. "Because that's not the way things are done. Ye've been here long enough. Ye ought to have that figured out by now."

"Can you not choose whom you love?"

"'Tis not so easy." She wrung her hands. "It doesna matter if ye are the greatest fighting knight in all of Christendom, the king will demand a commitment."

"I see." He stopped her and grasped her fingers in his very large palms—rough, protective palms. Palms she wanted to hold through eternity. Hands she never wanted to lose. What if he vanished in this very moment, in this chamber? She would melt and wither into a pile of worthlessness.

Curses.

He tugged her closer. "After you so eloquently pointed out that I was being too brash by assuming things I had no right to assume—"

"I must apologize for that."

He strengthened his grip ever so slightly. "I do not want an apology, m'lady. But I would be overjoyed if you would stand quietly whilst I try to explain."

She nodded, pursing her lips and trying not to cry.

"After our little *discussion*. I went for a long walk—walked where my father once stood. Saw what my father saw. And I realized I am not here for Andrew."

"Then why?" Blast, the words slipped out before she had a chance to check herself.

"I'm here because of my father. Because, in truth, I am half a medieval man and half-modern. That may not make sense to you, but by powers that defy the laws of physics I've been given a chance to experience life in his time, and I am certain I have a choice. I even think the medallion isn't functioning quite the same for me as it did for my mother."

"So…" She hesitated, waiting to see if Lachlan was going to stop her this time. When he didn't, she continued, "When are ye planning to leave?"

"And go back to what? A cuckold woman who has left me? A dojo I haven't seen in a year? I don't even have a place to live." He pulled her into his chest and wrapped those big, strong arms around her. "What I'm trying to say is, I love you, Christina de Moray, and there's no place I'd rather be than by your side."

A cry caught in the back of her throat. He wasn't leaving? She'd suppressed her feelings for so long they all bubbled to the surface with one effervescent trill. She buried her face against his chest, her stuttering heart flying as if it had wings. Tears of happiness flowed from her eyes as he hugged her close and kissed her hair.

"Did you hear me?" he whispered. "I love you."

"And I love ye, Sir Lachlan Wallace," she finally said in a shaky voice. Blessed be the stars, all of her hopes and dreams had come true upon this glorious day.

"Then let's go speak to the king together. Perhaps he will grant a Christmas wedding."

***

King Robert's cranky expression was the antithesis of the bubbles effervescing through Christina's insides. He sat in a padded chair elevated on a small dais with a red carpet runner at his feet and a gold embroidered canopy overhead. The epitome of a king.

In fact, he seemed much more like a grouch rather than a king preparing to celebrate Christmas with a queen who had been returned to him after years in captivity. He drummed his fingers on his armrest. "Lady Christina, I specifically recall saying I wanted to speak with ye alone."

Lachlan cleared his throat. "Forgive me, but that is my fault, Your Grace." He moved closer to the red carpet and bowed. "Please allow me to explain. I could not, in good conscience, allow Lady Christina to meet with you alone when I knew full well you'd be discussing her future nuptials. You see, I cannot possibly stand idle while any nuptials are discussed for the woman I love…unless they include me."

The king threw back his head with a belly laugh. "So ye think ye are worthy of this woman's hand?"

"Your Grace," Christina hasted to Lachlan's side. "This knight, this *champion* brought Andrew back to us in mind and body, and when no one else thought the lad would amount to anything."

"That he did," agreed the king. "But ye are a beautiful woman, Christina. There are many nobles in the kingdom who would vie for your hand."

"Nay." Christina shook her head. "I want no other. Ye ken what it is like to suffer alone for years and now I ken my heart. I have given the kingdom a fine heir. Please, Your Grace, allow me to choose love for once in my life."

Bruce looked to Lachlan and narrowed his eyes. "Do ye aim to marry her?"

He shot a panicked grimace at Christina. She tried to give him a reassuring nod. They'd discussed this. Lachlan knew what to say. In a brash move, he took her hand and threaded his fingers through hers. "I wish to ask your permission for Lady Christina's hand. I vow to care for her to the best of my ability for the rest of my life."

The Bruce stroked his fingers down his beard as if considering. "And ye, Christina, are ye absolutely certain this enormous knight is the man to make ye happy for the rest of your days?"

The bubbles nearly effervesced right out of her bodice. "I would have none other."

"Verra well. I am allowing this union only because Andrew's oration greatly impressed me this day. My word, if only all my knights would be so forthright, Scotland would rule all of Christendom." The king rose to his feet. "When shall we celebrate this wedding?"

"Christmas Eve?" Christina and Lachlan said together.

The king looked rather taken aback. "Christ's birthday? Is that done?"

"Why ever not?" asked Christina. She was growing fond of breaking the mold and doing things otherwise forbidden by outdated and nonsensical rules.

"Hmm. The pair of ye are eccentric, but I like that." King Robert slapped Lachlan on the shoulder. "Besides, the queen will be over the moon. She is planning to green the castle on the morrow and this will give her even more reason to lavishly spare no expense. I'll allow the ceremony...afore the feast."

Christina clapped her hands. "Would Sir Lachlan and I be able to contribute a gift of spectacular boughs for the great hall?"

"A *spectacular* gift, ye say?" The king arched his eyebrows. "I'm certain Queen Elizabeth would agree. The more boughs, the better."

***

Christina needed to do one thing before another day passed. An enormous smile stretched her lips when she beckoned Andrew into her chamber and asked him to sit. "There's something I've been wanting to give ye for over a year."

Andrew leaned back in his chair and crossed his ankles. Goodness, he'd grown tall. "A Christmas gift?"

"Nay, 'tis even more important than that." She'd hidden the items in an ornately carved wooden trunk at the footboard of the bed. Opening it, she pulled out a two-handed sword. "Every time I think of the strides ye have made in the past year, tears well in my eyes." She faced him and held it out. "This is the sword of Clan Moray, wielded by your father and your father's father. It was hewn in the Iron Furnace of Inverness with the purest ore in all of Scotland. Your father fought the English in Stirling and defended Ormond Castle with this weapon. Wear it with pride."

His face filled with amazement, Andrew stood and accepted the sword, reverently running his fingers down the flat side of the blade. "It looks new."

She beamed. "Malcolm honed it sharp for ye."

Holding it up, he took two hissing swipes through the air. "The balance is excellent."

"There is no blade hewn with better mastery than the weapon in your hands." She held up her finger. "But there's more." She pulled another item from the trunk. "This is your father's targe. Covered with oxhide, it is reinforced with strong iron rivets in the pattern of the sun. Follow the movement of the great ball of fire in the sky and ye will always find your way home."

"Holy Moses." Taking the targe, he admired the studded pattern, then slid his arm through the leather harness at the back and brandished it like a warrior. "A sword and a targe? Together with Jupiter, I will be feared throughout Scotland."

"Ye will, my son." She then took out a surcoat and brooch. "Wear the de Moray coat of arms emblazoned across your chest, and pin your cloak and plaid with your father's brooch. For my pride for ye stretches from sea to sea, and I stand tall to call ye my son."

Setting the targe on the table, Andrew accepted the other two gifts and stared at them. "These also were Da's?" he asked with a tremor in his voice.

"They were. I only wish he could have been alive to see ye knighted. His heart would have overflowed with so much pride, he would have knelt and kissed your feet."

"I wish I could have met him, too." Andrew rubbed his finger around the brooch. "What is the stone?"

"A rose crystal. And the French motto Tout Prêt means *finish everything.*" She firmly grasped his arm. "But ye are a de Moray and this brooch will serve as a reminder of its true meaning: *Go forth against your enemies, have good fortune and return with captives.*"

"I like it. Dear God, this is marvelous." Andrew dropped to his knees and kissed his mother's hem. "I am ever so grateful for your perseverance. Never once did ye give up on me and for that, I am truly honored to be your son.

Chapter Thirty-One

On market day, Christina and Hamish visited the fete below the castle walls and purchased all manner of baubles and ribbons for the tree whilst Lachlan and Andrew headed for the forest. With only two days before Yule, they needed to make haste, as the courtly feast of Christmas Eve was renowned to be the grandest in all the kingdom. And that would be their wedding day, their anniversary to celebrate for years to come.

To her delight, the lads brought back a glorious Scottish Pine that stretched all the way up to the gallery in the great hall. The queen and her ladies of honor had organized an impressive greening of the entire castle, however, their efforts in the hall were astonishing. Cedar bows draped across the gallery rail, secured with enormous red bows, filling the chamber with fragrance. In the giant hearth behind the high table, yule logs were stacked and ready to be burned to further fill the hall with delightful smells of the season.

Careful not to upstage the queen's efforts, Christina chose a rear placement for the tree.

The three of them stood back and regarded its pinecone shape. She grasped both her men by the hands. "'Tis perfect."

"I did a bit of trimming before we cut her down," said Lachlan.

Andrew inclined his head toward the crates of decorations sitting on the table. "I disagree, Ma. It willna be perfect until we've properly trimmed it."

Oh, how wonderful it was to have her son again. Possibly, last year, Lachlan's idea of bringing a tree into the castle and trimming it with all manner of decorations was the turning point for the lad. He surely enjoyed the season.

She picked up a roll of ribbon and handed it to him. "Are ye looking forward to the feast on Christmas eve? The king has hired the best minstrels in Scotland to play for us."

"I wish Aileen were here. She loves music and dancing."

"Aileen is a lovely gel, but ye are at court, son. 'Tis an opportunity to meet all manner of lassies. Might I even suggest ye ask the king's wee sister for a dance? Ye ken she has my name? The chambermaids told me they call her Lady Chrissy."

"Chrissy?" Andrew wrapped the ribbon around the bottom boughs. "I like that name, though I doubt anyone could be bonnier than Aileen."

Lachlan picked up the angel from the table. "Andrew, would ye go up to the gallery and top the tree?"

The lad glanced up with a look of surprise. "Ye want me to do it?"

"Of course. You found the tree, you should be the one to have the honor of putting up the angel."

Grinning, Andrew took it and ran for the stairs.

"I think Yule is his favorite holiday," said Christina.

Lachlan pulled a long curl from beneath her pink veil and twisted it around his finger. "It is mine for certain." He leaned toward her ear as he often did and lowered his voice. "Are you really happy with the tree?"

She giggled at his soft breath tickling her neck. "I love it, but I am more enraptured with ye and my son this season. I could not have possibly hoped for more."

"Have I told you how bonny you look in pink?"

"Nay." She drew her hands to her veil. "I didna think ye'd seen me in pink afore this."

"I say you look ravishing in all colors, m'lady…" He dropped to his knee and grasped her hand. "In my time, we do not ask the king's permission to marry. In fact, a man asks a woman to be his wife. He falls in love with her and nothing can change his mind that this is the woman with whom he wants to live out the rest of his days."

Tears welled in her eyes. Lachlan was always so full of surprises.

He licked his lips. "Christina, I love you with every fiber of my body. I promise to care for you and provide for you to the best of my ability. I promise to always love you even when you grow angry with me. I promise to sit by your side until I take my last breath. Will you do me the honor of marrying me?"

Clapping a hand over her mouth, she nodded and blinked back her tears. Could a woman succumb to too much happiness? "I will."

He slipped a ruby ring on her finger and she held it to the light. "'Tis stunning. The stone sparkles." She grinned at his bonny face. "And 'tis red like the colors of Yule."

He stood and pulled her into his embrace. Christina could spend the rest of her life cocooned in those braw arms. "I love ye."

"I love you and I always will."

"Och, ye pair send me up here on a task and ye start dallying," Andrew hollered from the gallery.

Lachlan held up Christina's finger and waved it at the lad. "I just asked your mother to marry me properly."

"I thought ye already asked her."

"Not the way I was taught." Turning, Lachlan clutched his arm around her shoulders. "So what do you say, Andrew? Do we have your blessing?"

"Ye want my blessing?" he asked with disbelief.

"Indeed, we do," said Christina.

"Well..." The lad's lips twisted into a grin. "I think 'tis a match from heaven and I'll be the first to raise my tankard in toast."

"Right, then." Lachlan beckoned him. "Let us finish trimming this tree, for tomorrow we are having a wedding."

Chapter Thirty-Two

Standing in front of the Christmas tree, Lachlan's hands jittered a bit as he watched Christina enter the great hall on the arm of her son. Her face, more radiant than any in all of Stirling, glowed as if she carried a candle in her hands. It made her face shimmer beneath her scarlet veil. He loved her in colors, blue, green, yellow, but today, red was his absolute favorite.

She smiled with warmth and love, and his heart squeezed. No, he hadn't landed on the battlefield to save Andrew. He hadn't landed on the battlefield to save Christina, at least not entirely. He'd landed there because it was meant to be—because his destiny lay with a bonny woman who would capture his heart and show him honor and respect on a uniquely deep level that had been lost in the twenty-first century.

Warmth spread throughout his chest while she walked toward him. Her tiny feet tapped the floorboards, her smile unwavering as she greeted him with crystal eyes filled with joy and ever-present mischief. He loved this woman more than life and nothing of this world could ever pull him from her side.

He'd purchased a lead box and placed the medallion inside—a coffin, he called it, and vowed he'd never put its leather thong around his neck again. Ever since their meeting with King Robert, Lachlan had feared something drastic would happen and he'd tumble through time. But when he opened his eyes this morn, there was no question as to his destiny.

As they joined hands, everything in the hall vanished except for Christina. The priest's voice chanting the Latin marriage vows was barely audible. Lachlan could see nothing but his bride's silvery-blue eyes and ruby lips revealing healthy, white teeth. To his joy, she'd even allowed a few mahogany ringlets to peek from beneath her delightful Christmas veil.

Together, they sealed the promise of their undying love and when the priest fell silent and blessed them with a sign of the cross, Lachlan wrapped his wife in his arms and kissed her for everyone to see. Their lips joined with an acceleration of heartbeats signifying the start of a new life. With Christina, he was home and he never wanted to let go. Never wanted to be too busy for her. Never wanted her to forget she was the pinnacle of his life and he adored her with every fiber in his body.

In a whirlwind of cheers, they were whisked to the dais to join the royal family.

The Christmas feast arrived with servants carrying trenchers piled high with course after course of richly spiced food. An ornate swan served on a platter as if it were swimming. Slices of venison and beef piled high. Bread with butter and twenty different flavors of conserve. To round out the diet as Lachlan so often preached, they were served with preserved apples, peaches, pickled cabbage and beets. Ale and wine and dessert port arrived with mince pies. Presented with more food than he'd ever seen in his life, they ate and ate until they could swallow not another bite.

All through the feast, Lachlan refused to take his eyes off his bride. In a year, he'd gone from the depths of despair, from self-doubt and self-loathing to the top of the world.

When the tables were pushed aside for the dancing, the minstrels surrounding the entire gallery picked up the volume along with the tempo.

Andrew stood and bowed to Lady Chrissy. "May I have the honor of the first dance?"

Blushing, the lass glanced to her brother and her guardian. When the king gave a nod, she hopped to her feet with an excited grin.

Lachlan slipped his arm around Christina's shoulders as they watched their son dance with the most important lass in the kingdom. "I think he looks pretty good."

"Thanks to Aileen's tutelage, else he'd be tripping over his toes like ye did the first time we danced together."

He gave her a nudge. "Hey, I caught on pretty well."

"Aside from the time ye nearly trampled me."

"Och, must you remind me?"

The king raised his goblet. "I do believe our two offspring look rather fine together."

Christina arched her brow with a surprised glance to Lachlan. "Indeed, Your Grace."

"And when will we see the bride and groom take a turn?" King Robert sipped his wine, smiling behind his cup.

Lachlan stood and offered his hand to his wife. "M'lady, would you do me the honor?"

She placed her dainty palm in his. "I shall."

Together, they joined the circle dance, slow as it may be. Lachlan liked the music and the moderate tempo. So many things about this era called to him—things he never would have imagined. But the most magnetic of all was the lass skipping alongside him. With Christina as his wife, he could tackle anything.

After the music ended, Lachlan kissed her hand. "When would it be appropriate for us to retire?"

She glanced to the dais with a worried cringe. "After the king and queen bid us a Happy Yule."

"Can't we slip away unawares?" he asked.

She chewed her bottom lip. "It would be terribly disrespectful of us—the king would be most upset."

"Perhaps if we go back up to the dais and start yawning?"

She smacked his arm with a chuckle. "Ye are incorrigible."

"Not at all. I am persistent and I'll not rest until I get what I want."

He tugged her hand and pulled her toward the doors. "I will make our apologies in the morning."

She resisted, sucking in a whistling breath. "It simply isna done."

"When did I ever follow the rules?" When she gave him a wee pout, he kissed her sassy lips. "Besides, not even a king would deny a bridegroom his bride."

Chapter Thirty-Three

The day after Christmas, Lachlan took Christina to Torwood Castle, explaining that he had an errand to do for his mother. After greeting Lord Forester and presenting him with a Yuletide gift of sweetbread, they were granted leave to stroll through the snow-dusted gardens.

At least Lachlan made a pretense of strolling through the gardens. As soon as they were alone, he took her hand and led her to the kitchens. Slipping into the rear door, he found a stairwell. "It must be this way."

"This is so mysterious. Are ye looking for Eva in the cellars?"

He pulled the lead box from a satchel draped over his shoulder. "I've hidden the medallion in here."

"Are ye planning to bury it?"

"Yes and I hope to high heaven she finds it." He glanced back at her and grinned. "This castle fell into ruins toward the end of the eighteenth century. Mum provided an endowment and worked to have it restored. She told me the only things remaining from the original fortress were the cellar foundations. The rest of the castle masonry that remained when she found it was dated to the sixteenth century. If I hide something in the cellars, she's more likely to find it."

Christina drew her hand to her forehead. "My heavens. So many hundreds of years. How do they ken when things are built?"

"It would take me the rest of my life to explain seven hundred years of progress. I think it's best if you just believe that they can tell by the style of masonry and by other tests which have been developed by chemists."

"Chemists?"

"Similar to apothecaries, but far more scientific," he explained while they continued, his gaze shooting through each chamber branching off from the chilly passageway.

"I should hope so. Apothecaries are Satan worshipers."

"Unfortunately, that is the errant view of medieval society, but they set the groundwork for future advancements." He stopped and faced her. "I haven't told you much about my time, but men have walked on the moon. If you want to travel from Scotland to...to any place in the world, you would fly in an airplane."

"A what?"

"It is like sitting in a chair in rows, say, six chairs across in a long sea galley that is enclosed on the top as well as the bottom, and rather than oars and a sail, there are wings."

Her bow-shaped mouth formed an "O". "Flapping wings?"

"No need for flapping. Jet fuel propels them."

"Fuel? Like an oil lamp?"

"Similar, but far more flammable. Anyway, people fly in planes and drive horseless cars—like covered wagons, but they travel far faster than a horse can run."

Shaking her head, she ran her fingers over her face. "Ye are right, 'tis difficult for me to believe, let alone imagine."

"Well, there's no need to worry. I don't miss any of it. Perhaps I wouldn't mind buying one of those destrier horses. They look a lot sturdier to carry someone my size." Lachlan continued to peer inside the vaulted chambers until he recognized an arched window. "Here."

"Have ye written Eva a missive?"

"I have." His heart twisted. The only thing he would truly miss with his decision to stay was he'd never share another Christmas dinner with his parents again. "I told her how happy I am to be with you and aside from Mum and my stepfather, I have nothing to return home for. I said I love her and will always cherish her in my heart, but I was meant to be with you."

Christina brushed a wee tear away. "She'll be heartbroken."

"Perhaps, but if anyone will understand, it will be my mother." The dirt floor in this cellar was packed solid, but at least it wasn't made of stone. He knelt down beneath the window and began to dig with his dirk. "It all makes sense to me now. She stayed with William until the end and when he was convicted, she had nothing left. Nothing keeping her here."

"Except, mayhap for the bairn in her belly."

He chuckled. "I'm certain she decided she was doing the right thing by me. I had an outstanding education and Mum had the support of my grandparents. Not to mention, in my time, it is rare for a woman to die in childbirth."

"Truly?"

He grinned. "Truly."

After digging a hole three times the size of the box, Lachlan checked inside to ensure the medallion was secured with his note, then sealed it, kissed it and placed it in the dirt. "Will you help me?"

Christina chewed her lip. "What should I do?"

"Hold my hand and concentrate on my words."

Kneeling together beside the hole, they grasped hands and closed their eyes. "Hiya, Mum. If you can hear me, please be happy. I now realize how much you loved my father and why you loved medieval history. I share with you in that love. I have married the bonny Christina de Moray and am returning the medallion, for I never want to wake up away from my true love, my wife, my dearest friend."

"That was beautiful." Christina cupped her hand on Lachlan's cheek and kissed him. "Thank ye for giving so much for me."

He kissed her. "Thank you for believing in me."

Before he pushed the dirt over the box, he looked inside one more time. "My God. It's gone."

Gasping, Christina reached inside and pulled out a slip of paper. "This vellum is so fine like nothing I've ever seen afore." She unfolded it. "'Tis from Eva. And look at the writing. How is it so smooth?"

"Ball point pens are another advancement that ceased the need for inkpots and quills."

Christina did nothing but take in a deep inhale and cover her mouth with her fingers. How could she possibly imagine all he had told her?

She doesn't need to. My wife is perfect just the way she is.

He took the note and read aloud:

My dearest son,

You cannot believe how overjoyed I am to hear you have found love and a life with Lady Christina. I always thought her to be a woman of fine character. You will be overjoyed to learn that her son, Andrew de Moray, becomes one of the most powerful men in Scotland and a fierce and loyal knight of Robert the Bruce. I am proud of you, Lachlan, and will miss you more than life itself.

Though we are not together in body, know that I will always be with you in spirit. I will be in the whistling wind and in your dreams. Think of me in the joy of watching snow fall and know that I am thinking of you always.

I wish you and your delightful bride all the happiness and joy that life will bring.

Merry Christmas, my son.

Love,
Mum.

Author's Note

Thank you for joining me for Lachlan and Christina's story. Though fictional, the novel is threaded with history. Andrew de Moray was, indeed, one of the English captives for whom Robert the Bruce negotiated a prisoner exchange. Andrew was captured from his mother's arms at the age of two and she was held prisoner by the English at Ormond Castle until King Robert's Scottish army liberated the kingdom.

In truth, Andrew de Moray was probably exchanged along with a number of other prisoners. It is thought he might have been present in November, 1314 when Robert the Bruce negotiated the exchange for his wife, Elizabeth de Burgh. The queen was captured in 1306 at Kildrummy Castle by Edward I and was held as a political prisoner under abysmal conditions in several locations in England until her husband negotiated her release with Edward II.

The Battle of Bannockburn marked a turning point for Scotland when Robert the Bruce finally gained a firm foothold to his right to the crown and reestablished the Kingdom's monarchy.

Other Books by Amy Jarecki:

Guardian of Scotland Time Travel Series
Rise of a Legend
In the Kingdom's Name

Young Adult Time Travel Adventure:
Time Warriors

The Kings Outlaws series
Highland Warlord
Highland Raider
Highland Beast

Highland Defender Series
The Fearless Highlander
The Valiant Highlander
The Highlander's Iron Will (a novella)

Lords of the Highlands Series:
The Highland Duke
The Highland Commander
The Highland Guardian
The Highland Chieftain
The Highland Renegade
The Highland Earl
The Highland Rogue
The Highland Laird

Devilish Dukes Series:
The Duke's Fallen Angel
The Duke's Untamed Desire

The Duke's Privateer

Highland Dynasty Series:
Knight in Highland Armor
A Highland Knight's Desire
A Highland Knight to Remember
Highland Knight of Rapture
Highland Knight of Dreams (a novella)

Highland Force Series:
Captured by the Pirate Laird
The Highland Henchman
Beauty and the Barbarian
Return of the Highland Laird (A Highland Force Novella)

ICE Series (romantic suspense)
Hunt for Evil
Body Shot
Mach One

Celtic Fire Series:
Rescued by the Celtic Warrior
Celtic Maid

Stand Alone Titles:
Defenseless
Virtue: A Cruise Dancer Romance
The Chihuahua Affair
Boy Man Chief
Highland Defender/Lords of the Highlands Series

If you enjoyed *In the Kingdom's Name*, we would be
honored if you would consider leaving a review. *~Thank you!*

About the Author

Amazon Bestselling Author, Amy Jarecki is a descendant of an ancient Lowland clan and she adores Scotland. Though she now resides in southwest Utah, she received her MBA from Heriot-Watt University in Edinburgh. Winning multiple writing awards, she found her niche in the genre of Scottish historical romance. Amy loves hearing from her readers and can be contacted through her website at www.amyjarecki.com.

Visit Amy's web site & sign up to receive newsletter updates of new releases and giveaways exclusive to newsletter followers: www.amyjarecki.com
Follow on Facebook: Amy Jarecki
Follow on Twitter: @amyjarecki

Printed in Great Britain
by Amazon

25859933R00182